AVID

READER

PRESS

ALSO BY SAMUEL HAWLEY

Ultimate Speed: The Fast Life and Extreme
Cars of Racing Legend Craig Breedlove

The Fight That Started the Movies: The World Heavyweight
Championship, the Birth of Cinema and the First Feature Film

The Imjin War: Japan's Sixteenth-Century Invasion
of Korea and Attempt to Conquer China

I Just Ran: Percy Williams, World's Fastest Human

Speed Duel: The Inside Story of the Land Speed Record in the Sixties

DAIKON

A Novel

Samuel Hawley

AVID READER PRESS

New York   Amsterdam/Antwerp   London   Toronto   Sydney/Melbourne   New Delhi

AVID READER PRESS
An Imprint of Simon & Schuster, LLC
1230 Avenue of the Americas
New York, NY 10020

This book is a work of fiction. Any references to historical events, real people, or real places are used fictitiously. Other names, characters, places, and events are products of the author's imagination, and any resemblance to actual events or places or persons, living or dead, is entirely coincidental.

First Avid Reader Press hardcover edition July 2025

AVID READER PRESS and colophon are trademarks of Simon & Schuster, LLC

Simon & Schuster strongly believes in freedom of expression and stands against censorship in all its forms. For more information, visit BooksBelong.com.

For information about special discounts for bulk purchases, please contact Simon & Schuster Special Sales at 1-866-506-1949 or business@simonandschuster.com.

The Simon & Schuster Speakers Bureau can bring authors to your live event. For more information or to book an event, contact the Simon & Schuster Speakers Bureau at 1-866-248-3049 or visit our website at www.simonspeakers.com.

Interior design by Ruth Lee-Mui
Map by Jeffrey L. Ward

Manufactured in the United States of America

1   3   5   7   9   10   8   6   4   2

Library of Congress Cataloging-in-Publication Data
Names: Hawley, Samuel Jay, 1960– author.
Title: Daikon : a novel / Samuel Hawley.
Description: First Avid Reader Press hardcover edition. |
New York : Avid Reader Press, 2025.
Identifiers: LCCN 2024050178 (print) | LCCN 2024050179 (ebook) |
ISBN 9781668083055 (hardcover) | ISBN 9781668083062 (paperback) |
ISBN 9781668083079 (ebook)
Subjects: LCSH: World War, 1939–1945—Japan—Fiction. | LCGFT:
Historical fiction. | Romance fiction. | Novels.
Classification: LCC PS3608.A89368 D45 2025 (print) | LCC PS3608.A89368
(ebook) | DDC 813/.6—dc23/eng/20241028
LC record available at https://lccn.loc.gov/2024050178
LC ebook record available at https://lccn.loc.gov/2024050179

ISBN 978-1-6680-8305-5
ISBN 978-1-6680-8307-9 (ebook)

To the memory of my mother, Anne Hawley,
who helped me to read

A NOTE FROM THE AUTHOR

THE ATOMIC BOMB DROPPED ON HIROSHIMA ON AUGUST 6, 1945, WAS CODE-NAMED LITTLE BOY. Its design—one mass of enriched uranium fired into another using what was essentially a gun—was relatively crude, especially in comparison to the bomb that destroyed Nagasaki three days later, which used a sphere of plutonium and a much more complex implosion triggering system.

While the design of Little Boy was simple, the 64 kilograms of uranium it contained was not. This material was so profoundly difficult to produce that virtually every book on the subject asserts that the bomb took all the uranium the United States had enriched up to that time. But according to a document at the Oak Ridge National Laboratory, where the work took place, "Beta Calutron Operations, June 24, 1944–May 4, 1947," significantly more uranium than 64 kilos was enriched prior to August 1945.

This enriched uranium was so precious that it was transported across the Pacific to Tinian Island in multiple shipments, lest it be lost. Half of it was sent by air on three C-54 Skymaster transports that arrived on Tinian on July 28—reportedly the only cargo aboard, 20-odd pounds in aircraft designed to carry 14 tons. The rest of the uranium and a crate containing the bomb were sent by sea on the USS *Indianapolis* and reached Tinian on July 26. A memorandum regarding this *Indianapolis* shipment ("Transportation of Critical Shipments," Major J. A. Derry to Admiral W. S. DeLany, August 17, 1945) refers to a heavy lead bucket containing the uranium and a crate just large enough to accommodate the 10-foot-long, 28-inch-wide bomb. Eyewitness accounts, however, suggest that there may have been more. Some crewmen remembered seeing not one bucket being carried aboard, but two. Others recalled the crate as being significantly larger. Lieutenant Lewis Haynes, medical officer aboard the *Indianapolis*, remembered it as "almost the size of this room."

Despite these inconsistencies in the historical record, the United States government has always asserted that only one Little Boy uranium bomb was delivered to Tinian in late July 1945.

JAPANESE EMPIRE, AUGUST 1945

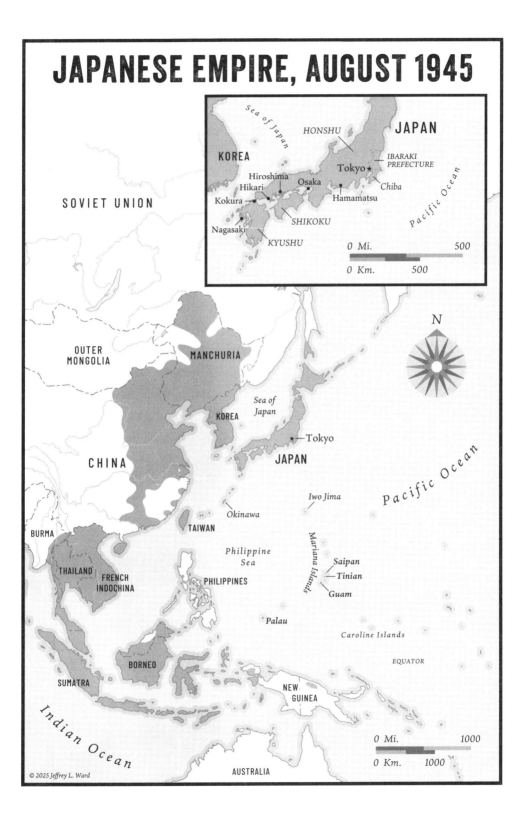

Sea of Japan

KOREA

HONSHU

JAPAN

IBARAKI PREFECTURE

Tokyo ★

Chiba

Hiroshima

Hikari

Osaka

Hamamatsu

Kokura

SHIKOKU

Nagasaki

KYUSHU

Pacific Ocean

0 Mi. — 500
0 Km. — 500

SOVIET UNION

OUTER MONGOLIA

MANCHURIA

Sea of Japan

KOREA

Tokyo

CHINA

JAPAN

Pacific Ocean

Iwo Jima

Okinawa

TAIWAN

BURMA

Philippine Sea

Mariana Islands

Saipan

Tinian

THAILAND

FRENCH INDOCHINA

PHILIPPINES

Guam

Palau

Caroline Islands

EQUATOR

BORNEO

SUMATRA

NEW GUINEA

Indian Ocean

0 Mi. — 1000
0 Km. — 1000

AUSTRALIA

N

© 2025 Jeffrey L. Ward

PROLOGUE

THEY JOINED THE LINE OUTSIDE THE WARFIELD THEATER, A MAN AND A WOMAN. THE PICTURE was *Camille,* starring Greta Garbo and Robert Taylor, "the most poignant love story ever told," according to the ad in the paper. It had not been his choice. He would have preferred to see Gary Cooper in *The Plainsman.* He liked Westerns. They were easier to understand. But she wanted to see *Camille,* and he wanted to please her. So he had taken the bus across the Bay Bridge and met her outside the Warfield for the six-thirty show.

The news from home wasn't good. It had been on the front page of the *Tribune* that very morning when he checked the time for the show: "Japan Cabinet Forced to Quit." The militarists were taking over. He would be returning to a Japan that was heading toward war. Would he be going alone? Or would she . . .

He glanced at her. She smiled back—the smile that never failed to flutter his heart, that promised to fill the void inside him that he now knew was there. How was he going to tell her? How was he going to express these feelings that were so overwhelming he didn't know how to put them into words?

They were almost to the ticket window. It was flanked by a life-size advertisement for the film, the two stars locked in a passionate embrace, *Camille* in red, the words encircled in lights: "Garbo Loves Taylor!"

Garbo loves Taylor.

It's so easy in the movies, he thought as they entered the theater.

She cried when Garbo died in Taylor's arms at the end and was still dabbing at her eyes as they left the theater, he walking her home. They continued in silence past City Hall. Then they were turning north on her street, and he knew he had no more than ten minutes left.

He began to walk more slowly, tension starting to build in his stomach.

He stopped.

She said, "Are you all right?"

He looked into her eyes, desperate.

"I . . ."

Nothing more came out. He struggled to get past the blockage, to kick it down, to get around it. He had to let her know or he would be returning to Japan alone. And that surely would kill him.

"I . . ."

His shoulders subsided. His eyes dropped to the ground. And then a thought came into his head and before he could reconsider he blurted out:

"Taylor loves Garbo!"

A look of surprise on her face, softening to a smile of understanding. She knew.

She wrapped her arms around him and laid her head on his shoulder.

"And Garbo loves Taylor," she whispered.

And they kissed.

ONE

MAJOR EDWARD T. HOUSEMAN LEFT HIS BARRACKS TENT AT 8TH AVENUE AND 125TH STREET—
the Columbia University district—and headed down the crushed coral
roadway in the direction of Times Square. It was eleven o'clock at night
and a half-moon was rising, painting the island bluish gray. He passed
a row of Quonset huts on his left, backed by miles of runways for the
B-29s. To his right lay the sea and the beach where he liked to go swim-
ming. Up ahead: the high point of the island, a hill known as Mount
Laso, where stranded Japanese soldiers were still hiding in caves. One
of them could be out there in the darkness right now, prowling for food
or an American to attack. It was a popular off-duty outing with some
of the boys to pack a lunch and load up the rifles and go hunting for
them.

The major turned right onto Broadway. He had chuckled at his
first sight of all these New York–style street signs when the 509th
Composite Group arrived on Tinian Island back in June. They had
been the idea of some joker in the engineer corps who had observed
that Tinian was shaped like Manhattan and that the roads should be
accordingly named. That was back when Houseman was just one part

of the 509th team, nothing but a cog in the wheel. He didn't feel like that any longer. And the signs didn't amuse him. The meeting at the base hospital a few hours before had dropped what seemed like the weight of the whole world onto his shoulders.

It had taken place at the bedside of the 509th's ailing commander, Colonel Paul Tibbets. Brigadier General Thomas Farrell, deputy to Manhattan Project head General Leslie Groves, was also present. Together they had filled Houseman in on what he needed to know, starting with the closely guarded secret that the weapon the 509th had been training for six months to deliver was a bomb that unleashed the power of the atom. Whatever that meant.

"This thing is big, Eddie," Tibbets had said, his voice raspy. "What I've been told is that we're looking at a destructive force equal to . . . " He paused to painfully swallow. "Equal to 20,000 tons of TNT."

Houseman would never forget that moment, looking down at Tibbets flat on his back and hearing those words. How could tiny atoms make an explosion equal to 20,000 tons of TNT? And what did 20,000 tons of TNT even look like? Would it make a pile as big as a house? No, probably bigger, more like a small apartment building. Someday, when all this was over, he would thrill his wife, Marion, and son Charlie with the story.

"So, Eddie." Tibbets reached out a hot, clammy hand, smiling to hide the disappointment Houseman knew he was feeling. "It looks like you're the guy who's going to end the war. But no pressure, okay?"

"Gee, thanks, Colonel," Houseman replied with a grin. "That's just what I need!"

The dark hump of the crew lounge emerged from the darkness. It was an olive drab Quonset hut like all the others, but some effort had been expended to make it look a little more like home. Shrubbery and a bit of lawn had been planted, and a sign erected out front, announcing it as Tinian Tavern. When the beer wasn't flowing, it was where mission briefings were held. Two armed guards were on duty outside, standing motionless in the moonlight as Houseman mounted the steps.

The crews were already assembled inside. A murmur rose when Houseman entered and walked to the front.

"All right, listen up." It was Houseman's mission voice. Discipline taking over. "Colonel Tibbets went into the hospital earlier today. Don't ask me why because I can't tell you. But I'm told he's going to be okay, so there's no need to worry. I repeat: the colonel is going to be okay. In the meantime . . . "

He paused, looking around at the intense faces of the men.

"In the meantime, we're going ahead with the mission. There's supposed to be a break in the weather, and if we don't take advantage of it, we could lose a whole week. So we go tonight. That's the word. The Gimmick is being transferred to *Wicked Intent*."

The Gimmick. Houseman glanced at the weaponeer who had just been assigned to his crew, a cold-eyed commander in the U.S. Navy named Samuel Filson. They were the only two men in the room who knew the nature of the weapon. For the rest it was still a mystery, referred to as the Gadget or the Gimmick. But his own crew would know soon enough. Houseman would fill them in on the way to Japan. He was looking forward to it. *Well, boys,* he would say, *it looks like we're splitting atoms today.* Then he would hit them with that bit about the 20,000 tons of TNT.

He winked at the crew members of the *Wicked Intent,* the guys he had been training with for six months, getting things to where they could drop a Gimmick on a dime. There was his copilot, John Morris, a killer at poker; navigator, "Billy" Boys, proud possessor of the foulest mouth in the Army Air Forces; tail gunner, "Pappy" de Gerald, sporting a cud of chewing tobacco in his cheek and spitting into a cup; flight engineer, "Hickey" Hicks; and bombardier, "Cy" O'Neill, who had dreamed up the clothes-snatching caper at the beach that had given them all such a good laugh.

"So that means it's us, guys," he said. "We'll be hauling this thing."

Houseman turned to the map pinned to the board behind him and got down to business. "All right. Primary target is Hiroshima. Secondary is Kokura. Third, Nagasaki.

"Weather ships." He turned to the crews of the three B-29s that would precede the strike team to radio back visibility conditions. "Take off at zero-one-thirty. Use the weather codes on the blue paper. No formation flying. Keep it spread out. You know the drill. Strike team. We go at zero-two-forty-five and proceed to Iwo. After rendezvous, it's compass heading 327 degrees, altitude 31,000 feet."

It took Major Houseman thirty minutes to get through the briefing, displaying the efficiency and focus that had made him the first choice to replace Tibbets in leading the historic mission. He ended with the synchronization of watches, then led the way to the mess hall for a breakfast he didn't want. He always felt queasy before missions, and this time was worse. He sat as far as he could from the smell of bacon and eggs as he spooned down a little oatmeal laced with brown sugar.

A hand on his shoulder. He looked up to see the flight surgeon.

"I hope you won't need these," the man said, handing Houseman a small pillbox. Inside it were ten cyanide capsules, one for each crew member in the event that the plane went down over Japan.

Houseman took the little packet of death and slipped it into his pocket. He figured the odds were in their favor, but he wasn't overly sanguine. In war, things went wrong. Throw a new weapon into the mix, a bomb never before used in combat, and the chance of a mishap became that much greater. Dummy gimmicks had already malfunctioned twice in practice drops off Tinian in the previous few days, one bomb tumbling unexploded into the sea and another detonating soon after leaving the plane. There was evidently some sort of fault in the proximity fuze.

Returning to his barracks tent, Houseman took a moment to say a prayer in private, asking God for steadiness and courage, for success in his mission, and for a speedy end to the war so that he could return home to New Jersey. He wanted to get to know Charlie, who was now nearly six. He also had a surprise for Marion, poker winnings totaling nearly two thousand dollars that would make a fat down payment on a house. But first he had to get through this mission.

When the time came, he pulled on his combat coveralls, collected his flight gear, and headed out to Tinian's North Field. The breeze in his face on the jeep ride felt good, taking the edge off the heat that the island had soaked up during the day. *Wicked Intent* was parked at the west end of Runway Able. He pulled to a stop under the scantily clad beauty painted on the nose, which would have been so much more lascivious if Billy Boys had his way. The crew lined up for a photograph, the prickly heat rash in Houseman's armpits now burning, for he was starting to sweat. A blinding flash exploded in the darkness.

"Okay, that's enough," said Houseman, annoyed. He groped his way up through the hatch and into his seat, a disk of light lingering on his retinas and overwhelming his vision.

Billy's voice behind him: "Goddamn it, I can't see a damn thing."

The stillness of the night was shattered by twelve 2,200-horse-power Wright Cyclone engines coughing to life, the three planes of the strike team. In addition to *Wicked Intent,* there was a B-29 that would drop instrument packages to measure the effects of the blast, and a second plane to film and take photos.

Wicked Intent led the way to the end of the runway and turned into the breeze. Houseman advanced the four engines to full power. The plane began lumbering down the crushed coral track, past the control tower, past the broken corpses and burned skeletons of B-29s that had crashed at this same moment, on takeoff, and been dragged off to the side. Finally, with less than a hundred yards remaining, Houseman pulled back on the yoke and eased the behemoth bomber into the air.

Three hours into the mission. The sun was up, a glorious dawn at 8,000 feet, the clouds to the east turning from purple to red, then glowing orange, then full daylight. Major Houseman was starting to feel hungry. He took out one of the bologna sandwiches he had brought, along with a thermos of coffee, and tucked in as he gazed down at Iwo Jima below.

It took fifteen minutes to rendezvous with the two observation planes that would accompany them the rest of the way to Japan. Houseman then led the way onto compass heading 327 degrees—northwest—and began a slow climb. "We're going to pressurize now," he informed the crew, his throat mike conveying his voice through the plane's interphone system. This was the signal for Pappy to squeeze into the tail gunner's compartment, for once the plane was pressurized for high altitude the access door would be sealed. With *Wicked Intent* stripped of all its remote-controlled cannons to save weight, Pappy and his tail guns were its only defense.

Another two hours and Japan itself was in sight, Shikoku, one of the four main islands, emerging from the mist up ahead. Houseman recognized the distinctive arc of south-facing coastline that looked like a bite had been taken out of the island. The cloud cover could be a problem, nearly 50 percent. It would be difficult to deliver the bomb with any accuracy if similar conditions were awaiting them over the target.

His headphones crackled: "Okay, I'm arming it now." It was the weaponeer, the stranger sent out from Washington, Commander Samuel Filson, his voice taut as a wire. The arming procedure involved his entering the bomb bay to remove the green plugs from the bomb and replace them with red ones. This would in turn switch the lights on the monitoring equipment hooked up to the weapon from green to red, indicating that it was live and ready to go. From this point on, it would be up to the radar countermeasures officer, Clifford Slavin, who should be setting aside his comic book about now, to ensure that enemy radar did not interfere with the signals emanating from the bomb, prematurely setting it off.

The first coded message from the weather planes was received:

"Y-3, Q-5, B-4, D-7." Translation: cloud cover over primary target more than 50 percent.

That meant Hiroshima was out. Houseman felt his stomach tighten. The odds were turning against them.

A second message came in, this one from the weather plane over Kokura: "R-7, S-1, B-2, A-3." Translation: cloud cover over secondary target less than three-tenths.

A wave of relief. Kokura was a go. Houseman spoke into the interphone: "Okay, it's going to be—"

A jolt rocked the plane.

Houseman turned to look at his flight engineer, Ralph Hicks, seated behind him. Hickey's eyes were on the cylinder head temperature gauges, his finger tapping on the glass. Then he was hitting the fire extinguisher switch and pumping fuel out of the Number Two tank.

"We got a fire in Number Two," he said. "I think she swallowed a valve."

"Can we still make it?" It was Commander Filson, crouched over his row of red lights. He was plugged into the interphone and had heard the exchange.

Houseman didn't reply for a moment. He had experienced an engine fire before in a B-29, but never so deep in hostile airspace.

His hand went to his throat mike. "If we can get the fire out, yes. How's it looking, Hickey?"

Hickey flicked the engine fire extinguisher switch again. No good. The cylinder head temperature needle remained stuck at 350 degrees. That meant in all likelihood that the fire was burning inside the cowling, where the fire retardant couldn't reach.

"It's still burning," he said.

Houseman's grip on the yoke tightened, his mind racing. The engines of the recently developed B-29 were not only prone to burst into flames, their crankcases were fabricated from a high-magnesium alloy to save weight—magnesium that, if it caught on fire, burned so hot that it could melt off the wing. And in the meantime it was producing a trail of black smoke that would be glaringly visible from the ground. The Japanese rarely attacked high-flying B-29s approaching singly or in small groups. They were too hard to bring down. But a B-29 trailing black smoke and clearly injured would be hard to resist. It was a target of opportunity, a real chance for a kill.

But they were so close. Less than thirty minutes and they would be over the target.

Houseman's eyes swept over the gauges. Airspeed barely holding at 189. Altitude: 28,000 feet and dropping. The *Intent*, running slower on three engines, was drifting lower, seeking denser air for support. To continue the mission would mean dropping the bomb from much lower than the 31,000 feet they had trained for. And they'd be too close when it detonated. They'd be knocked out of the sky.

He spoke to the crew: "That's it. It's an abort."

Filson reentered the bomb bay to replace the red plugs with the green, returning the weapon to safe mode. Back in the cockpit, Houseman was digging out a binder from beside his seat and flipping through to the page listing the codes for twenty-eight possible mission outcomes for transmission back to base. He ran his finger down the list to the one that he wanted, then spoke to his radio operator, Don Wood.

"Okay, Don. Send 25."

Number 25 meant *Returning with unit due to damage to aircraft.*

Houseman made the course correction, putting the bomber into a 180-degree turn. Down below, the dark green of Honshu, looking like crumpled tissue paper, began to rotate.

Wicked Intent came out of its turn, heading back south, altitude now holding steady at 25,000 feet. Number Two engine fuel tank was pumped dry and things were holding together. If the fire went out, they stood a chance of getting back to Iwo. If not, they were going down.

Major Houseman took out the pillbox he had been fingering in his vest pocket. He didn't want to hand out the capsules, but to do otherwise wouldn't be fair to the crew. They all knew how the Japanese treated downed airmen, going back to the Doolittle Raid and those eight guys who were starved and tortured and killed.

He leaned forward to the bombardier's seat and placed his hand on Cy's shoulder. "You might want to hang on to this," he said, holding out a capsule.

With *Wicked Intent* on autopilot, Houseman got up and began working his way through the plane, distributing a capsule to each man. He was on his way back to the cockpit when John Morris called from his copilot's seat, "We got company, chief!"

Houseman returned to his seat and snapped himself into his harness. "Okay, let's have it," he said.

"I count five fighters." It was Pappy on the interphone with his unimpeded view at the tail guns pointing back. "They look like Franks. Six o'clock. About six thousand feet down."

Houseman craned around, peering out his left side window, but couldn't see them.

There. He could see them now. They were definitely Nakajima Ki-84s. "Franks." They would be struggling on the edge of their maximum altitude. They wouldn't get much higher.

A series of blinks from the lead fighter. It was firing from too far out, a desperate move. No return fire from Pappy. He would be waiting until they were within a few hundred yards—if they made it that close.

Movement off to the left. Houseman raised his gaze to see a Tony, a Kawasaki Ki-61, no more than fifteen hundred feet out and just a few hundred feet down. It had broken away from the others for a separate approach.

"Nine o'clock low, Pappy!" he shouted. "He's coming right at us!"

The sound of Pappy's 50-cals. Houseman watched the first bursts of streaking bullets go wide.

The Tony kept coming, right into the face of Pappy's fire.

Half the distance gone now. Still no fire from the Tony. It just kept coming. Why wasn't he firing? Were his guns jammed?

A puff on the wing as the Tony was hit. Still no return fire.

Pappy must have got him!

The Tony wobbled but kept coming—so close now that Houseman could see the goggles, the oxygen mask, the tanned leather helmet of the Japanese pilot. That's when the realization hit him:

He's going to ram us.

The impact threw Houseman against the side of the cockpit, his head bouncing off the glass so hard that it left him momentarily stunned. As he regained his senses, he saw the horizon rising, up and up until the earth filled his field of vision. He stared, disoriented, as the mottled terrain began to rotate, wondering why the aircraft was pointing straight down.

A silvery mass entered his field of vision. It had a toppled-over "A" painted on it. It took a moment for him to process that it was the tail section. *Wicked Intent* had broken in two.

He fought with the controls, trying to level out using only the flaps. The mortally wounded aircraft slowly responded. The uncontrolled dive turned into a gentler downward spiral. But no amount of skill could arrest it.

In his final moments, with trees and rice fields coming at him, Houseman thought of Marion and Charlie and the house they were going to live in.

Then he saw a bright light.

TWO

THE B-29 CRASHED SIXTY KILOMETERS SOUTHWEST OF HIROSHIMA, IN YAMAGUCHI PREFECTURE near the coastal town of Hikari. The main part came down in a great smoking arc to litter fields on the banks of the Shimata River where it snaked out of the mountains, a flying shard nearly killing a farmer working in his rice paddy. As the man sat in shock on an embankment, others converged on the scene, followed by a local policeman.

It was the policeman, named Kinoshita, who hurried to the nearest military establishment to report the crash and the discovery of what appeared to be a large bomb in the wreckage. The base was home to 2nd Attack Squadron, Hikari Special Attack Unit, one of eleven such units in the Kure Naval District. After keeping Policeman Kinoshita waiting for some minutes, the Hikari SAU executive officer, Lieutenant Takeo Miyata, came to the gate. Lieutenant Miyata knew very well that the American B-29 had a tremendous carrying capacity, dozens of bombs. He therefore pressed the policeman about the bomb that had been discovered, asking if he had seen any more. Kinoshita was quite certain that he hadn't. "Only one," he said.

Lieutenant Miyata made his way back through the base to the

main workshop, where the kaiten, the manned torpedoes, were pre-pared. The job of investigating and disposing of the bomb required a competent man—competent, but not too valuable in case it exploded.

"Yagi! Where are you? Where's my hairy Korean!"

Petty Officer Second Class Ryohei Yagi looked up from the fuel pump he was repairing. He was no hairier than Lieutenant Miyata. And he didn't smell of garlic, another slur the lieutenant frequently used.

He came over to Miyata, wiping grease from his hands. The two men were the same age, twenty-three, but Yagi looked older, due to the lines etched on his face by his time in the engine room of an Imperial Navy oil tanker, back when the Imperial Navy still had ships. And then there were the ugly scars that snaked up his neck, a souvenir from the night his oil tanker went down.

"Yes, Lieutenant Miyata," Yagi acknowledged—a little too casually for the Navy, a little too proud.

The lieutenant's eyes narrowed. "Is today the day you lose that last bar?" He was referring to the single bar above the wreath and anchor on Yagi's petty officer second class insignia patch, one step above sea-man. Yagi had suffered much to ascend that one step.

"No, Lieutenant. I hope not," he said.

"Then straighten that back."

Yagi felt the anger stirring inside him. One day, if this war ever ended, he might pay Miyata a visit.

He swallowed the feeling down and straightened his back.

"That's better," said Miyata. "Now, I'm sending you on a little out-ing. That B-29 that came down—they've found the crash site, and a bomb that's got the farmers shitting their pants. I want you to secure the site and deal with the bomb. There's a policeman waiting at the gate who will show you the way. Understand?"

Yagi gave a curt nod and started back to his workstation to gather some tools.

"On the double!" roared Miyata.

Yagi picked up his pace.

Petty Officer Yagi took two men with him: Seaman First Class Kuni-yasu Nakamura, nineteen years old, and Ordinary Seaman Kotaro Wada, eighteen. Nakamura, a university student, had washed out of the profoundly difficult kaiten pilot training program and been reassigned to working on the craft, a tremendous disappointment. Yagi liked him. Nakamura had a sharp mind and was not given to resentful looks and loafing. He thought less highly of Seaman Wada, a slow-witted bumpkin and easy mark when they played Cho-han, Yagi expertly handling the dice. Nakamura, to his credit, rarely allowed himself to be fleeced.

The trio set out on bicycles, Policeman Kinoshita leading the way. It took them across the bridge spanning the Shimata River and through the center of the town of Hikari. It was a small place, not a likely target in itself for American bombers. It was home, however, to Hikari Naval Arsenal, where engines, cannon, bombs, and torpedoes were manufactured. The bombers therefore would surely come. It was only a matter of time.

They turned north and continued, the road angling back to follow the west bank of the river, clumps of bamboo screening the water and the train tracks on the opposite side. The going was easy, the road level, but Policeman Kinoshita was straining nevertheless. He was tired out from the fifteen kilometers he had already pedaled that morning. The civilian ration, reduced again and then again over the previous year, was also not enough to sustain any sort of physical effort.

Seven kilometers on and they turned away from the river into a narrow valley heading west. "There," said Kinoshita, pointing up the track they were following. PO Yagi had seen it already, tendrils of black smoke hanging over a stand of trees. He looked off to the right at the rice paddies filling the valley, about 500 meters across. A Buddhist temple overlooked the scene from a ravaged hillside on the left, the pine trees that had once surrounded it all gone. They had been cut down and the roots dug up to be distilled into fuel.

It was after passing the shrine that Yagi spotted the first piece of wreckage, an immense wheel with its supporting arm sticking up. It must have been thrown a great distance. He was starting to pick up smells now, acrid smoke from burning rubber, fuel, and scorched metal. Then they were past the trees and at the heart of the crash site, a mass of scattered wreckage, some of the larger pieces blackened by fire that had now almost burned itself out.

There were twenty or more people standing around, mostly farmers. Some were chatting in the shade, still excited by the crash and enjoying a respite from their labors. Others were moving about in the fields, picking through the wreckage. Those who were near enough to see the military outfits stood up and bowed as the navy men approached and dismounted.

Yagi set his heavy iron bicycle on its kickstand and offered his canteen to Policeman Kinoshita, who was struggling to catch his breath. The policeman urged Yagi to go first, then gratefully accepted the canteen with both hands and took a long drink. They refreshed themselves to the drone of cicadas, so loud that it seemed to envelop the whole area in a vibrating cocoon. Yagi mopped his brow and began surveying the scene.

The B-29 had first hit the ground off to the right, judging from the swath cut through the rice plants that were starting to ripen. Straight ahead—that was a broken remnant of a wing, some of the aluminum skin peeled away, exposing the bones of the frame. One of the engines, propeller sheared off, was still attached—a stunningly massive engine, larger than anything Yagi had seen on any Japanese aircraft. A second piece of wing lay farther off, electrical wiring trailing out like intestines. Somewhat closer, amid flattened rice plants, lay a huddled mass that looked like a pile of rags. It took a moment for Yagi to realize that it was a body, one of the crew.

The largest portion of the wreckage in sight appeared to be the central fuselage, with half the starboard wing still attached. Two farmers could be seen searching through it. No sign of the tail section. There was something very large farther up the track, however, something plowed into the hillside, partly obscured by the trees.

"The cockpit," said Policeman Kinoshita, noting the direction of his gaze. "And some smaller parts farther along. It's all through the trees. The bomb is farther down, against the embankment."

Yagi took out several sheets of paper from his knapsack, each one bearing a printed warning: "DO NOT TOUCH! BY ORDER OF THE IMPERIAL JAPANESE NAVY." He handed a dozen of them to Nakamura and a jar of paste to Wada. "Post these on the larger pieces. This site is off-limits."

The two men snapped a bow before hurrying off. "Hai!"

"And keep your eyes open for aircraft markings!" Yagi called after them.

He turned to Kinoshita. "All right, show me the bomb."

Kinoshita led the way up the track. As Yagi followed, he could hear Nakamura and Wada in the distance, establishing order: "Get away from that! Put that down! No one in this field!"

Yagi stopped first to examine the cockpit. It had been torn completely off in the crash, skipping on across the field and plowing partway up the hill, the last of its forward momentum arrested by the trees. An elderly Buddhist monk stood beside the track a short distance before it, rocking back and forth as he chanted over a second crumpled body, the remains of another member of the enemy aircrew. He took no notice of Yagi and Kinoshita.

The cockpit lay angled up the hillside, its ragged edges trailing wires and cables. The interior space was sealed off at the rear by a bulkhead with an access hatch on the upper side. Yagi tried the hatch, but it would not open. He put his shoulder against it and pushed, but it still would not move. So much the better. No one would get in. He took out one of the "Do Not Touch" notices and affixed it to the bulkhead, then continued on up the hillside to look at the nose, pulling himself up with the broken branches of the trees.

The entire nose of the aircraft was comprised of thick glass panels, now mostly covered with dirt. One had been knocked out, the open space large enough for a small person to squeeze through. Yagi, stocky of build, stuck his head in for a look.

He saw two bodies, pilot and copilot, strapped to their seats. The pilot, eyes partly open but quite dead, had his hands still locked on the yoke. The copilot was slumped sideways, hanging limp in his harness, blood down the front of his flight suit. A third seat, empty, was situated between them, lower down and farther forward. It was so close that Yagi could reach out and touch it. Who sat here? The bombardier? They were perhaps on a weather observation mission. Or taking reconnaissance photos. But why carry a bomb?

Yagi withdrew his head from the nose of the plane and looked around. Small pieces glinted in the undergrowth here and there: torn shards of metal, bits of wiring, a metal cylinder that looked like a thermos, a brown leather boot.

Policeman Kinoshita was right. It was all through the trees.

He affixed another "Do Not Touch" sign to the glass. There likely would be a good deal inside the cockpit of interest to the Imperial Navy. The warning alone should be enough to deter the local people from wriggling in through the broken-out panel, but still . . .

"Policeman!" he called out to Kinoshita, looking on from the track. "No one is to touch this."

Kinoshita jerked his head in acknowledgment. "Hai!"

Yagi began to descend the hillside on the other side of the cockpit, handing himself down from one tree to the next. It was then that he noticed the scraped and muddied image of a nearly naked woman painted on the aircraft's aluminum skin. He broke off an obscuring branch to reveal the picture more fully. An American movie star, displaying her bottom and looking alluringly over her shoulder. The picture was framed by two words, painted in red at a jaunty angle. He took out his notebook and copied down the twelve letters without understanding: *WICKED INTENT.*

"It's just over here," said Kinoshita when Yagi rejoined him. The policeman ushered him along the track for another fifty meters, toward a trio of farmers squatting on the side of the embankment, contemplating something below them down in the field.

"There," said Kinoshita, pointing toward whatever it was they were gazing at.

"You should move back!" Yagi called out to the farmers as he approached. "Move back at least one hundred—"

He looked down at the biggest bomb he had ever seen in his life.

"Get out of here," he said quietly. "Move."

The farmers scrambled to their feet and scurried away.

The bomb lay at the edge of the field, its nose buried in the chest-high embankment. It must have tumbled some distance, expending momentum, Yagi deduced. Otherwise it would have dug itself all the way into the earth. It was some seventy-five centimeters across, and three meters of its length was showing. Depending on how much of it was buried, it was possibly the length of two men.

"Only this one?" he said.

Kinoshita nervously nodded. "Only this one. Should I . . . should I guard the site?"

Yagi grunted and nodded. "Make sure that nothing is touched."

"Hai!" Kinoshita gratefully backed away, then turned and jogged off.

Yagi continued contemplating the bomb. For a B-29 to be carrying only one, and so large—it must be special.

He eased himself down the embankment to stand in the paddy among the rice plants. The realization that the bomb had tumbled violently before coming to rest was not a great comfort. It could have some sort of delayed fuze, after all. He stood very still, apprehensive before it, like it was a sleeping beast that might suddenly wake.

It was making no noise. He stepped closer and lowered his head toward the dirt-smeared black casing.

Nothing.

He pressed his ear to the metal, listening for the ticking of a timing device, the sound of an internal mechanism winding itself down.

Nothing.

He straightened up, starting to relax, and once again took in the immensity of the thing. He now noticed that under the dirt it was covered with inscriptions in chalk and white paint, each put there by a different hand, judging from the various ways the letters were formed—some in capitals, some cursive, some slanted, some straight. He had a passing knowledge of the English alphabet and recognized some of the letters: an E and an M and a P. He did not understand any of the words but could guess the intent. But for so many inscriptions to be on one bomb . . .

Yes, it was clearly special, worth investigating. He decided not to use the thermite charges they had brought along to detonate it in place.

A sharp intake of breath from Nakamura and Wada, returning at the double and getting their first look at the thing.

They descended the embankment, stepping lightly. Yagi began brushing dirt from the casing, revealing what appeared to be a large identifying number, L10, and more handwritten inscriptions.

"These look like signatures," said Nakamura, scrutinizing the various scrawls. He sounded out a few of the more legible names, pointing at them in turn: "John Morris . . . Samuel Filson . . . Edward Houseman, for Charlie." To all three men they were meaningless sounds.

Nakamura moved on to the largest inscription, printed in block letters, and read it aloud in halting English: "For . . . the boys . . . on . . . Han-cock Street . . . De-tro-it . . . USA." He puzzled over this for a moment, murmuring the Japanese word for "boys."

"A street of boys," mused Wada, looking over his shoulder.

"Detroit," said Yagi. "That's an American city." He remembered his father mentioning the place. Yagi senior had owned a garage in Osaka and often had occasion to service American cars, Fords and Packards and even a Cadillac that had been built in Detroit.

Steeling himself, Nakamura brushed off the dirt from another inscription and slowly read it aloud, syllable by syllable. "'To Emperor Hirohito, Special Delivery to where the sun don't shine.'"

He looked up at Yagi, pointing at the name. "'Emperor Hirohito.' That means Tennō Heika."

Yagi tried the rest of the inscription. "'Where . . . the . . . sun . . . don't . . . shine.'"

Nakamura attempted a translation.

Wada's eyes widened. "They're cursing the Emperor to a place of darkness. Near a street of boys. What could that mean?"

Yagi sent the two men back to the bicycles for the tool bag and shovels and put them to work excavating dirt from around the bomb. As they dug and sweated, he jotted down notes and began making a sketch. He then took over with the hand brush, cleaning off the last of the dirt from the now fully exposed bomb and beginning a detailed examination. It seemed sensible to gather as much information as he could, given the bomb's unusual nature. He also hadn't figured out how to go about disarming it. He in fact had very little experience in bomb disposal. What he knew came from a daylong lecture that had been part of his retraining at Kure Naval Yard after recovering from his burns. The class had been shown a 50-kilo American incendiary bomb and a few examples of British bombs recovered earlier in the war. That was the extent of the enemy ordnance he had seen.

The bomb was just over 3 meters long from its blunt nose to the boxlike structure at the tail. Yagi added the measurement to his sketch, together with the diameter, 71 centimeters, and the circumference, 2.23 meters. The rear structure had been crushed on impact, but its original configuration was apparent, crisscrossed vanes to stabilize the bomb as it fell. It was bolted to the casing and evidently could be removed. Some sort of plate lay beneath it, an access plate to the rear of the bomb. There were three shallow holes in it, possibly for a special tool to assist with removal.

Yagi worked his way forward, running his hand along the casing.

He came to a vertical seam in the metal, lined with bolts. A second seam lay another meter and a half farther on, making for three distinct parts to the casing. And positioned on this forward seam: a single steel shackle. This was where the bomb was suspended and thus marked its center of gravity. It was only a third of the way from the nose. That meant it was nose-heavy.

Where was the fuze? On the American incendiary bomb he had seen at Kure, it was inserted in the nose. Seeing the bolt and nut projecting from the front of this vastly larger weapon led him to think that it was similarly designed.

He removed the largest adjustable wrench from the tool bag and fitted it onto the nut projecting from the nose. He began to apply pressure as Nakamura and Wada looked on.

The nut didn't move.

Yagi braced himself and tried again, straining harder.

The nut didn't move.

He got down close to squint at the fraction of bolt projecting from the end of the nut. He could make out a bit of the thread, enough to verify that he was applying torque in the proper direction. Counterclockwise. The Americans did things the same, like on their cars.

He wavered, thinking he ought to switch his attention to the tail. No, the box-shaped vanes there would first need to be cut away. And that couldn't be done here in a rice field without an acetylene torch.

He returned to the nose.

He removed the heavy hammer from the tool bag, repositioned the wrench, and tapped on the handle to loosen the nut. It remained frozen. He increased the force of his blows, then tried tapping the wrench in one direction, then the other, trying to break whatever bond was preventing the nut from turning. No good. The nut wouldn't budge. Yagi let out a sigh of frustration and settled back on his haunches.

It was only then that he noticed Nakamura and Wada hovering behind him, their eyes wide with alarm from watching him use a hammer on a bomb.

Their fright goaded him on. It had been this way with him since he was a boy, when his family emigrated from Korea and his father, Yang Jae-sok, had adopted the Japanese surname Yagi. As an ethnic Korean in Japan, fully acculturated but still looked down on, Ryohei Yagi had developed a drive growing up to prove that he was braver and stronger and tougher than any Japanese boy. It was a trait that got him into numerous fights at school. By the age of sixteen, he could take on grown men.

"I hope you sent a letter home to your parents," he said, squaring his powerful shoulders and returning to work. He readjusted the wrench on the nut and bellied up close, both his hands bearing down on the handle. Wada, seeing what he was about to do, sucked in his breath.

"*Yosh!*"

Yagi brought his weight down on the wrench, one, two, three, four times. The nut held like it was welded in place. Instead, the entire bomb moved.

He paused to wipe away the sweat dripping into his eyes. A glance at Nakamura and Wada, looking on in terror.

"You two boys want to give it a try?"

Both men shook their heads.

Yagi got into position again to use his full weight on the wrench. He began heaving down again on the handle, grunting with effort. The bomb began rocking. Finally he felt the nut give way.

He paused for a breath, then resumed.

More movement. A definite turn.

But it wasn't the nut that was turning. It was the whole steel disk to which the nut was attached. It was unscrewing from the nose of the bomb like a giant oil drain plug from the crankcase of an engine.

Using less force, Yagi completed a full turn. The plate was a centimeter out now and rotating smoothly. Another turn and another, and the plug kept coming. Five centimeters, then eight, then ten—ten centimeters of high-quality steel with machined threads cut into the surface. Whatever this was—and it didn't look at all like a fuze—it had been manufactured with care.

It was getting hard to turn now. The emerging plug, solid steel, was heavy.

"Take the weight off the end," Yagi ordered.

Wada and Nakamura, moving stiffly from fright, positioned themselves facing the nose of the bomb and lifted up on the plug as Yagi continued to unscrew it.

A heavy metallic thunk, and the bomb shifted. The two seamen threw themselves backward. The plug had come loose. It was hanging at an angle from what was now a hole in the bomb's nose, apparently held in place by something farther inside.

With a great deal of struggle and straining, PO Yagi and his two assistants pulled the plug the rest of the way out of the cavity. It dropped into the dirt and they fell back, panting, Yagi's vision momentarily filled with flashing stars brought on by the effort.

Retrieving a flashlight from the tool bag, he peered into the exposed nose of the bomb. A polished tube, like a gun barrel, extended deep inside, sixteen centimeters in diameter and easily two meters in length. If there was any explosive material inside, he couldn't see it.

He got to his feet and looked down at the heavy plug they had removed from the nose. This was no fuze. It was a cylindrical assembly of several pieces of metal, held together by a thick rod with a heavy nut on each end. At the outermost end was the threaded plug that he had unscrewed from the casing. Next to it, in the center of the assembly, was a smaller piece of machined steel, angling down to a diameter of fifteen centimeters, then a thick gray metallic disk that had the look of coarse iron or perhaps tungsten carbide. And seated upon this, farthest inside . . .

There were six metallic rings, stacked one on top of the other. They were of varying thicknesses and crudely cast, which seemed odd, considering the precision evident in the rest of the bomb. The metal itself also seemed strange. It had a plum-colored patina, richer on some of the rings than others, and was quite soft, like lead. It yielded when Yagi pressed it with his thumbnail.

It was also extremely heavy. After removing the stacked rings from the assembly by unscrewing the innermost bolt from the rod, Yagi needed a good deal of strength to pick them up. The entire stack was only the size of a one-liter tin can, but he estimated that it weighed about twenty-five kilos.

He allowed his two men to handle the rings as they wondered what the material was.

It was Seaman Nakamura, remembering his high school chemistry, who suggested conducting a test.

THREE

PETTY OFFICER YAGI PEDALED AWAY FROM THE CRASH SITE WITH THREE OF THE RINGS OF unidentified metal lashed to the back of his bicycle. He took Seaman Nakamura with him. The test had been Nakamura's idea, after all. Seaman Wada was left behind to guard the unusual bomb.

Returning to Hikari, Yagi led the way into town, on past the post office and the train station to the local high school. It was closed, of course—nearly all schools in Japan had closed by early 1945—but there was an elderly caretaker on the premises who responded to Yagi's call from the front gate.

"Take us to the chemistry classroom," Yagi brusquely ordered, unlashing the plum-colored rings. He had them tied up in a cloth, like a little container of ashes.

"The chemistry classroom?" The caretaker appeared to be simple.

"The chemistry classroom!" Yagi snapped. "The chemistry classroom!"

The old man turned and shuffled off to fetch a ring of keys from the guardroom. Another creeping walk down an echoing hallway and a good deal of fumbling, and he unlocked a door.

Yagi scanned the classroom. It appeared to be largely intact. "Do the sinks work?" he asked. "Is the water turned on?"

"The water is on," said the old man. "But the pressure is low."

Yagi and Nakamura stepped inside. The caretaker, curiosity piqued, was eager to follow. Yagi closed the door in his face.

It was a laboratory classroom: teacher's desk and blackboard at the front, desks and chairs for thirty students in the center, a Formica-topped counter down one side and against the back wall. Dust lay thick on the desks and the dark wood of the floor and floated in the sunlight filtering through the grime-covered windows. It had been only two years since Nakamura had studied in a classroom like this.

A large glass beaker and a set of scales would be required. They found them in a cabinet under the back counter. The beaker was a three-liter model with precise graduations. The scales, a well-made German set, could measure weights of up to ten kilos. Nakamura set them both on the counter. Yagi meanwhile was looking through the books on a shelf at the front. He did not see the textbook Nakamura remembered, *Introduction to Chemistry* with a green cover. He found something just as good, however, a volume with the required table printed in the back.

With the book open on the counter, Nakamura placed the first of the metal rings on the scales. It was the thickness of only two fingers and not much wider than his palm. But it was remarkably heavy. Could it be even as heavy as gold?

He tweaked the scales and waited for the balance to settle. "Weight 3,965 grams," he said. Yagi jotted down the number in his notebook.

Nakamura held the glass beaker over the nearby sink and began to fill it with water, slowly dribbling in the final few drops until the level was at exactly one liter. Then he carefully lowered the ring into the water until it was resting on the bottom, fully submerged.

He squinted at the graduated markings on the glass. The water level had risen to 1.21 liters, perhaps a hair more. "Displacement is 210 cubic centimeters," he said.

Yagi jotted down the number and formulated the problem: *3,965 grams displaces 210 cubic centimeters of water. So 3,965 divided by 210 . . .*

He set to work on the longhand division. So did Nakamura, writing on the counter with a stub of pencil. Their answers, Nakamura finishing before Yagi, did not agree. They rechecked their calculations and Yagi found to his annoyance that he had been wrong. Nakamura was correct. The specific gravity of the metal ring was 18.88.

They turned their attention to the table in the back of the textbook. Water was listed at the top, with a specific gravity of 1. Aluminum was a little farther down at 2.6, copper at 8.8, silver at 10.5, lead at 11.5, mercury at 13.5. There was not much below that, just a handful of truly heavy substances down at the bottom of the list. Only one had a specific gravity in the range of eighteen: 18.8, to be precise. It came just before gold at 19.3.

"*Uran,*" Yagi read. The name was unfamiliar. He turned to Nakamura. "What do you know about uran?"

"Nothing," said Nakamura, slowly shaking his head.

Upon his return to Hikari Special Attack Unit, Petty Officer Yagi reported first to the executive officer, Lieutenant Miyata. Miyata then took him to Lieutenant Commander Sadayoshi Koreeda's office to report directly to the commanding officer of the base.

"Very strange," murmured Koreeda, scrutinizing Yagi's notes and sketch as the petty officer stood at attention in front of his desk. "And you found no explosive material inside?"

"Nothing I could see." said Yagi. "Just those rings of uran at the end of a long tube running through the center."

"And how do you know this is uran?" said Koreeda, eyeing the plum-colored rings Yagi had set on his desk.

Yagi explained the experiment he and Nakamura had performed and was rewarded with an appreciative nod. "It was Seaman Nakamura's idea," he added, hesitating only a little.

"Perhaps it's some sort of measuring apparatus," ventured Lieutenant

Miyata. "The prongs on the nose, they could be antennae. For relaying a signal back to the aircraft."

"Possibly. Perhaps." Koreeda considered Yagi's sketch for another moment, then shook his head. "No, a measuring apparatus would have a parachute attached. It would need to fall slowly as it took readings. I think this must be a bomb. A very strange bomb. The interior . . . it's just an empty tube?"

Yagi nodded. "Just an empty tube. Polished and smooth, like a gun barrel."

"And the outer casing?"

"Heavy steel. Painted black. In three sections, bolted together."

"Did these sections appear designed to break open?"

Yagi thought for a moment. "I don't think so. The casing is strong, hardly dented. The bolts would have to be removed to open it up."

"And you . . . you feel all right?"

Yagi's eyes darted to the commander's, realizing what Koreeda was thinking.

"I feel fine," he said.

"And your men," said Koreeda. "No ill effects?"

Yagi shook his head.

"Well, perhaps then we can rule out a biological weapon."

Koreeda picked up one of the uran rings and marveled again at the weight. He tapped it, tested its hardness with his thumbnail, then sniffed it.

He turned to his XO. "Lieutenant Miyata, send Yagi in a truck to recover this object. I want it brought back here. It is to be wrapped up in a tarpaulin. Double layers."

Dismissed from Lieutenant Commander Koreeda's office, Petty Officer Yagi fueled one of the base trucks with a precious quarter tank of diesel and set out with Seaman Nakamura and two new recruits to return to the crash site. They took the portable tripod hoist and winch from the workshop, together with additional tools and blocks of wood for stabilizing the bomb once they got it onto the back of the truck, and a tarpaulin for encasing it as per Koreeda's instructions.

To Yagi's amazement, the bomb was too heavy for the hoist and the winch, which could handle a maximum load of three thousand kilos. The only way to move it was to lift one end, put blocks under it, then lift the other end. In this manner the bomb was laboriously raised step by step up out of the rice paddy, a process that took more than two hours. It took another hour to raise it from the road up onto the back of the truck, the leaf springs straining when they took the full weight.

Twilight was coming on when the truck set out with its load for the drive back to Hikari, Yagi not exceeding twenty kilometers an hour and slowing to a walking pace on the rougher stretches. Arriving back at base, he reported first to Lieutenant Miyata, then proceeded with Miyata to the main workshop to get an accurate weight for the object using the heavy-duty hoist.

Commander Koreeda by this time had come over from his office for a personal inspection. After conferring with Miyata and reassuring himself that the object wasn't a biological weapon, he moved closer to look it over, then peered inside the open end using Yagi's flashlight, handed to him by Miyata.

"Total weight 4,300 kilos," the lieutenant informed Koreeda. The commander looked up in surprise at the number. It was four times the bomb load of an Imperial Navy heavy bomber.

Yagi, smeared from head to foot with dirt and sweat, had to make an effort to stand at attention beside the truck. Another few minutes, he glumly thought, and the mess hall would be closed. If dinner hadn't been set aside for him, someone was going to get punched in the head.

"All right," said Koreeda, returning the flashlight to Miyata, who in turn passed it back to Yagi. "Secure it in one of the old workshops down by the water. I want it well away from the main buildings."

Yagi released the tension from his back and climbed up into the truck.

He heard Commander Koreeda's voice behind him: "Well done, Lieutenant Miyata."

Returning to his office, Commander Koreeda drafted a cable. "Send this to Kure," he said, handing it to his clerk. "And to the Second General Army as well."

Kure Naval District, headquartered at Kure eighty kilometers to the northeast, encompassed the whole of southern Japan, including Hikari. The Second General Army encompassed a similar region. That Koreeda included it in his communication was in line with the Army-Navy Cooperation Agreement signed four months before.

The cable was sent. It read: *Possible new-type bomb recovered from B-29 crash site, Hikari, Yamaguchi Prefecture. Length: 3.04 m. Diameter: 71 cm. Weight: 4,300 kg. Metal tube like gun barrel, diameter 16 cm, runs through center. Metal rings removed from inside, 25 kg, identified as uran.*

The communication attracted little attention at Kure. Vice Admiral Kanazawa and his staff were still preoccupied with the devastation wrought by American and British aircraft, which had sunk every surviving large Japanese warship still in the harbor just two weeks before. No one even bothered to request confirmation of the remarkable weight, which Koreeda had half expected. The cable was routinely forwarded to the office of the Navy Chief of Staff in Tokyo, but no particular notice was taken there either.

Koreeda's message met with similar indifference at Second General Army headquarters in Hiroshima. The staff there had a myriad of more pressing things to worry about as they prepared for the coming American invasion and the final decisive battle for the homeland. As at Kure, the message was forwarded to Tokyo, in this case to the Ministry of War.

It was there, at the War Ministry, that someone finally took notice. His name was Lieutenant Colonel Shingen Sagara, an Imperial Army officer in the Ordnance Bureau. He was impressed by the reported weight of the recovered object, further evidence of the massive capabilities of the B-29. It was the final sentence, however, that attracted his particular interest.

"Uran," he murmured, running his thumb down the scar on his lip. Uranium.

He read the word with understanding. He knew what it meant.

FOUR

THE AIR RAID SIREN HAD SOUNDED THIRTY MINUTES BEFORE, BUT LIEUTENANT COLONEL Shingen Sagara had not gone to the underground shelter. He stood at his third-floor window in the War Ministry building, smoking a cigarette as he looked out. The Defense Section of the Ordnance Bureau, which he headed, occupied four offices at the front of the building and thus afforded him a view of Tokyo, looking south. He was watching the attack on the port area of Kawasaki in the distance, where black smoke was rising. The Americans were striking now with aircraft from carriers cruising within sight of the coast—striking with impunity during daylight hours and meeting minimal resistance.

The sirens stopped. First to leave the building was an officer Sagara recognized from the Personnel Bureau, his uniform creased and sweat-stained as usual and worn with all the grace of a rice sack. It irritated the colonel to see fellow officers dress without pride. He himself kept a generous supply of shirts in his office. In hot weather like this, he worked his way through two shirts a day, even three on occasion. An officer in the Imperial Japanese Army had no excuse for a slovenly appearance.

He returned to his desk and sank into his chair. The files and reports and memos heaped before him, which kept him working eighteen hours a day and sometimes longer, mainly concerned Operation Ketsu-gō, the defense of the homeland. The Ordnance Bureau was under tremendous pressure to meet the targets for the stockpiling of munitions at forward units on Kyushu, where the Americans would logically begin their invasion following the monsoon season. It was a difficult job, munitions production having been severely reduced by the air raids. What was being turned out, moreover, was often held up due to the state of the train lines, which were coming under increasing attack now that Japan's cities were mostly destroyed. To make any progress against these myriad problems took all the colonel's considerable organizational skills, together with a good deal of bullying, cajoling, and threats.

Stabbing his cigarette into the overflowing ashtray, the colonel noticed once again the document that had left his mind for a moment. *Unconditional surrender.* What an abomination! The very words increased his blood pressure and twisted his mouth into a frown.

It was a copy of the Allies' Potsdam Declaration, received four days before and made public in the newspapers, in censored form, that very morning. No real concessions were offered, only a demand for the emasculation and humiliation of the nation's armed forces, coupled with the assurance of utter destruction if Japan failed to comply. The whole thing was deserving of nothing but contempt. But that was not what upset the colonel. The Americans and the British were the enemy. Such behavior was to be expected. Sagara's anger was due instead to the rumor circulating at the War Ministry that morning that the Foreign Ministry was seeking Moscow's help in mediating peace terms. This confirmed Sagara's suspicions that Prime Minister Suzuki was being false with his assurances that the government would ignore the Potsdam Declaration. The wily old fox was just trying to keep the Army quiet while he worked behind the scenes to bring the war to an end.

Weakness. That was what it was. The way ahead had become

rocky, and the civilians, aided by a few misguided military men like Navy Minister Yonai, had lost all hope, all fiber, all spirit. Prime Minister Suzuki, Foreign Minister Tōgō, Admiral Yonai, and Marquis Kido whispering treason into the Emperor's ear—the entire lot of them were cowards. A few setbacks and they were ready to lie down and expose their backs to stinking streams of American piss.

That would not be allowed to happen, of course, not with the war situation far from hopeless. Yes, there had been strategic reverses and the Navy had been gutted, although the Army remained determined and strong. Yes, Japan's cities had been damaged, industrial output was down, and an enemy invasion was expected. The course of events had not unfolded in an optimal manner. But hopeless? No, certainly not hopeless. Victory remained within grasp. By continuing to fight, by meeting the coming invasion and showing a willingness to absorb heavy losses, the enemy would become mentally exhausted and be ultimately forced to concede.

Colonel Sagara cast the maddening document aside, facedown this time, and began fanning himself against the rising heat of midday. He had slept little the previous night, stretched out on a cot in his office. And the night before that, he had gotten no rest at all. It had left him fatigued and struggling to concentrate on the reports on his desk. He would have to take another tablet to get the work done. It was all leaving him run-down and haggard—enough to prompt even his wife, who hated him, to comment on his appearance when he visited his home a few days before to pick up clean clothes. And his mental state . . .

He opened a drawer, took out the little green bottle, and downed two of the tablets. It required two now to give him the boost that he needed.

Uran.

His mind went back to the word. He picked up the file he had requested from General Yasuda's office, the final report on Project Ni-Go, now bombed into oblivion. Sagara, as head of the Ordnance Bureau, had been aware of the research work being done at the Riken under Yasuda's aegis, the effort to enrich uran—uranium—with a view to making some sort of powerful bomb. That was why the cable from Hikari had caught his attention when he looked over the message center logbook the previous evening. A bomb recovered from a B-29 that contained uran . . . What were the Americans up to? Whatever it was, it demanded investigation. If his aide, Captain Kunio Onda, returned with worthwhile information, he would telephone the Riken and summon the head of Project Ni-Go.

The tablets were taking effect now. The colonel was feeling energized—so much so that he was unable to sit still. He jumped up and returned to the window.

Still no sign of the motorcycle outside. Captain Onda had left on it earlier that morning, after Sagara had phoned the Special Intelligence Unit in Suginami district to inquire about B-29 activity over western Honshu the previous day.

"Ah," replied the officer who headed the unit, "you mean the Special Task Planes."

"The Special Task Planes?" Sagara had no idea what the officer was talking about. Then, when the man began to explain: "Not on the telephone. I'll send someone over."

The colonel rolled his head and shoulders, trying to ease the ache in his neck. He could not remember injuring it. He lit another cigarette and returned to gazing out the window, smoking with one hand and fanning with the other. The city spread before him at the base of the hill had been reduced to the flatness of a Go board, almost total destruction, its network of roads and train lines and snaking rivers laid bare. The Ministry's west-facing offices looked out over a similar vista. So did the ones on the north of the building. So did the ones facing east.

Had Sagara been allowed to choose his own office, he might have taken one on the other side of the hallway, overlooking the secluded tranquility of the inner courtyard. Instead, he had been assigned an outer office facing the devastation of the city. The view had been disheartening at first, but in it Sagara had found inspiration. For one could not help but notice that there were only two areas that had escaped damage in the air raids: the War Ministry compound atop Ichigaya Heights, where he was now standing; and, just visible off to the left, the Imperial Palace. There was beauty and meaning in this, as Sagara reflected upon often and had emotionally expressed to his colleagues. As the physical husk of Dai Nippon was burned away in the air raids, the Emperor in his palace and the Imperial Army at Ichigaya stood out ever more clearly as the essential beating heart of the nation. This might never have occurred to him in an inward-facing office overlooking a cosseted garden and trees.

The throaty rumble of a motorcycle below. Colonel Sagara looked down, the cadence of his fan increasing, watching as Captain Onda dismounted from the Rikuo and straightened the khaki uniform he wore very well. The handsome young officer, seconded from the Army Air Service, had been a real catch.

Onda hurried toward the entrance, moving almost at a run.

"They're based on Tinian," began Captain Onda, closing the door and pulling a chair to Colonel Sagara's desk. "The Special Intelligence Unit has been reporting on them to the General Staff Office since June, but nobody there seems to have taken any notice."

Sagara knew the story only too well. Lack of interdepartmental cooperation, hidebound procedures, deskbound officers in blinders with the imagination of cows.

"Since early this year . . . "—Onda dug a map and some scribbled notes from his satchel and spread them on the desk—"since early this year the Intelligence Unit has been intercepting Morse code traffic from the American bombers on Guam and in the Northern Marianas. It's encrypted, of course, so we don't know what they're saying. But every signal from every aircraft has an identifying call sign that's sent in the clear. From that alone, we've learned a lot."

The captain turned the map around for Sagara to see. It was of the western Pacific, from Japan south to New Guinea, with Guam and the Northern Mariana Islands halfway between. "The B-29s based on Guam"—Onda pointed the island out as he consulted his notes—"use V500 call signs: V501, V502, V503, and so on, a unique identifier for each plane. The bombers on Saipan use V400 call signs, and for the ones on Tinian, it's V700. So we know where the B-29s are coming from—Guam, Saipan, or Tinian—just from these call signs. And by triangulating the signals we know where they're going, what cities they're going to attack."

Colonel Sagara grunted and nodded. He understood the principle of triangulating radio signals to obtain a position.

"About five weeks ago," continued Onda, "the Unit began intercepting new call signs from Tinian, planes using V600 identifiers instead of the usual V700s. There have been only a few of them, just ten or twelve. And they always operate on their own, never as part of a larger sortie. So we know they're not usual bombers, but used for some special purpose. That's why the Intelligence Unit calls them Special Task Planes."

"And the planes yesterday," prompted the colonel.

"Yes, yesterday." Onda turned to his second page of notes. "On August first, at 0205, signals from three Tinian B-29s were intercepted, call signs V670, V689, and V683, flying singly, heading north. One went to Hiroshima, another to Kokura, the third to Nagasaki. Then they turned back."

"Weather planes," Sagara surmised.

"Then, at 0320, signals from three more B-29s from Tinian were intercepted, following the same general route, heading to western Honshu, flying together. Here they are." Onda turned the paper around and pointed out the numbers. "V680, V665, and V691. They had almost reached Kokura when V680 turned away. The other two planes circled Kokura, then returned south."

Colonel Sagara leaned forward to examine the map, running his eyes along the route from Tinian to Kokura. Three planes on the outward journey, two going back. He turned to Onda's notes with their list of call signs.

V680. That was the B-29 that had crashed outside Hikari. That was his plane.

He steepled his fingers and touched his lips, softly caressing. Reconnaissance planes in the lead to report on weather conditions over three cities, followed by a single plane and support aircraft proceeding to one of those cities: Kokura. It was the sort of behavior that one would expect of a mission to deliver a very powerful weapon. But could the Americans actually have developed such a thing as a uranium bomb? The limited understanding he had derived from the file on Project Ni-Go was that it was merely a preliminary investigation, years away from the development of a hypothetical weapon. Could the Americans really be that far ahead?

The colonel lit another cigarette as he reexamined his options. He considered and rejected the idea of contacting Second General Army headquarters in Hiroshima and involving Field Marshal Hata. Hata, with overall authority over defenses in western Japan, could order the naval officer in charge of Hikari Special Attack Unit to transport the American bomb to Hiroshima for examination, where it would then be under Army control. Involving the Second General Army, however, posed several problems, starting with the possibility that Hata and his staff, mindful of the directive on Army-Navy cooperation, might not act decisively in the matter. They might not act at all. And if they did, what then? The weight of military bureaucracy would descend: stultifying interservice rivalry and a mass of red tape.

No, Sagara concluded, he would not inform Hata and the Second General Army. It would be better, given the war situation, for him to proceed on his own.

He glanced at his watch—it was just after eleven o'clock—then at Captain Onda. There was no point in sending him out of the office. His aide knew everything already, perhaps more than Sagara should have told him, but these were perilous times.

The colonel referred to the personnel list in his file on Project Ni-Go. It was headed by Dr. Yoshio Nishina, the "Ni" in the name of the project. He picked up the telephone and dialed the number at the top of the page. Six rings, then a young woman answered.

"This is Lieutenant Colonel Sagara at the War Ministry, Ordnance Bureau. Put Yoshio Nishina on the line."

"I'm sorry," the voice informed him, "but Dr. Nishina is away for a few days."

"Well, who do you have there? I need to speak to someone about the project."

The voice informed him that almost everyone involved with Project Ni-Go was now gone, reassigned following the destruction of the Riken in the air raids in April. The only project member still around was Dr. Kan.

Sagara ran his eyes down the list of Ni-Go personnel, twenty names in total. There he was. Keizo Kan. Separation Team. Team leader.

"Well, put him on," he snapped, irritation rising.

The woman set down the receiver. Sagara heard her voice calling in the background. The passage of three interminable minutes. Then the scrape of the receiver being picked up and her voice again.

"I'm sorry, but Kan-sensei is not in the building at the moment."

"Well, go and find him," barked Sagara. "Send him here. I want to see him at once!"

He hung up the receiver and pushed the Ni-Go file to Captain Onda.

"Keizo Kan," he said, tapping the name. "Find out what you can about him."

FIVE

KEIZO KAN WAS WORKING AMONG THE SWEET POTATOES, HIS FACE GLISTENING WITH SWEAT as he weeded the rows. He spent more time here these days, toiling with a hoe or on his hands and knees, than he did puzzling over matters of physics. The plot had been planted in May by one of his assistants, a young Tokyo University graduate named Nozaki. Nozaki had acquired a bundle of slips on a foray into the country and had planted them in the scorched earth beside the remains of Building 49, a dozen rows near the concrete steps that led up to nowhere. He had given them a good start by the time his summons for military service arrived, his greater scientific usefulness to the nation wiped out by the air raid that had destroyed Building 49, the home of Project Ni-Go, along with most of the rest of the Riken, on the night of April 13. After Nozaki's dismal send-off, his remaining colleagues giving three lackluster cheers of "Banzai," Kan had assumed the responsibility of tending the plot. It was one of several that now grew among the ruins of the largely abandoned research and development complex.

Kan began watering the plants, hauling pails back and forth from the tap nearest the water tank, which somehow was still standing. He hurried along at a shuffle, forearms straining, grunting like the workmen he had disdained in his youth. His flapping shirt was soon wet through. Sweat streaming down his forehead caused his Harold Lloyd eyeglasses to slide down his nose.

Watering finished, he sat on the blackened steps to rest. As he gazed at the plants and his breathing slowed, his mind went back to his home in Asakusa. It had been a nice little property near Senso-ji Temple, a well-built old house with space behind for a garden, six kilometers from the Riken, which he said he would walk every day for his health but rarely did.

The garden. They had planted flowers there together, grubbing in the dirt with smiles on their faces. Chrysanthemums. And cosmos. And roses. She liked roses. Then they sat on the back veranda and drank barley tea as they admired their work.

The back veranda. It had been their quiet retreat from the city, then their place of shared joy, for it was there that she had told him she was pregnant. It was in an evening in late spring, the sky shading from coral to violet. His eyes went wide at the news; then he burst out laughing and seized her in his arms. He had been so inept when they were courting, such an utter fool. And yet it had been his own awkward words that she now whispered, the words that had become the most meaningful expression of the love that existed between them.

Garbo loves Taylor, she had said.

And he had replied, no longer foolish: *And Taylor loves Garbo.*

He rose from the steps and returned to the tap to wash his face and meager torso and rinse out his shirt. He handled the garment with care, like fine silk. Wartime clothing had become so shoddy that it could not stand up to a vigorous scrub.

He was still at the tap when Miss Yokoyama found him.

"A Colonel Sagara at the War Ministry just called," she said. "He wants to talk about Project Ni-Go. He says it's urgent."

Kan straightened up, anxiety sweeping through his body. He had always had a nervous disposition, but lately it had become worse. He tried to reason himself back to calmness. If this colonel wanted to discuss Ni-Go, it was only natural that he should be sent for. In the absence of Dr. Nishina, he was the only one left at the Riken with intimate knowledge of the work that had been done. But why this interest now, months after the project's demise? Perhaps the summons was a trap, a way to get him to the War Ministry to be arrested. Kan often wondered why he hadn't yet been arrested, in the seven weeks since the Tokkō, the Thought Police, had come for his wife.

"You'll need to change your clothes," Miss Yokoyama gently prompted, for Kan was just standing there, seemingly lost. His mind had been badly affected by the strain of the past several months.

"Yes," replied Kan, looking down at his worn-out work pants, baggy and cinched up with a piece of string. "Yes, I must change."

He returned to his room in the surviving dormitory building to comb his hair and put on a presentable outfit, a People's Uniform minus the jacket because it was too hot. His prewar leather shoes, re-soled three times, were the only quality item of apparel he still owned. Beyond that there were a few books on a shelf, three dented metal bowls, a handful of utensils, some odds and ends, and an urn. That was the extent of Keizo Kan's worldly possessions.

Since time was pressing, Miss Yokoyama urged him to take Dr. Nishina's bicycle for the five-kilometer journey south through the city. It was the quickest way to get to Ichigaya, with streetcar service curtailed and electric trains no longer running into what was left of downtown. Dr. Nishina wouldn't need it. He was away until Sunday.

Kan exited the Riken's front gate, pumping hard at the pedals, past the weathered sign giving the facility's full name, Rikagaku Kenkyūjo, from which the contraction Riken was derived—the Institute of Physical and Chemical Research in Tokyo's Komagome district.

He passed the post office and the elementary school, now closed, and turned south at the police station. It had been the first place he had gone to look for his wife back in June. The way south along Hakusan-dori was clear now, the debris from the firebombings pushed into mounds along the side of the road. The pavement itself remained damaged from the intense heat. Kan had to weave from side to side as he went, skirting ruts and potholes, passing the occasional bicycle and cart but mostly people on foot. On both sides, through Komagome and past the Toyo University campus, through Maruyama Shinmachi and Hongo, there was nothing but ruin—empty shells of burned-out concrete and brick buildings, empty lots where wooden structures had been. Some of the scorched blank spaces, as at the Riken, had been transformed into vegetable gardens, a return to primitive existence in what had been until recently the world's third largest city.

Up ahead loomed the low tiers of Korakuen Stadium. Kan had brought his four-year-old daughter, Aiko, here to see the circus on New Year's Day in 1943. And he had returned with several of his coworkers for the sumo summer basho on a rare day off in 1944. The usual venue for the basho, the Ryogoku Kokugikan, had been turned into a military factory by then, and the wrestlers looked depressingly thin.

He continued on to the next corner and turned west to follow the train line, the Kanda River and Suidobashi Station on his left, the roof over the station platform burned completely away. A little farther along, he passed the district police station. He had been here as well. He had visited half a dozen police stations in the city—bowing low, his eyes downcast—as he made inquiries about his wife and learned nothing. Seven weeks and he still did not know why she had been arrested or where she was being detained.

There was only one road curving up Ichigaya Heights to the Imperial Japanese Army's walled compound on top. Kan dismounted and walked his bicycle up it, after being cleared at the guardhouse at the foot of the hill. By the time he reached the second guardhouse at the top he was starting to tremble. He gave his name to the guard in a quavering voice and was allowed to pass on, the guard pointing him to a large building off to the right.

Kan proceeded through the complex on foot, pushing the bicycle. It seemed irreverent, perhaps even criminal, to ride it up here. He looked around as he went, overawed by the two dozen buildings, the largest among them the Military Academy, Imperial General Headquarters, and the Ministry of War. It took him a moment to realize what was so striking. The entire compound, eight hundred meters long and five hundred meters across, was undamaged. Trees on the hillside leading up had been burned, but the buildings here atop Ichigaya Heights were untouched.

The War Ministry was painted in a patchwork of gray to break up its outline. It stood three stories high and was built in the form of a rectangle, a hundred meters long on the front and not much less on the sides. There were thirty-six windows on each floor across the front. Add the same number across the back, plus twenty-two windows on one side and twenty-two on the other, equals one hundred sixteen, times three floors.

Kan did the math in his head, trying to settle his nerves as he made his way to the building's front entrance. A tower rose above the stone portico to a height of six stories, a clock at the top, minute hand at twenty, hour hand at nine.

Four hours slow.

Or it had stopped altogether.

Keizo Kan was aware that he was visibly shaking as he bowed and stood in front of Colonel Sagara's desk. Sagara motioned him into a seat, ordered tea to be brought, then launched into an interrogation.

"Project Ni-Go," he began, tapping the file under his hand. "I'm going to ask you some questions."

"Yes, Sagara-chūsa," said Kan, looking down at his hands, pressed on the top of his knees.

"The explosive nature of uranium. Explain it to me."

Kan risked a glance up at the colonel. Sagara's eyes were on him, intense and unblinking, his finger tapping a rapid cadence on his desk. He seemed genuinely intent on getting an answer, not on making an arrest.

"Uranium," Keizo Kan stammered. "Uranium is ... It ... Uranium has—"

He stopped. He took a deep breath. He tried again.

"Uranium ... is mainly composed of uranium-238 atoms. Ninety-two protons and 146 neutrons equals 238. Uranium also contains a second type of atom in small amounts, less than one percent, uranium-235. Ninety-two protons and 143 neutrons equal 235. And there are also occasional stray neutrons."

He paused and drew in another breath. He was starting to calm down, his hands no longer shaking. He was more comfortable in his element, talking like this.

"When a stray neutron encounters a U-238 atom," he continued, "nothing happens. But when it encounters a rare U-235 atom, it attaches itself to it and the atom becomes U-236, which is unstable and breaks apart, releasing three additional neutrons and generating a small amount of energy. In natural uranium, nothing more happens after that, because there are so few U-235 atoms for the released neutrons to react with."

"Less than one percent," Sagara said.

Kan nodded. "Yes, less than one percent of U-235 in natural uranium."

"And in Project Ni-Go, you were attempting to increase that concentration."

"Yes, that's exactly right, Sagara-chūsa. If there is a greater concentration of U-235 atoms in the sample, the neutrons released in the first reaction will have a greater chance of encountering other U-235 atoms and causing them to split too. One atom splits to begin the process, the released neutrons cause two other atoms to split, then four, then eight, then sixteen, thirty-two, sixty-four, and so on."

Kan stopped, embarrassed by the realization that he was now talking so quickly. Colonel Sagara motioned for him to continue.

"This is called a chain reaction," said Kan. "The process, and the release of energy, increases exponentially, and it happens very quickly.

In a fraction of a second, trillions and quadrillions of atoms are fissioning, and the explosive release of energy is immense. It would exceed any bomb ever created.'"

"'A weapon powerful enough to destroy a whole city,'" murmured Colonel Sagara, thoughtfully nodding.

Kan recognized the line from the Project Ni-Go report he had helped write. "Yes, Sagara-chūsa. Exactly right."

"So, to create a uranium bomb, the proportion of these 235 atoms in uranium has to be increased." The colonel glanced down at the open file under his hand. "This Separation Team you headed, that was your task? To separate uranium-235 atoms? To create the material to make a uranium bomb?"

"Yes, Sagara-chūsa. The process is called enrichment."

"I see. And how much of this uranium-235 did you enrich?"

Kan sought a new position on his chair as he brought to mind the vast effort of building a thermal diffusion separator and trying to get it to enrich uranium hexafluoride. In theory it should have worked, neutrons being pulled away from some of the uranium-238 atoms as the hex gas rose through the separator so that the minute quantity of green sludge collected at the top contained an increased proportion of U-235. Even a small degree of enrichment would have been an achievement. But there had not been even that.

"None, Sagara-chūsa," he said. "None of the samples showed any increase in the proportion of U-235 when they were tested in the cyclotron. Or there was so little enrichment it couldn't be measured. It could have been due to leakage. The uranium hexafluoride gas we were using was corrosive and would eat through the tubing. But I believe we overcame that. I don't think that was the reason. I think the gap the gas passed through was the problem, the gap between the hot and cold surfaces that should have drawn the neutrons away. It had to be two millimeters wide, two millimeters precisely the entire length of the apparatus. And we couldn't achieve that degree of precision. Even the slightest warp in the—"

Sagara held up his hand to stop him. "So no uranium was enriched. Not even a gram."

"No, Colonel. It was an extremely difficult process. We didn't have enough time."

The office door opened and the colonel's aide, Captain Onda, quietly entered. He placed a file on Sagara's desk and took a position standing at his side. Sagara picked up the file and leaned back in his chair to peruse it, pausing twice to direct penetrating glances at Kan. The scientist, with mounting apprehension, had the distinct feeling that the pages being read were about him.

The colonel finished with the file and set it aside. "Yes, well, let's talk about the amount of U-235 that would be necessary to make a uranium bomb." He referred again to the open Project Ni-Go file on his desk. "In his report of March 1943, Dr. Nishina estimated that it would take ten kilograms of enriched uranium to build an atomic bomb. Ten kilos with the U-235 content enriched to ten percent. What are your thoughts about that?"

"I . . . I would support Dr. Nishina's estimates on that matter," Kan cautiously ventured.

Sagara flicked the end of his cigarette into the ashtray. "I want your honest assessment. Speak candidly, please."

"I was not directly involved in those calculations. The theory work was done by Dr. Nishina and the Theory Team. Tamaki's team. I was involved in the—"

Sagara brought his hand down hard on the desk, making Kan jump. "Speak candidly, please!"

Kan clasped his hands tightly and tensed his stomach, trying to stem the onset of renewed shaking. He did not succeed. Colonel Sagara, with a look of annoyance, leaned back in his chair and gave the scientist a moment to master himself.

Kan tried again. "I . . . I believe Dr. Nishina's estimate was correct for a theoretical explosion. He is a better mathematician than me and I can't fault his calculations. But . . . " He paused for another breath.

"But they were based on the assumption of an efficient explosion. An explosion in which most of the U-235 atoms would fission. In a real bomb, an explosion would not be so efficient."

"Explain that," demanded the colonel.

Kan held up his hands shoulder width apart. "When the bomb is detonated, two pieces of enriched uranium would be brought together . . . "—he brought his hands together—"the mass would become supercritical, and a chain reaction would begin among the U-235 atoms. Then the mass would blow apart"—he jerked his hands apart—"ending the supercritical condition before all the U-235 atoms had time to split."

Colonel Sagara's eyes were wide. "Wait a moment, wait a moment. These two pieces of uranium—how would they be brought together?"

"We made only a few theoretical sketches, Sagara-chūsa, but the general idea was to use a gun apparatus inside a bomb casing. To fire one mass of U-235 into another to initiate the process."

"'A metal tube like a gun barrel,'" Sagara murmured. He shot a glance at his aide, Captain Onda.

"All right," he said, returning to Kan. "So you believe that an amount of uranium larger than ten kilos would be needed to build a uranium bomb. Or an enrichment of greater than ten percent?"

"Both, Sagara-chūsa. More uranium and greater enrichment, since only a portion of the material would have a chance to fission."

"How much more?"

"I could only guess, Colonel. I would say at least double the estimate in the initial report."

"Twenty kilos at twenty percent enrichment?"

"Possibly. Perhaps more. There is no way of really knowing without experimentation with enriched uranium. And we didn't produce any. It was an extremely difficult process. We didn't have enough time."

"How much time would you have needed?"

"To perfect the enrichment process," Kan replied, carefully choosing his words, "and amass enough material for one weapon—that would take years."

"How many years? Two years? Two hundred years? Give me a number."

This was curious. Did the colonel envision launching a new atomic research project? Such an endeavor, at this late date, would be hopeless.

"Even ten years would be too optimistic," Kan ventured. "Twenty years, perhaps, assuming there was adequate funding, materials, and personnel. But realistically, I would have to say that it would take even longer than that. When you consider the current war situation—"

Dangerous ground. He stopped himself in mid-sentence.

Colonel Sagara did not seem to notice. "And what about the Americans? You know they have been doing their own research. Could they have mastered the enrichment process and created a bomb?"

Kan had no doubt of the answer. "No. Even for the Americans, it will take years."

The colonel fell silent and sat regarding Kan with his deep-set eyes. He referred again to the file that Captain Onda had brought him, then returned to his silent perusal of Kan, until the scientist was scarcely able to sit still on his seat.

The colonel finally nodded, evidently having made a decision. He retrieved a paper from beneath the Project Ni-Go report and pushed it across the desk to Kan.

"This came in last night," he said. "Tell me what you make of it."

It was a copy of a military cable. Keizo Kan read it, then read it again:

```
Possible new-type bomb recovered from B-29 crash site,
Hikari, Yamaguchi Prefecture. Length: 3.04 m. Diameter:
71 cm. Weight: 4,300 kg. Metal tube like gun barrel,
diameter 16 cm, runs through center. Metal rings
removed from inside, 25 kg, identified as uran.
```

He started to shake his head as he stared at the cable and absorbed its full meaning.

"Well?" said Sagara.

"No. Even the Americans couldn't do it," said Kan. "This must be something else."

"But it contains uranium," said the colonel. "And look: 'Metal tube like gun barrel.' We know the Americans have a uranium bomb project. We know they acquired a number of important Jewish scientists from Europe. And we know that this device was flown to Japan in a special plane."

Kan considered this for a moment. The biggest piece of uranium metal he had ever seen in his life had been the size of three coins placed one on top of the other. Twenty-five kilos of natural metallic uranium were therefore riches beyond imagination. And twenty-five kilos of *enriched* uranium . . .

"That's impossible," he said. "It can't be uranium. It must be a mistake."

Sagara stabbed his finger at the cable. "But it says *uran*. The Americans have the Shinkolobwe mine in the Belgian Congo. They have all the uranium they need. And we know they have been working on an atomic bomb project. Extremely large scale."

Kan sat with his head bowed, trying to think. It was unimaginable that even the Americans could have mastered all the problems so quickly and built an actual weapon. The number of separators alone, assuming they worked, would have to number in the thousands.

"If it is uranium in this bomb," he said, forestalling the rising impatience in Colonel Sagara's face, "then it must be natural uranium. U-238. Although I don't know what would be the purpose. A warning, perhaps."

"A warning . . . " Sagara considered this. Then: "Yes, well, you'll soon have an opportunity to find out. I'm sending you to examine it. You will return to the Riken and gather what you need. Captain Onda here will assist you."

Kan looked up, dismayed. "But my daughter," he heard himself say. "I can't leave her alone."

He lowered his head. Why had he said that?

"Your daughter?" Sagara sounded confused. He regarded Kan sharply for a moment, then his face softened.

"The woman at the Riken who answered the phone," he said. "Miss . . ."

"Miss Yokoyama," Kan quietly answered.

"Yes, Miss Yokoyama. She could look after your daughter. It would be for just a few days."

Kan slowly shook his head.

Sagara turned to Onda.

"Captain Onda, perhaps you could have your wife take care of Kan-sensei's daughter. I'm sure she wouldn't mind."

"Yes, of course," said Onda. "She would be glad to do it."

The colonel returned to Kan with a smile. "There. The problem is solved. You have no reason to worry. So you will proceed south and examine this American bomb, and you will communicate your findings back to this office. Directly to me, understand? Only to me. Discretion at this point is very important. And under no circumstances are you to reveal anything of this object's possible nature to anyone in the Navy. For now, this must remain within the Army."

Colonel Sagara pushed away from his desk and rose to his feet, indicating that the meeting was over. Kan reflexively stood up and bowed, but he made no move to leave when Captain Onda opened the door. His mind was racing, considering a gamble.

"Captain Onda will take you back to the Riken," Sagara said. "To get what you need."

Keizo Kan remained where he was, his head bowed.

Sagara's smile faded. "Is there something else?"

Kan inclined his head further. "Pardon me, Colonel, but it's about my wife."

"Your wife."

"Noriko Kan. She was arrested."

"Yes, so I've seen in your file. What was the charge?"

"I don't know, Colonel. The Tokkō took her away from the NHK Building on June seventh and I've been unable to find where she is. I've made inquiries but . . . " Kan's emotions were starting to well up. He fell silent and just shook his head.

"Well, that is very unfortunate. But I don't see how—"

Sagara stopped in mid-sentence. His face darkened into a scowl.

"Oh, I see. You want a favor in return for your service. So we're haggling like housewives in the market now, are we?"

"No, Sagara-chūsa, no. It's just—I've been unable to find out where . . . I thought—I thought if you could make inquiries . . . "

"If I locate your wife, then you'll do as you're told. Is that it?"

That was precisely it. But Kan didn't dare say so. He stood with his eyes downcast, aware of the colonel's balled-up fist in his peripheral vision.

"You realize that I could have you conscripted," Sagara said, his voice rising. "Is that what you want?"

Kan remained very still, looking at the floor.

"I could have you conscripted within the hour," Sagara continued, "and then give you an order. And if you refused to obey it, you'd be punished like any other soldier in wartime. Do you know what that means?"

Kan knew perfectly well what that meant. He could be shot.

"I don't think," said Sagara, "that that would improve your wife's situation. Do you?"

Kan stood frozen, staring at the gleaming toes of Colonel Sagara's boots. The idea of asking for a favor had come to him in an instant, the words tumbling out before he'd had a chance to consider. And now he realized that he'd made a mistake. The colonel, with his piercing eyes, gaunt face, and dangerous look, was clearly not the sort of man to grant favors, only to be obeyed. Kan would have to apologize and pray that he would be forgiven.

"Colonel . . . " Kan began to say. He did not get any further. Without warning, like a door thrown open, he burst into tears.

Sagara sourly regarded this display of emotion.

He let out a long, growling breath and turned to Onda. "Why is this man crying?"

"I'm sorry," Kan choked out, his head hanging in mortification as he struggled to regain his composure. He wanted to say that he would do what was required and slink away from the office. He wiped his eyes and cleared his throat. "I'm sorry," he tried again.

"All right!" Sagara erupted, throwing up his hands. "I'll make inquiries. Your daughter will be taken care of and inquiries will be made into your wife's situation." He smiled icily while his eyes continued to glare. "Now, will that get you out of my office and on your way to doing your duty?"

Keizo Kan bowed low, his back parallel to the floor. "Thank you," he managed to get out, his voice a husky whisper. "Thank you."

"All right, all right," said Sagara, waving him to the door. "Now go. Captain Onda will take you back to the Riken."

Kan gratefully hurried out of the office. Sagara resumed his seat behind his desk, Captain Onda standing by.

"Get him on the next plane to Hiroshima," the colonel instructed. "Then find out about this wretched woman of his." He referred to Keizo Kan's file for the name: "Noriko Kan."

"Yes, Colonel. And my wife will gladly look after his daughter."

Sagara cast Kan's file aside. "The man doesn't have a daughter. She's dead."

SIX

IT WAS FOUR O'CLOCK IN THE AFTERNOON WHEN THE TRAIN JOLTED TO A STOP IN HIKARI, ON the Sanyo Main Line near the southwestern end of Honshu. He was seven hours late, Keizo Kan anxiously noted, an image of Colonel Sagara's glaring eyes flashing through his mind. He retrieved his bag and the equipment case from the overhead rack and joined the line forming in the aisle between the hard wooden benches—mostly men in uniform, for this car was reserved for military personnel. "No civilians!" an imperious lieutenant had bawled at him when he boarded, obliging Kan to produce his War Ministry pass.

The scientist's journey had begun twenty hours before, with a ride west across Tokyo in the sidecar of a motorcycle to Tama Airfield. He was hustled onto a Nakajima twin-engine transport, the last passenger to be seated on the benches lining the sides of the compartment, and the only civilian aboard. The aircraft took off and banked toward the southwest, staying low—to avoid the attention of enemy fighters, the officer seated beside Kan explained. There was no window for Kan to look out to scan the sky for approaching destruction. He leaned back against the vibrating side of the aircraft and let his eyes drift closed.

It was only then, enveloped in the drone of the engines, that he was able to properly consider the object he was heading off to examine. If it was indeed a uranium bomb—an unthinkable proposition, but assuming it was—it would need to contain two masses of uranium: a projectile and a target; two masses to be brought together to form a critical mass. And if twenty-five kilos of uranium had been recovered from it without mishap, then there should logically be a second mass, a similarly sized mass, still hidden inside. So that meant possibly fifty kilos of enriched uranium, not twenty-five. Fifty kilos! The idea was outrageous. The Americans could not be so far ahead in developing an atomic bomb. If they were, the pitiful failure of Project Ni-Go would be too much to bear.

The Nakajima had made it as far as Nagoya when a report of enemy fighters in the area forced them to land. Kan and his fellow passengers spent the night in a hangar, camped out like refugees with their baggage, their uncomfortable rest disturbed twice by the wail of air raid sirens. They finally took off again the next morning, completing the flight to Hiroshima in less than two hours. From the airfield, Kan walked to Hiroshima Station to continue on to Hikari by train.

Hiroshima, he was surprised to observe, was virtually untouched by incendiary bombing. The year might even have been mistaken for 1942, when Japan was all-victorious, before things had gone so disastrously wrong. But the signs that it was August 1945, even here, soon became apparent as he made his way to the station. They were in the fire lanes torn through the heart of the city, bare swaths where houses had been dismantled to halt the fires that hadn't yet come. They were in the crude bomb shelter trenches and shoulder-deep "octopus holes" that had been dug beside streets and in the gardens behind houses for people to crouch in. They were in the desperation of the slogans plastered on billboards and painted on walls, urging to mobilization the "One Hundred Million," the collective population of Japan and its colonies of Korea and Taiwan. Nowhere did Kan see the exhortation *Ichioku Isshin*, "One Hundred Million Hearts Beating Together," so popular in the heady early days of the war. Instead it was *Ichioku Kirikomu* that he saw painted on the soot-blackened wall of a factory: "One Hundred Million Slashing into the Heart of the Enemy." And farther along, another slogan, even more recent, displayed beside a boarded-up sembei cracker shop. *Ichioku Tokkotai*, the four characters read: "One Hundred Million as a Suicide Squad."

He arrived at the station and joined other travelers waiting on the platform for the train heading south. A speech was blaring from a loudspeaker installed under the rafters. Kan moved as far away from it as he could and sat on his heavy case, fanning himself in the midafternoon heat. A formation of housewives under the command of a weedy policeman were drilling with bamboo spears on the other side of the tracks. Their anemic thrusts did not appear deadly.

" . . . The Okinawa Campaign must be viewed as the first step in a great victory. Yes, the enemy secured his hold on the island. But at a tremendous cost! Thanks in large part to the ardor and the spirit of the Special Attack Corps, more than six hundred enemy ships were sunk or otherwise incapacitated, many with all men and matériel on board. This teaches us a valuable lesson. It points the way forward to ultimate victory! When the enemy attempts to land on our home islands . . . "

Keizo Kan boarded the train.

Hikari was a small provincial town with a tiny station building, not the sort of place where one might be overlooked in a crowd. Kan looked around expectantly after alighting from the carriage, but no one seemed to be waiting to meet him. The train gathered steam and chugged off down the tracks. Other arriving passengers filtered away. Then the station was empty and he was alone.

The stationmaster gave him directions to the naval facility, east along the street that ran in front of the station, then across the bridge, about a kilometer and a half. Kan walked. The wooden equipment case was awkward and heavy, and his People's Uniform was sweated through by the time he arrived at the gate. He identified himself to the guard on duty, who made a call from the telephone in the guardhouse. After a few minutes a sailor came sauntering out to the gate. He had a hard face and was powerfully built under his sweat-stained shirt. He approached Kan with the hint of a swagger. There were scars on his neck.

"Keizo Kan-sensei?" he said.

Kan said that he was. The man made a perfunctory bow.

"Petty Officer Second Class Ryohei Yagi. I was in charge of recovering the object." He jerked his head in the direction of the administration building behind. "I've been ordered to assist you."

They proceeded onto the base, Petty Officer Yagi leading the way with Kan's small bag. Kan insisted on carrying the wooden case himself. The place was drab, unpainted wooden buildings and barracks, industrial structures fronting the river. A concrete quay nearly a kilometer long extended into the mouth of the river, creating a sheltered wharf where two small vessels were moored. The open water of the Inland Sea lay beyond.

Kan was led first to one of the barracks buildings, where a private room—Western cot, desk, and chair—had been prepared for his use. A bath was next, a rare treat for which Kan was grateful, followed by a meal brought to his room on a tray. White rice, a grilled piece of mackerel, miso soup, pickles—simple fare before the war, but the best meal the scientist had eaten in weeks. By the time PO Yagi returned, Kan's head was nodding. He was falling asleep.

The evening clouds were darkening as they made their way across the compound, Kan with the wooden case in his hand. A low rumble of thunder sounded in the distance. Yagi gave an account of the object's recovery and subsequent examination as they went along, adding a new detail that Kan found alarming. The petty officer had apparently delved deeper into the device in the past forty-eight hours.

They turned onto a cracked concrete roadway and followed it to a weathered building standing by itself near the fence at the southern edge of the base. It commanded a view of the Inland Sea, an expanse of gray fading into the distance to join with the sky. Kan paused for a moment to take in the view: the headland to the east; the small island a few hundred meters offshore; the large mass that lay to the west, a dark smear in the mist, the unseen sun setting behind it.

"Kasado-shima," said Yagi. He pointed southwest. "Kyushu is there. You can see it on a clear day."

He opened the double doors of the building and turned on a switch. Two naked bulbs hanging from cords bathed the interior in a warm glow. It was a large workshop, spacious enough to accommodate a truck, smelling of old dusty grease, turpentine, sawdust, gasoline. There was a workbench along one wall, a selection of greasy tools scattered about, the chains of a hoist hanging down from stout beams. And in the center: something large, hidden under a tightly lashed-up tarpaulin.

Yagi unfastened the cords and pulled back the canvas, revealing a heavy trolley, a bed of oil-stained railway ties on iron wheels. It held something that Kan had to admit looked very much like a bomb. A very large bomb. Two pieces of wood nailed to either side of the trolley bed held it in place.

Kan set down his burden and stood for a moment contemplating the object. Yagi leaned against the workbench, crossed his arms, and began contemplating Kan.

The scientist took a step closer to the thing. The casing, black, had been swept clean but still showed signs of dirt, caught in the crannies and seams that ran down its length. A large cavity was exposed in the nose. The component that had filled it—Kan assumed that this was what lay on the floor beside the trolley, the meter-long lump hidden under a scrap of canvas. This was what had brought him to Hikari. He reined in his excitement. He would proceed methodically, one step at a time.

He began to walk slowly around the object, moving away from the nose, tapping the casing here and there as he went. There was evidence of where several protuberances had extended from the black steel shell. They were now broken off or smashed flat, their original purpose unclear. A hoisting shackle was the only thing Kan recognized. Its location, well forward, indicated that the object was nose heavy.

He paused at a figure, L10, painted in large white characters on the left side. Some sort of identifier? Was this the tenth unit in a series?

He turned his attention to the handwritten inscriptions that PO Yagi had mentioned on the walk down. Some were still legible, not scoured off in the crash. *Samuel Filson, USN . . . Edward Houseman, for Charlie . . . For the boys on Hancock Street, Detroit USA . . . Sgt. Ralph T. Hickey . . . To Emperor Hirohito, Special Delivery to where the sun don't shine.*

He paused to consider this last inscription. It was the sort of thing, he realized with a chilling sensation, that an American would write on a powerful weapon before sending it to Japan.

"Can you read English?" asked Yagi.

"A little." Kan in fact knew English very well. He had done his doctoral work in physics in the United States, at the University of California in Berkeley. It was there that he had met his American-born wife Noriko, an English major, in 1936.

He continued along the casing, moving toward the tail, reading more inscriptions, mostly names. A twisted, flattened mass of metal lay on the floor at the rear of the object, some sort of stabilizing tail fin structure that had been cut away. An open cavity was exposed underneath, the end of a tube extending into the object. It was roughly the diameter of Kan's hand, fingers outstretched. The heavy steel plug lying on the trolley presumably screwed into the end.

"Yagi-heisō," he said. "You mentioned removing an explosive charge from the back."

The petty officer casually retrieved four tubular bags from the workbench. They drooped in his hands like fat, stubby worms as he showed them to Kan.

"Cordite," he said. "Total four kilos. About a meter inside after I unscrewed that steel plug. These wires were attached to the cordite. These points . . . " Yagi indicated the pencil-sized rods protruding from the end of the plug. "I figure they must be primers."

Kan examined the cordite and primers. More evidence. That was not good.

He moved around to the far side of the object. More inscriptions here: *F. A. Scudder . . . Lt. Howard Roach . . . Here's a hot one for you, Tojo . . . Stanley J. Rothstein*—

The name stopped Keizo Kan cold. He had known a Stanley J. Rothstein at the University of California. Everyone called him Stan or SJ. A fellow doctoral student in the Department of Physics, quite brilliant. Could this be the same man? Had Stan been recruited into the same type of war work? No, surely not. The population of the United States was more than one hundred million. There had to be more than one Stanley J. Rothstein in the United States.

Kan continued with his examination, a troubled look now clouding his face. Working his way back to the nose, he confirmed that it was solid by tapping with his knuckles. Unlike the rear two-thirds of the object, which rang hollow and was evidently bomb casing, the forward third appeared to be machined from a solid steel block. The scoring lines where it had been cut were clearly apparent.

The forward cavity was much larger than the hole in the tail. Kan bent down and peered in, using the flashlight that Yagi provided. The outermost portion, machined steel, shone like a mirror in the light, the space large enough to accommodate his whole head if he cared to insert it, which he did not. Then it narrowed to less than half the width—the same width as the tube opening in the tail. The tube evidently extended down the entire length of the object. Its first sixty centimeters here in the nose, not quite the length of Kan's arm, was some sort of collar or sleeve of a dark material—coarse grained, very hard, flecked with green. Sintered tungsten carbide, perhaps? Beyond this, the interior gleamed like the outermost portion of the cavity. Machined steel again.

No actual design for an atomic bomb had been produced in Project

Ni-Go, but the basic form such a weapon would take had inevitably come up in discussions. Kan and his colleagues understood that it would be a gun-type design, one in which a uranium-235 projectile was fired into a U-235 target to form a supercritical mass. Such a weapon would have at its heart a cylinder of machined steel, a gun barrel, to facilitate the firing—a cylinder like what he was gazing at now.

Kan looked down at the nose assembly, hidden under a piece of canvas. He used his toe to gingerly lift the edge of the fabric.

Stanley J. Rothstein . . .

Yagi stepped forward and pulled back the canvas.

"Screws in like the plug in the tail," he said. "A real heavy bastard."

The assembly consisted of a stack of four distinct components, each progressively smaller, held together on a thick rod. Kan's eyes immediately went to the small end—the innermost end when the assembly was inserted into the cavity in the nose. There were six rings here, covered on the outside only with a bright silvery plating. The rings themselves were of a gray metal with a plum-colored patina. He had never seen anything quite like it before.

"This is how it appeared when you removed it?"

"Yes," replied Yagi. "I put the outer pieces back on the rod after we did the testing. Uranium, that's what we figured. That plating—I don't know what it is."

Kan gazed down at the plum-colored rings. They were of the same diameter but varied in thickness, suggesting that they had been individually cast.

"Conducting a specific gravity test was very resourceful," he said. "Were you a teacher before entering the Navy?"

"A teacher!" One side of Yagi's mouth curled up in amusement and he made a dismissive snort. "I was a mechanic. In my father's garage in Osaka. Yagi Shokai."

Kan cast Yagi a glance, wondering if he had inadvertently offended the man. The petty officer met his eyes with a look of defiance.

"So you know cars," said Kan.

Yagi made a single nod. "Cars and trucks."

Kan squatted at the nose assembly, his knees popping like an old man's. He unscrewed the large nut from the end of the rod, removed the outermost ring and hefted it in his hand. It was extremely heavy, possibly four kilos, yet no bigger than the donuts he had enjoyed in the cafeteria at the University of California—a bit flatter, slightly bigger around. Although one of Japan's foremost uranium experts, he had never seen anything like it. His experience had been confined to handling uranium hexafluoride, which in solid form looked like white, crystalline rock salt, and to a lesser extent uranium oxide, a coarse yellow powder processed from uranium ore.

He opened the wooden case he had brought with him.

"Geiger-Müller counter," he said in response to Yagi's questioning look.

The counter was an old and familiar piece of equipment from happier days—and precious, with almost everything at the Riken now destroyed. It had accompanied Kan and his colleagues to Gunma Prefecture in 1938, on an expedition to collect cosmic ray data from inside Shimizu Tunnel, deep underground. And then there was the time Noriko had visited the laboratory with Aiko, a lifetime ago in 1942. Kan had taken time from his busy schedule to have some fun with his daughter, showing her this very counter, demonstrating how the rate of the clicking it made increased when he placed the Geiger-Müller tube in the wand near a glass of water containing a sodium isotope, which was radioactive.

"Now close your eyes," he had instructed. Aiko's eyes closed. He gulped down the water.

"The water is gone!" he exclaimed when Aiko opened her eyes and saw that the glass was empty. He led her on a search about the lab with the counter, checking under desks, in the corners, behind stacks of books and papers, muttering all the while, "Now where did that water go?"

Finally he passed the wand near his stomach, making the counter erupt with a flurry of clicks.

"It's in your stomach," Aiko had said, her eyes wide.

"In my stomach? Oh yes, of course. I drank it!"

He gave the wand to Aiko to pass over his belly. And Kan and his wife and his daughter had laughed.

The rings of plum-colored metal sparked a much more vigorous response than the water he had drunk. As Kan brought the Geiger-Müller tube in close, the sporadic clicks of background radiation increased to a flurry and merged into a harsh buzz, the needle on the gauge climbing past 200,000 counts per minute. It subsided when he moved the wand down the nose assembly, down past the tungsten carbide disk, then the outer steel pieces. He returned the wand to the rings. The counter began buzzing again.

Gamma radiation. The reading was high but in line with what would be expected. Coupled with Yagi's specific gravity test, the conclusion was clear.

Kan let it sink in. He started nodding his head.

"I think you're right, Yagi-heisō," he said. "This could be uran."

He would need to conduct his own testing, but he accepted it now. His mind leaped ahead instead to the next question: Had the U-235 content in these metal rings been significantly concentrated? As fantastic as it seems, could this uranium really be enriched?

If it was, the enrichment surely could not be very high, considering that the ring stack weighed twenty-five kilos and the upper range of Dr. Nishina's estimate for a supercritical mass was only ten. It would be possible to test them if he had use of the 26-inch cyclotron at the Riken. But it had been damaged in the fire in April, and in any event was more than 700 kilometers away.

A patter overhead on the tin roof. It was starting to rain.

Kan took no notice. He was considering the rest of the assembly, his mind completely absorbed. The outermost piece and by far the largest was the steel plug that screwed into the cavity in the nose, the threads spiraling down its sides catching the light from the naked bulbs overhead. It was really quite a beautiful piece of machined metal. Next to it was nestled a smaller steel disk, dinner-plate-sized where it rested against the outer plug, then angling down to the width of the tube that ran through the object. On top of this was another disk, same diameter but a different substance. It was dark gray with flecks of green, like the sleeve inside the nose cavity of the object. More sintered tungsten carbide? And then the six rings . . .

If they were enriched uranium, and assuming this was a gun-type bomb, then there would be a second uranium mass inside the tube, situated near the tail in front of the charges of cordite. Kan peered again into its depths with the flashlight. There did seem to be something down there, a long way inside, backed up deep in the hole.

He ran the wand of the Geiger-Müller counter along the length of the object. It gave an elevated response two-thirds of the way toward the tail.

He set the wand aside and looked around until he spotted a broom. He used the handle to probe the nose cavity, extending his arm partway in, but couldn't reach the end. He tried again, using a longer pole Yagi dug from a pile of wood in the corner. This time he encountered an obstruction at over two meters, in the back third of the object, around where the counter had made a slightly increased buzz. He removed the pole, measured the depth, and wrote it down.

The rain was picking up, a steady drumming now on the roof.

Kan moved to the rear end of the bomb—he was thinking of it now as a bomb—and inserted the pole into the opposite end of the tube. It descended to a depth of just under a meter. Subtracting these two distances from the overall length, he calculated that the obstruction was approximately fifty centimeters long.

He bent down and peered into the tube, using Yagi's flashlight. Whatever was in there caught the beam and reflected it back. He got down on his knees and inserted his hand into the hole. He couldn't help wincing as he did so, for it was like reaching into an animal's burrow. What was inside? A yellow-toothed rodent? An angry badger? A coiled-up snake? This was an entirely man-made construction of metal, not an earthen embankment, but Kan couldn't help thinking that something with sharp fangs was deep down in this tube, something untamed and unpredictable that might chew off his hand.

He reached all the way in but encountered nothing. The lights overhead flickered. He ignored them. He pressed his shoulder against the opening and stretched out his fingers as far as he could. They brushed against something. He pressed harder and stretched further, the end of the tube biting into his armpit. Whatever was in there, he managed to scratch it, then press it with his fingernail. It seemed very hard. Steel perhaps.

The lights flickered again, then went out. A power outage. Outages had become so common that it merited no comment. Kan removed his arm from the tube and stood up. He waited in the dark as his eyes adjusted. The lights did not return.

He joined Yagi at the open door. They stood side by side, looking out at the base and the river. Night had fallen. The base, the town, the arsenal complex across the river—all were in darkness. The only light came from the unseen moon overhead, a gossamer hint of illumination drifting down through the clouds.

Yagi took out a pack of Kinshi cigarettes and offered one to Kan.

"Ah, thank you," said the scientist. "We don't get many of these." The dry tobacco crackled as Yagi held out a match, momentarily illuminating their faces; then he lit one for himself. The flame disappeared. Darkness returned.

He would contact Colonel Sagara in Tokyo as soon as the power returned, Kan decided. He would send a cable, using the codes that Captain Onda had provided, giving as his preliminary assessment that the object could indeed be a uranium bomb. It was a bold assertion after such a short examination. And it would magnify still further Project Ni-Go's failure to produce a similar weapon. Kan had already decided to make it, however, even with less evidence than he had now, for the colonel seemed eager to believe it. Why? Was he so bent on atomic destruction from the skies? Or—

Kan caught himself. Even thinking such a thing was dangerous.

Or . . . was the colonel looking for a reason to surrender? If the Americans could command the destructive power of the atom, there was no better reason to end the war.

Kan swept the thought aside. The Imperial Army would never surrender. The Decisive Battle was coming when the Americans landed, and there was nothing he or anyone else could do about it. All that mattered until then was to make himself useful to the colonel. If he did, Sagara surely would be willing to get Noriko released. Wouldn't that be a reasonable reward for his service?

Kan had been clutching at the idea for the past twenty-four hours, the hope that he might be able to undo the damage that he had caused with his weakness. It had started with his delay in sending Noriko and Aiko away from Tokyo when the danger became clear. If he had insisted they go to Kanagawa to stay with his parents, the only thing lost would have been their house. And then, after that terrible night and the death of their daughter, he had been so overwhelmed by his own pain that he had given Noriko little thought. He had buried himself in his work at the Riken and been blind to her own suffering, which she bore more bravely than he did. How could he have been so selfish?

Emotion was welling up. He was becoming upset. He cleared his throat and concentrated on his cigarette. The drumming of the rain gradually returned him to the present.

"Yagi Shokai," he said, recalling the name of the garage Yagi had mentioned. "Did you work on American cars?"

"Mostly Fords," replied Yagi. "Dodge. Hudson. Buick." He drew in a lungful of smoke. His earlier gruff manner was falling away in the darkness. "We repaired a LaSalle once. A fat German businessman owned it. Beautiful car."

Thunder, no longer distant, rolled in off the sea. Overhead, the rain rose to a violent crescendo, pummeling the tin sheets of the roof, sluicing off the eaves to form a curtain of water in front of the door.

Kan's thoughts drifted back to Noriko. It made his heart ache.

SEVEN

THE CELL WAS FIVE SHORT PACES LONG, THE WIDTH SLIGHTLY LESS THAN THE SPAN OF HER arms. A thin, lumpy futon, alive with lice, was rolled up in the corner. It was to remain there, not to be used even as a cushion for sitting, between the blasts of the whistle that marked the start and the end of each day. No lying down. No sleeping. That was the rule. A bowl, a cup, and a toilet pail emptied twice weekly were the only other furnishings. There was no window, no electrical light. The only illumination was what came from the hallway through the fifteen-centimeter-square barred hole in the door—the door that she prayed would never again open. She would rather stay inside her cell, slowly starving, than for her door to be opened again.

There had been screams during the day, echoing down from the interrogation rooms overhead. Thankfully it was quiet now. With her eyes closed and slow, deep breathing, she was beginning to release some of the tension in her belly, enough for the hunger to reemerge from under the fear. The evening meal had been a piece of half-cooked pumpkin, thrust through the slot in the door by a silent orderly pushing a cart with wheels that squeaked. It would likely bring on cramps. The next meal—some sort of gruel, perhaps a lump of unsalted barley—would come in the morning. The war could not go on much longer, but at the rate her flesh was disappearing, she doubted she could last to the end.

Footsteps outside. The Toad or one of the other guards was making the rounds. She sat up straight, communicating alertness, her eyes submissively downcast from the shadow as it passed by the grating. She stared at the scabbed-over cigarette burns on the back of her hand and running up her forearm.

The footsteps faded to the end of the hall, then returned. It was only after she heard them scuff their way back up the stairs that she allowed herself to relax.

Weariness overcame her. It always did after a meal, during that brief respite from gnawing hunger. She lowered her head to her knees and let her eyelids drift closed, retreating back inside her mind, where she now spent most of her time. There were lights waiting for her there in the darkness, dim yellow flashes floating like fireflies in the night. She watched them for a time and they gradually grew brighter, like sparks from a fire, dancing up and flaring before drifting back down.

Greetings to all you GI boneheads. It's Humanity Calls. *With your favorite Radio Tokyo announcer, your very own sweetheart Sally. Did you miss me? Sure you did. I missed you, too.*

She had arrived on the sixth floor of the NHK Building at one o'clock that afternoon, her usual time. She had been finding the work difficult for the past two months, since the loss of their home and the death of their daughter. After the initial debilitating grief had come a feeling of emptiness that wouldn't leave her. Emptiness. And confusion. Keizo had urged her to take more time off from work, but she couldn't. She had received pressure from NHK to return, for she was one of their best announcers. And they needed her salary to adequately feed themselves.

The first task was to polish the script that Oita-san had prepared, turning his tortured English into something that sounded natural, something she could actually say. She was able to take great liberties, rewriting virtually the whole thing, for Oita-san had come to trust her. It was easy now that she knew the format, working in common American names, mocking taunts, and depressing items of stateside news from the list, fires and crashes and natural disasters.

Hi there, Pete! Hey, why so blue? I guess you must be feeling homesick. Well, don't let it get you down. Who wouldn't be homesick, stuck on that island out in the Pacific, thousands of miles from home. You're missing your wife, your mom and dad, and everyone else. That's okay. Your sweetheart Sally knows how you feel.

She had the script completed by two-thirty. She would read through it once or twice to practice and do some mouth exercises to get her voice in tune. Then it was time for the three p.m. broadcast of *Humanity Calls.* She always smiled as she read her lines into the microphone. It was a trick Oita-san had taught her to create a happy, upbeat delivery. Oita-san had taught her everything she knew about being a propaganda announcer, "a fighter in the ideological war," as he put it, "shooting shortwave bullets."

And that little boy of yours, Ted. You're wondering if he's okay. Well, he's thinking about you, too. And your mother, Frank—how's she doing? I hope she's well. But Sally won't lie to you. Bad things happen every day. Stars and Stripes just doesn't report it. It only dishes out the upbeat jive for you boneheads. So you didn't hear about the train wreck in Boise that killed all those people. Or the hotel fire in Sacramento. Or that airplane that crashed in—

Oh, but don't worry about that now. Your sweetheart Sally doesn't want you to worry. She doesn't want you boneheads to be blue. So let's get along and get to the music. Here we go, nice and slow, with Artie Shaw on his clarinet playing "Moonglow."

She liked the music they played on the broadcast. Artie Shaw, Benny Goodman, the Andrews Sisters, Tommy Dorsey. Owning such records and listening to such music could get an ordinary Japanese citizen into serious trouble. But here on the restricted sixth floor of the NHK Building, they were openly handled and played.

Fujimura-san appeared outside the glass window of the microphone booth and just stood there, staring at Noriko and getting in Oita-san's way. It was common knowledge that he was affiliated with the Tokkō, assigned to NHK to keep an eye on the American-born Nisei employees like Noriko who worked on the sixth floor. Why else did he have a private office when he seemed to do so little actual work? Noriko loathed him—his perpetually sour face, his open suspicion. He had even suggested that Oita-san was allowing Noriko too much freedom to write her own scripts, claiming that she could be inserting coded messages into her broadcasts. And then there was the way he treated the single women on staff, inviting them into his office and making advances, knowing that they would never dare to complain.

She shifted in her seat, pointedly turning away from the window to get Fujimura-san out of her field of vision. He eventually left.

This one's going out to Walter in 8th Marines Regiment, 1st Battalion. Hi, Walter! Summer's awfully hot on Okinawa, isn't it? But listen, bonehead, because here's a news flash. It's not half as hot down there as it is in your hometown, back in the good old USA, where that special lady is waiting.

Oh, you didn't hear? Well, she's found a new beau. Do the initials T. S. sound familiar? A friend of yours, perhaps? I hate being the bearer of bad news, Walter. But isn't knowing better than being kept in the dark?

I feel for you, kiddo. I really do. But keep your chin up, because Sally still loves you. Sweetheart Sally will never run around behind your back.

And so this one's for you, Walter in 8th Marines Regiment, 1st Battalion. A nifty number with a Spanish title. Here we go, nice and slow, with the Glenn Miller Orchestra and "Perfidia."

The seventy-five-minute broadcast ended at four-fifteen. The red light went out and Noriko left the booth. Oita-san gave her a smile and a nod. He had been worried about her since her personal tragedy, which was now so common. But she was doing well.

She returned to the desk she shared with another Nisei announcer, Ikuko Toguri, to collect her things.

Fujimura-san stuck his head out of his office. "Kan-san," he said, "I want to have a word with you."

Noriko stiffened. She didn't want to go into Fujimura's office alone. But she was a married woman. Surely he wouldn't.

She was mistaken.

"I know all about you," he said, closing the door and coming up behind her and placing his hand on her shoulder.

His hand descended.

Noriko wheeled about and struck him in the face.

The rap of a club on the cell door brought her back to the present. The thick-featured guard she thought of as the Toad was standing outside, staring at her through the grate. She sat up straight, demonstrating alertness as her heart palpitated. The Toad tapped again, twice. She scrambled to her feet and stood at attention. The guards sometimes insisted on this, keeping the prisoners in a constant state of apprehension.

The Toad moved on. His footsteps retreated. Noriko remained standing, listening as he continued down the hallway, pausing here and there to issue warnings with his club. One of the raps was repeated, followed by the guttural order, "Stand up!" Noriko had no idea who the unfortunate soul was who was being addressed. There were perhaps thirty others confined down here, but she had never seen or communicated with any of them. It was forbidden. She could hear them, however, the occasional cough during the day, snoring and cries and whimpers during the night.

The footsteps returned. Noriko remained standing at attention. The Toad passed by her cell door and continued on to the stairs leading up at the end of the hall.

The blast of the night whistle. Freed at last after fourteen hours of alternately sitting and standing, Noriko unrolled her futon and lay down. She heard a soft rustle from the next cell as her neighbor—man or woman, she didn't know—did the same.

The speed with which Noriko had been arrested left no doubt as to Fujimura's Tokkō affiliation. She had committed an unpardonable offense, an assault on a member of Japan's feared Thought Police. She never saw him again, but she heard his accusations repeated in the interrogations to which she was subjected, the claim that she had inserted coded messages into her broadcasts. She denied it. She tried to explain how Fujimura had made advances on all the Nisei and foreign women who worked at NHK on the sixth floor and treated them according to how compliant they were. Only the elderly American missionary known as Mother Topping seemed to escape his attentions. When he tried to take advantage of Noriko, she had rejected him and the present accusations against her were the result.

"Liar!" roared the interrogator, lunging out of his chair to spit the word in her face.

She repeated the story in a subsequent session and sparked a harsher response, a flurry of blows, then the cigarette burns. She didn't know if she would be strong enough to continue defending herself the next time she was questioned, for judging from the shrieks she had heard the treatment would only get worse.

Perhaps she shouldn't even bother. Perhaps she should just admit to the crime and accept the release from life that would no doubt swiftly follow. For there seemed little point in carrying on. Her Aiko was dead and didn't need her, her family was broken, and Japan itself was plodding inexorably toward annihilation. It would probably all be over, for everyone, by the end of the year. So it would only be a matter of leaving this life a little sooner. And the fact remained that she was indeed guilty. Not of treason. How did one even send coded messages via a radio broadcast? But of—

Her mind reeled away from the shame and the deeper horror behind it.

She gazed at the familiar dark stain on the floor, scarcely a foot from her nose. It formed the face of a man, head slightly turned, eyes downcast. There was only the vaguest hint of features in the mark but in the dim light her imagination brought it to life. It was her husband, Keizo, when she wanted him there, the shy and gentle soul she had married in San Francisco eight years before.

Should she have told him? No, what she had done could not be forgiven.

She lay in the darkness, listening to the sounds coming through the grating—the rustling, the breathing, the coughing, the weeping, the occasional sound of water as a toilet pail was used somewhere down the hall.

Here we go, nice and slow, with the Glenn Miller Orchestra and "Perfidia."

She had always liked the music they played on *Humanity Calls*. She squeezed her eyes tight shut and tried to conjure the tune.

So here we go, nice and slow. The Glenn Miller Orchestra with "Perfidia."

No music came.

EIGHT

THERE WAS TENSION ON THE THIRD FLOOR OF THE WAR MINISTRY THE NEXT MORNING. AN incident had occurred in the Matériel Section, where Colonel Shingen Sagara was now heading, involving a sub-section chief, an officer named Haga, who was setting a negative tone. He had been reported as making demoralizing comments and had struck a captain in the face who spoke up against him.

"Haga-shosa," Colonel Sagara said, intercepting the disheveled officer before he could spread his defeatism further. "Could I have a word?"

He took Haga by the arm and guided him to a secluded corner. The man had clearly been drinking, atrocious conduct while on duty but not uncommon these days. When Sagara left him some minutes later, the blood was drained from Haga's face and his fleshy lips were tightly pressed together—hopefully a permanent condition.

It was the second sharp reminder Colonel Sagara had had to deliver during the previous few days. He had known there were officers like Haga inhabiting the warren of offices lining the Ministry hallways, weak men promoted beyond their capabilities who were apt to break under pressure. Now, with the war situation becoming increasingly challenging, they were revealing themselves. But the Ministry, and the Imperial Army, must not be seen to falter. The Minister of War, General Korechika Anami, could be relied on to stand firm against the traitors on the Supreme War Council and in Prime Minister Suzuki's cabinet, thwarting their scarcely disguised aim to surrender. But Anami, for all his ability, could not monitor the conduct of every officer on staff. It was up to stalwarts like Colonel Sagara to step forward to keep creatures like Haga in check.

He returned to his office, annoyed at having had to spend his precious time herding cows. The work, as usual, lay heaped on his desk. On top of it all was the cable received the previous evening from Keizo Kan in Hikari, containing his preliminary assessment that the object appeared to be what the colonel had suspected. And beside it, Colonel Sagara's notes from the return telephone call he had just made. The static-filled conversation, the scientist struggling to speak in clouded terms, had yielded a crucial additional piece of information. There were numerous signatures and inscriptions written on the outside of the "object," and Keizo Kan believed he recognized one of the names.

The colonel reached for the telephone and put a call through to the Riken. The young woman, Miss Yokoyama, answered again. No, she informed the colonel, Dr. Nishina had not yet returned. She expected him back tomorrow.

"All right," said Sagara, keeping his irritation in check. "I want to know about the library there. Was it destroyed back in April?"

"Oh no, colonel," replied Miss Yokoyama, her voice brightening. "The library is still here in the building. It survived almost entirely."

"All right. That's excellent. Now listen. I want you to go through the journals relating to physics. Relating to physics, understand? From 19—" He paused to consider. "From 1936 to the most recent you have. Look for the name Stanley J. Rothstein." He carefully spelled it out. "Anything he might have written. Or any reference to him."

Sagara ended the call and made another, this time to the Imperial Japanese Army's Ninth Technical Research Institute in Tama district.

He repeated his instructions after confirming that the Institute's library was largely intact.

"Stanley J. Rothstein," he concluded. "Do you have it?"

"Yes, Colonel," came the voice from the other end. "I understand."

Colonel Sagara's patience lasted until ten o'clock in the morning. Then he could wait no longer. He telephoned the Ninth Technical Research Institute again, only to learn that their collection of foreign journals had been boxed up and sent to a secure location and therefore could not be easily searched. The colonel hung up in disgust while the clerk was still stammering his apologies.

He was about to place a follow-up call to the Riken when the telephone rang under his hand. It was Miss Yokoyama.

"I found the name," she reported, breathless. "Stanley J. Rothstein. There was only one reference."

Colonel Sagara picked up a pencil. "Read it to me."

"The whole paper? But my English isn't—"

"The title! The title!"

A rustle of paper and Miss Yokoyama began in halting English. "'A Classical Model for Nuclear Fission.' *American Physics Review*, March 1941. By Stanley J. Rothstein."

Sagara finished writing. "Anything else?"

"This information is given under his name." Miss Yokoyama resumed her slow phonetic pronunciation. "Norman Bridge Laboratory of Physics, California Institute of Technology, Pasadena, California."

Colonel Sagara ended the call and directed a shout at the door of his office. "Sugiura! English translation dictionary!"

A muffled "Hai!" from the colonel's clerk haunting the outer office. The door opened and the young man scuttled in with the book.

It took a moment for Sagara to clarify the term "classical model." "Norman Bridge" remained elusive. Why the connection between a physics laboratory and a bridge? Then he realized it must be a man's name, a commemorative name applied to the lab.

Stanley J. Rothstein. A physics researcher at the California Institute of Technology with enough knowledge of nuclear fission to publish a paper. Just the sort of man the Americans would recruit into a project to build a uranium bomb. And the same name was written on the bomb recovered from the crash site of the B-29, code V680.

The evidence was mounting. And with it a vision of possibilities was beginning to dawn, almost too dazzling to look at. Sagara's imagination ran free for a moment, then his faced darkened.

The object was in the possession of the Imperial Navy. That could not stand.

A part of the colonel's mind remained on the problem as he returned to working through the papers on his desk. He was reading a report from Tachiarai Airfield on northern Kyushu, revealing that stockpiling there was more than a month behind schedule. The next report concerned a bottleneck at a factory producing artillery shells, possibly a solvable problem. He put a telephone call through to the manager there.

Eleven-thirty. He set the receiver down after another call and started into the next file. He was finding it difficult to focus, his vision growing bleary. He stretched and tried to release the tension from his neck and shoulders, then leaned back in his chair and closed his eyes for a moment, the darkness spasming and jerking behind his eyelids.

An indigo sky, fading to violet and a band of orange on the horizon, a sea of lavender clouds soft underneath. They had climbed the sacred mountain in the night to watch the sunrise . . .

The colonel's head jerked up. He had drifted off for a moment.

He leaned forward, planting his elbows on his desk, intending to return to his work. But the sunrise lingered in his brain, and with it a memory.

It was of a class trip. He had been sixteen years old. Odd how that had crawled out of the depths of his brain.

They had made the ascent in the night, five hard hours from the Fifth Station, a physical test for their supple young bodies, followed by the spiritual reward of sunrise at the top. And then the long, leg-wearying slog back to the bottom, the dull gray trail zigzagging its way into the mist, the route at first utterly barren, then a return to stunted shrubs clinging precariously to the volcanic soil.

And then they were running. In high spirits from their conquest, they were running, racing to be first to the next rest station, Shingen Sagara and his friend Masao taking the lead. Running down Mount Fuji was not a wise course of action, Shingen's father would have told him. You're apt to lose your footing. You might fall.

And he did.

He tumbled for what seemed like a very long distance, head over heels, heels over head, arms and legs flailing, the camera around his neck striking his face and cutting him deep in the lip. He fortunately encountered no rocks before coming to rest on his back. He was badly shaken and lay still for a moment, taking a groggy inventory of the state of his body as he stared glassily up into the fog.

Masao was the first to arrive. He knelt down and began feeling Shingen's limbs with trembling hands, confirming that no bones had been broken. Then, with a rush, the others were there, whispering in horror to Masao, "Is he dead?"

"I'm not dead," said Shingen, closing his eyes as Masao administered to the cut on his face, gently washing away the soil with a trickle of water from his canteen. It hurt slightly. It was a precious moment. Shingen didn't want it to end.

The moment passed. Their ashen-faced teacher arrived.

Ashen-faced. Like Haga's face from earlier that morning. Is that what had stirred the memory?

The bleeding was stanched. Shingen was raised to his feet, Baba-sensei so relieved that he had not lost one of his students that he was dabbing tears from his eyes. And Shingen's classmates—they were hooting and carrying on like a pack of wild apes, fright and relief giving way to celebration and pleasure at having just survived this unexpected new adventure.

"Yah!" they exclaimed, brushing Shingen off and straightening him up to complete the descent. "Look at that cut! What a beauty! You'll have a scar now. Just like a soldier!"

His father wasn't angry about the broken camera. He was beyond being able to use it and in any event no longer had the energy to be angry. He just lay there in his bed on the tatami when Shingen returned home with his dirty pack and new stitches. He just lay there, quiet, in his room, surrendering to the tuberculosis, making no effort to fight it, making no effort to survive.

The colonel wearily pushed the memory aside, feeling the last of his own energy draining away. What he needed was a proper rest, but rest for him had become elusive. He had tried again the previous evening, returning to his billet in Ochanomizu, taking a bath and sipping a warmed bottle of sake before lying down for what he had hoped would be an uninterrupted six hours of oblivion. But sleep didn't come. He just lay there, exhausted, with disjointed images cascading through his brain, like a malarial fever without the sweat and the tremors. It had finally driven him to get up and get dressed and return to the Ministry well before dawn.

He tried to concentrate, but it was no good. Nothing more could be accomplished in this mental stupor. He had to rouse himself. He had to be sharp.

He opened the drawer of his desk and resorted yet again to the tiny green bottle. *Philopon* was printed in red katakana characters across the label, and *methamphetamine* small on the side. He had begun taking the tablets in the previous year, finding them a miracle for boosting his energy and focus in these increasingly difficult times. He also found them to have a certain aphrodisiac effect that was not unwelcome. But it had come at a price, the lasting disruption of sleep. And without sleep, he was needing Philopon tablets more and more.

"Yes, what is it? I'm busy!"

Colonel Sagara looked up as the door opened following the soft knock. His stern look switched to a smile and he rose to his feet.

"Oh, pardon me, Takeshita-chūsa. I thought it was my clerk. Come in, come in."

The visitor was Lieutenant Colonel Masahiko Takeshita, head of the Domestic Affairs Section in the Military Affairs Bureau, one floor down, opposite side of the building. They were only acquaintances, not friends, but Sagara was nevertheless glad to see him. Takeshita was excellently situated to know the latest happenings with the Supreme War Council and the Suzuki cabinet. His brother-in-law and confidant, General Korechika Anami, was the Minister of War.

Takeshita took a seat and accepted the cigarette Colonel Sagara offered. The two men settled back and smoked in silence for a moment.

"I understand there was some trouble down the hall," Takeshita began. "You had to reprimand one of the officers, I believe."

"Haga." Sagara snorted his disgust, expelling smoke through his nostrils.

Takeshita nodded his approval. "That was entirely proper."

A slight smile lifted the corner of Sagara's mouth at the memory of Haga's alarm. There was a moment there where he really could have shot the man in the head.

"I was only doing my duty," he said.

Another moment of silence. A meaningful pause. Takeshita was arriving at the point of his visit.

"Sagara-chūsa," he said, "the situation with the government is critical, as you know. General Anami is holding fast on the Supreme War Council, but this movement behind the scenes—I think we need to question Prime Minister Suzuki's sincerity about continuing the war. Don't you think?"

"I completely agree," said Sagara. "Suzuki is a fox. The man can't be trusted."

"This Potsdam Declaration has the politicians losing their heads," said Takeshita. "They're showing their Badoglio spirit. We're at the point now where even a small shift in the balance . . . " He left the sentence unfinished as he leaned forward to the ashtray to flick his cigarette.

Badoglio. Since the surprise capitulation by Italian premier Pietro Badoglio in September 1943, following Mussolini's ouster, the name had become a pejorative in Japan's Imperial Army, spat at those suspected of cravenly seeking surrender.

"It's regrettable," continued Takeshita, "but I think we'll soon reach a point where action will have to be taken. To prevent a wrong move."

Sagara regarded his visitor's face. "Are you referring to some sort of . . . change of course in leadership?" He did not use the term that initially formed on his lips: *coup d'état.*

"If it comes to that, yes." Takeshita drew in a final lungful of smoke and ground his cigarette out in the ashtray. "That's why I've come to you, to gauge your feelings. There are twelve of us now, mostly in the Military Affairs Bureau, and we're drafting a plan. An influential body on the outside has already been formed, the sort of patriotic civilians we'll need."

Sagara stubbed out his own cigarette. He set the butt in the ashtray parallel to Takeshita's.

"Takeshita-chūsa," he said, "accepting the Potsdam terms for surrender would be the greatest catastrophe ever to befall the nation. The spirit of Japan would not survive. And so of course I'll do whatever needs to be done to prevent it."

Colonel Takeshita nodded his approval. "I was hoping that would be your feeling. Now, here is how we're thinking we should proceed."

It took only a few minutes for Takeshita to outline the broad strokes of the planned coup. With the support of a handful of key Army commanders, seizing the capital and isolating the Imperial Palace would not be very hard.

"And what about General Anami?" said Sagara, asking the obvious question. "Has any of this been presented to him? What are his feelings?"

"We need to be careful about involving the General too early," replied Takeshita. "We must consider his position. But I can assure you that when the time comes, there is good reason to believe that the

General could be talked into accepting the premiership. For now, that's all I can say."

General Anami at the helm. That would be perfect. Sagara could think of no man better to lead a military government after Suzuki and the Badoglios were swept out of the way. Anami was beyond all doubt courageous, a rock cliff standing immobile against the thundering waves. Anami in charge would ensure the spiritual victory that must come in the end and greatly improve the prospects for a real victory, the physical victory that Sagara believed could still be achieved.

It was excellent news. And for Takeshita, General Anami's brother-in-law, to drop by at this very moment—surely that was providential.

This was the man.

"Pardon me, Colonel," said Sagara as Takeshita was rising to leave. "But there's something I feel I must tell you. If you could spare just a few more minutes of your time."

Takeshita resumed his seat.

Sagara retrieved the initial Hikari cable from the pile on his desk: *Possible new-type bomb recovered from B-29 crash site . . .*

He handed it to Colonel Takeshita and began to explain.

NINE

KEIZO KAN SPENT A RESTLESS NIGHT IN HIS BARE ROOM IN THE BARRACKS AT HIKARI SPECIAL Attack Unit, listening to the rain as it subsided, to the water dripping off the eaves, to the cricket that began to chirp outside his window. He kept thinking about Noriko as he lay in the darkness, wondering where she was and imagining the terrible things she must be enduring. When the visions became too upsetting, he focused on the black object in the workshop, to reason it into something other than what he feared it to be. A sensor, perhaps? A testing apparatus? Neither seemed plausible. A ruse of some kind, then? Equally unlikely. So why would the Americans place a mass of uranium at the end of a gun barrel inside a bomb casing—unless what they had made was a uranium gun bomb?

His mind went back to his own efforts to enrich uranium for just such a weapon, back to the Riken and Building 49. The two-story wooden structure had housed a cafeteria once. Kan and his half-dozen assistants, undergraduates from Tokyo University, began work on a thermal diffusion separator on the first floor. Kunihiko Kigoshi set up a lab on the second floor to manufacture uranium hexafluoride to feed into the apparatus. It had taken Kigoshi more than a year just to puzzle out the process and produce the first tiny crystals. It didn't particularly matter, however, for it had taken Kan nearly as long to build the separator. Obtaining basic things like copper tubing had caused major delays. Then, when the tubes finally arrived, they were found to be bent, making them unsuitable for use in such a precision apparatus. So more time had to be spent trying to make the tubes perfectly straight, an impossible task to accomplish by hand.

The separator was five meters tall when it was completed, rising up through a hole in the ceiling into Kigoshi's workspace above. Preliminary tests were conducted using argon gas. The results were inconclusive. Kan feared the separator was a failure and had to be completely rebuilt, but that wasn't an option. Finding the necessary materials was now even more difficult due to the worsening war situation. And there was even less time. In July 1944, with pressure mounting from the Army for a miracle weapon, Kan was obliged to go straight into tests with the uranium hexafluoride that Kigoshi was at last turning out. The rice-grain-sized crystals, benign as a solid, were placed in the receptacle at the separator's base and heat was applied, turning them into a highly toxic and corrosive gas. Would the copper tubing even contain it? Kan wasn't sure.

The separator was designed to take advantage of the fact that lighter atoms move more readily toward heat than heavier atoms. This was where the copper tubes came in. There were two of them, a smaller tube inside a larger one, with a precise two-millimeter gap in between. The inner tube was heated electrically and the outer tube was cooled by water, making the gap hot on one side and cold on the other. When uranium hexafluoride gas entered the gap, the tiny fraction of slightly lighter U-235 atoms it contained would gravitate toward the heated side, absorb the heat, and rise, while the preponderance of heavier U-238 atoms would stay closer to the cold side and descend. This would begin a convection process, U-235 atoms rising and U-238 atoms falling. Continue it long enough and the green smudge that solidified in the separator's upper collection chamber would hopefully contain a higher concentration of U-235. Pass the sample through the separator multiple times to increase the concentration, then repeat the process tens of thousands of times and you would have enough enriched, fissionable uranium to build an atomic bomb.

That was how the thermal diffusion separator was supposed to work. It was supposed to be the first of many separators turning out enriched uranium a gram at a time. But for some reason it didn't. None of the samples Kan produced up to April 1945 showed any sign of enrichment when tested in Nishina's cyclotron. Project Ni-Go up to that point had been a failure. And now the separator, the cyclotron, and most of the Riken were gone.

Kan could see it all in ghostly outline as he at last drifted off to sleep.

The air raid siren started to wail. It was the early hours of March 10. He turned the lights off but left the separator running. He used a flashlight to check the pressure gauge—still steady at forty—before evacuating the building.

He joined his colleagues who had been working into the night in the air raid trenches that had been dug on the Riken grounds the previous fall. No searchlights pierced the black sky, probing for enemy bombers. No distant drone of aircraft engines. He assumed—he hoped—it was another false alarm, for the sirens had been sounding almost nightly, two weeks after the last visit by the B-29s. Surely they would not return tonight, just five days before his wife and daughter were to evacuate to the safety of his parents' home in the country.

He slipped back inside to check on the separator. Another ten minutes passed and still nothing happened. He was getting impatient now waiting in the darkness, waiting for the second siren signaling the all clear.

It didn't come. What he heard instead was a hum.

The hum grew louder. The searchlights came on. He jumped down into the trench with the others.

The hum grew to a roar. The ack-ack-ack of anti-aircraft fire began, tracer bullets streaking skyward. Then the B-29s were passing over, flying low, their bombs already dropped. There was no whump-whump-whump of high explosives. It was incendiaries tonight, like the previous raid on February 25. He ventured out of the trench and stood beneath branches swaying in the stiffening breeze. It was blowing toward the southeast, where the sky beyond Ueno Park was starting to glow.

He followed the others up onto the flat roof of Building 43, one of the Riken's taller structures. From there he could see fires consuming the city. The Americans were bombing the flatlands between the Sumida and Arakawa Rivers, the district of densely packed factories and working-class homes known as Shitamachi, "lower city."

More B-29s were flying overhead now, leaving new fires in their wake. The destruction was spreading across the Sumida River into Nihonbashi and Kanda. A plane was seen to catch fire in the distance and spiral downward. The spectacle prompted clapping and cheering all around on the rooftop, even though it was impossible to tell whether it was an American bomber or a Japanese fighter that was crashing, whether it was friend or foe plummeting to death. Something massive exploded amid the conflagration, a fuel tank or munitions works erupting perhaps. The blast had the strange effect of momentarily illuminating blue sky in the middle of the night, a flash of blue sky glimpsed between the clouds, as vivid as day.

It's really quite pretty, isn't it? said a voice in the darkness.

It'll burn hot in a wind like this, said another. It's going to move right across there, unless they can stop it.

You can't stop a fire like that. It'll burn all the way to the river.

Then Asakusa's done for, the second voice said.

The dread that was quivering inside him burst into his chest. His home was in Asakusa, his family in the path of the flames. A series of images flashed through his mind: Noriko and Aiko squatting in the air raid shelter he had dug in the garden, a pit replacing the flowers; the water barrel he had placed against the back wall; the primitive firefighting implements that had been issued to civilians so that they could protect their houses. He saw Noriko and her maid Rie emerging from the shelter to fight the fires according to government instructions, battling the inferno with pails of water and a mop and soaked straw matting. He saw six-year-old Aiko in her padded air raid hood, scant protection against the ferocious heat and flames.

He turned and ran down the stairs and out of the building. No one on the roof seemed to notice him leave. They were captivated by the beauty of the spreading orange glow. He passed a colleague, Dr. Chosokabe, placidly smoking, alone on the steps.

Sit down here, said Chosokabe. Please try to stay calm.

He didn't stop. He ran out the main gate of the Riken, heading east with the wind that was rising. Soon he was wheezing, his chest congested and tight from the unaccustomed exertion. He continued to push himself on, fires burning less than a kilometer off to the right now, licking at the trees on the north side of Ueno Park.

He reached the Tohoku Main Line and passed underneath it. When he emerged from the underpass, he was confronted by a wall of flames to the east and the south, cutting off any direct approach to his home. Firefighters were battling to save a hospital on the leading edge of the blaze. Civilians, most of them women, were struggling to save their own homes, their tinder-box houses of wood beams and wood siding, tatami mats, paper-covered doors. Some were running about with brimming pails of water to fling at the flames, like raindrops at a volcano. Others were climbing up ladders to get onto their roofs, batting at the spreading fire with wet mops and throwing handfuls of sand with no effect whatsoever.

He headed north, trying to skirt around the inferno. He hadn't gone far when he heard renewed anti-aircraft fire and the drone of engines approaching. Then another wave of B-29s was passing low overhead, underbellies crimson, bomb bays open. He heard the incendiary bombs falling and breaking apart, then the hail of forearm-sized steel cylinders striking rooftops and the street and exploding on impact, sending pillars of flame shooting up into the air. A spatter of it struck him, a sticky gasoline substance aflame. His coat was on fire. He ripped it off and cast it away. When he looked up again, the way forward was blocked.

He turned to retreat, shielding his face and burning eyes from the heat.

Houses were ablaze now along the street he had just passed, fronted by flaming columns that were telephone poles, wires falling and sparking. He hurried along, retracing his steps, panic rising. By the time he reached the next street, Noriko and Aiko were no longer in his mind, only escape. He joined a throng of people desperately fleeing, wrapped in bedding and laden with armloads of possessions.

He was on a wider street now, flames leaping up from taller buildings on either side and arching over to meet at the top, forming a tunnel that was sucking in air to fuel the flames. Stinging debris carried by the wind striking his face. A woman with a cotton-padded air raid hood in flames on her head whimpering as she struggled to undo the tangled knot under her chin. A family scuttling along, holding hands. Hold on tight! Don't get separated! A man in a civil defense uniform waving his arms and shouting: Through the school! Through the school! Screams all around: It's hot! It's hot! A child's voice crying out in terror: Mother!

Keizo Kan woke with a start. He looked about the barracks room. It was morning.

Another knock on the door. It opened. It was Petty Officer Yagi with the required equipment.

They did not see Kyushu when they returned to the workshop at the edge of the Hikari Special Attack Unit compound. The view across the Inland Sea disappeared into gray mist. A handful of fishing boats were visible a short distance offshore, plying the waters around the small island. It was as far as the fishermen dared to venture, with enemy submarines lurking beneath the surface and enemy aircraft patrolling the skies.

The workshop door was locked, as PO Yagi had left it. He removed the padlock for Kan to enter, then went off to summon assistance. Removing the steel casing from the device would be heavy work. They would need extra muscle.

The first thing Kan did was to take a series of photographs of the object with the Leica camera he had brought, taking advantage of the

morning light streaming in. Then he began conducting his own specific gravity testing of the metal rings using the basic equipment he had
requested from Yagi. He was on the second ring when the petty officer
returned with Seamen Nakamura and Wada.

"You are entirely correct, Yagi-heisō," said Kan. "Uranium. No
doubt about it."

He methodically continued, testing two more rings as the three
navy men patiently waited. When he was done, he stacked the rings
in the corner, as far away as possible from the bomb-shaped object
itself. He did not know what was inside the thing, the obstruction in
the gun barrel he had probed the previous evening. But if it was more
uranium . . .

"We'll leave these here," he said. "It would be best not to touch
them."

He turned to the bomb, examining the rows of bolts that held the
casing together. The central portion of the casing was comprised of
two panels, 180-degree arcs sandwiched onto either side, seams at the
bottom and at the lifting shackle at the top.

He pointed to the left-side panel. "Shall we begin here?"

Twenty-four bolts had to be removed to free it. Some yielded to
the wrench when Yagi applied mighty strain. The rest had to be cut
away with a hacksaw. Yagi, Nakamura, and Wada took turns with the
blade until they were all glistening with sweat, then went to work with
hammer, chisel, and crowbar prying at the warped metal. Kan, conscious that he was no match for their fitness, spared himself the embarrassment of helping by jotting down notes and adding detail to the
drawing he had started.

The panel at last sprang free and clattered to the floor, sending Yagi
jumping back with a curse.

"This doesn't look like a bomb," he observed, sucking blood from
his nicked finger as he peered into the cavity he had exposed.

It was packed with electrical equipment, wires, and connectors.
The cavity on the other side was found to be identical after the second

panel was removed. The largest components were four identical black boxes that encircled the girth of the object. Each was stamped with a unique code, a combination of letters and numbers, and bore several labels in English, the largest one impressed on a metal plate riveted to the box. Yagi pointed to it as Kan took a photo of the interior space.

"What does that say?"

"'Warning: High Voltage,'" Kan translated. "'Disconnect power before removing cover.'"

"High voltage." Yagi's eyes followed the cables that ran from each of the black boxes to a smaller white unit positioned at the end. "Those must be batteries, then."

Kan examined the black boxes more closely. There were two terminals on each, one marked "Transmitter Antenna," the other "Receiver Antenna." An eight-pin electrical plug labeled "To Control Box" was situated in the center. Was this some sort of recorder? Perhaps. But recording what? It could also be an electronic triggering apparatus. But why would there be four of them?

He took another photo, close up.

They paused to refresh themselves from the bucket of water, standing at the open door to catch whatever breeze was wafting in off the sea. After two hours of work, Nakamura and Wada were no longer stiff in Kan's presence. They casually loitered. A streak of white appeared in a break in the clouds overhead.

"B-29," said Nakamura, taking another drink. It was the second time they had seen a high-altitude condensation trail that morning, a single line pointing northeast.

They returned to work. As the navy men sawed at and pried off the rest of the casing, Kan undertook a more detailed examination of what had been exposed. He was struck by something that had escaped his notice before: fingerprints. Greasy smudges and black smears on interior surfaces, a few bearing the distinct impression of ridges. Seeing them, he imagined American scientists, engineers, builders, bending over this very space just like he was now doing, sweating in the heat as he was now sweating, their hands sore and nicked and dirty, stained with oil and lubricant, leaving fingerprints just like his. The sense of their presence, for a fleeting moment, was eerily strong.

Had one of them been Stanley J. Rothstein?

He noticed something else as well: The interior had a makeshift quality about it, evidence that the builders had made adjustments as they worked. There were bolt holes that had been redrilled where two surfaces had not lined up. And there—the corner of that bracket had been filed down to fit into that tight space. And were those hammer marks on the edge of that flange? In outward appearance this object bore no resemblance to the separator Kan had built at the Riken. But in these small evidences, he recognized the same experimental nature of his own work.

This thing, this device—it had not come from a factory.

It had been painstakingly assembled by hand.

By midafternoon the outer casing had been completely stripped off and the interior space emptied of its complex components. What remained of the object, its essential core, was a thick cylinder—the tube that had run through the entire length—connected to the heavy nose component machined from solid steel. It looked like a gigantic club, a two-meter-long handle with a monstrous bulb on the end. Kan, nearing the end of his second precious roll of film, photographed it from both sides.

Before proceeding further, he probed the tube with the pole he had used the previous evening and marked the location of the obstruction on the outside with chalk. He ran the wand of the Geiger-Müller counter over the spot. It gave only a slightly elevated reading. If the obstruction was a strong radiation emitter, the two-centimeter-thick walls of the steel tube were absorbing most of the rays.

"What are you doing?" asked Seaman Nakamura. He and Seaman Wada were watching over his shoulder.

Kan smiled and shook his head. "I don't really know."

The two young men hurriedly stepped back as Yagi returned. He was carrying a galvanized iron water pipe, somewhat rusty. He stood it on end. It extended more than a meter over their heads.

"That will do nicely," Keizo Kan said.

He eased the rod into the front of the tube, the end attached to a wooden block to keep it elevated to center. He fed it down, down, more than two meters down until it encountered the obstruction.

"Be very careful," he instructed Yagi. "Just gently to start."

Yagi, using a heavy hammer, delivered a tentative tap onto the end of the pipe. The modest release of energy passed down its length into the obstruction and did not move it at all.

He struck the pipe again, and again, progressively harder, the clang of metal on metal making Kan and Nakamura and Wada all blink together.

Still no movement.

Yagi cast the hammer aside in disgust. He went to the corner, rummaged through the larger tools, and returned with a sledgehammer, a determined look on his face.

"Let's see how it likes this," he said.

He began cautiously, gripping the sledgehammer close to the neck. Still nothing. He shifted his grip downward and started swinging from farther back, until Kan was wincing and shying away.

"Nakamura," Yagi barked. "Take over."

Kan relinquished his steadying hold on the pipe to Nakamura and stepped back, rubbing his hands. Nakamura repositioned the pipe. Yagi brought the sledgehammer farther back.

A metallic clang.

Another. Another. Whatever was stuck in the tube remained tightly wedged.

"Come on, you bastard," Yagi murmured.

Nakamura pulled the pipe back, gave it a twist, and repositioned it up against the obstruction. Yagi took a fresh grip on the sledgehammer, lined it up, made a few trial movements, then brought it back, all the way back, and struck a resounding blow.

"It moved," he said.

Two more blows and the obstruction broke free. With a series of taps Yagi drove it back down the tube to the rear end, where Wada stood ready to catch it. Wada braced himself, feet apart, cradling his hands underneath the object as it appeared.

It was too heavy for him. It fell to the floor.

It was a metallic plug—it was hard not to think of it as a projectile— the width of Kan's outstretched hand and the length of his forearm from the fingertips to the elbow. His first reaction as he gazed down at it was relief, for it appeared to be a cylinder of copper, not another uranium mass. But then he realized that what he was seeing was only a thin exterior sheathing, a series of bands, presumably intended to hold the interior elements together and ensure a snug fit inside the tube.

He took two photographs from different angles. Then Yagi, at Kan's direction, went to work at the copper sheathing with a screwdriver and pliers, prying it up and peeling it off as the scientist and the two seamen watched over his shoulder.

Released from the encasing bands, the plug—the projectile—fell apart on the floor.

"There you go," said Yagi. "Uranium. It looks just the same."

There were nine rings of the metal, the same plum patina as the rings retrieved from the front of the tube, coated on the inside with the same silvery plating. Behind them was a tungsten carbide plug identical to the sleeve of the material in front, the same green flecks. And behind that: steel.

Yagi stood up with a grunt and stretched until his back cracked. Keizo Kan, lost in thought, took no notice. He was turning the rings over in his hands, examining them, assessing them, adding them to the basic design that was coming into focus.

They varied in thickness like the uranium rings in the nose— again, individually cast—but were thinner and substantially larger, large enough to fill the whole tube. Individually, they seemed to weigh about four kilos, making the entire stack of nine rings heavier than the forward uranium assembly—at least thirty-five kilos in total, perhaps as much as forty. And the thin silver plating, it was on the inner surface of each ring, not on the outside as with the rings in the nose.

Kan fetched his wooden case.

The Geiger-Müller counter produced the same vigorous reading as the forward uranium mass, more than 200,000 counts per minute, when he held the wand over the scattered rings. He stacked them together, one on top of the other, returning them to their original configuration, and inserted the wand into the hole in the center. The click rate soared in intensity, an angry buzz, the needle on the counter leaping to the top of the scale.

Kan yanked the wand out and kicked the stacked rings over, scattering them across the floor.

The three navy men eyed him curiously. Yagi said, "What did that mean?"

Kan didn't answer. The workshop had receded as the bomb—for it was a bomb—filled his mind. The ten-centimeter hole in these rings—it matched the width of the uranium rings in the nose. When the projectile was fired down the gun barrel, this rear stack of rings would not smash into the ones in the nose, it would slide onto them, hastening and controlling assembly into one solid mass. Assembled, the silvery inner plating on the rear rings would come into contact with the plating on the exterior of the forward rings, now nestled inside. What was the purpose of that? And what were these four small nubs, no bigger than the end of his little finger, that were attached to the outermost ring?

Yagi and Nakamura went to the water pail at the open door of the workshop for a drink. Seaman Wada remained where he was, gazing at the uranium rings on the floor. He picked one of them up. The thickest and heaviest one. He hefted it, marveling at the weight.

Kan didn't notice. He was imagining a theoretical nuclear chain reaction, how it would begin. The silvery plating . . . was it some sort of initiator? A substance that would create a burst of neutrons when the two masses of uranium came together?

Wada, uranium ring in hand, began wandering toward the back of the workshop.

Kan didn't notice. The ring configuration of the uranium filled his mind. Why rings? Because it facilitated the mating of projectile and target upon firing. But there was more. It also allowed for a larger mass of enriched uranium to be assembled and maintained in a subcritical state, for a ring presented far more surface area than a solid slug—surface area from which neutrons could escape. If this mass of uranium had been cast as a solid projectile or with only a small hole in the center like the rings in the nose, the surface area would have been greatly reduced and—

He glanced up. Cold washed over his body. Wada was bending over the stack of uranium rings from the nose that Kan had placed out of harm's way in the corner. He was comparing them, noting how the larger ring in his hand appeared to be exactly the right size to fit onto the stack.

The scientist opened his mouth to shout a warning just as a blue flash engulfed the garage and a wave of warmth struck him. A crackling sensation passed through his body and the Geiger-Müller counter let out a shriek. Wada reeled back, the ring flying from his hand. The blue light vanished. The Geiger-Müller counter subsided.

The young seaman, recovering from his initial shock, looked over at Kan in dismay. "Pardon me! I'm sorry! I'm sorry!" He repeatedly bowed, then began rubbing his hand.

Kan stood frozen, his eyes locked on the uranium rings on the floor beside him. He became aware of a metallic taste in his mouth, like tinfoil on a piece of chewing gum touching a filling. And a sharp, chlorine-like smell. Ozone.

Click . . . click . . . click. The Geiger-Müller counter was reading only background radiation. The workshop was very still. Outside, cicadas were buzzing.

"Bakayaro!" Yagi strode over from the water pail and gave Wada a clout in the head. It seemed the proper thing to do, even though he did not know what the young seaman had done.

"Outside," Kan said. "All of you. Go outside."

Yagi, spitting curses, shoved Wada and Nakamura through the door. Left alone, Kan continued to stand very still, as if any sudden movement might reawaken the beast. Finally he forced himself to take a small step. The uranium did nothing. The unimaginably ferocious power of fission had apparently retreated back inside the rings.

He bent down and touched the ring Wada had dropped. It was burning hot.

He approached the nose assembly and held his hand close to the stacked uranium rings. Heat was radiating off them as well. He pulled his hand away and stepped back.

There was no longer any doubt.

"Genshi bakudan," he whispered.

Atomic bomb.

TEN

THERE WERE NINE OF THEM SEATED AROUND THE TABLE IN THE AIR RAID SHELTER BENEATH the War Ministry building. The concrete space, lit by three naked light bulbs, was a uniform gray, the only splash of color the red markings on the first-aid kit affixed to the wall. The ventilation fan was turned on but ineffective. The shelter was growing warm from the heat of the nine bodies, the air filled with smoke from a half-dozen cigarettes.

Most of the men present were from the War Ministry's Military Affairs Bureau, foremost among them Colonel Masataka Ida, Major Kenji Hatanaka, and Colonel Masahiko Takeshita, who was presiding. Colonel Genga Goto from the Economic Mobilization Bureau was also present. They had begun meeting like this, clandestinely, following the receipt of the Potsdam Declaration on July 27. Their purpose was to approve a plan of action should the government make a move toward accepting the Allied powers' terms of surrender.

Major Hatanaka was speaking, his voice hoarse with fatigue and excitement. Colonel Sagara, invited by Takeshita to attend, gripped his legs in an effort to keep his hands still as he listened, approving of the younger officer's zeal. It was regrettable that Hatanaka had come to the meeting looking disheveled, but he had clearly been busy. He had prepared the draft plan for a coup d'état that now lay before them, outlining the necessary movement of troops and the neutralization of key government figures.

Hatanaka's plan met with general approval. Much would depend on the Imperial Guards, headquartered on the grounds of the Imperial Palace. It was agreed that Hatanaka should approach their commander, General Takeshi Mori, to gauge his feelings. With the Guards on their side, other commanders throughout the country would fall into line once the coup was in motion and General Anami's support was made clear. Colonel Takeshita, Anami's brother-in-law, would formally enlist the general's backing.

"Prime Minister Suzuki. Foreign Minister Tōgō. Marquis Kido." Takeshita finished by reading out a list of civilian leaders suspected of seeking peace behind the scenes. The defeatists who would have to be dealt with. The Badoglio clique.

"You've forgotten Baron Hiranuma," came a voice from the opposite end of the table, referring to the president of the Privy Council. "We all know he's whispering treason into the Emperor's ear."

A murmur of agreement. Colonel Sagara joined in.

"All right. Baron Hiranuma," said Takeshita. He added the name to the list of those to be isolated or killed.

Colonel Ida spoke up: "What about Admiral Yonai?"

Admiral Mitsumasa Yonai. He was a key member of the Supreme War Council, the Navy's counterbalance to General Anami, who represented the Army. According to rumors, Yonai favored surrender.

"The Goldfish Minister," sneered Colonel Goto. The derogatory nickname had been given to Yonai following the destruction of the Navy. Without ships, the admiral was about as useful as an ornamental goldfish in a pond. "I say he goes."

"No," said Takeshita. "We need Yonai to keep the Navy in order. When General Anami steps forward, he'll fall into line."

Silence. Sagara noted uneasy looks. Some of the men present

seemed to be expecting a more open and immediate show of support from Anami.

"The General *will* step forward," Takeshita assured them. "When the time comes, he will do what's needed. But until then, he must be discreet."

He folded his notes and tucked them back into his pocket. "All right. If there's nothing else, I'll ask Colonel Sagara to speak now. There has been an interesting development he's going to tell you about."

Takeshita settled back in his chair and nodded to the colonel.

Sagara cleared his throat and looked around the table. He didn't want to be here. For what he was planning to do, however, he needed support.

He began with an explanation of how the Special Intelligence Unit in Suginami-ku was using the call signs from intercepted radio traffic to track B-29s flying to Japan, and how an unusual new bomber squadron had recently been identified, based on the island of Tinian. It was small, perhaps only ten aircraft. And it seemed to be tasked with some sort of special mission.

"What is that mission?" he said. "The SIU doesn't know. But I believe I have discovered the secret."

Sagara had everyone's attention now. He paused to refer to his notes.

"Four days ago, on August 1 at 0205, three of these Special Task Planes were monitored taking off from Tinian. They flew singly to Hiroshima, Kokura, and Nagasaki."

"Observation planes," someone suggested.

"Correct," Sagara affirmed. "Then, at 0320, three more Special Task B-29s followed. All three followed the same route toward Kokura. One of them turned away just minutes before reaching the city. The other two circled Kokura, then returned to Tinian. The plane that turned away is I believe the same B-29 that was observed trailing smoke by a civilian lookout at Tosa. I believe it is the same B-29 that was brought down in a ramming attack by an Imperial Army

Air Service pilot stationed at Hofu. I believe it is the same B-29 that crashed on Wednesday morning in Yamaguchi Prefecture, near a naval facility, Hikari Special Attack Unit. So it was our friends in the Navy"—Sagara said this with a facetious smile—"who were the first on the scene. They recovered a very large bomb from the wreckage, 3.04 meters long and weighing more than four tons. It was found to contain a large amount of uranium. I believe the purpose of the Special Task Planes was to deliver this weapon."

He paused again and looked around the table. Judging from the blank expressions, the significance of the word *uranium* was lost on everyone present.

"Did you say four tons?" asked Colonel Goto, zeroing in instead on the bomb's tremendous weight.

Sagara nodded. "Four-point-three tons, yes. But it's the uranium that was inside it that's most important. It was recovered at Hikari Special Attack Unit and reported to Kure headquarters and the Navy Chief of Staff, but I don't think the Navy has grasped what it means. The cable was also forwarded here to the Ministry, and I happened to see it. An act of providence, I am sure.

"In any event, I sent a man from the Riken to Hikari to examine this bomb. Quietly. Discreetly. I received his latest report a few hours ago. He is convinced it is a uranium bomb."

More blank looks. Colonel Ida was the first to speak.

"What is a uranium bomb?"

"It is not a conventional weapon," Sagara replied. "It uses the power of the atom. My knowledge is not deep, but I'll try to explain." He went on to outline the thermal diffusion work that had been done at the Riken and the idea of enriching uranium to create a fissionable product. He explained the concept of two pieces of enriched uranium being fired into each other to create a nuclear chain reaction. And then the exciting conclusion:

"My man has informed me that there was a mishap in handling the uranium removed from the weapon. It caused some sort of initial reaction, a release of energy that generated heat and created a flash of light. It left no doubt in his mind that the device is a uranium bomb."

Silence.

"This reaction," said Colonel Ida. "If it continued, the result would be an explosion?"

"A massive explosion," said Sagara, nodding. "Powerful enough to destroy a whole city. Kokura was the target."

The news sent a pall over the room. It was more bad news, another setback to swallow. Ida closed his eyes and lowered his chin to his chest.

"It doesn't matter!" exploded Major Hatanaka, looking around at the dispirited faces. "This changes nothing. It doesn't matter what weapons the Americans have. We will break them with our will!"

Colonel Sagara liked the younger officer more and more. He had the spirit of a samurai warrior, fighting to the death with a river to his back.

"You don't understand, Hatanaka-shōsa," he said. "This is good news."

He looked around the table. "The Americans appear to have succeeded in making an atomic bomb, yes. But they could not have made more than one. My Riken man is quite sure about that. Producing concentrated uranium is too difficult and too time-consuming for them to have made more than one of these weapons. In time they may make a second. But until then . . . " He smiled. "Until then, they have delivered it to us, whole and intact."

Silence around the table.

"This is providence," Sagara continued, his eyes starting to shine. "From the moment I read this cable from Hikari with the word *uran*"— he held up the paper—"the story about Tokimune Hōjō and Mugaku Sogen has been running through my mind. For we are facing the same threat from the Americans today that Japan faced six and a half centuries ago from the Mongols. And now we have in our hands the means of an equally terrible deliverance. For Hōjō it was the divine winds of the typhoon that destroyed the Mongol fleet. For us . . . "—he looked around the table—"for us it will be a uranium bomb. Nuclear fission."

More silence. And only dour looks. Colonel Sagara felt a pang of annoyance. He had just revealed something profound and his fellow officers were just sitting there. No reaction. Like cows.

"You paint a pretty picture," said Colonel Goto at last. "But I can't believe it's anything more than a dream. This thing—supposing it really is a uranium bomb, as you call it. How can you know it will work?"

"I just told you," Sagara shot back. "The material began to react. It proved itself."

"But we didn't build it," Goto went on. "The Americans did. Have we tested it? No. Is it even a viable weapon? We don't know."

"I believe you said it weighs four tons?" said Colonel Ida. "Then deploying it could also be a problem. Our bombers can't carry four tons."

Colonel Takeshita, watching Sagara's face darken, interjected: "Let's assume that the bomb is a viable weapon, and that it can be delivered. Perhaps, Sagara-chūsa, you could tell us your thoughts about how it could be used."

Sagara was glowering at Goto and rubbing his arms. It felt like ants were crawling on his skin. The Philopon tablets did that.

"The bomb will work," he said, "because it is Japan's destiny for it to work. Goto-chūsa might not be able to understand that. But I do."

Goto crossed his arms and leaned back in his chair. He and Sagara had crossed paths before and did not like each other. Sagara referred to Goto behind his back as "Valentino" because he was so ugly. Goto had reciprocated, much to Sagara's annoyance, by nicknaming him "The Ghost" on account of his increasingly hollow-eyed look.

"And the target you propose," prompted Colonel Takeshita.

Sagara tore his eyes from Goto and forced himself to be calm.

"My initial thought," he said, "was to use the weapon against the Americans when they attempt to land on Kyushu after the monsoon. We hold our forces back and let them establish a beachhead. But then we don't draw them into the interior for a defense in depth, as we planned. Instead, we detonate the uranium bomb over their beach-head. Complete annihilation. But now I'm thinking—"

"You're assuming the Americans will mass their forces on a single beachhead," said Colonel Goto, cutting him off. "Look at their Nor-mandy operation. That covered at least fifty kilometers of coastline. Can your bomb deal with all that?"

Sagara's hands balled into fists. His eyes were blazing. Colonel Ida spoke up before he could respond.

"That would mean holding this weapon in reserve for two months or longer," said Ida. "If it really is viable, we should be considering targets that we can hit *now*, when it will do us some good. Would it be possible to use it to dislodge the Americans from Okinawa?"

"An even worse idea," huffed Goto. "Okinawa is one hundred ki-lometers long."

"Guam, then," said Ida. "Or Tinian. Send the bomb back where it came from. If it can destroy a whole city, it could wipe out the north half of the island, the whole airfield complex that the Americans are using to send B-29s to Japan."

"Military targets!" said Major Hatanaka, slapping his hand down on the table. "Why talk of military targets when the Americans are destroying our cities? If this bomb can destroy a whole city—"

"Wait a minute, wait a minute!" cut in Colonel Goto. "Sagara-chūsa, did you not say that this thing was recovered by a naval unit?"

"That's right," said Ida. "So what are we talking about? We don't even have the weapon. It's in the hands of the Navy."

Sagara imagined lunging out of his seat at Goto and clawing out his eyes, then going to work on Ida. But he couldn't afford to lose control of himself now. For they had arrived at the crux of the matter. He took a deep breath and forced himself to be calm.

"You are correct," he said, digging his fingernails into his thighs. "The bomb is currently at the Special Attack Unit at Hikari in

Yamaguchi Prefecture. It's in the hands of our colleagues in the Imperial Navy, but they don't know what they have. Now, we could simply inform them, and leave it to the Navy to make the most of this
heaven-sent gift. But if we did that, we all know what would happen.
The weapon would never be used. Against *any* target. It would just
disappear, tucked away by Admiral Yonai and the Badoglios to prevent
it from steeling the nation's resolve."

He looked around at all the faces. "I don't think we should let that
happen. Do you?"

"The Navy will never turn it over," said Goto. "Asking them to do
so would be pointless."

"I agree," said Sagara. "Entirely pointless."

Colonel Takeshita's face was now showing concern. "Just what are
you proposing?"

"What I'm proposing is that I go down to Hikari and take charge of
the uranium bomb as a representative of the Ministry of War."

"But that could cause a serious conflict," said Takeshita.

Sagara shook his head. "It would be a tactful operation. No con-
frontation. I'll go there myself."

Major Hatanaka spoke up. "Sagara-chūsa said that the B-29 carrying the bomb was brought down by an Imperial Army pilot. One
of our own sacrificed his life in a body-crashing attack to bring down
that plane. That alone should give us priority in the matter. The Navy
merely happened upon the crash site and picked through the pieces. If
any trouble arises from the Colonel taking possession of the bomb, he
should remind them of this."

"Wave the Army-Navy Cooperation Agreement in their faces,"
someone suggested. "That should end any protests they might care to
make."

Colonel Ida nodded. He had no love for the Navy.

Neither did Goto. "Agreed," he grudgingly said.

Sagara turned to Colonel Takeshita at the head of the table.

Takeshita was stroking his clipped mustache, his head bowed, as he considered. He was the direct conduit to General Anami. It all depended on him.

"You didn't mention this before," he pointedly said.

"It occurred to me only this morning," Sagara lied. "I realized that involving the Navy would mean squandering this golden chance."

Takeshita looked around at the others. Sagara appeared to have the backing of everyone present.

"All right," he said, turning back to Sagara. "What do you need?"

ELEVEN

THE DOCTOR WAS SHROUDED IN A GOWN, GLOVES, AND FACE MASK AS HE EXAMINED SEAMAN Wada. Keizo Kan, Petty Officer Ryohei Yagi, and Seaman Nakamura, looking on from the foot of Wada's cot, were not similarly protected. They were confined along with Wada in the empty barracks. Hikari base commander Koreeda had ordered them all quarantined.

"Please relax," the doctor instructed Wada, feeling his pulse. The young seaman, his face drawn and gray, did his best. The doctor squinted at the second hand on his watch, sweating under his gown as he counted fast.

"One hundred and ten," he said. "Very high."

He wrapped the blood pressure cuff around Wada's left arm, the good arm clutching a towel, and began pumping the bulb. He pumped a long time before releasing the air and watching the mercury fall.

"Please try to relax," he said, pumping the cuff tight again for a second reading.

Wada tried. The doctor removed the cuff and set the apparatus aside.

"One hundred and eighty-eight over one hundred and five. Very high."

Kan found the man's admonitory tone annoying. It reminded him of the doctor who had passed off his own breakdown as a form of hysteria, a product of his imagination.

The doctor began feeling under Wada's neck and along his jawline, probing the lymph nodes.

"Any tenderness here?"

Wada forlornly shook his head.

The doctor produced the chopstick he used as a tongue depressor and peered into Wada's mouth. He pulled up Wada's shirt and poked his gloved fingers into the seaman's liver and kidney.

"Any pain?"

"No."

The doctor moved to Wada's solar plexus and belly.

"What about here?"

Wada winced. "A little."

He suddenly lurched upright in his cot, holding the towel to his mouth, and heaved. Nothing came up. A few more dry heaves, his whole body straining.

He lay back, gasping from the effort.

The nausea had come over Wada an hour after the incident the previous afternoon, as he was sitting in the shade outside the workshop, now locked up with the disassembled bomb sealed inside. Yagi had ordered him to remain there, away from the main part of the camp, while he went to report to Lieutenant Miyata, who in turn reported to Lieutenant Commander Koreeda. Keizo Kan had insisted on going with him to telephone his own report to the War Ministry in Tokyo. It was his fault that Wada had been exposed, and he felt guilty leaving him, even for a short time. If he had warned him of the danger or taken adequate precautions, it never would have happened. He expected, however, that trouble was coming. If he didn't communicate his findings to Colonel Sagara now, he might not get another chance.

When he returned to the workshop, Wada was doubled over, vomiting into the grass. Kan recorded this latest development in his notebook, adding to the observations he had set down in an unsteady hand after the initial shock of the incident passed. As far as he knew, nothing like this had ever before been reported. The results of extreme radiation exposure were of course well known, the horrific bone loss and malignant tumors suffered by those who ingested radium back when it was believed to be healthy. He had seen a photograph of the amputated right hand of radium discoverer and radioactivity research pioneer Marie Curie, two fingers missing and the others covered with lesions after a lifetime of handling the substance. It had probably also killed her, her death attributed to a rare disease of the blood. But these were the outcomes of long radiation exposure, lasting for years. What had happened in the workshop had lasted for only a second, but the effects were immediate, starting with the tingling and numbness Wada reported feeling in his hand. And now this nausea.

Wada's stomach was soon emptied, but the heaving continued as he was moved into quarantine at Koreeda's orders. Kan assured the commander that the bomb was not a biological weapon and that Wada's illness was not contagious. His inability to explain what it was, however, left Koreeda fearing the worst. He ordered Yagi, Nakamura, and Kan to join Wada in isolation before placing a call to Vice Admiral Masao Kanazawa at Kure Naval District headquarters.

Wada's violent dry heaving continued through the evening and on into the night. The spasms finally subsided just after dawn, leaving him wrung out and exhausted. Whatever had been ailing him seemed to be releasing its grip on his guts. His hand, however, the one that had held the uranium ring, was worse. Now it was red and inflamed under the wet compress and ointment that had been applied. The doctor was treating it like a burn.

Kan recorded it all.

. . .

Examination over, Wada returned to gazing sadly at the open window. Barked commands and shouted responses could be heard from the kaiten pilots performing their morning calisthenics outside. "I should be on duty," he said.

The doctor ignored him. He turned to Yagi, Nakamura, and Kan. "And you? Any symptoms?"

"Nothing," Yagi said curtly, rolling a pair of dice in his hand. "I'm fine."

"Nothing. I'm fine," echoed Seaman Nakamura.

Keizo Kan, his arms tightly crossed, was slow to respond. He did not feel fine. His head was aching. Was it merely stress or something else? He had been at least four meters away when it happened, Yagi and Nakamura perhaps double that distance. What was the effect of a neutron and gamma ray burst at four meters, a burst so massive it had generated light and instantly heated the uranium rings? He had no idea. And then he had stupidly touched the hot ring.

The doctor noted his hesitation. "Any nausea? Any discomfort?"

Kan shook his head.

The doctor left. Kan watched him strip off his gown, mask, and gloves as soon as he was outside and confer with Commander Koreeda, who was just returning. Koreeda then borrowed the doctor's mask and, holding it over his nose and mouth, entered the barracks and called Kan to the door.

"I've spoken with Vice Admiral Kanazawa," he said, "and he is communicating with the Navy Chief of Staff in Tokyo. In the meantime I've been instructed to question you and gather more information."

He looked into Kan's eyes. He said, "I wonder if you've been entirely forthcoming with us."

Kan was unable to hold the commander's gaze. He looked down.

"Kan-sensei, the Army and the Navy must cooperate. That's the directive. If the War Ministry has instructed you otherwise, someone there is disobeying an Imperial order."

Kan hesitated, remembering Colonel Sagara's admonition for secrecy. "I'm sorry, Commander. I'm in a . . . it's a difficult situation."

"Caught between the Army and the Navy. Yes, I can see that."

Koreeda regarded him for another moment, then jerked his chin at Wada inside. "What happened to the seaman?"

Kan glanced over his shoulder. Nakamura was out of earshot, sitting with Wada. Yagi, pocketing his dice, had approached when Koreeda entered and was standing nearby.

"I don't know for certain," Kan replied, keeping his voice low. "But his condition isn't contagious. I can assure you of that."

"Yes, so you told Lieutenant Miyata. But isn't it curious that you know his condition isn't contagious yet would have us believe you don't know what his condition is?"

Kan's eyes dropped again to his scuffed shoes.

"Come now," pressed Koreeda. "If I don't get a truthful answer, I'll have no choice but to keep you confined here. What happened to the seaman?"

Kan's eyes remained down. The Navy, he knew, had funded its own atomic bomb research, Project F-Go, to explore the centrifuge method of uranium enrichment. He had exchanged data with F-Go's head scientist, Kyoto Imperial University professor Dr. Bunsaku Arakatsu. With a report of the incident now on its way to the Navy Chief of Staff, it was just a matter of time before Arakatsu was consulted and everything was revealed. It therefore seemed pointless to dissemble with Koreeda. It would serve only to keep him confined here in the barracks, unable to carry out Colonel Sagara's orders.

"Very well," said Koreeda, turning to leave. "Consider yourself detained. Indefinitely."

"Radiation poisoning," Kan blurted out. "I believe Seaman Wada has been exposed to a large amount of radiation."

Koreeda turned back. "Radiation poisoning," he repeated, unsure of the term.

"There are several kinds of radiation," said Kan. "X-rays are one.

If you have had an X-ray photograph taken of your body, you have received a small amount of X-ray radiation. It doesn't do any harm. Gamma radiation is another. I believe Seaman Wada received a large amount of gamma, large enough to make him sick."

"And it's not contagious?"

"No. Definitely not contagious."

Koreeda hesitated a moment, then lowered his mask.

"So is that the nature of this bomb? To generate radiation? A kind of poisoning weapon?"

Keizo Kan had not considered this. A radiation poisoning weapon? No, that seemed unlikely.

"Poisoning would be only a by-product," he said. "I believe the real purpose would be to create an explosion. A large explosion. It's called *genshi bakudan*."

"Atomic bomb," repeated Koreeda slowly. He considered the term for a moment. Then: "How large an explosion?"

Kan didn't know the answer. According to the accepted calculation at the Riken, one kilogram of enriched uranium had the energy potential of 1,700 tons of conventional explosives. But that was purely theoretical.

"It's difficult to say," he replied.

"Bigger than the Blockbuster?" Koreeda was referring to the well-known monster bomb the British had used to pulverize the Germans.

The American bomb contained sixty-four kilograms of uranium, so that meant a theoretical energy potential of more than 100,000 tons. What did a 100,000-ton pile of conventional explosives look like? Would it even be possible to detonate such a mass all at once? In reality, an atomic explosion would not be nearly so efficient as to realize its entire energy potential. But if only a half, a quarter, even a tenth of the atoms in the uranium rings were to fission . . .

Kan slowly shook his head. "I believe it would be much more powerful than that."

•   •   •

Lieutenant Commander Koreeda rescinded the quarantine order, releasing Kan and the three navy men from the barracks. Seaman Wada was moved to the base infirmary for what was hoped would be his recovery. His nausea was subsiding, but his affected hand appeared to be getting worse, swelling even more and turning bright red. Nakamura went off to find some ice to ease the pain it was causing his comrade.

Keizo Kan's first concern was to prepare the uranium rings to be safely transported. "We need lead," he said to Petty Officer Yagi. "We need to place the two ring assemblies into separate boxes lined with lead."

Yagi led the way across the compound toward a grouping of ramshackle warehouses alongside the river. They passed the assembled ranks of kaiten pilots, now standing at ease in front of their commander as he delivered a speech. They were all young, aged eighteen to perhaps twenty-two, every one of them robust-looking and brimming with health.

"We underestimated the enemy's will," Kan heard their commander saying. "We thought he wouldn't fight so hard. Well, he fights hard, doesn't he? We know that now. He loves his country and he has his own national spirit, just like you. So you must strengthen your Japanese spirit. You must love your country even more and fight even harder!"

"Wada doesn't look good," said Yagi. "Do you think he'll recover?"

Kan shook his head. "I don't know."

They continued on.

"Gen-shi ba-ku-dan," Yagi murmured the syllables thoughtfully. "So that's what it is."

Kan turned on him and stopped. "You weren't supposed to hear that. Your ears are too sharp."

The rebuke made no impression on Yagi at all. "So how does it work?" he pressed. "'Atomic.' What does that mean?"

Kan raised his hands to his head in exasperation. "This is supposed to be a secret!"

Yagi thrust his face at him, threatening. "Listen. I've sweated over that thing for days. And now one of my men is sick. Don't tell me it's a secret!"

They stood nose to nose. Kan managed to maintain his indignation for three seconds before backing down. He had already disobeyed Colonel Sagara's orders in revealing what he did to Commander Koreeda. The damage was already done, if the colonel found out.

"All right," he said. "But please, be discreet. Let's not even call it a bomb. Can we do that?"

Yagi shrugged. "We can call it whatever you want. With the outer casing off, it looks like a big horse cock. How about that? Let's call it the Horse Cock."

Kan gave him an annoyed look.

"The Eggplant, then," said Yagi. He snapped his fingers. "No, the Daikon. It looks like a big black daikon radish. Let's call it the Daikon."

The word gave Kan a pang of unease. He didn't know why. He let out a weary sigh and nodded.

"All right," said Yagi. "It's the Daikon. Now how does it work?"

They continued on across the compound, Kan explaining in whispers the basic concept of atomic fission and his deductions of how the . . . Daikon was intended to function.

"So it *is* a gun barrel," said Yagi. "To fire the two parts of uranium together. And all those other parts, the wiring, the electrical units—that's the triggering mechanism? All that just to detonate it automatically? Remotely?"

"That's what I'm thinking," said Kan. "The—" A final sigh of capitulation. "The Daikon was probably designed to explode at a certain altitude above the ground. Multiple systems to safeguard against failure."

Yagi was shaking his head. "Now that's what I don't understand."

"Detonating it above the ground? Because that would cause maximum damage."

"No," said Yagi. "I mean making it so complex. Just to save the lives of one or two men."

They had come to the wharf and turned toward a grouping of rust-streaked, warehouse-like buildings. There were five training kaiten moored in the oil-filmed water, their tops painted white. Another thirty, painted black for combat, were sitting on chocks in the tin-roofed structure Yagi led the way into. It was Kan's first good look at the unusual weapon. It was fifteen meters long and one meter wide and had a hatch and periscope sticking up at the center—the Navy's Model 93 torpedo, elongated just enough to accommodate a man.

"Get off your lazy asses!" roared Yagi, making Kan jump. "Get back to work!"

Knots of men leaped up from the corners where they had been idling and threw themselves back at a half-dozen partly assembled torpedoes.

"One-point-six-ton warhead," Yagi said with obvious pride, noting Kan's interest. "It can lift a destroyer right out of the water. Break its back. But the welding—"

He raised his voice so that it boomed through the building. "We're going to fix every leak!"

A dozen voices affirmed in unison, "Hai!"

"We're going to send our comrades off in perfect weapons!"

"Hai!"

"Orita! Watanabe!" barked Yagi.

Two of the seamen broke away from the kaiten they were working on and reported to Yagi on the double, arms tight to their sides.

Yagi handed them the sketch Kan had made. "Ten-millimeter lead sheeting. Cut these pieces. Exact. Understand?"

The seamen hurried off. Kan's gaze returned to the kaiten.

"It's hard to imagine a man could fit inside," he said.

"Getting in isn't so hard," said Yagi. "It's staying in that's the problem. Not many can stand it for more than just a few minutes. Too claustrophobic. Those men out there . . . "—he gestured toward the parade ground—"they have to be able to sit in one of these things for hours."

Kan approached the nearest kaiten and began walking around it. Even elevated on chocks, it came only to his chest.

Yagi lifted the hatch. "Go on, take a look."

Kan peered down into the cockpit. There was a backrest but no seat. The pilot sat directly on the hull, surrounded by valves and tubes and hard metal edges, the periscope eyepiece a handbreadth from his face. It was so much worse than what he had imagined for Tetsuo, one of his nephews, who had crashed his explosives-packed aircraft into an American ship off Saipan. Kan had congratulated his sister in the approved manner on the glorious sacrifice of her son after hearing the news. She had thanked him with a grateful smile and tears in her eyes.

"How does the pilot see?" he asked. "Surely the periscope doesn't work underwater."

"He takes a sighting on the target through the periscope on the surface," explained Yagi. "After he dives for the final approach, it's all done blind. Underwater navigation. Pure calculation. And he's all alone, with only a flashlight." He paused, then added: "It takes a special kind of crazy fool to do that."

Kan noted something in the petty officer's voice. A hint of reverential emotion? Looking down into the kaiten, he felt nothing but horror. At least Tetsuo had seen his target as he made the final dive in his plane. A kaiten pilot, steering blindly toward a moving target—what was his actual chance of success?

They proceeded to a jumble of wood piled against the back wall and selected some scraps and odd lengths for the boxes. As they began marking and sawing out pieces, Kan's mind went back to his telephone call to the War Ministry in Tokyo. He had spoken cryptically and the line had been bad, but Colonel Sagara had grasped his message—and also his meaning when Kan cautiously inquired about his wife.

"That person is in—" Sagara snapped, the last word lost in a burst of static. "Now there's no reason for you to bring up this matter again. Do you hear me?"

Kan hadn't dared ask the colonel to repeat himself. Had he said

Noriko was in Iidabashi? It had sounded something like that, but Kan hoped he was mistaken. Iidabashi was just north of the Imperial Palace in what was left of downtown Tokyo—a dangerous place to be held, already thoroughly bombed. But then Sagara's next sentence: *Now there's no reason for you to bring up this matter again.* Did that not imply that he would be satisfied with the action being taken? As Kan pondered the phone call and Sagara's words, his feeling began to gravitate slightly toward hope.

Yagi was awash with sweat now as he worked with the saw. Kan, looking on, felt the fingers of his right hand—the hand that had absorbed the heat coming off the uranium ring Wada had dropped. A definite tenderness was apparent on the tips of the index and middle digits, as if they had been burned.

He looked at his fingers. Only a slight redness.

He checked his watch. Twenty-three hours since exposure.

He took out his notebook and jotted this down.

That person is in . . .

Where was Noriko?

He prayed she was safe.

TWELVE

THE BLAST OF A WHISTLE. SIX O'CLOCK IN THE MORNING. NORIKO KAN WEARILY ROSE FROM another restless night. She rolled up her futon and pushed it against the wall and went through the motions of straightening the clothes that she lived in. Fourteen interminable hours lay ahead of alternately sitting and standing on the hard concrete floor, alone with her anxiety, confined with her thoughts.

She started with sitting. She spent hours each day staring at the concrete when she wasn't dozing, staring until the cracks and stains took on the form of identifiable objects: the outline of a mountain with the moon rising behind it; the head of a horse-insect; a child's footprint; the dead eye of a fish. And then there was the splotch that she always returned to, the face of a man, slightly turned away, a friendly presence locked up with her inside her cell.

She smiled, remembering the time during their awkward courtship when she taught Keizo to drive. His lack of coordination working the clutch and the gearshift had made her laugh so hard that she hurt his feelings. It was her first glimpse of his sensitive nature. When she realized what she had done, she won him back with a playful kiss on the cheek. She had been only twenty-one years old, nine years younger than Keizo, a mere sophomore while he was a doctoral student. But she was the confident one, the leader, as she helped him in his struggles with English and every other aspect of American life. It was from that moment in the car that she knew that Keizo was the man she would marry.

And then the shoe was on the other foot. After their marriage, she returned with Keizo to Japan and experienced devastating culture shock of her own, starting with those first months living with his parents: his difficult and domineering mother, who she realized was the source of his shyness; his indulgent father, who was proud of the academic success of his son. Then it was Keizo who helped ease her struggles. He protected her against his mother's abuse, then scraped money together and moved them into a home of their own. He helped her improve her Japanese accent and adjust the things that marked her as foreign. He comforted her when life in Tokyo overwhelmed her and reduced her to tears.

Footsteps jerked Noriko back to the present. She got to her feet and stood with head bowed. The guards insisted on prisoners standing when they made their first rounds in the morning. She heard the footsteps pause somewhere down the hall and the warning tap of a baton on a cell door.

The footsteps continued. Another pause. Another tap.

The footsteps stopped outside her door. A shadow appeared at the grating. Was it the Toad? She didn't dare look. She kept her head down, communicating submission.

The footsteps passed on. She continued to stand for a time, her eyes closed. Then she started scratching. Being denied the ability to wash had been its own kind of torture for the first two weeks. Now, after two months, she didn't give it much thought. She just scratched.

The squeaking wheels of the cart. Breakfast was coming. She seized her bowl and moved to the door. Hesitate when food was served, and the man would pass on and you would receive nothing. Attempt to call him back, and the only thing you would be eating would be a guard's fist or his club or his boot.

The hatch in her door was opened from the outside. She thrust her bowl through and something was ladled into it. Then, strangely, something more was added. Noriko pulled her bowl back and looked down at the most generous meal she had ever received in this place, the usual thin gruel that was served in the morning with a supplemental scoop of something dense sitting in the middle, a concoction of soy and peanut residue and bits of unidentifiable green. She stared at it for a moment, confused, then retreated to the corner and started greedily eating. When she was done, she felt almost full.

She licked out the bowl and washed it with a small amount of water, which she drank. Then she sat with her back to the wall, puzzling over why she had received extra food. Was the man with the cart new? Had he made a mistake? Was it a trick?

A trick seemed most likely. Her eyes kept darting to the door, half expecting that it would burst open and she would be taken upstairs to face more accusations. *So you're not just a defeatist and a traitor. You're a pig! A greedy pig!*

Yes, it was a trick. They were trying to raise her spirits so they could smash them back down.

Her anxiety rose. Then the panic seized her. It was the start of madness. She knew that. Confined in this small space, caught between the torment of her thoughts and her fear of what lay beyond the door—it was becoming more than she could bear.

It was starting to unravel her mind.

The scrape of the key in the lock came at midmorning.

She scrambled to her feet as her cell door opened. A man in civilian clothing stood there, not one of the guards. He looked like a clerk.

"Noriko Kan?"

Noriko didn't answer. She stood with eyes downcast, frightened and confused.

"Is your name Noriko Kan?"

She nodded. The clerk said nothing further. He waved her out of the cell and directed her toward the stairs.

There was daylight one floor up, the first daylight she had seen in weeks. It was painfully bright and made her squint. A hallway extended in both directions. The room where she had been interrogated was to the left. She did not want to go to the left. She prayed she would not have to go that way as she mounted the last step.

The clerk led her to the right, down the hall and around a corner. She found herself at the head of another corridor lined with cell doors. She kept her eyes down as they walked along it, not daring to glance through the row of gratings but sensing human presences locked up inside.

They reached the end, another corner, and the clerk opened a door.

"Five minutes," he said, motioning for her to enter.

Noriko held back. She could see white tiles through the door.

"Quickly. Five minutes."

She cautiously entered. The door closed behind her. Tiled floor and walls, mildewed corners, taps with basins underneath, two drains.

It was a bathing room. She was being allowed a bath.

She quickly undressed and began filling one of the basins, then a second to soak her soiled clothes. The water pressure was low, but it was enough. There was even the luxury of a sliver of coarse laundry soap.

She worked quickly, scrubbing herself all over and pummeling her clothes, the filth coming off everything turning the cold water gray as it flowed down the drain. She was gasping when the clerk knocked on the door and called in all too soon: "Finish now."

She grabbed her clothes from the basin, squeezed out the water and struggled to get dressed without tearing the wet fabric.

The door opened.

"That's long enough. Come out."

She had not been able to button up her blouse. She pulled it closed and headed for the door.

"Thank you," she said as she exited. "Thank you."

She stood in her cell, feeling anxious and confused as the clerk's steps faded away. The extra food, and now a bath—what did it mean? Was it all just a trick? Or had her situation improved? She had never been formally charged with a crime, after all. Perhaps there was a limit on how long someone could be held without charge. She had assumed the Tokkō could do whatever they wanted, but perhaps not. Perhaps they had reached the limit on the torment they could inflict.

Tendrils of hope were growing in her mind as she carefully pulled off her wet clothes and wrung them out and hung them from the door. She would sit naked in the corner until they were dry, then put them back on.

She closed her eyes and allowed herself to be carried away, away to the back garden, surrounded by flowers. They were helping Aiko take her first steps. Keizo propped her up and gently released her. *Come on, you can do it!* One, two, three tottering steps, then a gurgling laugh as Aiko fell into her arms and Keizo was clapping and—

The footsteps returned. They did not belong to the clerk. They were heavier and sharper, the clop of iron-heeled boots. Noriko lurched up and seized her damp clothes and frantically started dressing. But it was too late.

The door opened. It was the Toad, pistol on his belt, club in his hand. His glare turned into a smile when he saw her state of undress.

He leaned back out the door and looked up and down the hall, making sure no one was there.

He entered the cell and closed the door. Noriko huddled before him, clutching her clothes to her body, her soul dropping down through the floor.

There was no hope. It had all been a trick.

The Toad approached. He stuck his club under her chin and forced her to look into his face. "So, you think you have friends," he sneered, keeping his voice low so it wouldn't carry.

He pulled back and started looking her up and down. He ran his club down her bare arm and along the diminished curve of her hip.

He started pushing the club between her legs. She resisted. He gave her a warning rap on the hand. It hurt, but still she resisted.

He stepped back and struck her on the shin. It was a practiced blow, sharp enough to cause agony without breaking the skin. Noriko cried out and dropped to the floor, clutching her leg.

The Toad looked down at her and smiled. "Do you see your friends here?" He looked around the room, feigning confusion. "Where are they? I don't see them."

He cracked the club across her other shin. Noriko let out a strangled cry and rolled into a ball, clutching her legs with one hand, covering her breasts with the other. The Toad watched her with satisfaction, seemingly pleased to have caused so much pain with so little effort.

He squatted down beside her, thrusting his face into hers, breathing stink.

"You have no friends here," he whispered. "There's only me. Understand?"

THIRTEEN

THE TRANSPORT, A MITSUBISHI KI-57 WITH FADING CAMOUFLAGE PAINT, WAS SUITABLY LARGE for Colonel Sagara's purpose. In addition to the three-man crew, there was room for a personal guard of four soldiers, enough to provide manpower and make an impression while still leaving cargo space for the return trip.

They took off from Tama Airfield in the dark, just after two o'clock in the morning. The destination was the airfield at Yuu in Yamaguchi Prefecture, on the Inland Sea up the coast from Hikari. Estimated flight time: three hours.

Sagara remained upright in his seat, his right leg jiggling up and down in the dark, his fingers strumming his thigh. He needed a tablet but would wait a little while longer. His mind kept jumping from what lay ahead to the telephone call he had received back at Tama Airfield from Captain Onda just minutes before takeoff, reporting renewed activity among the Americans' Special Task Planes. After five days of silence, V600 call signals had been again intercepted by the Intelligence Unit, three aircraft departing from Tinian and heading toward Japan, either southern Honshu or Kyushu. Were they weather planes? Were they reconnaissance aircraft? Would three more B-29s with V600 identifiers follow as before?

The copilot emerged from the cockpit with a thermos. "Biwa-ko!" he shouted above the roar of the engine, pointing down.

Colonel Sagara decided he had waited long enough. He swallowed two Philopon tablets with the lukewarm tea the copilot offered. The methamphetamine burned in his stomach as he looked out the window— a small price to pay for the energy and confidence it would bring.

They were passing over Lake Biwa, lost in the blackness, then a scattering of pinprick lights indicating the presence of Kyoto. The ancient city, Sagara knew, remained untouched by American bombing. An oversight? Almost certainly not. The Americans did not spare civilians and cities. They had some plan for Kyoto. Perhaps it would be next.

He leaned back, remembering his honeymoon in Kyoto in 1934. What a ludicrous week! His wife had not appealed to him at all—it was an arranged marriage—and the feeling was mutual, judging from the minimal effort she made. Within two years, still childless, she stopped making any effort, after discovering that her husband's tastes lay elsewhere.

He was feeling better now. Yes, much better. And sure of his plan. A smile spread across his face as he envisioned it unfolding. He was certain it was going to work.

The flight proceeded without incident, the Mitsubishi landing on the dirt runway at Yuu Airfield as the sky was starting to lighten. A truck was waiting as Sagara had ordered. It would transport him and the soldiers the rest of the way, thirty-five kilometers south and west along the coastal road to Hikari.

The flight crew was to refuel the plane and await his return.

Keizo Kan scrutinized his right hand, peering at it over the top of his glasses. Some swelling was now apparent, but the redness no longer seemed to be spreading. The tenderness on the fingertips persisted and was accompanied by a mild tingling sensation. He opened his notebook and jotted down the time and the progression of symptoms, after the ominous entry he had made the previous night: "loss of appetite; difficulty eating; mild nausea."

He proceeded to the base infirmary, taking his camera, to check on Seaman Wada. The young man was lying in bed, his injured hand resting in a pan of chipped ice. He tried to sit up when Kan entered.

"Pardon me, Sensei," he said, apologizing yet again. "I'm very sorry."

"No, no, please just rest." Kan placed his hand on the young man's shoulder, urging him to lie back. "Any more nausea?"

Wada shook his head and smiled weakly. "Nothing really."

"Diarrhea?"

"No. I'm fine."

Kan smiled encouragement. "Good, good." He felt Wada's forehead. Hot and clammy. He bent down to look at the hand. "I'm afraid it's causing you pain."

Wada hesitated. "A little."

He was lying, of course. Kan could see the pain in Wada's drawn face. He hid his concern as he examined the seaman's hand, so swollen now that the flesh had burst open and was oozing clear liquid. Its color was also evolving, the uniform bright red of yesterday shading into a waxy gray blue. Kan had never before seen gangrenous flesh, but he imagined that it might start out looking like this. And all from a split second of exposure. What fundamental damage had it done? What did it mean? Perhaps he should ask the doctor to take a blood sample.

"The doctor says it's only a burn," said Wada.

"I'm sure he's correct. It certainly looks like a burn." Kan held up his camera and smiled again. "May I take a photo?"

Wada nodded. Kan adjusted the aperture and focus and clicked off two shots, one from each side, using up the last of his film. He felt the need to document the process, even though he didn't know what use it would be.

"Well," he said, snapping the camera back into its case, "if the stomach upset and diarrhea have passed, I should say there's nothing to worry about. All that remains is for your hand to get better."

He bid Wada an awkward farewell, feeling doubly guilty now, the photo of Marie Curie's radiation-destroyed amputated hand lingering in his mind.

He was descending the steps of the infirmary building when base commandant Koreeda's clerk spotted him and hurried over.

"Kan-sensei," the man said. "You are required in the Lieutenant Commander's office!"

There was a heavy truck parked in front of the bungalow-style administration building housing the office that base commandant Koreeda shared with his executive officer. Four Imperial Army soldiers, hard-faced veterans, were standing on the veranda, Arisaka rifles over their shoulders. Keizo Kan warily skirted around them as he followed the agitated clerk up the steps.

"Precautionary security," said the clerk. "That's what he said."

He opened the door to the office and stepped aside for Kan to enter. Koreeda's executive officer, Lieutenant Miyata, was sitting behind his desk, looking as perturbed as the clerk. Seated facing him was Colonel Sagara in high boots and full uniform, smoking a cigarette. The clerk closed the door.

"Ah, there you are, Sensei," Colonel Sagara said, rising to greet the scientist with affected good humor. "Come and help me clear this up. Lieutenant Commander Koreeda unfortunately isn't here at the moment and Lieutenant Miyata is under some misapprehension. I'm sure you consulted fully with the Commander about the object you were sent to investigate. Yes?"

Kan looked nervously between the two men, unsure of the game that Sagara was playing. He had breached his instructions for secrecy with what he had revealed to Koreeda, but at the moment the colonel seemed to want an affirmation of full consultation.

"Yes," he tentatively replied.

"And you informed him that the Army would be taking charge of it. By War Ministry order. You explained this. I'm sure he must have understood this."

"Yes," Kan said. "I believe so."

"I'm sorry, Colonel," said Lieutenant Miyata, struggling to stand firm against an army officer who greatly outranked him. "But the object can't be released without Commander Koreeda's order. I'm sorry."

Sagara blew out a lungful of smoke, squinting at the embattled lieutenant through the haze. He carefully stubbed out his cigarette in the ashtray beside him and placed it next to the first one he had smoked.

"Lieutenant Miyata," he said, leaning back in his chair. "This is a War Ministry matter. That makes it a matter of national importance. Commander Koreeda would understand this if he were here. It's unfortunate that you're unable to grasp what I'm sure your commanding officer would see in an instant."

Miyata was looking desperately unhappy. "I'm sorry, Colonel," he stammered. "There's nothing I can do. Please understand."

"There really is no more time to discuss it. I'll just ask you one last time for your cooperation. Do I have it? Yes? No?"

"Please, Colonel, I can do nothing without Commander Koreeda's—"

Sagara's face twisted with sudden fury. He lurched up out of his chair and placed his hands on Miyata's desk, looming over the lieutenant, his eyes blazing. Kan took a step back, as shocked as Miyata, thrown back in his chair.

Whatever passion had seized the colonel passed. His shoulders relaxed. He straightened his uniform and looked around the office, then through the open door behind Miyata into the empty inner office and Koreeda's desk.

He turned to Kan. "Get the corporal."

Kan, still shaken, scuttled to the door. The toughest looking of the soldiers waiting outside answered his whispered summons.

"Corporal," said Sagara when the man entered. "The lieutenant here is not to leave the office. He is to remain at his desk with the door locked. He is not to use the telephone or communicate in any way with anyone. Understand?"

The corporal snapped a nod. "Hai."

Miyata, the color returning to his face, at last found his voice. "But, Colonel—" he started to protest, rising out of his chair.

The corporal unshouldered his rifle and leveled it at his chest. "Sit down."

Miyata subsided into his seat, shock returning to his face.

"Pardon my crudity," said Sagara, "but there is really no time. Now, where is the object? As a representative of the Ministry of War, under General Korechika Anami, I am taking control."

Miyata's mouth opened, but nothing came out.

"It's down by the water," said Kan. "The building is locked."

"The key," said Sagara, beckoning to Miyata. "Give me the key."

The lieutenant fumbled in his desk drawer and produced a key. Sagara took it and led the way out of the office. He closed the door before the hovering clerk could see in. Kan heard it lock behind them.

Sagara motioned his three remaining soldiers to the truck. He turned to the clerk, who was looking suspiciously between Sagara and Koreeda's locked office door.

Sagara waved him into the truck. "You too. I may need you."

The truck made its way through the base, past the exercise field and barracks buildings to the workshop near the south perimeter fence. Kan sat in front, sandwiched between the driver and the colonel, deeply troubled over what he had just witnessed. The look he had seen in Sagara's face, the rage in his eyes—it was as if some sort of insanity had flared up inside him.

Kan cast a furtive glance at the colonel, whose thigh was pressed against his. His other knee was jiggling up and down as he stared straight ahead. His face appeared normal. He had apparently returned to himself.

The Inland Sea was sparkling in the distance when they arrived at the workshop, the cloud cover burning off in the rising sun. Sagara jumped down from the front seat and took an impatient step forward. Then he thought better of it and handed the key to the clerk who had alighted from the back.

"Open the door."

"This thing is dangerous," said the clerk. "One of our men is sick."

"Yes. Now open the door."

The clerk reluctantly removed the padlock, swung the double doors open, and stepped away. Sagara signaled to the driver to turn the truck around and back up.

He entered the building with Kan.

The disassembled carcass of the bomb lay exposed on the floor, just as Kan had left it. The scientist watched Sagara eagerly looking around, taking in the various components: the curved steel sections of the bomb's outer casing; the crushed fins that had been removed from the tail; the myriad of electrical components, switches, and wiring; and at the center, the long steel gun barrel with the bulbous mass on the end that was the heart of the bomb.

"The uranium," Sagara said. "Show it to me."

Kan pointed to the two lead-lined boxes he and Yagi had fabricated the previous day. He'd had them placed apart in opposite corners, painting "Do Not Touch" on the top for good measure.

"These were in the nose," said Kan, "25.6 kilos." He removed the lid from the smaller box to reveal the six rings inside. He pointed to the box in the opposite corner. "The projectile is there—38.5 kilos. They should be safe so long as they're kept apart."

Sagara picked up the top ring and turned it over in his hands, marveling at its weight. "This accident," he said, gazing at the plum-patinaed metal. "What happened? What did you see?"

"I was preoccupied," said Kan, dropping his head as he recalled the scene. "The seaman picked up one of the rings from the rear and brought it to this mass from the nose. Too close. There was a flash of light."

Sagara's eyes brightened. "Light," he murmured. *Hikari.* "In a town called Hikari."

Kan noted the look with deepening unease. "Yes, bluish light. And a wave of heat. The uranium—it was hot when I touched it."

"And this made him sick?"

"Vomiting within ninety minutes. There must have been a tremendous amount of radiation to have had such an immediate effect. And his hand . . . " Kan shook his head.

"And this convinced you that this uranium is enriched."

"Yes. I had no way to be certain before, but there can be no doubt now."

"So we owe the seaman our thanks," said the colonel. "His mistake was a crude test." His face darkened. "And you?"

Kan did not know how to answer. In addition to the other symptoms he had already recorded, he was now feeling an urge to empty his bowels. But it could be unrelated. His bowels sometimes loosened when he was experiencing stress. Like now.

"I was more than four meters away," he said.

"Your health. I'm asking about your health."

"Nothing to speak of. I'm fine."

Sagara grunted and nodded. "Good. I need you."

He returned the uranium ring to the box and called to the soldiers outside. "You! Load this box into the truck. And that one over there."

"They should be kept apart," said Kan.

"Keep them apart, do you hear?" Sagara barked as the soldiers strained to pick up the heavy little crates.

He turned his attention to the rest of the bomb. "All right, what else do we need? We'll be taking a plane, so weight is limited. We can manage a thousand kilos, perhaps a bit more."

Kan pointed to the club-shaped core of the bomb, the machined piece of steel comprising the nose with the attached gun barrel extending from the rear. "This." He indicated the assembly that fit into the nose cavity. "And this. But they weigh much more than one thousand kilos."

"How much more?"

"Nearly two tons."

Sagara winced at the figure. "It's only a gun barrel. Why do we need it?"

"It's quite complex, Sagara-chūsa, more than a simple gun barrel. There's tamper material in the nose, a tamper inside a steel shell to contain it. I believe this is to contain the assembled critical mass to maximize the effect of the—"

"All right, all right, we'll find a way."

Sagara turned to the electrical components arranged on the floor. "What's all this?"

"I believe most of it has to do with remote detonation after release from the plane." Kan pointed to the four small white boxes. "Those are batteries. And these—" He indicated the four larger black units, one of them partly disassembled. "These may be some sort of radar unit. I think the Americans intended to detonate the bomb above the ground."

Sagara scanned the mass of parts, his hand tapping his thigh. "To manually detonate the device, none of this would be required. Correct?"

Kan nodded. "I believe so."

Sagara gave the order for the gun barrel assembly to be loaded. The truck was backed fully into the workshop and the three soldiers began fumbling with the hoist. It was soon evident that they did not know what they were doing. Observing the colonel's rising irritation, Kan asked the clerk to get Petty Officer Yagi.

"Quickly!" Sagara barked.

The clerk hurried off. Sagara began poking through the mass of electrical components, giving the radar units particular attention. Kan, standing beside him, kept glancing anxiously through the door toward the center of the base. He half expected to see a rank of sailors marching toward them, heavily armed.

Sagara made up his mind. "We take it all."

PO Yagi arrived at a jog, still chewing the last bite of his breakfast. He slowed to a walk, his eyes warily going from the gaunt officer in the uniform of an army colonel to an obviously anxious Keizo Kan.

"Petty Officer Second Class Ryohei Yagi," he said, coming to attention, stone-faced.

"Where is Commander Koreeda's clerk?" said Colonel Sagara, looking around.

Yagi glanced over his shoulder for the clerk. The man had disappeared.

"I don't know."

Sagara let out a growl of aggravation. His eyes went back to Yagi. "Show my men how to work this hoist. I want all of this loaded."

Yagi stood there, confused, looking from Sagara to Kan.

"Move!" roared the colonel. "I'm from the Ministry of War in Tokyo! I have direct orders from the War Minister, General Anami!"

With Yagi overseeing, the gun barrel assembly was wound with chain and hoisted onto the back of the truck, the vehicle's leaf springs creaking as it took the weight. Colonel Sagara was visibly sharing Kan's anxiety now, looking around for signs of trouble. Had Koreeda's clerk gone to get help? Was Koreeda's executive officer still under guard in the office? It was imperative to get away before something unpleasant occurred.

The truck was loaded, the gun assembly lashed down, the four radar units and other components tucked in alongside. PO Yagi, breathing hard from the effort, stepped back, waiting to be dismissed.

"Get in," Sagara ordered, motioning him to the back of the truck with the soldiers. "I need you to help load the plane."

Yagi faltered, but only for a moment. Sagara was a colonel in the Imperial Army, comparable in rank to base commander Koreeda. The petty officer climbed up into the back with the soldiers. Sagara waved Kan into the cab beside the driver. The truck roared to life.

That's when Kan remembered. He ran back into the workshop and swept up the four small parts that he had forgotten on the workbench, the radioactive nubs that had been attached to the projectile's outermost uranium ring.

"Get in! Get in!" Sagara roared.

Kan shoved the nubs into his pocket and climbed up into the cab,

Sagara following. The driver ground the engine into gear. A jolt and they were moving, rolling back up the road through Hikari Special Attack Unit, Sagara on high alert, looking for trouble. They passed several men and were given curious looks, but no one tried to stop them.

Still no sign of the clerk when they reached Commander Koreeda's office, where the base XO had been left under guard. Sagara got out, marched up the steps, and knocked on the locked door. The door opened. He disappeared inside.

In the front seat of the truck, Keizo Kan was watching the clerk hurrying toward them.

"Lieutenant Commander Koreeda is coming," said the clerk in deep agitation. "I've spoken to him on the telephone. He says the truck must not leave."

Kan could only stare at the man, speechless.

"Step back," said the soldier behind the wheel, completely nonplussed.

"That is Commander Koreeda's order," said the clerk, holding his ground. "You must not leave. That is his order!"

The office door opened. Colonel Sagara appeared, followed by the soldier who had been guarding Lieutenant Miyata. The soldier closed the door and turned the key, locking Miyata inside.

"Colonel," said the clerk, intercepting Sagara as he came down the steps, "I have spoken to Commander Koreeda on the telephone. He's coming. He'll be here shortly. Until then he has ordered that nothing must be taken from here."

Sagara swept past him, heading for the truck. "I'm afraid I'm pressed for time. Convey my regrets."

"Please, Colonel—"

"I'm afraid not. War Minister Anami was very insistent."

He climbed up into the cab beside Kan and slammed the door shut. The soldier who had been guarding Miyata scrambled over the tailgate into the back and sat beside Yagi. The truck started off.

The clerk, ignored and left behind, frantically raced up the steps and tried to enter Koreeda's office. The door was locked. He banged on it but got no answer. He looked about, trying to figure out what to do.

He ran back down the steps and chased after the truck. He caught it as it was slowing at the gate.

"If I could see the War Minister's order," he said, coming up to Sagara on the passenger side.

The truck stopped. The sentry came out. Sagara turned a look of astonishment on the clerk.

"What did you say?"

"The War Minister's order," stammered the clerk. "His written order. If I could just see it."

Sagara's astonishment turned to outrage. He climbed down out of the truck and screamed into the clerk's face: "What is your name!"

The terrified man stiffened to attention. "Ensign Nobuo Yamada!"

"Ensign Nobuo Yamada! Are you questioning me?"

"No, Colonel. But if I could just see the order—"

"Is an ensign, an *ensign,* questioning a lieutenant colonel in His Majesty's Imperial Army? A lieutenant colonel acting on orders from the Minister of War?"

"No, Colonel!"

"Well then, Ensign Yamada, raise the gate! If you value your well-being and the well-being of your family, raise the gate!"

The clerk, his face a mask of misery and confusion, looked from Sagara back to the administrative building with the XO locked inside, then back at Sagara glaring at him like a ferocious temple statue of the thunder god Raijin.

The last of his resistance crumbled. He stepped away from the truck and motioned to the sentry to raise the gate.

The drive back to Yuu Airfield took forty-five minutes, Colonel Sagara wincing and rubbing his temple as he urged the driver to maximum speed. It was clear to Kan beside him that the colonel was in some sort of pain, perhaps brought on by the stress.

"We take only what's essential!" Sagara instructed when they arrived at the airstrip. "The rest can follow later!"

Loading the two-ton gun assembly onto the Mitsubishi transport was a challenge. A trolley hoist from one of the camouflaged hangars was used to move it to the cargo door of the aircraft, but getting it aboard took sheer muscle, the four soldiers and Yagi and the three-man flight crew all pushing and pulling and straining as Sagara called out for haste. In the distance, the muffled sound of waves beat on the shore.

"Too heavy," said the pilot, wiping the sweat from his brow.

"The soldiers will be left behind," Sagara said. "They can travel back separately."

The pilot shook his head, doubtful.

"Did you fuel the plane?" asked Sagara.

"Fully fueled," said the pilot.

"Well, pump half of it out. We can refuel at Itami."

The pilot conveyed the order to the ground crew. The fuel cart was wheeled back alongside the plane. Men started pumping by hand.

Kan climbed into the aircraft to unpack the uranium rings. Leaving the lead-lined boxes behind would save an additional fifty kilos. He divided the front and rear ring assemblies in two and secured them at opposite ends of the compartment, held in place with wire so they couldn't be moved.

Something caught his eye as he emerged from the plane. It was a trail of condensation, so high that the aircraft tracing it across the sky was a silvery speck. The excited cry of his daughter Aiko came into his mind as he paused to gaze skyward: "B-san! B-san!" When B-29s started appearing singly like this over Tokyo in daytime they were assumed to be observation planes and did not instill fear. Children like Aiko would point and dance about and shout, "B-san! B-san!" It was like spotting a rare bird.

He turned to see Colonel Sagara approaching. He had something in his hand.

It was a small packet of headache tablets. Sagara had secured them from the airfield administration building to ease the throbbing that had started inside his skull back at Hikari. He shook out four tablets and sourly chewed them as he came up to Kan.

"The soldiers stay," he announced. "And they're pumping off fuel, so we should be able to manage."

He offered Kan a cigarette and lit one for himself, feeling tense but elated. He had successfully decoyed Lieutenant Commander Koreeda away from Hikari and had dealt with his XO in an efficient manner. Perfect, really. The corporal striking Lieutenant Miyata in the head with his rifle butt before they left—that was unfortunate but not a problem. The man was going to raise the alarm and had to be silenced. He had slipped and fallen, cracked his head on the desk. That's what Sagara would say. And his account would be corroborated by the corporal. For Miyata to claim otherwise would be evidence that his wits had been addled by the accidental, self-administered blow to the head. And in the meantime the plane was loaded with his prize. He was almost under way.

The right side of his mouth curved up in a lopsided smile.

Kan observed it. The colonel seemed in good spirits. If there was ever a time to take the gamble, to act on the idea that had been forming, it was now.

"Sagara-chūsa," he said, hesitant, his eyes on the ground. "When we spoke on the telephone, the line wasn't clear. You said where my wife was being held, but I couldn't quite catch it."

Sagara didn't respond. His gaze had fallen on Petty Officer Yagi, sitting in the shade of the nearby hangar, his work done.

"The petty officer there," he said. "He was in charge of the detail that recovered the bomb? That identified the uranium inside it?"

"Yes, he's the man," Kan replied, glad to give Yagi his due recognition. "Yagi-heisō was also very helpful with my investigation."

"What have you told him?"

Kan suddenly grew cautious. He shook his head. "Nothing, Colonel. I told him nothing."

Sagara's eyes narrowed as he regarded Yagi.

"Yagi-heisō!" he called out.

The petty officer looked up. He flicked away his cigarette, rose, and walked over. Sagara's right hand casually dropped to the polished leather of his holster.

Kan noticed this with rising alarm. Yagi had been a witness to Sagara's actions back at Hikari. He was a loose end. Could the colonel really be that ruthless?

Yagi came up and stood at attention.

"Yagi-heisō," Sagara said, regarding him. "Kan-sensei here tells me you've been very helpful."

Yagi stood with his eyes straight ahead. Sagara considered him for another moment, then started looking around, his hand still on his holster.

He casually unsnapped the flap securing his pistol.

"Sagara-chūsa," Kan blurted out, "I'll need assistance."

"And you'll have it," said Sagara, his hand now on his gun.

"I'd like Yagi-heisō. He has been extremely capable and—"

A burst of bluish light filled the whole sky, as if a cosmic flash-bulb had been set off in the heavens—a flash so intense, so powerful, it seemed to explode inside Keizo Kan's brain. It swept across the airfield with a burning heat that made his skin prickle, then retreated inside a colossal cloud that was rising along the coast to the north, a luminous, roiling mass of yellows and oranges enveloping a beating heart of purples and reds.

Kan and Colonel Sagara, PO Yagi, the soldiers, the flight crew—all turned to stare open-mouthed at the writhing, billowing apparition. It rose higher and higher until it was passing through the scattered wisps of low-lying cloud, its living colors gradually fading to dead gray and dead slate, dead sand and dead brown. A halo momentarily materialized around the top, intensified to a beautiful violet, then faded.

Thirty seconds had passed.

The airfield became a beehive of activity, personnel hurrying around. Doors were pushed back all along the low line of camouflaged hangars, revealing fighter aircraft, Kawasaki Ki-45s, "Dragon Slayers," hidden inside. Army Air Force pilots, pulling on jackets, goggles, and leather helmets, raced to their planes hoping for orders to take off. "The fuel dump at Iwakuni!" one of them called to his comrades. "They must have bombed the fuel dump at Iwakuni!"

A minute had passed.

Cawing overhead. Kan looked up. A crow flapped drunkenly by and heavily landed, half falling from the air. It staggered, teetered, lost its balance, fell over. It struggled to get back on its feet, flapping its wings in the dust.

The cloud was kilometers high now, its top spreading out as the atmosphere thinned, giving the whole the appearance of a mushroom. There was no more inner luminescence. It was entirely gone. The column extending down to the earth was beginning to bend. The cloud was starting to tip.

Two minutes had passed.

A deep, rumbling thunder washed over them from the north, a slowly building deluge drowning out the sound of the waves. Volume increasing, it overwhelmed the air with its presence until the windows in the airfield buildings were sympathetically buzzing, then the buildings themselves, then the ground underneath. Kan and Sagara and Yagi and all the men bearing witness could feel the vibrations rising through their bodies. They could feel it in their extremities, feel it in their bones.

Two minutes. It had taken two minutes for the sound to reach them. With dawning realization, balanced on the edge of a dreadful abyss, Keizo Kan seized on the number, calculations unfolding on an almost subconscious level. The speed of sound at sea level was 340 meters per second, a third of a kilometer per second, a kilometer in three seconds. So a two-minute delay . . .

"Forty kilometers," he whispered, gazing in awe at the cloud.

"Hiroshima," Colonel Sagara said.

FOURTEEN

THEY STOOD TRANSFIXED BY THE MUSHROOM CLOUD RISING IN THE NORTH, COLONEL SAGARA and Keizo Kan and Petty Officer Yagi together. It was nearly ten kilometers high now, the column contorted and eroded by air currents. It was so vast that, even at a forty-kilometer distance, it seemed to loom over their heads, the whole of Yuu Airfield engulfed by its shadow.

"That's no fuel dump," said Yagi.

The breeze was picking up.

Sagara wheeled about and ran to the Mitsubishi transport. "Finish it!" he called to the pilot, waving the fuel cart away from the plane. "We leave now!"

The breeze strengthened into a stiff wind. It blew from the same direction as the flash, the same direction as the cloud the light had given birth to, the same direction as the ground-shaking thunder. It swept across the airfield, raising swirls of dust from which Kan and Yagi were forced to shield their eyes. Then it died away, leaving the air still.

Colonel Sagara called from the plane. "Yagi-heisō!"

Yagi trotted over, Kan anxiously trailing behind.

"Yagi-heisō," Sagara began, producing an envelope from his pocket, "by the authority—"

The wind returned, this time from the opposite direction, like a gigantic inhalation following an expulsion of breath. It blew back across the airfield, racing home toward the north, and snatched the envelope from Sagara's hand. Kan lunged for it and caught it as it flattened against the side of the plane. Then he was doubled over like everyone else, shielding his eyes from the stinging flurry of dust. Then it was gone.

Sagara snatched the envelope back. Had the scientist noticed that it was empty? Sagara gave him a hard, warning look.

"Yagi-heisō," he said, holding up the envelope like an instrument of unassailable power, "by the authority of the Minister of War, you are reassigned to assist Kan-sensei in his work. You're coming with us."

Yagi looked confused. "But I'm stationed at Hikari," he said.

Sagara stepped into his face. "Stand at attention!"

Yagi straightened his back, eyes front.

"This is a War Ministry order! Understand? A priority matter! Your commanding officer will be informed when we land. Now get on the plane!"

The fuel cart was wheeled away. The Mitsubishi's engines roared to life. There were only three passengers aboard: Sagara on the floor on one side of the compartment, using a parachute for a cushion; Kan and Yagi on the other; the bomb components secured to the floor between them. The transport taxied to the end of the runway, turned into the erratic breeze, and began its takeoff, a lumbering, elephantine acceleration, engines straining, the entire airstrip used up before it took to the air.

The pilot set a course due north after reaching an altitude of five hundred meters, following Sagara's instructions to fly over the site of the blast. Within minutes the Imperial Navy airfield at Iwakuni was visible on the left. Sagara peered down at it through the window on his side of the compartment, confirming that the facility and its fuel dump were intact.

Rain began to beat against the window. It ran down the glass, leaving a black residue in angled streaks. Sagara was just starting to notice and puzzle over its meaning when the cockpit door opened and the copilot beckoned to him in alarm.

Sagara pulled himself up, his face flushed deep crimson, and staggered forward, the plane now starting to lurch. The pilot, he discovered, was flying blind, the view through the windshield obscured by whatever filth was suspended in the rain.

"We should turn away," the man said, his knuckles white on the yoke.

Before Sagara could respond, they were through it, the force of the wind beating the black rain from the glass, leaving a streaked but visible view. And there, up ahead and a few degrees to the right . . .

Hiroshima.

The city straddled the mouth of the Ota River, where it broke into six tributaries flowing into Hiroshima Bay, like skeletal fingers hanging from a cadaverous wrist. It had been wholly intact up to a few minutes before, untouched, overlooked in the months of American bombing. It was not untouched now. The city lay in ruins, a field of destruction, countless plumes of smoke rising from fires.

The Mitsubishi once again entered turbulent air, the buffeting nearly throwing Sagara off his feet. He staggered back to his place on the floor, removing the small packet from his pocket and chewing the remaining headache tablets, the throbbing inside his skull having reached a tearing crescendo. He had never been prone to migraine headaches, but he was surely having one now.

Squinting with the pain, he stared out the window at the city he had visited twice since the spring, the headquarters of the Second General Army and a major troop assembly area and military stockpiling center. It was all gone now. The warehouses, the arsenals, the oil and gas storage plants, the communication centers and factories, the hundreds of barracks—all gone. Gone, too, were the homes of Hiroshima's large civilian population, the schools and the shops, the hospitals and parks, government buildings, places of employment. The entire city of Hiroshima had been reduced to ruin beneath a pall of smoke by a single bomb dropped by a lone Special Task Plane.

He cast a hard look across the compartment at Kan. The scientist had misled him with his assertion that there could be only one bomb. It was now clear that the Americans had built at least two. And if they had two, why not a third? And a fourth? The Americans had mastered the technology of atomic weapons. And the devastation below was proof that they had no qualms about using them against Japanese cities.

Kan, his face pressed to the opposite window, did not notice the colonel's sharp look. He saw nothing but the overwhelming vista below him. It wasn't the same as the destruction he had witnessed in Tokyo, a city methodically reduced to ashes and piles of black rubble. Hiroshima had been laid waste *in an instant*. And the city hadn't merely been burned. It had the look of being crushed, swept away, effaced down to the dirt. A few more substantial buildings were still standing, scorched and blown-out shells, but virtually everything else, every house, every shop, every wooden structure was . . . *gone*.

He fought to push his horror away and come up with some sort of estimate of the power of the bomb, to do something useful. The damage he was seeing extended six or seven kilometers inland from the harbor, where a freighter lay on its side and numerous smaller craft were overturned. It stretched an equal distance in an east-west direction before washing up against the barren hills flanking the city. That made the total area of destruction something in the vicinity of thirty square kilometers.

Yagi nudged him in the side and leaned close to his ear. "Did a daikon do this?" Yagi cocked his head at the gun barrel assembly lashed to the floor. "Same as this?"

Kan glanced across the compartment at the colonel. Sagara, massaging his temples, could not have heard over the engines.

He leaned close to Yagi. "I think so."

Yagi returned to looking out the window, shaking his head and grimacing as he gazed down.

The Mitsubishi completed its traverse and made a banking turn over the hills to pass over the city again, dropping lower for a closer inspection. Kan began making out details he had been unable to see on the first pass: figures climbing to the crest of the hill from a neighboring valley, while others gathered at the top, looking down; a cemetery on the slope descending to the city, grass smoldering all around it; a broadcasting tower snapped off; electrical lines downed and sparking; flattened houses burning, no one fighting the flames; black objects floating in the first finger of the river; more black figures scattered about. Then the Mitsubishi was down to one hundred meters, almost skimming the ground, and Kan began to see the full horror.

He saw a man clawing frantically at the smashed remains of a house; a second figure, burned black but still alive, sitting beside him; a third figure, down on all fours, vomiting like a dog.

He saw people who looked like skinned rabbits crowding the banks of the next tributary of the river, wading into the water to ease the pain of their burns; more bodies floating facedown in the water, drifting with the current; a woman caught against the girder of a bridge, a child strapped to her back, another clutched in her arms, all dead.

He saw a man lying on his back gazing skyward, his face swollen to twice the normal size, his mouth torn from ear to ear in a hideous grin, his stomach ripped open and entrails spilling out. A bony dog was eating.

He saw twenty or more forms moving about on the playing field of a school, black and red creatures. Were they schoolgirls? Their clothes were torn off, their skins peeled away and hanging like rags. They were shuffling in a circle, eyes swollen shut and arms raised as if beseeching to heaven, as if they were performing some sort of horrific Obon dance of the dead.

Kan turned away from the window and squeezed his eyes shut. This was more than the destruction of war. This was more than the hatred of men. Hiroshima had been annihilated, pulverized, transformed into a hellscape, complete with lost souls writhing in torment.

Only something otherworldly could have done this.

Something demonic had been unleashed.

He reluctantly turned back to the window to bear witness. The smoking remains of Hiroshima Castle were passing below, dozens of bodies strewn about, most still, a few attempting to crawl; the military airfield where Kan had landed, a line of destroyed planes still smoking; the station where he had caught the train to Hikari, platform roof toppled; the field where he had seen the women drilling with spears, the grass burnt black, a seared horse dragging its innards. Then they were climbing over the western hills and the city was gone.

He settled back onto the parachute on the hard floor, the vibrations of the engines passing up through his body.

Thirty square kilometers.

His estimation of the area of damage returned to his mind. Those glimpses of horror—they extended over thirty square kilometers. Or more.

Awe entered into Kan's confused thoughts, the realization that the Americans possessed a weapon that no military on earth could resist. And then something else: a feeling of shame. Was it shame that he and his colleagues at the Riken had achieved so very little? They had not only failed to develop a uranium bomb for Japan. They had given up after the first few clumsy attempts, consoling themselves with the assumption that developing such a weapon, even for the Americans, would take decades. What a miscalculation! What a spectacular delusion! The idea occurred to him as Hiroshima faded behind them that he and everyone associated with Project Ni-Go should consider killing themselves—which only deepened the shame, for he had always disdained such notions as old-fashioned. He also suspected that he lacked the courage to do it.

But what if Project Ni-Go *had* succeeded? Kan had never really considered that outcome. He had immersed himself in experiments and theories and never gave any thought to the real-world applications, so distant was the prospect of developing an actual bomb. But now, having seen what Hiroshima had become, having seen what could be on his hands . . .

If only he could get Noriko freed. They would escape into the mountains or to some remote place and never come back.

He glanced across the compartment just as Sagara was slipping a tablet into his mouth from a little green bottle he had extracted from his pocket. Kan recognized what it was: Philopon. The drug had come to be widely distributed in Japan over the past three years as a stimulant that allowed the user to work longer hours for the good of the nation. Several of Kan's colleagues swore by its powers—and one or two of them had begun behaving erratically after prolonged use. He wondered if the colonel's shocking behavior back at Hikari could have been due to his overuse of these methamphetamine tablets. Whatever the cause, a dangerous, almost manic side to the man had now been revealed. The thought of pressing him about Noriko, in his current state, quickened Kan's pulse and made him doubly anxious.

The plane continued northeast, staying low to reduce the risk of being spotted by enemy fighters from the aircraft carriers that were known to be only a short distance offshore. Kan looked down at the green fields, the serene hills, the secluded valleys, so many places to hide. Obtaining food would be the biggest problem. But there would be fish in the rivers. And he had a little money . . .

The copilot appeared ninety minutes into the flight. "We can make it back to Tama!" he shouted to Colonel Sagara over the roar of the engines. He pointed toward the rear of the aircraft. "Tailwind!"

Sagara nodded his satisfaction. The copilot passed around a thermos, then headed back to the cockpit. Passing Kan and Yagi, he pointed to the window.

"Kobe!"

Kan pressed his face to the streaked glass, looking down as the obliterated port slipped astern and Osaka, second in size only to

Tokyo, came into view. The entire southern half of the city, from the Yodo River to the port of Sakai, was a wasteland.

He glanced at Yagi, looking down beside him. There was anguish in the navy man's face.

"Can you see your neighborhood?" he asked.

It took Yagi a moment to orient himself, picking out familiar landmarks. There was Osaka Station, the Castle, the ribbon of the Tokaido Main Line.

"On the south side of the river," he said. "Near the fourth bridge."

He scanned the desolation as the plane passed over but could not settle on where his home had stood. It was down there somewhere in that square of brown, an empty lot now, the wooden structure and all the neighboring houses consumed in the flames back in March. The small neighborhood park was gone too, treeless, devoid of all green. So was the tofu shop on the corner he had walked by every morning, steam billowing out. So was the produce vendor, the butcher shop, the bookseller, and everything else.

At least he could recognize Naniwasuji-dori. He followed the main street along, burned-out buildings on both sides, to the approximate place where his father's garage had once stood. A letter from his sister had related how it burned on the same night as their home, and how their father had died fighting the flames. Yagi had hated his father, who'd always been harsh with his discipline. But he had wept bitter tears at the news just the same. If only the old bastard had—

The fifty-caliber bullets tore through the fuselage a half second before they heard the explosions. Machine-gun fire. The Mitsubishi banked violently to the left, tumbling Kan across the compartment with Yagi and pinning them with Sagara against the opposite side. They grabbed whatever they could and hung on as the plane took evasive action against whatever had just attacked them. Kan, his eyes wide with terror, took in the four large holes in the walls of the aircraft, sky showing through. There were two on one side near the ceiling, two opposite near the floor, each big enough for two fingers to fit through. Whatever had swooped down on them had come from above.

The Mitsubishi took another wild lurch and started weaving back and forth, forcing Kan to hang on. Another burst of machine-gun fire closing in, followed by the scream of an engine and a flash outside the opposite window.

Yagi scrambled across the compartment to look out. "Hellcat!" he cried.

Kan stared at the new holes that had been punched through the skin of the aircraft, one of them close to the smaller stack of uranium rings. He recalled a comment made by one of his Riken colleagues, an enthusiast on the subject, about the Hellcat being the deadliest fighter the Americans possessed.

The transport was flying low now, scarcely fifty meters up, skimming the trees. There was no room for evasive action. They were defenseless and lumbering and pinned to the ground against a vastly more maneuverable enemy armed with two twenty-millimeter cannons and six machine guns. The Hellcat would finish them on its next pass.

"Come on, you bastard!" roared Yagi, looking up through the window. He smacked the side of the plane. "Come and get me!"

Kan's eyes met Sagara's. The colonel stared back at him, hollow-eyed, frozen. They would all be dead in less than a minute, burned alive in a fireball as the Mitsubishi smashed into the trees. A portion of Kan's brain registered a cough in one of the engines.

The transport lurched upward, barely clearing a hill. Another cough from the engine.

Yagi threw himself across the compartment to look out the opposite window. "Ha!" He wheeled about with a shining face. "He's leaving!"

Sagara seemed to come back to life. He turned to the window to scan the skies overhead. Kan did the same. He saw the Hellcat climbing back up into the ether, rejoining a line of five other fighters, specks at one thousand meters. They were heading east, back out to sea.

"Returning to their carrier," Sagara exulted over the engines. "Out of fuel! He must have been using up his ammunition!"

It took Kan a moment to process this information. When it finally sank in, he had a hard time prying his fingers from the handhold he had locked on to. He turned to Yagi with a weak smile of deliverance.

There was a tear in the petty officer's shirt. A shard ripped from the fuselage by one of the bullets had scythed through the fabric.

"Your shirt," Kan said, pointing.

Yagi glanced down with surprise. He examined his skin. No blood.

He stuck his fingers through the rip and grinned. "Look at that. Almost got me!"

The Mitsubishi limped on for another fifteen minutes, following the coast to land at the Army Air Force airfield at Hamamatsu. The damage, a severed oil line and wrecked fuel pump, would take at least twenty-four hours to fix. Colonel Sagara made hurried arrangements for the onward journey, then commandeered a private office and placed a call to the War Ministry and Colonel Takeshita.

"It's done," he reported. "I have it."

"What's happened down there?" Takeshita snapped back. He sounded harassed.

Sagara, caught up in his success, didn't notice the tone. He cupped his hand around the mouthpiece. "We flew over the city. I saw it."

"You saw it?"

"I saw it. Total destruction."

Silence at the other end of the line. Then: "What are you talking about?"

"Hiro—"

Sagara stopped himself, realizing it had been only three hours. News about Hiroshima must not have reached Tokyo yet. Something else was troubling Colonel Takeshita.

"Pardon me, Takeshita-chūsa. Is there a problem?"

"Yes, there's a problem! We've just received a protest from the

Navy Chief of Staff that one of your men struck an officer of the Imperial Navy. A rifle butt in the head! Is that true?"

Sagara felt his blood pressure rising. He didn't answer.

"You said you would be discreet!" Takeshita shouted through the line.

"The man tripped and fell," Sagara managed to get out through clenched teeth.

"That's not what he says. He says he was struck in the head! And what did you mean by that just now, 'Total destruction'?"

Colonel Sagara was struggling to keep himself from exploding. He had just accomplished a magnificent thing single-handed and here was Takeshita quibbling about his tact. There was a great deal he could say to that, but he didn't. He kept it all in.

"Hiroshima is destroyed!" he roared. "It no longer exists!"

He slammed down the receiver.

Keizo Kan and PO Yagi were passing along the edge of the airfield in company with a young sergeant, on their way to the mess hall for a much-needed meal. Yagi, in high spirits, lit a cigarette and passed it to Kan, then lit one for himself. Kan, recovering from the terror inside the plane, was starting to feel it too. A smile played across his face as he drew the smoke into his lungs and the nicotine went to work. He was glad simply to be living.

He faltered as they passed a row of fighters, parked out in full view. They looked utterly insubstantial. Yagi had noticed them too.

"Paper on a bamboo frame," explained the sergeant, noting their dubious looks. "That and some scraps. It's getting hard to find men willing to fly these things, I can tell you."

Kan and Yagi exchanged a glance. The sergeant savored their bemusement for a moment, then threw his head back and let out a laugh.

"They're dummy planes," he crowed, after enjoying his joke. "They're to draw the Americans in where we want them." He indicated the flight paths attacking fighters would take on strafing passes over the airfield. "This way and that way. Right into our guns."

"Kan-sensei!"

The scientist turned to see a young soldier hurrying toward them from the nearby administration building.

"The Colonel wants you!"

Kan's heart began to beat in his ears.

"You will be continuing on by train," Colonel Sagara said as soon as Kan entered the office. "Tama Airfield. That's where you'll work. You will install the weapon in an aircraft for a no-return mission. Manual detonation. The simplest arrangement. And I want it done quickly. Understand?"

The order was shocking. Kan felt a pang of anxiety as he struggled to maintain his resolve.

He took a deep breath. This was the moment.

"Colonel," he said, dropping his eyes to the ground. "About my wife—"

"You're not here to talk about your wife! I don't want to hear anything from you but 'Yes, sir!' and 'No, sir!'"

Sagara started pacing around in front of Kan, his fists clenched.

"First you say, 'Oh, the Americans couldn't possibly have a uranium bomb.' Then it's, 'Oh, the Americans couldn't have made more than one.' Well, now we know they made two! And don't tell me they couldn't have any more because I know now that your predictions are worthless!"

Kan stood with his head bowed, his palms pressed to his thighs. Sagara glared at him, clearly expecting some sort of answer.

"Well?"

"Sagara-chūsa, please," Kan heard himself say. "About my wife—"

Sagara lunged forward and slapped him in the face, sending his glasses flying.

"You stupid civilian!" he spat, standing over Kan who was bent over, clutching his nose. "You have no idea the importance of what is happening here, no inkling of the great events that are unfolding. The nation is in peril and you're trying to haggle!"

Kan wiped the seeping blood from his nose with the back of his hand. His heart was no longer racing. He felt remarkably calm. The blow had somehow shocked his nerves into abeyance.

He picked up his glasses. There was a crack in the right lens. He straightened up.

"When we spoke on the telephone, the line wasn't clear." He spoke softly, continuing as if the blow hadn't happened. "You said where she was being held, but I couldn't quite catch it."

"Ibaraki," the colonel snapped. "A detention center in Ibaraki."

"What is the charge?"

"There's no charge! It's the Tokkō. They can take as long as they want."

"If there's no charge, then perhaps—"

"Then perhaps I can get her released. Is that it?"

Kan kept his eyes submissively down. "Yes, Colonel. I would consider it a great favor."

Sagara seemed to swell with anger. His hand dropped to his holster. "You insolent . . . "

He drew his pistol and pointed it at Kan's head. "Do you realize that I could shoot you for that?"

Kan bowed his head even more.

"Attempting to extract a favor from an officer in His Imperial Majesty's Army. And refusing to obey an order." Sagara cocked the pistol and pressed it to Kan's forehead, forcing him up. "I could shoot you dead for that."

Kan didn't move. He felt the barrel press into his skull.

"I could shoot you dead where you stand."

Kan didn't move.

Sagara shoved the barrel hard against his head, forcing him to take a step back. The scientist maintained his submissive posture but didn't abandon his passive resistance. They stood facing each other in this manner, a tableau of the moment before execution, for what to Kan seemed a very long time.

The pressure of the barrel finally eased.

The pistol came down. Kan could feel the circular imprint it had left on his forehead.

"You stupid bumpkin," Sagara said. "You know nothing about the Special Higher Police."

"No, Sagara-chūsa."

"Dealing with the Tokkō is no easy matter."

The tide seemed to be turning. Kan dared to look up.

"But with your influence . . . " he began to suggest.

Sagara glared back. He aimed the pistol again at Kan's head and the scientist knew it was over. He felt a sinking sensation, like his heart and stomach were dropping out of his body and down onto the floor.

Sagara angrily thrust his pistol back into its holster. He glared at Kan for another moment, then struck him again in the face, this time with his fist, knocking him down.

"You wretched, dirt-scrabbling farmer."

Kan drew himself up onto his knees, blood dripping from his nose onto the floor. He remained there, kneeling like a servant in front of his master, his eyes on the toes of Colonel Sagara's boots. He tensed his stomach, preparing himself for a kick.

It didn't come. Instead the boots staggered. Then he heard a groan.

He dared to look up. He saw Colonel Sagara slumped against the desk, his hands pressed to his temples.

Kan rose and helped Sagara to an armchair against the wall. The colonel, clearly in agony, allowed himself to be led.

"Should I send for the doctor?" Kan whispered.

Sagara, eyes squeezed shut, shook his head and waved him away. Kan stepped back and remained at a submissive half bow, waiting for whatever had seized the colonel to pass.

It finally did. Sagara began taking slow, deep breaths, massaging his head.

"You will work at Tama Airfield," he said, his voice low. "You will prepare for me my atomic divine wind. And I will see that your wife is released."

Kan bowed deeper.

"Yes, Colonel. Thank you, Colonel. I'll do my best. You have my word."

Sagara was coming back to life now. He carefully hoisted himself to his feet and stood still for a moment, rubbing his left arm, flexing his hand.

He took a few tentative steps.

He straightened his uniform and turned to Kan, a look of contempt on his face.

"You and your American wife . . . you make a fine pair."

FIFTEEN

THE FREIGHT TRAIN JOSTLED AND SWAYED ITS WAY THROUGH THE DARKNESS, FOLLOWING the Tokaido Main Line northeast along the coast toward Tokyo. Keizo Kan and Petty Officer Yagi sat side by side with their backs to the plank wall of an empty boxcar, the uranium bomb, the Daikon, secured to the floor at their feet, illuminated by the soft glow of a shaded lantern. It was hot and they were both sweating. Yagi was stripped to the waist as he dozed.

There was no sleep for Kan. Between his sore nose from Colonel Sagara's blow, the worry gnawing at his brain and the cramps gripping his guts, he could not relax enough to drift off.

He felt the tips of the fingers on his right hand, the fingers that had touched the burning hot uranium ring. The tingling was verging into discomfort. And now these abdominal cramps. Was it just his nerves? His high-strung nature? Bad digestion, perhaps? Or something more?

He held his watch up to the dim light. Nine o'clock in the evening. It had been six hours since the onset of this new symptom.

He breathed in the musty aroma of jute that permeated the box-car. It was a smell he associated with the warehouses of Saito Trading, the family business begun by his grandfather, brought to great success by his father and now wrecked by the war. Keizo had never been interested in joining the firm, and his father thankfully had not pressed him, supporting him instead in his academic pursuits. Private tutors had been hired to pave the way to Tokyo Imperial University, the best in the country. Then doctoral studies in America under the great minds at UC Berkeley—all paid for by his father, a significant financial burden. Keizo had been glad to leave it all behind, to leave Saito Trading to his bullying elder brother Keigo, Keigo who had inherited their father's forceful side and none of his gentleness, which had gone wholly to Keizo. Keigo *liked* to prowl through warehouses and bellow at workers, to argue with suppliers and buyers to squeeze out the maximum profit. But that wasn't in Keizo's nature. He preferred physics. There was beauty in physics, a way to see the sublime symmetry of nature. There was immutability in physics, universal laws spanning space and time and governing everything that existed. But above all, there was mystery in physics. Kan often had the sense, especially earlier in his career, that he was standing knee-deep on the edge of an ocean of knowledge where unimaginable secrets lay hidden. What would be discovered out there?

And now this.

He regarded the sinister mass at his feet, the Daikon under its shroud of canvas. Pure destruction.

He closed his eyes and rested his forehead on his knees and let his mind drift back to Hamamatsu—to the bomb being loaded onto a truck for transport to the rail line; to Colonel Sagara, the wildness returning to his eyes, climbing into the back seat of a fighter. Kan was glad that Sagara had decided to fly on ahead. The sooner he was back in Tokyo, the sooner he could act on his promise to get Noriko freed. She might even be released the next day. Where would she go? Almost certainly to the Riken. That was where they had lived following the loss of their home, squeezed into a small room in the workers' dormitory that hadn't burned down.

She had no other place to go.

• • •

He moved the gramophone into the closet and hung a quilt over the door to keep the neighbors from hearing. Western music had been banned. The records they had brought from San Francisco could get them into trouble, so they had to go. They put Aiko to bed and together squeezed into the small space and spent the evening listening to the disks one last time. They listened to "Blue Moon" by Glen Gray and the Casa Loma Orchestra, then he removed it from the turntable and broke it. They listened to "Seventh Heaven" by Abe Lyman and His Californians, then he broke it. They listened to "The Words Are in My Heart" by Russ Morgan and His Orchestra, then he broke it. It was a sorrowful occasion. They spoke little. They stared at the floor.

A certain constraint now existed between them. His recruitment to Project Ni-Go had no doubt played a large part. His work at the Riken consumed more and more of his time and obliged him to be careful about what he revealed at home. Then Noriko had started working at NHK, pursuing a career of her own and leaving Aiko with a neighbor. And then there was the mounting pressure for her to evacuate Tokyo with Aiko and go to Kanagawa to live with his parents. He didn't blame Noriko for not wanting to go. His mother's capacity for finding fault with her American-born daughter-in-law was seemingly endless and often bordered on cruel. But the worsening war situation was leaving them little choice.

They listened to "Dancing Under the Stars," then he broke it.

They listened to "Living from Day to Day," then he broke it.

They listened to "It's Love I'm After," then he broke it . . .

The train took a hard lurch, jerking Kan from a doze. Yagi, roused from a deeper sleep, stretched and yawned like a cat. He got to his feet to peer out a crack in the side of the boxcar as they slowed.

The train jolted to a stop. There was the sound of the huffing engine up front, then the crunch of boots on gravel outside.

The metal screech of a bolt. The door slid open. A rat-faced soldier looked in, handed Yagi a thermos and two small packets, and stepped back to close the door again.

Yagi stuck his foot out to stop him. "Leave it open. It's hot in here."

The soldier gave him a threatening look. "Move back."

Kan scrambled to his feet, the urge suddenly strong. "Excuse me, I need to go outside for a moment."

The soldier slid the door shut with a bang and bolted it from the outside.

"Excuse me!" Kan knocked on the side of the boxcar. "I need to step outside for a moment!"

"Hey!" roared Yagi, banging on the planks with his fist. "The Sensei needs to go!"

No good. The soldier was gone.

"Bastard," Yagi muttered, returning to his spot and slumping back down. He set one packet aside for Kan and went to work on the other, two balls of millet wrapped in seaweed with a salted red plum. He took a big bite, then looked up at Kan's obvious discomfort.

He motioned toward the end of the boxcar. "Go down there. A little shit won't bother me."

Kan faltered, eyeing the dark corner. Then urgency overcame embarrassment. He scurried to the spot, clutching his stomach, and managed to get his trousers down just in time.

"Pardon me," he said when he was finished, washing his hands in the pail of water that had been provided before they set out. Yagi ignored him and continued sucking his teeth. Kan sat back down and opened his food packet and started gingerly eating. A jerk and a screech and the train was moving again.

"Why'd they have to lock us in here?" muttered Yagi. "Treating us like prisoners . . . "

He got up and returned to the crack in the wall to peer out. He stiffened, apparently having spotted someone outside.

"Hey!" he called out. "Where are we!"

No answer.

He started walking down the length of the car like an animal in a cage, striking at the plank sides with his fist. He reached the end and started back up the other side, still striking. Then he stopped, a pair of planks attracting his particular interest. He banged on them a few times, verifying that they sounded rotten. Then he stepped back and kicked them out, opening a half-meter-wide hole in the side of the car and letting in a warm breeze.

"That feels better," said Kan as Yagi sat back down. "But won't you get into trouble?"

Yagi snorted. "That? It was like that when they locked us in here."

He took out his dice and started rolling them in his hand, expertly manipulating them with his fingers. The hypnotic movement seemed to relax him. His scowl slowly dissolved.

He helped himself to more cold tea from the thermos. Draining the cup, he began to lazily wave it around, making circles in the air, rotating his wrist.

He dropped the dice into the cup and began to swirl it, making the dice swish.

He brought the cup down with a smack on the floor of the boxcar, the dice hidden underneath.

"Even!"

He lifted the cup, revealing the dice. A six and a four, equaling ten. Even.

He swept the dice back into the cup, swirled it around and brought it down again with a bang.

"Odd!"

He lifted the cup, revealing a one and a six, equaling seven. Odd.

"You're good," observed Kan, swallowing the last of his millet.

"I listen to the sound of the dice," said Yagi, swirling the cup close to his ear. "It takes practice. Even or odd, the sound is a bit different."

Kan gave him an incredulous look. "Really? You can actually hear it?"

Yagi burst out laughing. "Of course not! It's just luck. Come on, let's play."

It took Yagi ten minutes to relieve Kan of the coins in his pocket. Being a good sport, he returned them, then won them all back again.

• • •

Three o'clock in the morning. A thundering downpour, then the train was slowing again. Kan and Yagi stood side by side at the hole Yagi had kicked in the side of the boxcar, gazing out at a dripping, desolate rail yard, then a sign creeping by announcing that they were passing through Numazu. It was only a modest-sized town, but the B-29s had not overlooked it. The entire moonlit nightscape was a ruin, brick buildings reduced to burned-out shells, wooden structures reduced to ashes. Numazu had been razed by conventional bombing just as thoroughly as Hiroshima had been obliterated by the atomic bomb.

"This used to be a pretty town," said Kan.

"You've been here?" asked Yagi.

Kan nodded in the dark. "Before the war."

It had been in 1938, the year after his return from the United States. Kan had passed through Numazu with Noriko after a trip to the hot springs at Hakone, the onsen where she had conceived. She was pleased after counting the weeks back to figure that out. And then came their baby, their beautiful little girl. They had no difficulty choosing a name. They both agreed she should be Aiko, meaning "child of love."

They were through the town now, the train picking up speed. Then they hit a bad section of track that almost knocked Kan off his feet. It was in that moment, Yagi supporting him as they staggered back to their seats on the floor in the circle of light from the lantern, that Kan realized that he felt a closeness to this strange man who differed from him in almost every conceivable way.

"Those must have been painful," he said, nodding toward the burns on Yagi's shoulder and neck. "How did it happen?"

Yagi made the dismissive *humph* that Kan now recognized as one of his usual sounds.

"I hope you don't mind me asking."

"Mind?" Yagi took out his cigarettes. "Why should I mind?" He tapped one out and lit it, handed it to Kan and lit another for himself.

They smoked in silence.

Suddenly Yagi broke out in a song, making Kan jump. "'I fought and fucked all across the South, and then I came home to Mother!'"

He settled back with a wistful smile, then noticed Kan's bemused look.

"A little song one of my pals dreamed up," Yagi explained. "Ryuji Sakamoto. 'Filthy' Sakamoto. He's dead. They're all dead now."

He lowered his head, a look of sadness clouding his face. He fought it off with another snatch of song: "'When the Navy's in town, the ladies lift up their gowns.'"

He fell silent. The look of sadness returned.

"It must have been difficult," Kan said. "Losing your friends."

Yagi concentrated on his cigarette, smoking it down to nothing and crumbling the stub with the callused ends of his fingers.

He turned to Kan. "So, do you want to hear my war story?"

"Yes, I'd be interested. If you don't mind."

"*Humph.* There you go again—'mind.'"

Yagi took out his dice, settled back, and began.

"All right. So, I was an able seaman on an oil tanker. The *Iro.* Worked down in the engine room. You know what an oil tanker is like?"

Kan shook his head.

"Well, it's not like an aircraft carrier or a battleship, I can tell you. Or even a cruiser or a destroyer. Floating fortresses, that's what those are. Palaces. You at least have a chance. But in a stinking oil tanker . . ." Yagi shook his head.

"We were in the Caroline Islands for most of 1942. Truk, Rabaul, Bougainville, Tulagi—we sailed all around down there. Even Port Moresby in New Guinea."

A chuckle.

"Ugly women down there. You know that saying 'A sailor has a woman in every port'? Well, I'd have said, 'Not in Port Moresby! No thank you!' But after you've been away for a while . . . *humph!*

"Anyway, we got it the first time in the Marshall Islands, out of Jaluit. Torpedo from an American sub. That was February '43. Eight thousand tons of fuel in our tanks and we get hit by a torpedo. We should've been blown sky high, right? But we weren't. Two months of repairs to keep us afloat, then we were taken under tow back to Kure. Almost made it, too, when another sub caught us. Two hits this time. And we *still* didn't blow. The luckiest unlucky ship in the Navy, that's what we said. Six months on shore for repairs, then we're off again for the South and I'm thinking: *Yagi, this is it. Your luck is used up.*"

He fell silent for a moment, remembering.

"We'd lost the Carolines by then. It was Kalimantan now, taking on crude oil at Balikpapan and convoying to Palau. That's where we got it again. Another American sub. That made it three times. We got to Palau, but they were right on us. Hit the port first, bombed and strafed the whole place. That's when I had my first good look at a Hellcat. We were anchored in a lagoon on Peleliu, so they missed us. But they sniffed us out the next day. *BOOM.*" Yagi clapped his hands. "Direct hit to the engine room. Lifted us right out of the water."

"The engine room," said Kan. "But you were . . . "

Yagi shook his head. "I was on one of the anti-aircraft guns up on deck. We were shorthanded, so they had me on the twenty-millimeter when we were at anchor. I was firing at that Hellcat as it's coming at us. The next thing I remember I'm in the water and I'm drowning and the *Iro* is burning. Burned for two weeks before it sank. Forty-seven men dead. Captain Kitamura, everyone in the engine room. But not me."

"Drowning . . . " Kan repeated the word. He looked at Yagi intently, thinking of his daughter, Aiko, wanting him to continue.

Yagi remained silent, the dice motionless in his hand.

Kan gently prompted. "That must have been . . . Was it . . . "

"A boy I knew drowned when I was eight," said Yagi. "My father told me it was a peaceful way to go, I suppose because I was upset and he wanted to settle me down. And like a dumb kid I believed him. But there's nothing peaceful about drowning. Sheer panic, that's what it is."

He paused, remembering, anguish coming in his face.

"There were three of us in the water," he continued, his voice quiet. "Me and Tokage and Ensign Kaneko. Flailing around. Clawing at each other over this one piece of wood." He shook his head sadly. "The animal in you, it comes out when you're drowning. You can't help it . . . I was just stronger than them."

They sat together in silence, staring at the floor, lost in their thoughts.

Yagi was first to turn away from the darkness.

"And *that*," he said with forced levity, "was the fourth and last time we were hit. And here I am. So I guess four is my lucky number." He used the pronunciation *shi* for four, which also meant death.

"I was shipped home after that, spent the rest of the year in the hospital and was promoted to petty officer first class. They said it was because I shot down that Hellcat. And to encourage people like me. Ha! And yes, the burns were painful. Then I was reassigned to Hikari, and I became petty officer *second* class."

"What do you mean, 'people like me'?" asked Kan.

Yagi remained silent for a moment, then waved the question away. "It doesn't matter."

He started rolling the dice in his hand.

SIXTEEN

HEY, GI. ARE YOU LISTENING? ARE YOU OUT THERE? BECAUSE YOUR SWEETHEART SALLY HAS something to tell you. Sally doesn't want you to worry, but the little lady you thought was waiting back home is sitting down to write you a letter. Up at the top of the page she's writing "Dear Charlie." Or is it "Dear Robert"? Or "Dear George"? Or "Dear Sam"? But that's not what she's really thinking. Do you know what she's thinking? She's thinking, "Dear John."

Stop it. Stop it.

It felt like Noriko Kan was losing her mind, the way the radio broadcasts kept playing inside her head. A symptom of the isolation and strain, no doubt. And the lack of sleep. She had not slept well in months. It had started with the air raids in late 1944 and had only gotten worse. She would close her eyes and drift into a doze, hovering on the boundary between conscious and unconscious, and there she would stay. If she sank deeper, into more complete relaxation, something would rouse her up with a start. The experience was unpleasant. Perhaps that was what was driving her insane, the drifting into unconsciousness only to jerk back awake, the repeating of the exhausting process again and again.

She shifted, searching for a less uncomfortable position. Where was the evening whistle? Surely it was time for the evening whistle. She wanted desperately to unroll the futon and lie down, just to stretch out her aching body, if not to sleep.

She tried to concentrate on something else. The shadow of Senso-ji Temple near their house in Asakusa took form in her mind. She and Keizo had often walked there in the first years of their marriage. The first time with Aiko . . . that was when they bought the omikuji fortune paper. They had shaken the hexagonal box, worn by generations of hands, until one of the long sticks inside protruded from the hole in the end. "Number seventy-one," she said, reading the number on the stick to the old woman in the booth who was dispensing fortunes as she ate her lunch. Keizo handed over a coin, and the woman, still chewing, extracted a paper from one of the numbered drawers at her side.

"Ah, we're doomed," said Keizo, chuckling at the line of characters at the top. "Look at that. 'Number Seventy-One. Misfortune.'"

The poem beneath, about dark clouds obscuring the moon, suggested trouble ahead. But the more specific auguries weren't entirely bad. They read them together, going along with the old custom. Travel to the south was to be avoided. There would be a long sickness, but the patient would recover. An awaited person would come. And a business venture would start slowly but eventually prosper.

"What do you say?" said Keizo, grinning at her in amusement. "Shall we open a shop?"

They folded the paper lengthwise into a long, narrow strip and tied it to the branch of a nearby pine tree, explaining to Aiko that this would leave the misfortune behind at the temple.

Was the pine tree still there?

You see, she's found herself another man. There are so many to choose from, some of them right on her street. She got feeling blue one day—

Stop it! Stop it!

Where was the evening whistle?

Or was it perhaps still only morning?

The crack of a club striking the door made her jump.

"Stand up!"

It was the Toad, glaring at her through the grate. Noriko Kan jumped to her feet and stood with head bowed. The sudden exertion made stars dance before her eyes in the gloom.

The sound of a key in the lock. The Toad was opening the door. But she had been sitting, not lying down. She hadn't broken the rules.

He pushed the door open and remained in the hallway. "Come out!"

Noriko didn't move. Her limbs were frozen.

"Come *out!*" The Toad punctuated the command by striking the door again with his club.

Noriko obeyed.

The Toad stood behind her, his mouth close to her ear. "Be careful what you say," he said. "Be very careful."

He marched her down the hallway and prodded her onto the stairs leading upward, up to the place she was afraid to return to, the un-marked door with the dark square at the center where a label had been.

The Toad knocked.

A muffled voice inside: "Come in."

The Toad opened the door. "The prisoner!"

He pushed Noriko inside, gave a curt bow, and turned away, clos-ing the door.

It wasn't the Tokkō captain this time seated behind the table. It was an older man, late fifties, a civilian with the look of an office manager or government official.

"Sit down," he said blandly, without glancing up from the files he was perusing. Tendrils of smoke snaked from a cigarette in the ashtray by his right hand.

Noriko's legs were quaking so badly that she was unable to move. She stood there, staring at the floor. The stranger finally noticed her hesitation.

"Sit down," he repeated.

His voice and manner seemed benign. She risked another glance at his upraised face. It had none of the Tokkō captain's look of menace and contempt.

"Please." He motioned Noriko to the chair. "Sit."

She willed her legs to step forward. She lowered herself onto the edge of the chair facing the table. She sat very still with her knees pressed together, hands clutched protectively against her abdomen, head down.

"Are you being treated adequately well?" the man asked, his eyes returning to the file.

There was only one possible answer. "Yes," Noriko said in a small voice.

"Good, good."

The man fell silent as he continued to read, pausing now and then to pick up his pen and make a notation. He finished the first page, turned it over, and started the next.

"The Imperial Army has taken an interest in your case," he said, starting on the third page. "I've been asked to clarify a few things."

The Imperial Army has taken an interest in your case . . .

The words hit Noriko like an electrical shock. Her husband, Keizo, had worked closely with the Army. He knew high-ranking officers. Perhaps . . .

She risked another look up at the stranger, suddenly hopeful. He was underlining something, two precise strokes.

He set his pen down. He leaned back and fixed her with an unwavering gaze.

"So. You were born in America."

He spoke politely, not the tone of her previous interrogations.

"Yes," Noriko acknowledged in a whisper, keeping her head down.

"A little louder, please."

"Yes," she repeated.

"San Francisco." He retrieved his cigarette from the ashtray and drew in a lungful of smoke. "I've been there. A beautiful city." He smiled and added in English: "Golden Gate Bridge. Fisherman's Wharf."

Noriko didn't know how to respond. It was unwise to say anything positive about the United States. She remained silent.

"Your father was from Shizuoka-ken, I see. Where exactly?"

"Mishima."

"And when did he emigrate to the United States?"

"In 1908." Noriko had already gone over all this multiple times with the Tokkō captain. "He worked at my uncle's lunch counter. Then he started his own."

"A chain of lunch counters, I see here," said the stranger, tapping the file.

"Only three."

"And an import-export business. I would call that successful."

Noriko's face darkened. "My father lost everything in 1942. He was forced to close his business, and my family was sent to a prison camp." That was the last news she had received from America, in a letter from her mother that had somehow reached her via Hong Kong.

"Was that when you decided to give up your American passport?"

Noriko nodded.

The stranger jotted down a note. "Yes, well, before all that, your father *was* successful—successful enough to send you to the University of California. English literature and business courses. It was there that you met your husband, I take it."

Noriko nodded.

The stranger let out an exasperated sigh. "We'll get through this faster if you'll be forthcoming."

"He was a doctoral student," said Noriko quickly. "I interviewed him for the student newspaper. We were married in 1936, and I returned with him to Japan the next year."

A rustle of paper. The man was consulting the file.

"Keizo Saito. He took your family name. Kan."

"Yes. My husband is a second son, and I have no brothers. He agreed to be entered into our family register to continue the name."

"But you had no son to perpetuate the family name. Only a daughter. Pity."

Noriko only nodded.

The stranger continued. "Where did he work, your husband? After you returned to Japan?"

"At the Riken. For Dr. Nishina at the Riken."

"Yes, at the Riken. What did you know of his work?"

Noriko hesitated. "I knew very little."

"Did he tell you about it?"

"He said he was investigating cosmic rays. I didn't understand."

"What about later? After 1943?"

"He didn't talk about his work then."

"Never? Did you know he was involved in a secret project?"

Noriko thought carefully before responding. "Yes, I knew."

"What do you know about it?"

"Nothing. My husband never talked about it."

"Nothing? You know nothing?"

"No, nothing. I know nothing."

"You never questioned him? You never tried to find out?"

"Never. He told me his work was sensitive and that I shouldn't question him about it. So I didn't."

"You weren't curious?"

"I suppose I was curious. But I never asked."

"Did you ever see any of his papers? Anything that might have given you an idea of what he was involved in?"

"No. Never. He never brought papers home."

"I find that difficult to believe. Surely he brought something home. Perhaps you took a glance at it? An innocent glance? By mistake?"

"Never," Noriko replied, emphatically shaking her head even though it wasn't true. Keizo had been careless with his papers. "Never. My husband was extremely careful. He never brought anything home."

The stranger finished his cigarette and crushed out the butt. He extracted a pack from the pocket of his short-sleeved white shirt, tapped out another, and slowly, deliberately, lit it.

"Is that so."

His chair scraped back. He stood up and paced the length of the room, thoughtfully smoking.

"Is that so."

He turned at the wall and paced back to stand behind Noriko's chair. She cringed, anticipating that the session might turn violent, that this stranger might have a hidden malevolent side.

"And yet," the man continued without raising his voice, "here you are. Arrested. You were accused of being insincere, a defeatist, a traitor. And you are imprisoned here. Let's talk about that."

Noriko pressed her clenched fists into her stomach. "It had nothing to do with my husband."

"No?"

"It was at my place of work."

"Your place of work. Tell me about that."

Noriko took a long, quavering breath. "I worked at NHK," she began. "In the Front Line Section. There were about twenty English speakers there, overseas Japanese like me. Nisei. And some prisoners of war. We broadcast English-language programs." Her voice trailed off.

The stranger, still behind her: "Go on."

"I started as a typist in 1942. I was reassigned as a writer and announcer in 1943. I worked on *The Zero Hour* and *The Hinomaru Hour*. And on *From One American to Another* occasionally. And in January this year I became the main announcer on *Humanity Calls*."

She stopped, her eyes on the open file on the table, presumably all about her.

The stranger, still behind her, placed his hand on her shoulder, making her jump. "Go on."

"We played American music," Noriko said quickly. "The sort of music American soldiers and sailors would like. And we broadcast news reports and messages from prisoners. I read the introductions to the music and made various comments. The 'platter chatter.'" Noriko spoke the phrase in English. She paused to catch her breath, then continued more slowly.

"The broadcasts were written to have propaganda value. 'Sowing seeds of loneliness and homesickness among the enemy by shooting psychological bullets.' The Front Line Section chief explained it like that. I used the name Sally. I was Rose in some of the earlier broadcasts. Then I changed my name to Sally."

"Sally. I see. So that was the purpose of your work, 'shooting psychological bullets.' Did you sincerely and loyally work to fulfill this purpose?"

"Yes."

"You did?"

"Yes, I did."

"And yet you were denounced as unpatriotic, as working to undermine the war effort."

The man at last left his position behind Noriko's chair and returned to his seat. Noriko's eyes flashed up at him and then retreated to her clasped hands. His face remained impassive.

"I tried to explain . . . " She fell silent. She couldn't go on.

"Yes?"

Noriko squeezed her fists tight. "I tried to explain before, but the officer became angry."

The stranger drew in a meditative lungful of smoke and slowly expelled it. "Yes, well, tell me now."

Noriko hesitatingly began to explain about Fujimura, the undercover Tokkō man assigned to Radio Tokyo on the sixth floor; about the advantage he took of the Nisei women; about the advances he made on her and his anger when she refused him.

"And so this is why you attacked him," said the stranger, addressing the top of Noriko's bowed head.

"I only slapped him."

"Because he made unwanted advances."

Noriko nodded.

"Very spirited. I can't say I blame you. But Fujimura isn't the issue just now. He was removed from that position." The stranger consulted a page in the file. "Reassigned on July second. His accusations against you were dropped."

Noriko's head jerked up. She looked the stranger full in the face, shocked.

"You seem surprised."

She swallowed. "Yes."

"Yes, well, the other reports against you remain." He extracted a page and set it on top of the file. "This is the problem."

"I don't understand," said Noriko. "What other reports?"

The stranger looked down at the paper and started to read. "'Noriko Kan has been heard by her coworkers to express pro-American sentiments. Noriko Kan has actively attempted to undermine war spirit among her coworkers.' And more in that vein."

Noriko shook her head, emphatic. "But that's not true."

"Mary Hasegawa and June Ikeda. These were coworkers of yours?"

"Yes."

"And you're saying these reports they made against you are false?"

"They're not true."

"Then why were they made?"

Noriko's heart was beating hard, blood thundering in her ears. She dropped her eyes. "I don't know."

"You don't know? You have no idea why they would make false reports against you?"

Noriko didn't respond. She could feel her cheeks burning.

"Kan-san, I've been given the authority to rectify your situation, but I really can't unless I get to the bottom of this. Fujimura was removed from your office. He was no longer there to bully your coworkers. So why did they make these accusations against you? Why, if they weren't true? Do you claim to have no idea?"

I've been given the authority to rectify your situation . . .

Noriko glanced up again. She saw no duplicity in the man's face. She felt a pang of hope.

"You have no idea?" the stranger repeated.

"No," she said in a quavering voice. "I have an idea."

"All right. Then tell me."

Noriko's eyes dropped back to her hands. She had not told the Tokkō captain her secret even when she had been the most frightened. What had happened in the office that day . . . it was as if someone else had taken control of her body.

"It's shameful," she said.

"Please set aside your feelings. It's the only way for you to get out of this place."

She hesitated, struggling with herself.

She took a wavering breath and started to speak.

"There was a Filipino man in our section." She stopped. She took another breath. "His name was Fernando Reyes. He was brought to Japan as a prisoner of war and became a resident alien after the Philippines joined the Co-Prosperity Sphere. And he was . . . "

Noriko stopped. Even with her blood so depleted her face felt like it was glowing. She turned in her chair until she was partly facing away.

"He was very handsome," she continued quietly. "And very active among some of the younger Nisei women. In one of the empty offices. Do you understand?"

"I believe so," said the stranger, sounding mildly perplexed.

"And two of these women became quite infatuated with him. They developed strong feelings. And one day . . . " The shame of it was intolerable. Noriko stopped.

"Go on." The stranger's voice was soft, almost gentle.

"One day, I found myself alone with this person."

"This Filipino. Reyes."

"Yes. I found myself alone with him. In the empty office. And the door was locked." Noriko turned farther away, raising her hand to hide her face. "And I did something foolish. Something very foolish. I don't know why it happened. I wasn't myself. And when the other women found out—he must have told them—they gossiped. And . . . "

Her voice trailed off.

The man was slowly nodding now. "These women who were infatuated with this Filipino," he said. "I take it they were Mary Hasegawa and June Ikeda."

Noriko nodded.

The man heaved a long sigh. "All right. I see now. Jealousy. I think I understand."

He stubbed out his cigarette, extracted a sheet of paper from his satchel, and started to write. He worked industriously with his pen for ten minutes, line after line of characters filling the page. Noriko cast him anxious glances, mortified that he was committing to writing the secret that caused her such shame. The incident—for that's what it was, an isolated incident, not an affair—remained inexplicable to her even now, after weeks in solitary confinement to reflect. After the horror of losing her only child, for which she felt to blame, she had then betrayed her husband in a moment of madness. She had been trying to find . . . She was trying to feel . . . what? She didn't know. She had never been inclined toward infidelity before. So why had she done it? Had her journey through hell on that night in March somehow left her irredeemably corrupted?

The stranger finished writing. He screwed the cap back onto his pen.

"This may take some time," he said, gathering up his papers and returning them to his satchel. He stood up and went to the door. "I'd like to see the captain now," he said to the Toad, who was waiting outside.

The door closed.

Footsteps disappeared down the hall.

Noriko was left alone in the interrogation room for more than an hour, exhausting herself with emotions careening between hope and despair.

When the footsteps finally returned, her heart raced so fast that the beats seemed to trip over themselves.

The door opened. It was the Toad, face hard, eyes angry. He seized her by the arm and yanked her up and shoved her down the hall toward the stairs without a word.

She was not returned to her cell. She was instead prodded outside—outside into daylight that she had not seen in weeks, extraordinarily bright. After her eyes adjusted, she saw a patch of grass. And trees. Green trees. She saw fields in the distance, green fields, and beyond them a line of hills, an exquisite shade of grayish blue through the haze. She saw an overcast sky overhead, and the hint of an orb that was the sun trying to break through. She saw flowers lining the roadway leading to the main gate, pink and white cosmos with bright yellow centers. The aching beauty of it all, mixed with a deep dread of where she was heading, gave her a curious light feeling, like she was floating along.

They passed a battered, dust-covered car, the driver coaxing its charcoal-fired engine to life. The stranger who had interviewed Noriko was in the back seat, patiently waiting.

"I'm sorry about this," he said as the Toad hurried her past. "But they insisted, you know."

They continued along the length of the prison building, the car coughing and choking behind them as it slowly drove off. They came to a smaller structure with large front doors like on a garage. Behind it, in a secluded exercise yard—hard-packed earth, chin-up bars, rusty barbells and dumbbells—stood the Tokkō captain. There were two other men with him. The captain was wearing a sword.

"Bind her," he said. His voice was flat—no frenzy in it like in his interrogations. He and his two companions stood very still.

The Toad produced a length of cord and tightly trussed Noriko's hands behind her back.

"Blindfold."

A rough piece of burlap was knotted around her head, covering her eyes. The light was blotted out now. Noriko could smell the jute.

"On her knees."

A kick to the back of Noriko's legs. It dropped her hard and she toppled over.

"Get up," ordered the Toad, speaking for the first time. He grabbed her by the hair and lifted her onto her knees.

She knew what was coming. There was no point in resisting. She started to shake.

A slow, distinctive sound, close to her ear, a *shush*. It was the captain drawing his sword.

"It would be better for you to keep very still," came his voice. "And to hold your neck straight."

Noriko tried to comply, but she couldn't. She was shuddering too badly. She could hear the captain moving around behind her, the rustle of his uniform fabric as he loosened his shoulders, the swish of his blade as he made a few practice strokes.

"Straighten her up."

The Toad seized her by the arm, pulling her up, his other hand prodding her in the spine. She tried to remain straight. But it was hard not to cringe.

Movement behind her. The captain was taking his position.

"Yosh!"

He was ready.

A calmness descended upon her, accompanied by a hollow feeling, like she was only a shell. Then, with a sensation of tearing, she was rising out of her body, enveloped in a circle of light, rising into the air so that she was looking down at herself. She saw the captain standing behind her, his sword poised. She saw herself kneeling in the dirt, a pathetic figure. And she saw a second light, mauve and violet, glowing in the lower part of her torso.

A sharp, guttural cry. Noriko watched as the blade descended and stopped at the nape of her neck.

"Well done!" A different voice, one of the others.

"Passable." This from the third man, less enthusiastic. "It might not have gone through, though. Two strokes, perhaps."

A sense of falling. Noriko found herself back in her own body. She slumped forward, a fog filling her brain.

"Straighten her up!"

The Toad's hands on her again, yanking. "Keep your neck straight!"

The captain's movements behind her sounded quicker. Swish, swish, swish. Three practice strokes of the blade.

"Yosh!"

A pause, then the cry, higher this time. The icy touch of steel on the back of her neck.

"Ah, that was a good one."

"Splendid. A clean cut, I think."

"I believe it was." This was the self-satisfied voice of the captain. Then: "All right, get rid of her. Get her out of my sight."

Noriko felt herself being yanked upward. Her legs seemed boneless. She fell down.

"Stand up!" barked the Toad, hauling her back to her feet and this time propping her against his body, which smelled of sweat. The blindfold came off. Noriko squeezed her eyes shut against the light. Sharp pulls at her hands now. The binding cord fell away.

"Move!"

She staggered forward, propelled by a push in the back, and fell down.

"Stand up!"

The Toad yanked her up again. This time her legs managed to support her weight.

"Move!"

She took a step forward, struggling for control of her muscles. She weaved from one side to the other, partly bent over. Another push.

"Move!"

She continued on in this manner, pushed and staggering and

occasionally falling, back to the main building, then down the road leading to the front gate.

"Open it!" called out the Toad as they drew near the guardhouse. A young sentry appeared, gave Noriko a distasteful look, and complied. A final push propelled Noriko through. She again lost her balance and sprawled in the dirt.

This time the Toad left her. "Go!" was all he said, standing in front of her, his hands on his hips. "Get away from here. Go!"

Noriko got onto her hands and knees. The sentry, expressionless, was watching. She got her right foot under her, then her left, and slowly stood up.

"Go!"

The Toad scooped up a handful of gravel and threw it. Most of the grains and pebbles struck Noriko in the chest.

"Go! Get out of my sight!"

She heard his words but could not process the meaning. She stood in the middle of the road, facing the prison, not knowing what to do, her hand shielding her face.

"Bakayaro!" spat out the Toad, scooping up another handful of gravel and throwing it hard. "Go! You've been released! Go!"

Biting stings on her arms, her neck, the back of her hand. She took a step backward.

"Go!"

She took another staggering step back from the gate, then another. The Toad, muttering curses, bent down for more gravel. Another stinging shower struck her.

She turned her back on the prison and started walking away.

SEVENTEEN

THE FIRST LIGHT OF MORNING WAS PAINTING THE SKY OCHER WHEN THE FREIGHT TRAIN screeched to a stop and the boxcar was decoupled and left on a siding. Two fresh soldiers, barely eighteen, were assigned to guard it. They started to protest when they saw the hole kicked through the side of the car, now revealed in daylight, but Petty Officer Yagi's glare intimidated them into silence. Yagi sent them off to refill the thermos and find something to eat, then helped Keizo Kan down out of the boxcar to relieve himself behind a nearby shed. After finishing the hot tea and the few food scraps the soldiers returned with, Yagi challenged them to a contest of throwing stones at various targets to pass the time. Kan considered the navy man as he watched, envying the easy way he seemed to adapt. The events of the past several days had not seemed to ruffle Yagi at all. The stone-throwing continued, rocks thocking off boxcars and poles, until a bowlegged rail yard worker came stumping over and angrily told them to stop.

An hour's wait with the sun coming up, then the onward journey continued, due north now on the Sagami branch line following the Sagami River, the boxcar attached to a rusty relic of a truck, engine wood-fired, wheels converted to run on rails. Kan and Yagi sat in the open door, their legs dangling out, gazing at the Kanto Plain, the vast expanse of fertile flatness extending from Tokyo on the coast of central Honshu to the mountains inland. The view was of fields of ripening rice and millet and barley, farm settlements, vegetable plots. An elderly woman looked up from her garden and stood motionless, watching them pass.

Kan's eyes returned to the distant mountains. A popular song from before the war came into his mind. Life had been so much easier then, a summer hike in the hills.

He started softly singing, hardly more than a whisper:

Let's cross the hill,
The sky is clear and sunny.
With joyful hearts,
Blood resounding in our chests.
Let's praise our youth,
As we head off,
Crossing the hill of distant hopes.

Yagi sighed with pleasure. "Ah, 'Crossing the Hill.' I haven't heard that in a long time." He joined in with his rough, booming voice.

Let's cross the hill,
The November sky is brightening,
With joyful hearts,
A fountain in our chests . . .

The town of Atsugi crept past at twenty-five kilometers an hour, a dismal place, houses dilapidated, shop signs broken and askew. The bigger town of Hachioji was next, "Seven Lives for My Country" painted multiple times on a wall facing the tracks, the fading characters unskilled, evidently the work of schoolchildren. Tachikawa appeared off to the right, an industrial center, much damaged.

Then they were crossing the Tama River.

Then they were there.

Tama Airfield. Home of the Imperial Army Air Service's maintenance training center and aircraft testing department. It should have been a prime target for enemy bombers, but the 1,200-meter-long runway, hangars, and ancillary buildings all were undamaged. The Americans had overlooked it out here on the edge of the Kanto Plain. The airfield, operational only since 1940, did not appear on prewar maps.

Yagi and the two soldiers jumped down onto the siding. Kan followed more slowly, favoring his right hand. He looked around at the airfield's shabby, dark buildings, mostly unpainted wood, and up at the sky, clouds now moving in. Had it really been only five days since he had passed through here en route to Hikari?

A bicycle approached. The rider was Captain Onda, Colonel Sagara's aide.

"Kan-sensei!" he called out, excited and cheery. "You've arrived!"

Onda dismounted and turned to PO Yagi.

"Petty Officer Ryohei Yagi?"

Yagi responded with a casual nod.

Onda passed the bicycle to one of the soldiers and looked into the boxcar at the Daikon, a lump wrapped in canvas. His eyes went to the hole kicked in the side of the car, then back to Yagi and Kan.

"It was like that when we got on," said Yagi, shooting a warning glance at the two soldiers.

They both nodded confirmation.

"Yes, well, welcome to Tama Airfield," said Onda. "You'll be working here."

He stepped closer and lowered his voice. "Hiroshima . . . this is really the same sort of weapon?"

Kan nodded. "It seems so."

"All that power from just one bomb." Onda shook his head in wonder. "They're saying that eighty percent of the city was destroyed."

The number stirred images burned into Kan's brain—his glimpses of horror flying over Hiroshima; deeper memories of the firebombing of Tokyo in March, one hundred thousand killed in one night.

"I don't know how anyone could have survived it," he whispered. "Casualties must have been terrible."

"Seventy thousand dead is the estimate," said Onda. "So not as bad as Tokyo. But people are still dying. Oh, and the reports of parachutes just before the flash—some sort of instruments were dropped as well. What do you make of that?"

Kan thought for a moment. "To measure the effects, I suppose."

Onda nodded as he pondered this possibility. Then he started peering intently at Kan, then at Yagi. "And you're all right? The Colonel mentioned that there was an incident at Hikari and you might have been injured."

"I'm fine," said Kan, covering his right hand.

"Perfectly healthy," said Yagi.

"Excellent." Onda turned to the engineer leaning out the cab of the truck-locomotive. "Take it onto that siding!" he shouted, pointing toward a divergence from the tracks up ahead.

The driver put the truck into gear and chugged off, trailing exhaust, hauling the boxcar toward the hangars facing the runway.

It was the biggest airplane Kan and Yagi had ever seen up this close. Neither man had known it even existed. It was called the "Mountain Range" bomber, the Nakajima G8N Renzan, based in large part on the American B-17. The fuselage alone, twenty-three meters long, was as large as a blue whale. Its wingspan, 32.5 meters, four massive engines, 8,000 cumulative horsepower, made it much bigger. The behemoth looming over them filled up the hangar. It conveyed such a feeling of mass that it was hard to imagine it could get off the ground.

"The Renzan," said Captain Onda as they walked around it. "Long-range land-based bomber for the Imperial Navy. Only five completed before production was shut down in June. They sent the Army this one and it's been just sitting here, a prime aircraft going to waste. So Colonel Sagara has requisitioned it for the mission. Isn't it magnificent? Fully armored, self-sealing tanks, range 7,500 kilometers, maximum bomb load 4,000 kilos."

He turned to Kan with a grin. "Did you hear that, Sensei? Maximum load 4,000 kilos. I think that should be more than sufficient, wouldn't you say?"

Kan tore his eyes away from the plane. Each of the blades on its four propellers was as tall as a man.

"Yes," he said. "I believe so."

Yagi was equally enthralled as he counted the guns: two cannons mounted in a turret atop the fuselage behind the cockpit, another pair in an underbelly turret toward the rear, two machine guns in the nose, two more in the tail, and openings on either side of the rear fuselage for waist guns. The Renzan was an airborne fortress.

He pointed to the twenty-millimeter turret guns. "Are those Type Ninety-Nines?"

"Exactly," said Onda. "You know it?"

Yagi nodded. "I had some time on one of the Ninety-Nines on our ship."

"Yagi-heisō shot down a Hellcat," said Kan.

"Did you!" Onda looked at the navy man with renewed interest. "Well done! We won't be using a full crew of course, so some of the guns are going. The navigator can man the nose gun, the flight engineer the top turret gun there, maybe one more. The main thing is that there is plenty of room for *that*." Onda jerked his head toward the boxcar parked on the siding nearby.

"For the Daikon," Yagi prompted.

Onda chuckled. "Excellent. A code name. Yes, plenty of room for the Daikon. That will be the responsibility of you two, to prepare the Daikon and install it in the aircraft. An interservice project, Yagi-heisō. Full cooperation, with you representing the Navy."

Kan observed a flicker of pride break through Yagi's usual taciturn look, then saw his eyes suspiciously narrow. And he knew why. If Yagi, a mere petty officer second class, one step above seaman, was the extent of Navy involvement, wasn't that a slight to the service? He scrutinized Onda's face for any hint of sarcasm but saw none.

They skirted the Renzan's chest-high rear wheels and continued around to the starboard side. There were two men on a scaffold, applying paint to the underside of the wing. Black paint. It gave Kan a sudden feeling of dread, the awful realization that men would take off in this aircraft with the intention of never returning.

"The pilot," he said, lowering his voice. "Has someone been chosen?"

Onda smiled and modestly lowered his head. "Colonel Sagara has granted me the honor of volunteering. I flew with the 81st Reconnaissance Squadron before joining his staff."

"Oh," Kan exclaimed, taken aback. He controlled himself and gave the proper reply. "Then I should offer you my congratulations."

Onda nodded his thanks.

"Congratulations," said Yagi, his voice flat.

A moment of awkward silence. Finally Kan asked, "And the rest of the crew?"

"Nothing decided yet apart from me," said Onda. "But I think we can expect to offer five more places. The Renzan would normally take a crew of ten, but for this mission a crew of six should be enough. Colonel Sagara intends to invite a volunteer from the Navy, Yagi-heisō. To make it even more of an interservice operation. I told him that would be a splendid idea."

Yagi grunted.

Onda slapped his head. "Oh, I almost forgot." He placed his arm around Kan's shoulder for a private word. "About your wife, you'll be pleased to hear that the Colonel has taken steps to improve her situation."

Kan's eyes grew wide, his heart skipping a beat. "She's been released? Is she free?"

Onda smiled and nodded. "You see? We're not unreasonable in the Imperial Army."

Kan stepped back and made a low bow. "Thank you, Onda-tai-i," he said, his voice cracking with emotion. "Thank you. Thank you."

"Oh, there's no need to thank me. It was the Colonel's doing. It was all Sagara-chūsa. Now, you must be hungry. What do you say to some lunch?"

A meal was brought to them in the office built against the inside wall of the hangar. They ate in silence, Yagi and Onda wolfishly slurping. Halfway through the meal, Kan realized that he too was actually enjoying his food and that his lower abdomen was no longer causing discomfort. Surely this was confirmation that the cramps he had experienced were due not to radiation exposure, but to nervous tension—tension that had now fallen away with the good news that Noriko had been freed.

He couldn't help smiling and giving Captain Onda another grateful nod. He would do what was expected, installing the Daikon on the plane. Then he would return to Noriko and put Onda and Sagara and their desperate mission out of his mind.

The meal finished, they settled back with cigarettes and tea, Kan taking surreptitious glances at Onda. There was no apprehension in the man's face, only enthusiasm and a satisfied smile. The prospect of sacrificing his life on a suicide mission did not seem to disturb him at all.

Kan's gaze shifted to a map on the wall, which he had noticed Yagi contemplating. It showed the farthest extent of the Japanese empire in 1942, from the Aleutians in the north to New Guinea in the south, from the Marshall Islands in the Pacific to Burma in the west.

"Have you chosen the target?" he asked.

Onda hesitated, then shook his head. "All I can tell you is that it will be a long mission and will be flown over enemy-held territory to a great extent. So getting there without being spotted—I think we can manage if we fly at night. That's why we're painting the plane black, to make it more difficult to see at night. We fly at high altitude, under the cover of darkness, and there will be no risk of being seen before the final approach."

He leaned forward to grind his cigarette into the ashtray, a decorative affair with a dial thermometer attached.

"But now the timing," he said, his brow furrowing. "That could be a problem. We need to be able to see when we arrive at the target, so that means getting there precisely at daybreak. If we're early, we'll arrive in the dark and won't be able to see. If we're late, it will be full daylight and we'll be exposed." Onda waved his hand at the Renzan filling the hangar outside the office. "We know what it can do, how long the journey should take in normal conditions. But at high altitude, things can be unpredictable. The air currents up there can be strong, so I really don't know what to expect. A headwind or a tailwind—that could add or subtract an hour or more to the journey. And that kind of uncertainty . . . " He frowned and shook his head.

The mention of air currents brought to Kan's mind another research project, funded by the Imperial Army far more lavishly than Project Ni-Go. He had heard it spoken of on several occasions, usually with a touch of envy, when Ni-Go's tight budget was being discussed. Perhaps it would be helpful to Onda. He was deeply thankful for Noriko's release and wanted to appear helpful.

"Are you aware of Project Fu-Go?" he asked.

"Fu-Go?" Onda shook his head. "Was that some sort of weapon?"

"Balloons," said Kan. "They did a great deal of research into high-altitude air currents."

EIGHTEEN

COLONEL SAGARA LAY ON THE COT IN HIS WAR MINISTRY OFFICE, AN INTRAVENOUS BOTTLE feeding fluid into his arm. It had been thirty-six hours since his return from Hikari, and he was feeling much better, although his left side was still weak. The spell he had suffered had likely been a stroke, the doctor had told him, possibly brought on by severe dehydration. But if he took care, he should expect to fully recover.

The colonel had no intention of taking care. The situation was too critical for that. It had started with the news received during the night that the Soviet Union had declared war on Japan. The latest reports from the Kwantung Army, which Sagara was going through as he waited for the bottle to empty, were all bad. Soviet forces were crossing into Manchukuo all along the frontier. Soviet mechanized units were driving hard across the steppes. Japanese forces were being pushed back.

Sagara cast the pages aside and picked up the newspaper. There, on the front page, was the first authorized report of Hiroshima's destruction, released for publication in newspapers that morning to dispel the rumors that were swirling around.

"New-type bombs were used by a small number of B-29s that raided Hiroshima on Monday morning," read the announcement. "They were reportedly dropped by parachute and exploded before reaching the ground, causing considerable damage to the city. The explosive power of the new bomb is now under investigation, but it is considered that it should not be made light of. Authorities assume that more of these bombs will be used against Japan and are therefore speedily preparing countermeasures. In the meantime the public is advised to wear light-colored clothing, preferably white, as this seems to mitigate the effects of this weapon. Adding a roof to entrenched positions and liberally covering it with dirt is also recommended, as the effect of the bomb does not appear to penetrate soil."

The communiqué, based in part on eyewitness accounts, contained several inaccuracies that Sagara was content to let stand, starting with the statement that multiple bombs had been dropped. It was better to encourage the public to think this. The truth that a single bomb had wrought so much destruction might cause undue agitation. As for the safety recommendations, he had no reason to doubt them. Multiple reports from Hiroshima confirmed that the bomb had not penetrated more than two or three centimeters into the ground. The roots of plants at this shallow depth appeared untouched. And white clothing, strangely, did indeed seem to offer some sort of protection. Photographic evidence of this had been received at the War Ministry the previous day, including an image of an eleven-year-old boy who had been injured at a distance of four kilometers. His exposed face, arms, and shoulders were all badly burned. But his torso, covered by a white singlet, was unmarked.

The boy was also blind, his retinas seared beyond any hope of recovery. He had been gazing up at the parachutes when the bomb detonated, facing the flash that Sagara had observed at Yuu Airfield forty kilometers away. Even at that distance the light had seemed to fill the whole sky.

Light. *Hikari.*

The colonel thoughtfully nodded.

A weapon of light.

He had recovered a weapon of light from a town named Light. A coincidence? No. It was a sign.

The door opened. It was his clerk.

"Your car is ready, Colonel. Shall I get the doctor?"

Sagara stiffly got up and yanked the needle from his arm. "Don't bother."

He kept his eyes down as he crossed the lobby, moving as quickly as he could, walking with a slight limp. He did not want to invite any encounters. He had already had an unpleasant moment with Colonel Takeshita, in a renewed state of agitation over his actions at Hikari. Mustering all his patience, Sagara had begun again to tell his version of events and his justifications, only for Takeshita to rudely cut him off.

"I don't want to hear it!" Takeshita removed a paper from his pocket. "Do you know what this is? An official summons to the War Minister's office! General Anami, *my brother-in-law,* has sent me an official summons!"

Sagara exited the War Ministry and climbed into the back seat of his waiting staff car. "Nichigeki," he ordered.

The driver turned around, doubtful. "The Nichigeki music hall, Colonel?"

"Yes, the Nichigeki! Go!"

Sagara settled into his seat and began to thumb through the information on Project Fu-Go that he had extracted from the War Ministry files. The project was dead, canceled back in April. But perhaps some value might be squeezed from it yet, if its data on high-altitude air currents, requested by Captain Onda, contributed to the success of the mission.

He looked out the car window.

They were passing the moat of the Imperial Palace, stone walls just beyond.

•   •   •

The Nichigeki Theater was in Yurakucho, near the southeast corner of
the Imperial Palace. Colonel Sagara had been told he could meet two
former staff members here when he'd called the Technical Research
Institute to ask for further information on Fu-Go. The massive Art
Deco structure, once the largest and finest theater in Asia, had been
battered in the air raids but was still standing. It rose to a height of
seven stories above the rubble-strewn street and descended an additional three floors underground, making it one of the few buildings
in the city with enough interior space to accommodate the unique war
work that had been done here.

The main entrance door was unlocked by a guard, releasing a pun-
gent odor from inside. He returned a minute later with an Imperial
Army major named Kishi and a civilian meteorologist Kishi intro-
duced as Mr. Yonetsu. They had both worked here until four months
before and had just been ordered back to gather up any sensitive materials. They had been informed that the colonel might be stopping by
and were glad to answer his questions.

As Kishi and Yonetsu led the way through the lobby, Sagara realized
that the smell he had initially noted permeated the whole building—
something boiled and earthy, with undertones of turpentine and mil-
dew. He glanced at the posters still adorning the walls as they passed,
the largest being for the 1942 smash hit film *The War at Sea from Hawaii to Malaya*. The thought occurred to Sagara that this was a good
omen. Then they were entering the cathedral-like auditorium and he
was looking around.

Light angled down from the broken windows high up on the walls,
no longer covered with thick velvet curtains. The shafts of illumination, motes of dust drifting about, revealed a hall from which all the
seats had been stripped, exposing the bare concrete floor. In the center
of this space, watched over by the seats in the balcony, lay the scattered
remnants of a workshop and the deflated corpses of a half-dozen immense white balloons.

Fusen bakudan. Balloon bombs. These were the remains of Project Fu-Go.

"Ten meters in diameter when inflated," said Major Kishi. Yonetsu stood a respectful step back.

Colonel Sagara bent down and hefted the edge of the nearest balloon. Like everything else, it was covered with a layer of dust.

"Washi paper," said Kishi. "Four layers glued together with potato paste. Initial fabrication was done mostly in schools. We used high school girls. When the balloons were finished, they were sent here and to the Ryogoku Sumo Hall for inflation testing. After we checked them out, they were shipped to launching stations along the coast."

Sagara nodded as he took it all in. "What sort of payload?"

"One hundred forty kilos," said Kishi. "Including the ballast. The actual explosive material—most carried an incendiary package, twenty kilos, and a fifteen-kilo anti-personnel bomb."

Sagara gestured toward some tanks lining the far wall. "Is that the gas you used?"

"Hydrogen, yes. It's what finished us off, when the B-29s knocked out our hydrogen plants. No more gas. The program had to be suspended in April."

April. A bad month, Sagara mused. "How many were launched altogether?"

"More than nine thousand," said Kishi, swelling with pride.

"And how many actually reached a target?"

Kishi deflated a little. "We estimated about ten percent. But we're not really sure."

Sagara frowned as he looked about at the detritus of the project. According to the information he had read in the car, each balloon had cost ten thousand yen to manufacture. More than nine thousand balloons launched, each costing ten thousand yen, with 10 percent reaching a target, a figure he was sure was inflated. It added up to a very costly failure.

"All right," he said. "Tell me about these air currents you studied.

What would an aircraft encounter, heading south from Japan at high altitude over the Philippine Sea?"

They moved to a glue-stained worktable at the foot of the stage, a convenient shaft of light falling upon it. Mr. Yonetsu, the civilian meteorologist, took over, producing a large map and spreading it out. It showed the entire Pacific Ocean, the east coast of China and Japan on the left, Hawaii in the center, North America on the right. He then unrolled a semi-transparent sheet of onionskin paper and spread it out over the map, superimposing a series of wavy lines on top.

"We developed this chart of high-altitude air currents from the work Professor Oishi began in the 1920s," he said. "He published his findings in Esperanto, so hardly anyone took notice outside Japan. Even now, the Americans are only starting to learn about this. From their B-29 pilots, flying so high."

"The Americans probably think they discovered it," said Major Kishi. "But we've known about it for twenty years."

"Now, the air currents over the Philippine Sea," continued Yonetsu, pointing to the lower left side of the map. "This was peripheral to our research. But we did determine that the general airflow at high altitude here is in a northerly direction. So a plane flying south from Japan— to Manila, for example—could be expected to encounter a headwind. Possibly a strong headwind. A headwind on the outward journey and a tailwind on the way back."

Colonel Sagara was studying the map. The lines indicating airflow sweeping up from the Philippine Sea to Japan merged with a much larger mass of lines extending all the way across the Pacific. They formed what looked like a vast river of air flowing from Japan to the United States.

He traced his hand along the lines. "These are the air currents you used to carry your balloon bombs across the Pacific?"

Yonetsu nodded. "Yes, Colonel."

Sagara's gaze returned to the Philippine Sea.

He was drawn back to the lines moving across the Pacific. Project Fu-Go may have been a costly failure, but it had been bold.

"They always move in this direction?" he asked. "East to west?"

Another nod from Yonetsu. "Yes, always east to west. At high altitude the air currents are quite predictable across the Pacific."

High-altitude air currents blowing across the Pacific Ocean. East to west.

An idea began to form in Sagara's mind. He placed his hands on the table and leaned over the map, tracing the lines with his eyes.

High-altitude air currents blowing east to west. Always east to west. From Japan to the United States.

The idea came into focus.

A powerful tailwind . . .

Sagara looked up sharply. "What altitude are you talking about?"

"It varies," replied Yonetsu. "But approximately from 8,000 to 12,000 meters. For the balloons, we considered 10,000 meters ideal. If they rose much higher than that, they could overexpand in the heat of the sun and explode. Too low and they drop out of the current."

"That was the greatest challenge," said Kishi. "Automatically adjusting the ballast. During the day, when it's hot—"

"And the velocity of these currents," interrupted Sagara. He tapped the inscription on the onionskin overlay. "What do you mean by 'high speed'?"

"Again, it varies," said Yonetsu. "They're highest in winter—"

"Forget about the winter. Tell me about now."

Yonestu produced another paper, columns of numbers, and laid it beside the map. "Well, at an altitude of 10,000 meters, air current speeds of around 200 kilometers per hour could be expected."

"Blowing from Japan all the way to the United States," said Sagara.

"Exactly. Given ideal conditions, we estimated that a balloon could reach the west coast of the United States in as little as thirty hours. That would be in winter, of course, when the currents are strongest. The average traverse time would be perhaps double that."

"And from Tokyo to here." Sagara stabbed the map with his finger. "How far?"

"About 8,500 kilometers," said Major Kishi. "If you could plot the most direct course across the Pacific, following the curvature of the Earth. But in a balloon floating freely, it's actually longer. More than 9,000 kilometers."

Sagara brought his hand down on the table with a triumphant slap, making the men jump.

But if it was a plane!

He stopped himself from blurting it out. He removed a paper from his pocket. On it were written the specifications for the Renzan bomber, which he had previously checked. Service ceiling: 10,200 meters. Cruising speed: 370 kilometers per hour. Range for a one-way mission: 7,500 kilometers.

He added 200 to the Renzan's speed: 570 kilometers per hour! He snatched up a pencil from the worktable to do the calculation, but somehow he couldn't.

"What is 8,500 divided by 570?" he snapped, annoyed by his brain's unaccountable slowness.

Major Kishi reached for his pen. Before he could uncap it, Yonetsu said, "Just under fifteen."

A smile spread across Colonel Sagara's face.

The Renzan was capable of a fifteen-hour flight.

It could be done.

The dreaded summons from General Anami, the Minister of War, was awaiting Colonel Sagara when he returned to his office. He took two Philopon tablets to brace himself before venturing downstairs.

Anami did not look up when Sagara entered. The colonel stood at attention before his desk, ignored, as the door closed behind him and the War Minister continued to write. Anami was in shirtsleeves, the strength he had developed from decades of archery practice visible in his shoulders and forearms. The bristles on his close-cropped head were graying. His shirt collar, Sagara noted, was frayed.

"I had quite an unpleasant call from the Navy Chief of Staff," said Anami at last, still without looking up. "Because of you. I was obliged to apologize on behalf of the Imperial Army. But he still wants you broken."

He finished writing and looked up at Colonel Sagara at last. Sagara inclined his head to show his contrition. He knew his Hikari mission had caused trouble. But to hear General Anami speak of it extending to the highest echelons—that was unsettling. Thankfully the Philopon was doing its work.

"In normal times," Anami continued, "you'd be facing a court-martial now. Don't you think?"

Sagara didn't respond. Anami let the threat hang in the air.

"But these aren't normal times," the general continued. "So consider yourself reprimanded. And you will write a letter of apology, addressed to the Navy Chief of Staff. Now sit down."

Sagara bowed deeply and took a seat on the hard chair facing the general's desk. Anami leaned back, rubbing his neck as he took a deep breath.

"All right," he continued, his tone a few degrees warmer. "Colonel Takeshita has informed me about this uranium bomb you've recovered, and about your plans to use it against Tinian Island. To destroy the Special Task Planes. I told him I found the whole thing doubtful. A salvaged weapon, one we know almost nothing about . . . How confident are you that it could actually work?"

"Very confident, General," Sagara replied, struggling to contain his excitement. "The weapon is extremely simple, nothing more than a gun firing one piece of uranium into another. If we fire it manually, all risk is removed. Detonation is certain. And we already know the uranium is highly reactive, because there was a mishap in handling it at Hikari. The reactive process was accidentally initiated, very briefly. It created a flash of light."

Anami nodded slowly as he digested this. "It still seems unlikely. But you need only one aircraft for this mission?"

"Yes, General. The Renzan bomber at Tama Airfield. It's just been sitting there, going to waste. But about the target, General, a better alternative has just presented itself. A more appropriate target, one that will shake the Americans to their core. They've been firebombing our cities. And now they've used this same weapon—I'm sure it's the same weapon—against Hiroshima. And now we can do the same. A city for a city. There are air currents blowing across the Pacific, from Japan to the United States—"

He fell silent. Anami had retrieved a paper from his desk and was holding it out.

"I take it you haven't heard," said Anami. "The Americans just used another new-type bomb. Nagasaki was attacked at eleven o'clock this morning."

Sagara read the terse report, his heart sinking. Three B-29s spotted, flying high. A flash of light. A mushroom-shaped cloud. Radius of immediate total destruction 1.6 kilometers. Fires still burning.

"Forget about alternate targets," said Anami. "There can be only one target: Tinian Island. If you can do it, I want those Special Task Planes and everything around them destroyed."

"But General, we can reach the United States. If we use the air currents—"

Anami held up his hand for silence.

"Enough. It's not just about striking back at the Americans now. It's about maintaining our spirit. I don't need to tell you how delicate the situation is on the Supreme War Council. Keeping the surrender talk in check has become extremely difficult. And now this." He motioned to the Nagasaki report Sagara had placed back on his desk. "This is only going to embolden the surrender faction. How can I argue that we have to maintain our resolve, that the Army can still defend the country, after news like this? And what if it happens again? If the Americans use another one of these bombs to destroy a third city, perhaps Kyoto . . ."

Anami wearily shook his head.

"If there is any way to prevent it," he continued, "we have to do so. So make your target Tinian Island. That's an order."

He picked up his pen and returned to work. "You're dismissed."

Sagara rose and bowed and turned to leave.

"Oh, and Colonel."

Sagara turned back.

"The Navy Chief of Staff's office wants to interview those two men," said Anami. He consulted a paper and read the names. "Keizo Kan and Petty Officer Ryohei Yagi. To corroborate your story. Make them available, will you?"

NINETEEN

THE JOB OF PREPARING THE RENZAN BOMBER HAD CONTINUED AROUND THE CLOCK SINCE Keizo Kan's and PO Yagi's arrival at Tama Airfield. Two of the four engines, eighteen-cylinder Nakajima Homares, were being overhauled, fuel pumps and compressors tested and replaced when found less than perfect. Bearings had been repacked with grease, fuel lines and electrical systems inspected, along with all flight controls leading to the wings and the tail. As darkness came on, tarpaulins were placed over the gaping holes in the roof of the hangar so that work could continue in blackout conditions. A fresh team of mechanics came on duty. They worked on the plane all through the night and into the next day, testing and checking and then checking again.

The Daikon was secured in a walled-off corner inside the hangar, a storage room that had been converted for Kan into a workshop, a guard placed outside the door. The gun barrel with the bulbous mass of machined steel attached to the end, totaling nearly three meters in length, lay on a trolley that could be wheeled out to the Renzan when the time came to install it. The target rings of uranium-235 had already been inserted back into the nose, Yagi and two mechanics taking on the heavy work, Kan doing his best to assist. The forward half of the Daikon was now complete. The next step was to reassemble the projectile, using the larger stack of uranium rings, and to insert it into the rear of the gun barrel. But first there was something Kan needed to understand.

It involved the four nubs that had been attached to the projectile assembly, at the rear end of the stack of uranium rings. They were tiny, smaller than the end of his little finger. But he knew from the moment he saw them that they were important. This was confirmed when he removed them from the assembly and discovered with the Geiger-Müller counter that they were highly radioactive, much more so than the uranium to which they had been attached. What purpose did they serve?

The quest to understand them took him back to a more innocent time, to his studies under Dr. Robert Oppenheimer at UC Berkeley. Pure theory.

So you want to be a physicist.

Kan smiled at the memory. That had been Oppenheimer's greeting when they first met in Room 219 in LeConte Hall, Kan invited to explain the research he had done in Japan.

Mostly childish, had been Oppenheimer's devastating assessment. He turned away to light one of his ever-present cigarettes, not noting the shocked look on the face of his newest graduate student.

But this research you did on cosmic rays, he continued. *A courageous piece of work. I think you might do well here.*

Kan studied the nubs for a long time, turning them over in his hand. All four were identical. They consisted of two pieces of gray metal, shades slightly different, separated by a thin layer of what appeared to be gold. Could Oppenheimer's mind be behind them? Or perhaps his old classmate, Stanley J. Rothstein?

It was only after separating one of the nubs that Kan was able to deduce their purpose. Although similar in appearance, the two metal halves were very different. One half was light. A specific gravity test revealed it had a density of just 1.85 grams per cubic centimeter. Apparently it was beryllium.

And the other half, a soft metal, yielding to Kan's thumbnail—this was where the high levels of radioactivity came from. Its specific gravity was 9.2, in the vicinity of lead.

But lead wasn't radioactive.

Polonium was.

Kan closed his eyes, visualizing the uranium-235 projectile fired into the U-235 target to form a critical mass. A critical mass in the presence of beryllium and polonium, kept separate from each other by a thin layer of gold. The beryllium and polonium would crush together when the projectile smashed into the target, creating a burst of neutrons that would accelerate the chain reaction at the critical moment, ensuring that more of the U-235 atoms fissioned before the mass blew apart. That would greatly enhance the explosion.

"An initiator," he murmured.

So then what was the silvery plating on the inside surface of the projectile rings, the plating that would come into contact with the identical plating on the exterior of the smaller rings in the nose? Kan's initial conjecture that this was an initiator was wrong. But perhaps . . .

The final piece of the puzzle fell into place.

The plating was titanium, or cadmium, a neutron *absorber*. It would rein in the chain reaction for a fraction of a second when the two uranium masses came together, allowing supercriticality to build. Then the initiators on the trailing edge of the projectile would crush together as they smashed into the assembled uranium mass, beryllium and polonium melding to create a neutron burst.

Boom.

The process was elegant. And the discovery pleased him. The hint of a smile came into Kan's face as he joined the beryllium and polonium pieces back together with a small daub of glue.

He was finding his right hand, red and swollen, increasingly painful to use.

•   •   •

The hangar was empty when Kan exited the workroom. The Renzan had been towed outside and was parked in the daylight. He had been so caught up in his thoughts that he had hardly heard the engines being tested.

He walked over to the plane, becoming aware that his legs felt weak. Mechanics were working on the outboard starboard engine. Another pair of men were atop a scaffold, brushing black paint onto the front of the plane. The bomb bay doors were open, sparks raining down.

Kan ducked underneath the aircraft and looked up into the bomb bay. Yagi and another man were perched inside, welding an iron cradle to the frame of the Renzan for the Daikon to rest on. Another shower of sparks.

"I think we're ready to finish the assembly," Kan said, shielding his eyes.

"Almost done," said Yagi.

More sparks raining down. Kan stepped away.

One of the mechanics working on the engine was descending from his stepladder. Kan noted a look of frustration on his face.

"Is there a problem?" he asked.

The mechanic fetched his canteen. "The fuel is shit. We got barely fifteen hundred horsepower from this one." He took a long drink. "Did you hear the news?"

Kan nodded glumly. "Now we have to fight the Soviets, too."

"No, I mean Nagasaki. The Yankees used another new-type bomb."

"Nagasaki?"

"It's gone." The mechanic took another drink and screwed the cap back on his canteen. "They wiped it out."

Kan stood frozen, the vision of Hiroshima flooding back into his brain. First Hiroshima and now Nagasaki. Counting the weapon in the hangar behind him, that meant the Americans had succeeded in building at least three atomic bombs. And if they could build three, they could build more. They possessed a destructive power that was almost without limit and were unleashing it against Japan.

He jumped at the touch of a hand on his shoulder.

It was Captain Onda. "Let's go into the office," he said.

"Yagi-heisō!" Onda called up into the bomb bay as they passed. "Come to the office! I have good news!"

"Yes, it's true," said Onda, closing the door. "The Americans attacked Nagasaki yesterday, just before noon. From what we're learning, the effect was more or less the same as at Hiroshima."

"Nagasaki," murmured Yagi. "I knew guys from there."

"Has this changed Colonel Sagara's thinking?" Kan asked hopefully. "About the mission?"

Onda gave him a sharp look. "Changed his thinking? How?"

"It just seems . . . " Kan stopped to consider his words. He tried again. "I was wrong about the Americans' ability to build this type of weapon. I advised Sagara-chūsa incorrectly, and for that I'm sorry. I realize now that the Americans are far beyond what I ever imagined could be possible. And so I wonder if the mission might be considered . . . futile."

Onda's eyes grew wide. "Futile! Our mission is even more critical now!"

He went to the map on the wall showing the Japanese empire in 1942.

"You asked about our target." He stabbed his finger at the Mariana Island chain in the middle, almost directly south from Tokyo. "It's here. The B-29 that crashed outside Hikari, the one carrying the device Yagi-heisō recovered—it took off from here. Tinian Island. So did the B-29 that attacked Hiroshima. So did the plane that attacked Nagasaki. If the Yankees have more of these weapons, then this is where they are. Here." He tapped the speck on the map. "Tinian Island. So that's why our mission is even more critical. If the Americans have more of these bombs, we have to stop them. Do you understand now?"

Kan lowered his head, abashed. "Yes. I see."

Onda unfolded a second map he had been carrying and smoothed it out on the desk. It showed the island itself, twelve kilometers long by six kilometers wide, a large airfield situated at the north end.

He pointed out the airfield. "The bombers took off from here. V600 Special Task Planes. This is where they're based, at Tinian's North Airfield. Previously our airfield. It's much larger now, covers the whole north end of the island. The Yankees expanded it for their B-29s."

Kan looked up from the map. "What are V600 Special Task Planes?"

Onda explained. He then gestured toward the Renzan parked outside the hangar. "With that, we'll destroy them. The reports we've gotten from Hiroshima confirm your estimates, Sensei. About thirty square kilometers of almost total destruction. If our bomb is as powerful, it will easily destroy the entire airfield complex, the whole north end of the island."

Kan bent down to study the Tinian map more closely. Onda was probably right. If the Americans possessed additional atomic weapons ready for immediate use, they were likely here. The northern part of the island was approximately five kilometers by five, well within the limits of the devastation he had witnessed at Hiroshima. Unlike Hiroshima, moreover, there were no surrounding hills to contain the blast. Judging from the minimal contour lines depicted on the map, Tinian's north end was relatively flat. The Daikon would wipe it clean.

But wouldn't the Americans just build more bombs? And use a different airfield?

"What we're hearing from Nagasaki," Onda was saying, "is that the bomb was detonated above the ground, like at Hiroshima. We have estimates of between 500 and 800 meters. What do you say to that, Sensei? I'm thinking we should detonate in that range."

Kan didn't know enough about the power of the bomb to come up with any sort of useful calculation. "That seems sensible," he replied. "You may as well follow the Americans' lead."

"Why not detonate it close to the ground?" asked Yagi.

Kan shook his head. "That would excavate a large crater. Wasted energy, throwing up all that dirt. Detonating it above the ground would be more effective."

"Coming in with some altitude will also make our task easier," said Onda.

Kan became aware of a strange sensation, a sort of déjà vu. It felt odd talking so matter-of-factly about detonating an atomic bomb over an actual target. What would the island look like after? How many people would it kill? What nightmarish scenes would he be helping to create?

"And now," said Onda, straightening up, "about the good news I mentioned. In addition to me as the pilot, we now have a copilot, a navigator, and a flight engineer. All first-rate men. That just leaves two positions still vacant."

He paused, looking from Kan to Yagi. Something important was coming. This was confirmed by Onda's formal tone when he resumed.

"Petty Officer Second Class Ryohei Yagi, as a representative of the Imperial Japanese Navy. And Dr. Keizo Kan, as a representative of Dai Nippon's loyal civilian army. You are hereby offered the opportunity to accompany me on this mission to destroy the Special Task Planes on Tinian Island, this glorious mission in defense of our homeland."

Yagi's face hardened. He lowered his head.

Kan beside him seemed to wilt. He looked with dismay at Captain Onda, his mouth agape, his eyes wide. "But, Onda-tai-i," he stammered. "One moment, please. This—I—I can't—"

"Pardon me, Captain," said Yagi, looking up. "I don't know anything about aircraft. And I believe the Sensei's knowledge is limited too."

"Yes," Kan quickly added. "I know nothing about planes."

"No flying knowledge is needed," said Onda. "You two will be responsible for the bomb. For the Daikon. No one knows it better, wouldn't you say? You even gave it a name!"

He turned to Yagi. "Yagi-heisō, you'll also man the tail gun when we make our final approach. You mentioned having experience with an anti-aircraft gun aboard your ship. You shot down a Hellcat! What better experience is there than that? And with any luck we won't need to use the guns at all. Only if we encounter trouble—which I don't think we will, flying at night and approaching the target at dawn. So you'll be able to spend almost the whole flight sitting beside the Sensei in the radio compartment. To assist him. Only when we're on our approach will I need you on the tail gun, to keep away any fighters that might attack us. And when the final moment comes . . . " Onda turned to Kan. "When that moment comes, Sensei, it will be your job to operate the trigger."

Onda was smiling, as if he had just bestowed on them a precious gift. "It is Colonel Sagara's particular wish," he added, "that both of you be offered this honor in recognition of your service. May I inform him of your eager acceptance?"

"But . . ."

It was all Kan could get out. He cast a frantic look at Yagi. The petty officer was stone-faced, his mouth tightly closed.

"So may I inform the Colonel that you have volunteered?" pressed Onda. "That you have gratefully accepted this honor?"

Silence.

Onda's smile faded.

He inclined his head toward Yagi and lowered his voice. "It really is a rare opportunity for you, Yagi-heisō. A chance to redeem the honor of the Navy after the loss of so many ships. After the loss of almost *every* ship, in fact."

Anger came into Yagi's face.

Onda kept pressing. "I've even heard Admiral Yonai referred to as the 'Goldfish Minister,'" he said. "I found that very offensive, a top admiral being insulted that way."

The lines in Yagi's forehead deepened. The muscles in his jaw stood out as he clenched his teeth.

"But a steady nerve is required. A special kind of courage. Courage that not everyone possesses."

Yagi's lips turned white as he pressed his mouth shut.

"If you don't feel up to the task, however—"

"My duty!" Yagi blurted out, directing a glare at Onda. "Please thank the Colonel!"

"Excellent!"

Onda turned to Kan.

"Sensei?"

Kan met the eager gaze with a glassy look of panic, the frozen stare of an animal caught in a trap as the hunter approaches. There was of course a way out. He did not have Yagi's pride. He could embrace his cowardice and refuse to volunteer and save himself. But that would mean condemning Noriko. Colonel Sagara would see to it. This was his revenge.

He lowered his head. His shoulders sagged.

"Please thank Colonel Sagara for this honor," he said, his voice little more than a whisper.

"I knew it!" exclaimed Onda, seizing Kan's hand and shaking it hard, then doing the same to Yagi's. "This is splendid! Together we'll deliver a crushing blow to the Yankees!"

They stood in silence after Captain Onda left them, Kan overwhelmed by the chasm of terror that had opened before him. He was no kamikaze hero. He was only a weak civilian, a middle-aged man who could not keep his legs from shaking.

Yagi sprawled in the chair behind the desk, put up his feet, and casually lit a cigarette. He leaned back and started blowing smoke rings, unperturbed.

"What's wrong with you!" snapped Kan, suddenly annoyed. "Don't you know what just happened? Don't you care? We're going on a suicide mission!"

Yagi snorted smoke through his nose. "No, I don't care. Because I won't be going."

"But we just volunteered!"

Yagi looked at Kan sharply, his mouth curling into a smirk. "You still haven't figured it out?"

"Figured what out?"

"You can't smell me?" Yagi rubbed his chin, which needed shaving. "Look at the stubble."

"What are you talking about!"

Yagi lurched out of the chair and thrust his face into Kan's, his eyes wild and wide. Then he hunched over like a monkey, arms out from his sides, and started hooting and hopping about.

"*Ooh-ooh-ooh-ooh.* Look at Yagi. Look at the hairy Korean. Yagi smells like garlic. *Ooh-ooh-ooh-ooh.* Look at the dirty Korean."

Kan took a step back. He knew the navy man was strange but now he seemed crazy.

Yagi straightened up and came at him again. "I'm Korean! My name was Yang Byeong-il! I was born in Keisho-do!" He threw his head back and spat out a laugh. "Do you really think they'll let a Korean go on their mission? On their *sacred* mission? I'll be bad luck! Yamato race only! I'll stink up the plane!"

Yagi's anger subsided. He picked up the cigarette he had dropped, thrust it between his lips, and started pacing about, Kan staying out of his way.

"You just watch," Yagi continued. "There'll be a scramble to get me replaced as soon as they find out. And then they'll look like fools."

He viciously ground his cigarette into the ashtray and turned to face Kan with a sneer.

"And you . . . " Yagi bobbed his head up and down, mockingly cringing. "'Oh, thank you, Captain Onda. Thank you for releasing my wife.'" He straightened up and glared. "Do you really think he did that? Or that colonel? Do you really believe them? Wake up! Don't be a fool! The bastards are lying to you!"

He stormed out of the office, leaving Kan feeling sick.

TWENTY

NORIKO KAN WAS LUCKY SHE WASN'T LYING ALONGSIDE THE TRAIN TRACKS, HER NECK BRO-
ken, a leg snapped, an arm twisted under her at an impossible angle.
She was lucky the conductor hadn't thrown her from the train.

She hadn't known what she was doing when she staggered away
from the prison, driven off by the Toad, a trickle of blood down the
back of her neck where the Tokkō captain's sword had broken the skin.
The shock and confusion cleared only slowly as she hurried down the
road, instinctively heading away from the outskirts of an unknown
town, fleeing into the countryside, fields on both sides. Every time she
passed someone, a farmer in a paddy, a man with a cart, a half-dozen
soldiers, she expected to be stopped and questioned and marched back
to prison. But no one accosted her. She continued on, unmolested, a
half-starved wraith no one bothered to notice, a ghost on the edge of a
tattered society exhausted by war.

The road crossed railway tracks. She paused to consider, forcing
herself to be logical, to think clearly. The sun was too high to give her
a clear sense of direction. The surrounding terrain, however, was flat,
suggesting she was near the sea. And those low hills toward which the

road was heading—they would rise inland, away from the coast. So that direction was west. And the railway tracks angling off to the left were heading generally northeast and southwest.

She decided to follow the tracks—southwest, for she did not want to return to the town she had just fled. They continued straight, passing fields of ripening rice, plots of cabbage and leeks and daikon radishes, the occasional farmhouse.

After a time, her strength fading, she came to a stream. A heap of withered cabbage leaves lay on the bank. Someone had washed cabbages here after harvesting, discarding the coarse outer pieces. Realizing with a pang that she was desperately hungry, she began poking through the mass and eating whatever wasn't spoiled, chewing on the left side of her mouth, for her teeth on the right side were sore. Somewhat revived, she washed the blood from her neck and combed her tangled hair with her fingers. Then she forced herself to stand up and move on.

She had walked no more than a kilometer when a scattering of buildings appeared up ahead, then a small country station, a sagging open-air shelter of gray boards. Uchihara, the faded sign read. The name meant nothing to her. An elderly man was dozing on a bench, his arm protectively around a burlap sack bulging with produce. Noriko steeled herself and approached.

"Excuse me," she said. "Where is this place?"

The man sleepily opened his eyes and swiveled his head toward her. "Uchihara," he said.

"I'm sorry, I don't know it. I'm lost."

The man raised his chin toward the tracks.

"Joban Line."

The Joban Line. Noriko felt her heart soar. The Joban Line left Tokyo's Ueno Station, heading north. She must be in Ibaraki Prefecture.

"Excuse me, but which way is Tokyo?"

The man raised his chin down the tracks in the direction Noriko had been walking. She wanted to ask more questions—*How far is it to Tokyo? When is the next train?*—but she didn't dare. She retreated to the other side of the shelter, placing a wall between herself and the man, facing the road.

Ueno Station. That was only a short distance from the home she had left in June for her final fateful trip to the NHK Building downtown. The realization swept away the last of her confusion. For whatever reason, she had been released from prison to make her way home. To return there, she had to continue on down these tracks to Ueno. She had no money, no travel certificate, no ration book, no identifying papers to show. But somehow she had to traverse these tracks to Ueno.

The train, a crowded local, chugged into view an hour later, as the sun was sinking behind the trees. Noriko climbed up the steps into the rearmost carriage but didn't try to find a seat. She remained standing near the stinking toilet as the train laboriously built up speed, considering the possibility of slipping back out the door and climbing up onto the roof when the conductor appeared, if she had the strength. The train reached the next local stop, then the next, and still no conductor. Finally exhaustion forced her to sit on the floor and rest her head on her knees.

A nudge from the toe of a boot roused her. She had fallen asleep.

"Ticket."

Noriko scrambled to her feet and stood before the conductor.

"Where are you going?" he said, eyeing her with suspicion. She was ragged and looked like a tramp.

"Ueno Station," she stammered. She was trembling now.

"Do you have money to pay for a ticket?"

Noriko stood frozen before him, her head bowed.

"No."

"So you're stealing." The conductor seized her arm and turned her toward the door. "Riding the train without a ticket is stealing."

Noriko's legs gave out. She crumpled to her knees, a pathetic figure. The conductor looked down at her with disgust.

He left her where she was until the next stop, then ordered her off the carriage.

• • •

She set out following the train, which had now disappeared, on and on until it was twilight. She had no energy left now. She needed rest and something to eat.

She wandered away from the tracks, following a raised path between fields of golden grain, soon ready for harvest. She tried stripping one of the drooping heads—it was barley—but found it impossible to eat the coarse handful. She paused to scour the low bank on either side of the path, looking for edible greens. She found nothing. Then she spotted a glow in the distance, the flickering light of a building. She made her way toward it.

It was a thatched-roof farmhouse, lantern light showing through oiled-paper windows. And off to the side, a garden plot: daikon radishes and mustard spinach and sweet potatoes, leeks and cabbages and onions all in a jumble. Could she take something and slip away? She was sorely tempted but she was also afraid. There had been reports in the newspapers of farmers beating thieves to death. But if she just took something and quickly went away—

A dog started barking. It was tied at the back of the house. She hadn't seen it. The sudden noise breaking the silence made her heart race. She turned to flee, but something told her not to.

She approached the front of the farmhouse, the dog now apoplectic. She knocked on the door.

It was opened by a woman with a creased, sun-darkened face.

"Please," Noriko said quickly before the door could be closed. "I'm very hungry. Please give me something to eat. I have no money, but please . . ."

The woman stared at her, suspicious. "Shiro!" she bawled at the dog. "Be quiet!"

The barking abated to whines.

"Please," Noriko repeated, her eyes downcast. "I'm going to Tokyo. I can't go on without something to eat. Please."

The woman continued to look her up and down, deciding.

"Wait there," she finally said, pointing to a bench against the wall under the eaves. She disappeared inside, sliding the door closed.

Noriko eased herself down and leaned back against the wall of the farmhouse, listening to the woman moving about and conversing with someone inside. "A beggar," she heard her say. Then a male voice, too low to make out.

The door opened.

"Here," said the woman, thrusting out a bowl. "Leave it there when you're finished and go."

It was a small battered metal basin, the sort scraps would be put in to serve to the dog. Noriko bowed low and expressed her thanks and took the bowl with both hands. It contained a scoop of barley and rice in the remains of a fish stew. She forced herself to eat slowly, sitting alone in the darkness.

The door opened again, letting out the lamplight. A grizzled older man emerged, squatting in the doorway to watch Noriko eat.

"Catfish," he said, gesturing toward her bowl. "I caught it."

Noriko bowed. "Thank you. It's delicious."

The man gazed out into the night for a time. Then: "Do you know where Hiroshima is?"

"It's in Chugoku," said Noriko. "On the western end of Honshu."

"Ah, a long way off, then. I heard a strange rumor about it today. Something about a—"

"Close the door!" the woman bawled from inside. "You're letting in mosquitoes!"

The man's whole body contracted into a ball of rage, which he vented into the night with a bellow: "Be quiet!" Then he obediently pulled his head back in and closed the door.

Noriko finished her meal in the dark, listening to the couple bickering inside. Fatigue was overtaking her now. She wanted nothing more than to curl up on the ground and go to sleep, but she knew that she couldn't, that the woman wanted her gone.

"Thank you," she called out, setting the empty bowl on the veranda. "I'm leaving now."

She made her way south, following another path that seemed to angle back toward the train tracks. She proceeded slowly and with care, for it was now fully dark under the barest sliver of moon. She knew she couldn't go far, not in this blackness, not on the verge of dropping from fatigue.

She continued on until she came to the remains of a pine grove, most of the trees cut down. It did not provide much shelter, but there were a few patches of fallen needles that were soft. She found a comfortable spot against a gnarled trunk and sat down.

The cicadas were quiet. Their droning had given way to the chirping of crickets, joined by the croak of a frog hidden in a crevice nearby. Noriko closed her eyes and rested her head on her knees and allowed herself to be carried along by the night sounds. As she relaxed, images began to race through her mind—the Toad's face leering through the cell door grating, the stranger who interviewed her, green fields passing the train, the conductor's stern look—and looming behind them, the Tokkō captain with his sword and his mock execution. She could still feel and even taste her terror as she waited to die. And then that moment when the blade was descending, that moment when she rose into the air and was looking down at her own mortal body, that moment when she saw that there was something inside her, a second light, a second spirit.

The nausea she had been feeling made sense to her now. The realization had been there all along.

She was pregnant.

She lay down on the bed of pine needles and curled up.

She was drifting away now.

She fell asleep.

It had been the coldest winter in forty years, people were saying. February 25 had brought a blanket of snow, transforming Tokyo from wartime bleakness into a vision of sparkling white. It lasted until the afternoon, when squadrons of B-29s appeared high overhead and began dropping bombs, the biggest raid yet. It razed a large swath of the city between the Imperial Palace and the Sumida River and started a dozen smaller fires elsewhere, one scarcely a kilometer from the Umamichi neighborhood in Asakusa-ku, where their house was located. By the end of the day ash was drifting over the city and the cobalt-blue sky was obscured by a haze of black smoke.

Noriko agreed to evacuate to the countryside after that, to bow to the danger that had been steadily increasing since the end of November. She would give her employers at NHK appropriate notice, then take Aiko to live with Keizo's parents in Kanagawa Prefecture in the middle of March. She had put off going for as long as she could, for she dreaded living under the same roof as Keizo's mother, a sour-faced woman with an inexhaustible capacity for criticizing her American-born daughter-in-law. This was what she told Keizo, and it was entirely true. She didn't mention that she was also reluctant to give up her job and her identity as an NHK announcer, a valued position for which she was paid as much as her husband. The thought of going from that to existing under her mother-in-law's thumb was almost more than she could bear.

The ruins were still smoking on February 26 when the cable was sent to Keizo's parents. Notice was given at the radio station. Train tickets were purchased. Then, five days before the planned departure, the American bombers returned.

The sirens began wailing shortly after midnight. They were sounding almost nightly now, warning of dangers that didn't come, so there was no panic. Everyone was growing accustomed to the drill. Noriko wearily rose and carried Aiko out to the shelter Keizo had dug in the garden, a chest-deep hole with a roof of tin sheeting covered with dirt where the flowers had been. If this was like the warning of two nights before, or the night before that, they would spend an uncomfortable hour or two in the hole, then the all-clear siren would sound, releasing them to return to their beds.

They hunkered down with Rie, their maid, all three of them with padded hoods shrouding their heads and shoulders, a government recommendation for surviving explosions and flying debris. Aiko went back to sleep, huddled in the quilts they had brought, for it was a cold night and a stiff wind was blowing. The firefighting equipment was close at hand—water-filled barrel, straw matting ready for soaking, sand pail, grappling hook, long-handled broom, ladder for climbing up onto the roof to douse any flames. Noriko had practiced the procedure several times with her neighbors, rushing to put out hypothetical fires on rooftops before they could take hold. She hoped she would not have to do so in earnest. She hoped that tonight was just another false alarm.

It wasn't.

The B-29s when they came sounded different, their droning louder than before. This was because they were flying lower, at an altitude of scarcely two thousand meters. Their arrival was heralded by searchlights piercing the night sky, then the barking of anti-aircraft guns, the batteries in the park at Shoten-cho and farther west at Korakuen and Ueno. Then the bombers were passing overhead, hundreds of them, a deafening roar. They did not leave high-explosive blasts in their wake. What Noriko heard instead was an approaching whisper, followed by what sounded like a sudden downpour striking the roofs. It was the sound of thousands of small metal cylinders raining down from the sky to release jellied gasoline on impact. Within moments the sky was glowing crimson. Houses were burning, showers of sparks dancing up to spread the conflagration. The sky grew brighter, as bright as day.

Noriko emerged with creeping dread from the shelter. The fires seemed to be all around them, choking smoke in the air, the temperature rising like on a hot summer day. She heard shouts from neighboring houses and the narrow alley out front and knew instinctively that their only hope was to run. She dashed inside, a thousand thoughts flooding her mind, their house full of possessions, everything they owned, what she should take. The interior was eerily bright, as if daylight was shining through the windows. She stood there for a shocked moment, not knowing what to do. She grabbed her ration book and a small bag of rice and ran back outside.

"We have to leave," she said, thrusting the rice at Rie and sweeping Aiko up in her arms. She led the way back through the house and out the front door into the street, Rie following with the rice and the quilts. The writer who lived next door, Mr. Ukita, was frantically loading things into a cart— books and dishes and mosquito nets, utterly useless. He gave Noriko a wild look and plunged back inside. Noriko turned and hurried away. They had to get out of this narrow alley, away from these wooden houses, out of this tinderbox maze.

The main street was full of people, most loaded down with suitcases and bundles, everyone heading west toward Ueno, where the fires seemed less intense. Noriko joined the exodus as more B-29s were passing over, the roar of their engines deafening, their undersides illuminated red from the flames, then blue when they were caught in the beam of a searchlight. More steel cylinders filled with jellied gasoline rained down, thousands upon thousands of them. Soon the way ahead was blocked by flames. Panicked people were turning back now, transforming the street into a struggling, screaming mass of bodies as they tried to flee in the opposite direction.

Noriko was becoming tired carrying Aiko but didn't dare set her down in the crush. She turned south, thinking of the local middle school, now closed. It was the most substantial building in the neighborhood, an island of concrete in a sea of wood. She reached the railway overpass, the school a hundred meters farther on, only to find the way blocked by an inferno. A firebreak had been cleared on both sides of the tracks, but it made no difference. Flames leaped up all around. Several large shelters had been dug in the underpass but were already full, people squeezed in tight.

"Please take my child," Noriko pleaded. No one responded. There was no room.

The furnace heat was now so intense that Noriko's clothes were sparking, on the verge of catching fire. There seemed nowhere left to flee now, but they couldn't stay here. She wrapped herself and Aiko in one of the quilts and plunged onward, going she didn't know where. She pushed past people wailing in terror, people on fire and screaming, people sitting on the ground chanting to the Buddha for mercy. The updraft was so strong that it was difficult to hang on to the quilt that was their only protection.

Now it was on fire. Noriko beat it out with her hands. She heard a shriek and glanced back to see Rie burst into flames. She kept running.

Her desperate flight brought her to a large tank filled with water, one of many that had been placed around the city for firefighting. It was already packed with people, hunkered down so that only the tops of their heads were showing. One man had dragged in his bicycle and was hanging on to it as another tried to wrest it from his grasp so he could climb in. Noriko tried to lift Aiko into the water.

"My child!" she cried. "Let in my child!"

It was no use. There wasn't room. Noriko pushed past the arms trying to fend her off and thrust the quilt into the water. She draped it back around her and Aiko dripping wet, a momentary relief from the heat, and raced on into a tide of trapped people surging back toward the west. She ran into a house, its door hanging open, hoping to escape through the back, but was driven back by more flames. She tried another, then one on the other side of the street.

There, in a courtyard, people in line at a hole in the ground leading down into a sewer or drain. She rushed to join them. When her turn came, she lowered Aiko into the stink, then followed, crawling through what felt like filth, praying that the way ahead led under and away from the fire. The heat inside the concrete blackness was intense. Whimpering and moaning and gasping close in her ears. "Keep moving, keep moving," a hoarse voice was saying.

A ring of light framing Aiko's body in front, growing to meet them, illuminating the sides of the drain. Just another few meters. Then they were out.

She put Aiko on her back and scrambled out of the ditch, stepping on trampled dead bodies. She no longer had the quilt. Where was it? She looked around. It was gone.

A glimpse of water ahead, glowing red. The Sumida River. She ran toward it. She arrived to find hundreds of people fighting to get onto Kototoi Bridge. The opposite side of the river was a wall of fire, so there was no point crossing over. There was no escape there. The goal seemed to be to get to the middle of the bridge, as far as possible from the wind-fanned flames leaping up on both sides.

Noriko left the roadway and headed for the bank of the river, intending to wade into the water. Thousands of others were doing the same. She was carried along by the press of bodies, Aiko, frozen with fear, clinging tight to her back.

Pushed from behind, Noriko entered the water, warm from the fires. The pressure forced her in deeper, past her waist, until she was up to her chest. Splashes farther out in the river, strangled cries of "Help me! Help me!" People were jumping from the bridge above to escape being crushed against the superheated steel railings.

"Please," Noriko gasped, for she was being pushed in deeper. The water was up to her chin now. She was fighting to keep her head above water.

Aiko was starting to struggle.

"Please . . . "

Her toes were barely touching the bottom.

"Please . . . "

The bottom dropped away.

She awoke to the sound of seagulls. It was morning.

She rose from her bed of pine needles and looked about at her surroundings, unseen in the darkness the previous night. The immediate vicinity was ravaged, pine trees cut down for firewood, roots dug up for fuel. The glint of water beckoned in the distance. Walking toward it, she came to a large lake, an expanse of marsh extending out from the shore, herons wading in the shallows, smaller birds flitting about. A dozen or more boats were out on the water beyond, scudding along under rectangular white sails that were so immense they made the vessels look inconsequential. Noriko recalled seeing a picture of these unique crafts, using the wind to trawl for fish on Lake Kasumigaura.

She stared out at the lake.

She felt Aiko's hands clutching at her neck, at her shoulders, pushing her down.

. . .

Yellow grass rising above her, swaying in a hush of breeze.

A green grasshopper clinging to a stem, hanging on.

The white of an egret traversing a bowl of gray sky.

Her clothes were muddy and wet with rain. How long had she been lying here? Was it hours? Or days?

She winced as she got to her feet, her whole body aching. She looked out at the lake, at the boats moving along under their giant sails. They had been out there fishing for centuries.

She continued on along the shore until she came to a stretch of beach where clear water was lapping. No one was around apart from the crews on the boats, who were too far off to see. She removed her shoes and her clothes and waded into the lake and started bathing, caressing her abdomen, the life growing inside her. How was it possible after what she had suffered? And yet it was. She could feel it.

She lay in the long grass and let the warm air dry her before getting dressed. Refreshed, she turned away from the lake and headed west toward the train line. The path led her past a series of lotus ponds, a riot of green with pink flowers scattered on top, then on into fields. The town to the north—she knew now that it was Tsuchiura, seventy kilometers north of Tokyo.

She came to the train tracks and turned south.

She kept walking.

TWENTY-ONE

KEIZO KAN FOUND CAPTAIN ONDA IN THE TAMA AIRFIELD ADMINISTRATION BUILDING, SEATED in an empty office, working at a desk.

"Excuse me, Onda-tai-i," he said, sticking his head through the door and apologetically bowing.

Onda looked up from his maps and scribbled figures and air current chart. "Ah, Sensei. Come in. I've just been finalizing our plans. We'll be leaving tomorrow evening. So not much longer to wait."

"Tomorrow evening?" Kan felt the blood drain from his face.

Onda didn't notice. "If we take off at ten-thirty, that should get us to Tinian just as the sun is rising at six. Was there something you needed?"

Kan struggled to steady himself. "I was hoping to make a telephone call."

Onda's eyes narrowed. "To whom?"

"To the Riken. To see if my wife has arrived. You said that she has been released."

"Yes, I did. She has."

"I'd like to make sure she has arrived safely."

Onda considered for a moment. He frowned. "A letter would be better."

"I'd like to assure myself with a phone call," Kan persisted.

"She's been released, as I told you. Don't you trust Colonel Sagara?"

No, Keizo Kan thought.

"Please, Captain," he said. "I only want to assure myself that she's there."

An annoyed *tsk* from Onda, a deep breath, then he stood up. "Don't mention where you are. Not a word about any of this."

"Of course not," said Kan.

Onda led the way to another room with a telephone on a table and stood by as the scientist dialed the operator and waited for his call to go through. Kan turned his back for a bit of privacy. His heart was pounding as he counted the rings.

Miss Yokoyama, Nishina's secretary, answered when he reached ten. "Kan-sensei!" she cried. "Where have you been? We've been worried!"

Kan, acutely aware of Onda's presence, made an evasive reply. "I'm phoning to see if my wife has arrived."

"Your wife? No. Why would she—" Miss Yokoyama stopped herself, flustered.

"Her situation," Kan said. "That matter has been corrected. I was hoping she had returned."

"No, she hasn't. But that's excellent news. Shall I get Dr. Nishina? He's back now. Would you like to speak to him?"

A heavy weight of disappointment descended on Kan. He lowered his head.

"Shall I get Dr. Nishina?" Miss Yokoyama repeated.

"No, that's all right. But please give him my regards. And thank you, Yokoyama-san. Thank you for all the kindness you've showed me."

"Kan-sensei . . . " Miss Yokoyama's concern carried through the telephone line.

"Goodbye." Kan hung up the receiver.

"There," Onda said. "Now you've had your call."

Kan didn't reply. He just stared at the phone.

Onda's face softened as he saw the scientist's distress. "Please don't worry yourself," he said, walking him to the front entrance of the building. "Your wife has just been delayed, that's all. She'll certainly arrive there tomorrow. And writing a letter would be so much better, don't you think?"

Kan descended the steps and started back to the hangar, Onda's cheery final words ringing in his ears: "We have just thirty more hours!" He passed the trainee barracks, now mostly abandoned, the mess hall and training school buildings, all of weathered unpainted boards. Off to the right, beyond the front gate, he could see the road heading east to Tokyo and west toward the mist-shrouded mountains. On the far side of the road were inviting green fields and a peaceful hamlet on the Tama River. If only he could just walk away . . .

The Daikon was now installed in the Renzan bomber and almost complete. Kan and Yagi had finished the job an hour before, the scientist trying to ignore the pain in his hand as they worked inside the walled-off corner of the hangar. The first step had been to reassemble the three elements that made up the projectile: the stack of nine enriched uranium rings; the tungsten tamper behind the rings; and behind the tamper, the rear steel plug. Before mating them together, Kan restored the four beryllium-polonium initiators to their original position at the rear of the uranium stack, explaining their purpose to Yagi in general terms. He had ceased keeping any secrets from him.

With the whole assembly firmly wedged together, they had then wrapped it in a thin sheet of copper, the same metal Kan had peeled away at Hikari during his initial examination. They trimmed the sheet to size, bent it around the assembly, heated it, and ran a bead of solder down the seam. As the encasing copper cooled and contracted, it tightened onto the uranium rings, tamper, and steel, returning them to a solid projectile, a pristine, even beautiful thing.

It was the length of Kan's forearm almost to the end of his fingers and weighed ninety kilos. Yagi, straining mightily, could not get it inserted into the rear of the gun barrel, even with Kan using what strength he had to assist. The fit was too snug. Finally, with the help of two mechanics and a great deal of grunting and sweating, they got the projectile lined up and inserted and pushed into place down inside the tube.

All that remained now was the explosive charge that would blast the uranium projectile down the gun barrel to mate onto the uranium target. Cordite would be used, the same material that had been removed from the bomb at Hikari. It was the obvious choice. Cordite had a rapid burn rate and high peak pressure, so it would propel the projectile and assemble the critical mass at maximum speed. The salvaged American cordite was at hand, but Kan had decided it would be imprudent to reuse it. A supply of Japanese cordite had been obtained through Captain Onda. They had packed four kilos of it into a silk bag and placed it up against the projectile once it was in place. The breech plug was then screwed onto the rear of the gun barrel, sealing the end.

The Daikon, resting on its trolley, was wheeled out to the plane.

"Well?" Yagi, perched up inside the bomb bay of the Renzan, looked down as Kan returned. "Did he let you make the call?"

Kan nodded, letting his disappointment show. "She wasn't there."

"Just like I thought. That's what I told you."

Yagi lowered his hand and helped Kan climb up inside beside him. The tension between them following Yagi's outburst the previous day was gone. The navy man had become friendly again—friendly enough to urge Kan to ask Onda to make a call to the Riken to check on his wife. That was the way Yagi was, Kan now understood. He was like a volcano or geyser. He could erupt, then settle back down as if nothing had happened.

"Any mention of me?" Yagi casually asked.

Kan shook his head.

Yagi craned his neck, making it crack. It had been twenty-four hours and still no mention of removing him from the mission. Hadn't they checked his navy record? It would be there.

They resumed their work on the Daikon. It was already in place, secured to the cradle of struts that had been welded to the frame of the aircraft. Yagi was now stringing a wire from the tail end of the gun barrel to the radio operator's compartment above, located near the midpoint of the aircraft, at the trailing edge of the wing. Since there would be no radio operator on the flight, the space had been allocated to them. When this was done, they climbed up into the compartment to install the switch that would serve as the trigger. The firing mechanism was as simple as that—a guillotine switch wired up to a primer in the end of the bomb, which was in turn connected to the cordite charge nestled up against the projectile. Lift the locking bracket on the guillotine switch, throw the switch, and the bomb would explode. Kan affixed a note to the switch—Do Not Touch—after it was in place. That and the locking bracket were the extent of safety precautions. They also left the triggering wire disconnected from the bomb. They would wait until the last moment to connect it. Just before takeoff.

Takeoff.

Kan checked his watch.

In twenty-nine hours . . .

The terror of what lay ahead returned to him in a rush. He sank into the left-hand seat he would occupy during the flight, the triggering switch screwed down to the radio operator's desk directly in front. He looked up through the glass window above the two seats and struggled to push the black vision away.

Yagi was behind him, peering through the small rear door opening onto the next compartment extending to the back of the plane—largely an empty space now with the waist guns removed. Beyond it, at the very back of the plane, was the tail gun. Yagi had been given an orientation to the weapon and allowed to fire a few bursts when the Renzan was towed to the firing range.

"You know, I visited Korea once," said Kan, for something to say.

"My father went on a trip to Keijo and took me along. He was trying to interest me in the business."

Yagi closed the door and settled into the seat beside Kan's. "Then you've seen more of Korea than me," he said. "I was only five when we came to Japan. What sort of business?"

"Importing soybeans, mostly. My father did well with Korean soybeans. Top quality for miso." A wry smile. "But he didn't have much luck with me. I didn't want to get my hands dirty."

"Don't want to get your hands dirty, eh?" Yagi raised his hand and slapped the air. "*Smack!* My father would have sorted you out."

They fell silent. Kan returned to gazing up through the glass at the broken roof of the hangar. The receding panic left an empty feeling in his chest.

Yagi let out a wistful sigh. "I couldn't get away fast enough, but I wish I could go back there now. We had some times in that garage."

"It must have been hard," said Kan. "Your father starting a business like that."

"Hard!" Yagi snorted. "'No Korean businesses here!' 'Oh yeah? Think you can drive us out? Think again, fuckers!' My father and me—we *fought* those bastards for that garage." He held up his right fist, displaying a depressed knuckle. "See that? I was sixteen years old when I did that. Broke my hand smashing a guy's nose."

Silence. Kan returned to gazing up through the glass at the low, scudding clouds.

He closed his eyes, feeling weary. He heard Yagi draw in a long breath and slowly let it out.

"Are you sure Onda didn't say anything about me?" said Yagi.

Kan shook his head.

They descended the ladder and exited the Renzan. Soon it would be time for dinner. Yagi went off to the airfield bathhouse. Kan returned to the barracks room they shared and took out his notebook.

The weakness that he had begun to notice a few days before was now becoming acute. Installing the bomb had left him worn out and light-headed, even with Yagi doing most of the work. He wrote out this observation in his notebook, his handwriting clumsy, then added an update about the deterioration of his right hand, which was causing him pain just gripping the pen. He expected that it would continue to swell, as happened to the unfortunate Seaman Wada at Hikari. What had become of Wada? Had he recovered?

Kan closed the notebook, stared at it for a while, then wrote on the cover: *Send to Dr. Yoshio Nishina, Institute of Physical and Chemical Research, Komagome, Tokyo.*

He returned the notebook to the satchel beside his carelessly rolled futon. PO Yagi's futon beside it was much more neatly stowed. Shipshape.

He reflected on Yagi. They had been together for not much more than a week, but he had already developed an affection for the volatile young man. And now he felt sympathy, too, for he understood the wounds beneath Yagi's bravado and anger. Kan was well aware of the discrimination Koreans faced in Japan, no matter how well they assimilated. It had taken its worst form following the Great Kanto Earthquake in 1923, when Koreans were accused of looting and arson and many were killed. Kan had a vivid memory of being surrounded and threatened by a vigilante mob when he went out with his father to view the earthquake damage. They had been mistaken for Koreans because his father had a beard.

There was nothing he could do to save himself. Any attempt would doom Noriko, and he would rather face the terror than do that. But perhaps there was something else he could do.

He looked at his watch.

Twenty-eight hours to go.

Kan waited until later that evening, when Captain Onda was alone in his room.

"Excuse me, Onda-tai-i," he said, keeping his voice low, confidential. "But there's something I need to tell you about Petty Officer Yagi."

TWENTY-TWO

KEIZO KAN AND PO YAGI WERE PERCHED UP INSIDE THE BOMB BAY OF THE RENZAN, HUNCHED over the end of the Daikon. They had already tested the triggering wire, using the plane's electrical system and a light bulb. All that remained was to attach the wire to the primer at the back of the weapon—the primer that would set off the charge of cordite that would blast the uranium projectile down the gun tube.

Kan was no longer taking the lead in the work. His inflamed right hand was causing him pain, which was making him clumsy. He was holding the flashlight, illuminating the end of the bomb for Yagi. Watching Yagi work, he was struck yet again by the crudity of what they were doing. It was almost ridiculous, applying what was essentially a light switch to a mass of uranium-235 the manufacture and complexity of which he could scarcely imagine.

We're like monkeys, Kan thought, the memory of Yagi's hooting coming into his mind. *We're like monkeys playing with something we don't understand.*

"Wait."

Kan snatched the wire from Yagi. He touched the end to his tongue, making doubly sure that no current was passing through it, that the Renzan's electrical system was truly shut down.

"It's dead," said Yagi, annoyed, snatching it back. "How many times do you have to check?"

A loop and a twist and the job was done. The Daikon was live. All that it would take to set it off was to throw the switch in the compartment above them—the switch that Kan had doubly secured in the closed position by wrapping a piece of wire around the locking bracket.

They climbed out of the bomb bay and stood on the grass, looking at the plane parked in front of the hangar. Its transformation into a kamikaze atomic bomb was complete. The cowlings were back in place on its overhauled engines. The openings in the fuselage for the waist guns, now removed, had been sealed. And the entire aircraft, from nose to tail, from wing tip to wing tip, was painted black, merging into the lengthening shadows beneath as the sun descended toward the hills in the west.

Kan looked at his watch. Just after five o'clock. Six hours until takeoff.

The sun . . .

He realized with a pang that he would never see it again.

He glanced at Yagi. The navy man was anxiously chewing on the side of his thumb, for he still had not been removed from the mission. Kan's approach to Captain Onda the previous evening had resulted in nothing. He had not saved Yagi. A part of him felt bad about it. But another part, a larger part, felt relieved. For it meant that he wouldn't have to do it alone. Having Yagi beside him would make the coming ordeal a little easier to bear.

A fuel cart was wheeled alongside the Renzan and the ground crew began manually pumping. The wing tanks, inboard and outboard, could hold a total of 10,780 liters of fuel, weighing 8,090 kilos. And it all had to be pumped in by hand.

"All set?"

It was Captain Onda approaching.

"Yes, Onda-tai-i," said Kan. "Please make sure no one touches the switch."

"Already done," said Onda. Kan had been warning him about the switch all through the day.

He examined Kan's face, then took his red and swollen hand and gave it a close inspection. His eyes returned to Kan's. "How do you feel? Are you all right?"

Kan nodded. "I think so."

"Because we just got word about that seaman at Hikari. The one who got sick."

"Seaman Wada?" asked Yagi.

"Yes, I think that was his name. He's dead."

Kan's eyes grew wide with dismay. Yagi scowled.

Onda took out his Philopon bottle.

"Here. Take one of these. It will do you good."

Kan mechanically took a tablet and swallowed it.

Yagi did the same.

Kan could feel his mood lightening as he sat in his room in the barracks, referring to his notebook as he penned a letter to Dr. Nishina explaining the images on the exposed rolls of film. Various angles of the bomb prior to disassembly; shots of the uranium rings removed from the nose; the bomb disassembled; the projectile intact; the projectile with copper sheeting removed; Seaman Wada's injured hand, the skin burst open and leaking fluid—it was all there. When he was done, he packed up the film, the camera and the letter and set them alongside the precious Geiger-Müller counter for return to the Riken.

The door flew open and Yagi stormed in. Kan knew instantly what it meant. Before he could register his feelings, the navy man had him by the throat and was roaring into his face.

"Why did you tell Onda I was Korean! Why did you tell him I should be removed from the mission!"

"I was trying to . . . spare you," Kan managed to gasp.

Yagi continued to glare, his eyes murderous, his grip choking.

Finally his hand relaxed. He let go.

"I'm sorry," said Kan, rubbing his throat. "It was the only way I could think of to spare you. I thought you'd want it. So you wouldn't have to go."

"But I'm still going!" said Yagi, throwing up his hands.

Kan's face fell. "Onda didn't remove you?"

"No! He just gave me a lecture about what a great honor it was for me and 'my people.' 'We were enemies once, but now we go into combat as brothers.' That's what he said!"

Yagi gave the wall a backhanded blow with his fist, shaking the boards and sending a cheap print of Mount Fuji crashing to the floor.

A muffled voice in the hall outside. Then a knock at the door. It was one of the guards who always seemed to be lurking.

"Is everything all right in here?" he asked, looking in.

"We're fine," said Kan. "Everything is all right."

The final banquet for the crew was held in a private room above the officers' mess. The three remaining members had arrived now and were present: Captain Yoshino, copilot; First Lieutenant Kamibeppu, navigator; and First Lieutenant Otani, flight engineer. Introductions were made and the six men started eating. It was an excellent meal specially laid on by the cooks: pure white rice unadulterated by millet or barley; miso stew with seaweed, tofu, and clams; a variety of pickles and other side dishes; and as the centerpiece, a huge sea bream sprinkled with coarse salt and grilled to perfection. Captain Onda ate with gusto. PO Yagi began mechanically, then showed mounting enjoyment as the Philopon tablet did its work. Kan found himself enjoying the meal too. He was feeling a remarkable sense of renewal, his dread beaten down, the mission ahead more a source of manageable fear than stark terror. He finished eating and stretched, his spine pleasantly cracking, then gave his scalp a reviving massage. When he lowered his left hand, he was disconcerted to see a tangle of hair caught between his fingers. He brushed it away under the table before any of the others could notice.

So now you're losing your hair.

Only a modicum of sake was served—it was three hours to take-off and heads had to be clear—so the meal did not become boisterous. Two songs were sung to wind up the celebration, "Companion Cherry Blossoms" and "Until the Enemy Raises the White Flag," Onda displaying a fine voice, Kan and Yagi subdued. The dishes were then cleared away, a map was spread on the table, and the crew gathered round as Onda conducted a briefing. The navigator, Kamibeppu, poring over the chart, draped a comradely arm across PO Yagi's shoulder.

The finalized plan would take them well out into the Pacific to stay clear of the American presence around Iwo Jima. They would then turn south at latitude 24 degrees and proceed to a point 100 kilometers to the east of Tinian Island. Here they would turn east in a direct line to Tinian, descending from their cruising altitude of 10,000 meters to below 100 meters to stay beneath the Americans' radar. In the last few minutes, on the final approach, the dawning sun behind them, they would ascend to 700 meters to maximize the destructive effect of the bomb. Making allowances for possible headwinds, Onda estimated that the 2,350-kilometer journey would take seven and a half hours.

Briefing finished, the crew retired to their assigned quarters to make final arrangements and write their last letters. For Kan, all that remained was to pen a will declaring that he had no outstanding debts or loans and was leaving all his earthly possessions, such as they were, to his wife. He then steeled himself to write Noriko his farewell, assuming that it would somehow reach her. His request to make another telephone call to the Riken had been flatly refused.

"You will be surprised to learn," he wrote, "that I have died in a military manner in battle. I am surprised myself, writing these words. I have volunteered for a no-return mission that it is hoped will change the course of the war, a unique mission that involves my area of specialization. I am not at liberty to reveal more here. A full account no doubt will be provided to you when you receive this letter. I pray that I will do my duty and acquit myself honorably at the decisive moment."

He paused. The next part would be hard.

"Dearest beloved Noriko," he continued, "thank you for being a good companion and a kind wife to me. And thank you for our precious child you bore us. I will soon be with Aiko in the next world and together we will—"

The image of Noriko distraught as she read this came clearly into Kan's mind. Emotion welled up inside him, overwhelming the composure and lightness of spirit the Philopon tablet had granted. He turned away to hide his tears from Yagi, who was seated across the table.

Yagi didn't notice. He was struggling with his own feelings. He had been all set when Captain Onda finally called him aside for a word, no doubt to remove him from the mission.

It was you who pressed me to join, you cloven-foot fucker!

Jokbari. Cloven foot. It was the term Yagi's father had used in private for the Japanese people he worked with and lived among and secretly hated. Yagi was going to spit it right in Onda's face, then drop him with his fist if he tried to get physical. He had done it to others, one swift blow to the chin. There was that seaman on the *Iro* who had tried to push him around. And that Dutch prisoner of war at Balikpapan, for no reason, when he was drunk. Yagi had regretted doing that.

But the insult hadn't come. He was still being included on the mission.

Come on, Onda! Where's my insult? Yes, I'm Korean. My name is Yang Byeong-il. I have Yi Sun-sin in my blood!

The camaraderie he had experienced at the farewell banquet had meant something to Yagi. He couldn't deny it. And the songs they had sung together had almost moved him to tears. It wasn't just the words. It was the feeling that he was being included without reservation in the group.

And Kamibeppu's arm across his shoulder . . .

Don't be a fool, Yagi! You're being used!

Yes, he was being used. But it was too late now. His pride had led him into a trap—a trap from which the only escape was to demean himself and confirm every insult he had ever endured.

Yes, the petty officer backed out at the last minute. Lost his nerve. We gave him a chance to prove himself, but he's Korean, you know.

Yagi looked across the table at Kan, laboring at his letter with tears in his eyes. He picked up his pencil and addressed a letter to the only immediate family he had left, his younger sister.

"Dearest sister," he began. "Please excuse this hastily written letter. I will soon be setting out on a special mission which you will no doubt read about in the newspapers. There will be nothing left of my mortal body, so I will leave fingernail and hair clippings to be placed in the white box. When you receive it, please remember me without tears."

Yagi's own eyes now were misting. A tear escaped down his cheek. Annoyed, he brushed it away.

"I am sorry for not being able to do anything more to help you beyond the insurance money," he continued. "Please work hard and be cheerful and live a long life. Give my regards to Arima-san when you see them. And if you ever run into Nobuhiko, tell him—"

The door opened. It was Captain Onda.

"Thirty minutes," he said.

Eight o'clock in the evening. Colonel Sagara arrived by motorcycle. He had to struggle to get out of the sidecar and onto his feet, waving off the helping hand of the driver. He donned his cap and straightened his uniform, then set out with Captain Onda to inspect the black bomber parked in the waning twilight.

He paused to admire the large rising sun emblem that had been painted on the rear of the fuselage, discreetly in maroon to meld into the black. He continued on, walking with a limp, clutching his left hand, his arm oddly akimbo.

"You've done an excellent job, Captain Onda," he said as they completed their tour. He looked up at the sky. "What do you think of these clouds?"

"I've been worried," said Onda. "But they appear to be breaking."

Sagara continued to gaze up. "Yes . . . Any trouble with the navy man and Kan?"

"No, Colonel. They've been very useful."

"Good. I want them on the plane."

Sagara turned to Onda, his face now intense. "All right, now listen. His Majesty spoke to the Supreme War Council and said that he wants the war to end. I could hardly believe it, but War Minister Anami has confirmed that it's true. It was a trick Prime Minister Suzuki arranged, asking the Emperor to give his opinion to break the deadlock."

Onda gravely nodded. He knew that important meetings had been taking place at the Imperial Palace. But for the Emperor to intercede—that was unprecedented.

"It's treason, of course," Sagara continued, "the Badoglios using His Majesty that way. And now they've sent a cable to the Allies, saying they're willing to accept the terms of surrender. I've just heard this from Colonel Takeshita."

Onda's eyes widened with horror. "No . . . "

"They won't get much further. They're going to be stopped. But this mission needs to be a success. Do you understand? We need a victory that the War Minister can use to smash the traitors back into line. Can you give me that victory?"

Onda straightened to attention.

"I think so, Colonel. We had some trouble with one of the engines, but it seems to be functioning now. A lot will depend on the weather. If we encounter . . . "

Onda's voice petered out. Sagara's expression had hardened. He did not want to hear it.

"We're ready," Onda said, snapping a nod.

•   •   •

Ten o'clock. A table covered with a white cloth was set up in front of the Renzan. On it lay a sake bottle, six cups, and six strips of white cotton, hachimaki on which *Shichisho Hokoku*, "Serve the Nation Through Seven Lives," had been brushed in black ink. The Renzan's crew stood in a line in front of the table, Captain Onda in the middle, Keizo Kan and PO Yagi side by side at the end.

Colonel Sagara walked to the front. He surveyed the men before him—the Renzan crew at the fore, their faces dimly lit by the shaded lanterns flanking the colonel, the mechanics who had worked on the plane dark shadows behind.

"Most of you," he began, "don't know the significance of this aircraft you have helped to prepare. So I'll tell you. It's equipped with a new-type bomb many times more powerful than any conventional weapon. It is so powerful that it can destroy whole cities, sink entire fleets, level whole islands. The Americans have used such a weapon against us twice. At Hiroshima. And at Nagasaki. Now it's time for us to strike back."

Sagara paused and looked around.

"These six men . . . "—he gestured toward the crew—"these six courageous warriors are about to fly this weapon south to the Marianas. They will use it to destroy the airfield complex on Tinian Island where a large part of the Yankees' bomber strength is located. This will be a major blow! It will cripple the enemy's ability to launch strikes against Japan. This single aircraft and these six men will do that tonight to protect our homeland! Could there be any greater glory? I envy them for it. And I revere them!"

A wild fervor was coming into Sagara's face. It was the dangerous look that Kan had seen before. He dropped his own gaze, then glanced at PO Yagi beside him. Yagi was staring straight ahead, his face hard, no sign of emotion. Kan admired him for it. He was sure his own face was revealing his fear.

"But that's not all," Colonel Sagara was saying. "For we are not fighting only enemies without. We are also fighting enemies within, enemies occupying the highest levels of our own leadership who have lost their courage and seek to surrender. I tell you now with complete frankness, these traitors would pray for the failure of this mission so that they can bow to the Allied powers' call for our surrender. But that won't happen! This mission *will* succeed and these treasonous voices will be silenced. And we will continue to prepare for the decisive battle! For that is where we achieve victory in this war. When the Yankees invade, we will break them with our fighting spirit. Our resolve, the collective will burning inside every man and woman and child in this country, will crush them. The Yankees will find themselves drowning in a sea of blood and it will horrify them, so that they will be forced to withdraw. Because if they don't, we will fight them, the Japanese people will fight them—*until we eat stones!*"

Eat stones. It was an old expression. It conjured up the image of a samurai warrior fighting to the death on the field of battle, slashing at the enemy until he fell facedown, mouth agape, in the dirt. Kan recalled the term from his youthful reading. He recoiled from it now. Then his mind returned to the colonel's previous revelation: *enemies occupying the highest levels of our own leadership who have lost their courage and seek to surrender.*

He had not known this.

He glanced up at Sagara. The colonel had fallen silent and was looking at the crew, from one face to the next, his eyes blazing almost in challenge.

Sagara's eyes met Kan's. And Kan saw the madness. He held the colonel's gaze, unable to look away, afraid that he would reveal himself if he did.

"Captain Onda!" Sagara called out, breaking the spell.

Onda stepped forward and stood at attention. Sagara handed him one of the hachimaki cloths to tie around his head, then served him a drink in the small cup. Onda downed it, replaced the cup on the table, and stepped back into line.

"Captain Yoshino!"

The copilot stepped forward to receive his headband and toast. Sagara continued down the line until he came to PO Yagi. Kan observed the colonel hesitate slightly. Then it was his turn.

"Dr. Kan!"

He stepped forward. He tied the hachimaki crookedly around his head, hampered by his painful hand. He received the cup and gulped down the contents. He could not keep a look of surprise from his face when he realized it was only water.

"The death toast," Sagara quietly explained. He seemed almost gentle. "Water to signify a pure soul."

He leaned closer, his mouth to Kan's ear. "Your wife will be taken care of, Sensei. You have no need to worry."

Kan bowed deeply. "Thank you," he whispered, momentarily overcome. He resumed his place in line, feeling confused.

The ceremony was over. It was ten-fifteen. Fifteen minutes to takeoff.

"A photograph," said Colonel Sagara. He began shepherding the crew over to the Renzan. The sergeant who had driven him out to the airfield jogged over to the motorcycle and returned with a camera and flash apparatus.

"Stand a little closer," the man instructed, lining up the crew in the darkness.

Kan stood solemn-faced in front of the plane and the maroon rising sun, flanked by copilot Yoshino and PO Yagi, both looking robust.

"There will be a bright flash," said the sergeant. "Please don't close your eyes. Ready? Three-two-one . . . "

A white light exploded in Kan's vision. Yagi murmured a curse beside him.

"One more, please," said the sergeant.

Kan heard the voice, the click of metal as the spent bulb was removed and another inserted. But he could not see a thing, only the white disk of light lingering in his vision, refreshed with each blink.

His stunned retinas began to recover. Shadows started to become apparent.

"Ready? Three-two-one . . . "

Another explosion of light plunged him back into blindness.

The sergeant's voice: "Thank you!"

A voice rose from the assembly, leading the cheer: "Tennō Heika . . . Banzai!"

Two dozen voices responded: "Banzai!!"

"Banzai!"

"Banzai!!"

"Banzai!"

"Banzai!!"

Kan stood helpless, bedazzled, waiting for his vision to clear.

He felt a hand on his shoulder. It was Captain Onda.

"Come on, Sensei. It's time."

TWENTY-THREE

THE RENZAN'S FOUR ENGINES COUGHED TO LIFE, BELCHING BLACK SMOKE, THEN RISING TO A collective roar. The chocks were removed and the throttles advanced. The bomber started taxiing through the night toward the south end of the runway where it would begin its takeoff, bouncing over ruts and potholes in the poorly maintained ground.

In the cockpit, bathed in red light to preserve the crews' night vision, Captain Onda's knuckles were white on the yoke as he steered. The shortage of fuel had not allowed him a practice flight, and the size of the bomber was still unnerving, the view from his right-side pilot's seat comparable to looking out a second-story window. But he only had to get the behemoth into the air. He would not have to land it.

Ten meters back, Keizo Kan sat in the radio operator's compartment, at the desk on the left, Petty Officer Yagi to his right. They were wearing rabbit-fur-lined flight suits that the crew had donned before climbing into the plane. The bulky outfit was hot here on the ground on a sultry August evening, and the plug emerging from the hip added to the discomfort. But it would all be needed shortly, together with the fur-lined leather helmet and oxygen mask that Kan had not yet put on.

When the unpressurized Renzan reached high altitude, the air would be thin and the temperature would fall to well below freezing.

Kan looked around the small compartment. The lamp over the desk, red filter in place, gave everything a flat, washed-out appearance. In the forward bulkhead he was facing was the door opening onto the bomb bay and the catwalk leading forward to the flight deck. At the base of the bulkhead, emerging from a hole near the floor, was the wire. It was connected to the Daikon's manual trigger, the guillotine switch mounted on the desk at which Kan was sitting, a bracket across it locking it down in the "off" position. When the time came, all Kan had to do was remove the precautionary twist of wire he had added, lift the locking bracket, and throw the switch. That was it.

We are also fighting enemies within, enemies occupying the highest levels of our own leadership who have lost their courage and seek to surrender.

Kan continued to ponder Colonel Sagara's startling remark. He must have been referring to a division on the Supreme War Council. This mission he had been coerced into joining—Kan had assumed it was an act of futility on the inevitable path to Japan's destruction. But what if that path wasn't inevitable? What if there was another possible outcome? What if the Supreme War Council was split, with some of its members arguing for surrender? Kan did not consider them enemies if that was the case. If they sought to end the war, shouldn't he want to help them?

His eyes returned to the guillotine switch. He imagined reaching out and retracting the locking bracket. He imagined throwing the switch and closing the circuit. He imagined the pulse of electricity passing through the wire, the charge detonating in the gun barrel below him and driving the uranium projectile into the target.

The bomber reached the end of the runway and turned into the gentle breeze wafting down from the hills. Looking forward from the cockpit, Captain Onda saw only shadows as he advanced the throttles, pushing the Renzan's four engines to full power. Then soft points of light began to appear, blinking on to form parallel lines leading forward into the darkness. They were shaded lanterns held by airfield personnel lining the runway, a pair of men every hundred meters to guide the aircraft on takeoff. They had taken up position as the crew boarded the plane.

A throbbing sound on the left. Engine Two was not running smoothly. Onda checked his gauges. The rpms were low, barely 2,200. He waited as the flight engineer, Lieutenant Otani, increased the fuel-air mixture. The throbbing subsided.

Onda released the brakes. The big plane started moving, engines straining. Slowly, heavily, it gathered momentum, pounded every time its wheels hit a rut, Onda using the entire length of the runway to get his speed up to 180 kilometers per hour.

The last pair of lanterns marking the end of the runway was approaching. Onda pulled back on the yoke. The nose lifted off the ground, a final jolt, and they staggered into the air. Ahead lay the western hills rising from the Kanto Plain. Onda kept the Renzan in a steady climb to 800 meters.

"Landing gear up."

A whine below as the wheels retracted. A banking turn to the left, the Renzan coming about as it continued to climb. Entering scattered clouds now, altitude 2,000 meters.

The last wisps of clouds disappeared, leaving only a canopy of black dotted with stars. Altitude 5,000 meters, rate of ascent slowing. Onda, watching the creeping altimeter needle, realized that they would not be able to reach 10,000 meters as planned. The engines were underperforming. This was concerning. Maximum altitude was not critical to the mission, but ground speed was. They needed to maintain 320 kilometers per hour to reach Tinian at dawn.

A turn to the left, the aircraft easing onto the course it would follow for the first half of the flight, bearing 150 degrees, south-southeast. Altitude 7,000 meters. Onda was feeling the cold now. Unseen down below in the darkness, the Japanese coastline was slipping away.

•　　•　　•

In the radio operator's compartment, Kan retracted the red filter from the lamp on the desk, bathing the space in a more natural warm glow. His left ear was hurting. He worked his jaw, trying to relieve the pressure.

A crackle in his earphones. Captain Onda: "Kan-sensei. Yagi-heisō. Make sure your suits are plugged in. And you should have your oxygen masks on."

Kan clipped his mask into place. It smelled vaguely of vomit. He plugged the cable emerging from his flight suit into the socket by his seat and turned up the rheostat to get the electricity flowing. Within minutes his suit began to feel warm. Outside the aircraft the temperature was ten degrees below zero.

A jolt passed through the plane. It made Kan jump, like something had touched an exposed nerve. A pause, then the Renzan began to vibrate and buck. These were the air currents Onda had told them in the briefing to expect, the headwinds that could add an hour or more to their flight. The turbulence lasted a few minutes, then subsided as they leveled out at 8,000 meters.

It all depended now on the navigator, Lieutenant Kamibeppu, to plot their course in the darkness and get them to the target. Kan visualized him doing it now, crouched in the glass nose of the plane, using a sextant to take fixes on the stars, then working with compass, flight calculator, and chart. They would continue on their present heading for 1,300 kilometers to latitude 24 degrees, then come onto bearing 170 degrees, south by east, for another 1,000 kilometers, to latitude 14.5. Then they would turn due west to Tinian, the rising sun to their back.

One o'clock in the morning. They had been in the air for two hours.

Kan slipped his watch back into the pocket of his flight suit, contemplating Colonel Sagara's words and the terrible choice that he was now seeing before him.

We are also fighting enemies within, enemies occupying the highest levels of our own leadership who have lost their courage and seek to surrender.

If steps were being taken to surrender, the success of this mission would only prolong the war, which he hated. Kan had no doubt about that. He himself would help to prolong the war and in turn the suffering of the Japanese people, everyone that he knew. But if he detonated the bomb now, before they reached the target . . .

He was a dead man anyway. They were all dead. So why not just do it?

Navigator Kamibeppu's voice in his headphones: "Thirty degrees."

Kan looked over at Yagi. The petty officer's eyes were closed, but he was awake, his gloved right hand rhythmically moving, rolling in his imagination the dice he had neglected to bring. On the ground, in a quiet moment, Kan would have asked him what he thought. It would be easier if they did it together. But here, enveloped in the roar of the engines—what could be said beyond a few shouted words?

Kan returned to gazing at the guillotine switch, an arm's reach away, directly in front of his face. To stare at it until dawn surely would drive him insane.

Another glance at Yagi. His eyes were still closed.

Kan pulled off his left glove and leaned forward and removed the wire from the switch, the extra precaution he had added back at Tama Airfield. All that remained was to lift the locking bracket and throw it. Should he do it now? He leaned back and pondered this for a while, visualizing the moment, his heartbeat thundering in his ears, louder than the engines.

He began to breathe deeply, trying to make himself calm. The dryness of the air flowing through his mask didn't help. To divert his mind, he counted the aircraft's ribs visible in the compartment and estimated how many there were in the entire length of the airframe. Were they made of aluminum? He contemplated the element, its nucleus of fourteen protons and thirteen neutrons, its outer shell of thirteen orbiting electrons, its melting point of 606 degrees, its vaporization point of

2,500 degrees. The detonation of the bomb would generate temperatures much greater than this, temperatures perhaps greater even than the surface of the sun. It would turn the plane into vapor and him along with it, and Yagi beside him and Onda up front with the rest of the crew. Kan and these men, already parts of a single machine, would then become united in the most intimate way, transformed into a gas and their atoms commingled, some to drift down to become part of the ocean, some to be carried along with the air currents. By this time tomorrow, remnants of his being could be in China or Russia or back home in Japan. He could be wafted across the Pacific to Hawaii or America or the Amazon jungles, or on to Europe, India, Australia, Tibet.

Or would he drift higher? Kan looked up through the glass panel in the fuselage over his head, at the stars, a wash of tiny points of light. A blurred line cut across them from the crack in the lens of his glasses, the result of Colonel Sagara's blow. Perhaps he would float his way up there, beyond the bounds of the Earth, on and on through the desolation . . .

He continued on like this as the minutes crept by, then an hour. Yagi remained motionless beside him, his eyes occasionally open, occasionally closed, his right hand going through the motions of rolling the dice. What was he thinking? It occurred to Kan that they were trapped in a version of hell—an iron-ribbed, claustrophobic version of hell where the roar of the engines was the howling of demons.

Finally, after an eternity, Kamibeppu's voice in his earphones: "Twenty-five degrees."

Captain Onda turned off the autopilot and eased the Renzan onto its new heading for the second leg of the journey, almost due south to Tinian's latitude of 14.5.

He checked his watch. A quarter after three o'clock in the morning. Only fifteen minutes behind schedule. The headwind they were facing was more moderate than he had allowed for, largely offsetting the poor performance of the engines.

Confidence rising, Onda leveled out the plane onto heading 170 degrees. They had now passed the halfway mark of the mission, 1,300 kilometers behind them, just over one thousand to go. If their luck held for another three hours, they would reach Tinian on schedule, at dawn.

In his position behind the cockpit, flight engineer Otani began pumping fuel from the outboard tanks into the dedicated inboard tanks for Engines Two and Three, which were now down to 25 percent. The larger dedicated tanks for Engines One and Four would be good for another hour.

Engine Three began throbbing. Otani increased the fuel-air mixture but could not coax it back to smooth function. Instead, the engine started to knock—so loud it was audible in the cockpit over the roar of the other three engines.

It was the fuel from one of the outboard tanks, starboard side, numbers six to nine. Something was wrong. Otani could visualize what was happening inside the engine, the premature combustion of gasoline inside the chambers. He could see the results on the rising pressure and temperature gauges.

He started shutting the outboard tanks down, trying to isolate the problem.

The knocking continued.

Captain Onda was watching the airspeed and altitude gauges. The Renzan, robbed of even more power, was slowing and drifting lower. A dozen possible causes flashed through his mind. Blocked fuel line. Broken fuel pump. Failed fuel injector. Clogged air filter. Clogged strainer. Or was the problem the fuel itself? One of the mechanics back at Tama Airfield had made a guarded comment about it. But the barrels pumped into the tanks had been clearly marked Number One gasoline. Onda had inspected the labels himself. Number One gasoline was the reduced standard for top-grade aviation fuel set the previous year but was still perfectly sufficient, octane 91.

The descent continued. They were now skimming the wispy tops of clouds at 6,000 meters. Then the clouds swallowed them and the night sky disappeared.

Navigator Kamibeppu turned back from his position in the nose. "I can't see anything! I can't get a fix in this!"

Onda flashed a glance at Yoshino. If they couldn't stay above the clouds for Kamibeppu to take star sightings, that would mean continuing on dead reckoning alone, which would make finding Tinian almost impossible. They *had* to stay above the clouds. But that would mean pushing the engines even harder. And that could be fatal.

Onda set his hand on the throttles.

Keizo Kan stared at the guillotine switch. It had become hateful to him. He wanted to smash it. He wanted to rip it from its mounting and stomp on it with his boots. Then his anger gave way again to his fear and he heard his heartbeat running wild in his ears. Then another surge of anger—at himself, at his fear, at his weakness.

He took deep breaths to steady himself.

You coward! Just do it!

It would be over so fast he wouldn't feel a thing. A flash of light and he would be gone.

He pulled off the fur-lined glove from his injured right hand. He wanted to feel the pain. He leaned forward and lifted the locking bracket from the switch, the metal brittle with cold.

He settled back in his seat and resumed his contemplation. The Daikon's trigger was now unencumbered. A single motion would end it all.

Do it. Just do it. One second and it will be over.

Kan continued to stare at the switch, not noticing the increasing whine of the engines, not noticing PO Yagi's eyes open beside him.

Yagi looked up through the glass over his head. They seemed to be flying in clouds. He could feel the Renzan slowly climbing.

He glanced across at Kan. The scientist was staring straight ahead, an intense look on his face, completely absorbed. And his glove was off, revealing his swollen right hand.

Yagi followed Kan's gaze to the trigger. He saw that the locking bracket had been lifted.

Kan leaned forward. He was reaching for the switch.

Yagi lurched out of his seat. "What are you doing!" He was pulled back by the plug of his flight suit.

He yanked it out of the rheostat and threw himself at Kan.

A shudder passed through the plane.

TWENTY-FOUR

"IT'S NUMBER THREE," SAID THE FLIGHT ENGINEER, LIEUTENANT OTANI. HE WATCHED AS THE needle on the pressure gauge dropped and the temperature soared.

Captain Onda eased back on the throttles, but it was too late. Another cough, followed by a muffled explosion and a lick of flame illuminating the night, and the propeller on Number Three ground to a halt.

Otani had already hit the extinguisher switch and shut off the flow of fuel to the engine. Onda adjusted the port throttles to balance the power and keep the plane level on three engines, two on the left side, one on the right. The needle on the airspeed indicator dropped below 300 kilometers per hour. They were losing altitude as well, the Renzan seeking denser air for support. It settled at 4,000 meters, in the midst of dense cloud.

The mission had just failed. Without Kamibeppu's star sightings and accurate navigation, the chance of finding Tinian, a speck in the ocean, was extremely remote. Morning would come, they would conduct a futile search for the island, their fuel would run out, and they would crash into the sea. Onda could see no other conclusion.

Should he continue? Make the desperate gesture? That would be the honorable thing.

But that would mean wasting the heaven-sent weapon.

He hesitated, dreading Colonel Sagara's rage.

He spoke into the interphone: "We're turning back."

In the radio compartment, Keizo Kan heard the words through a fog of confusion. He felt the aircraft bank as it went into a turn.

PO Yagi was looming over him, pressing him into his seat. Keeping one hand on Kan's chest, Yagi reached out and flipped the locking bracket back onto the Daikon's triggering switch. Then he was in Kan's face, snarling: "Don't touch it!"

Kan stared at him blankly. Had he actually been about to set off the bomb? His mind was in such turmoil that he didn't know.

He nodded weakly. "It's all right. I'm all right."

Yagi's grip relaxed. He made Kan switch seats, moving him farther away from the trigger. Then he restored the twist of wire around the locking bracket as a further precaution.

Kan was returning to himself now. He became aware of a burning in his right hand. It was freezing. He pulled on his glove and settled into his seat, feeling shattered.

Humph. Yagi's familiar sound. Kan looked over to see the petty officer rocking back and forth as if releasing the hours of tension, his expression somewhere between a scowl and a smile.

They continued northwest by dead reckoning for two and a half hours, halfway back to Tama Airfield at reduced speed, coddling the three functioning engines. A tense moment when flight engineer Otani began pumping fuel from the outboard tanks to refill the dedicated tanks feeding Engines One and Four. More throbbing, this time from Engine One, but a catastrophe was averted. They continued on with six of the eighteen outboard wing tanks shut down. There was clearly something wrong with the 1,400 liters of fuel they were holding. They didn't dare burn it. Getting back home would be a close thing.

Six o'clock in the morning, the sun breaking above the horizon. Captain Onda took the Renzan down to 2,000 meters, out of the clouds, hoping to spot the Ogasawara Islands and fix their position.

The islands were nowhere to be seen. Kamibeppu went to the back of the plane to scan the rear horizon from the tail gunner's position, passing through the compartment where Kan and Yagi were seated. He saw nothing, only gray ocean.

"Is everything all right?" Kan asked as Kamibeppu returned to the flight deck.

"Halfway there," the navigator replied.

Onda took the aircraft back up into the safety of the clouds, altitude 3,000 meters. It was as high as he dared push the plane. They continued on through the white.

At 8:05, Kamibeppu's dead reckoning put them within sight of the coast of Japan. Onda took another Philopon tablet to stave off his mounting fatigue, then signaled to copilot Yoshino that they would make another descent out of the clouds. Soon flashes of ocean began to peek through the mist. Then, like a curtain swept back, the view ahead cleared.

They all recognized the graceful arc of shore in an instant. They were nearing the north end of the Chiba Peninsula, 100 kilometers off course.

"Heading 320," said Kamibeppu, making a quick calculation. "We're 230 kilometers out."

Onda felt a wave of relief. Less than an hour to go. They had enough fuel. They would make it.

He banked the Renzan to the left. An armada of ships came into view. Hulking battleships. Cruisers. Destroyers. And aircraft carriers, more than Onda could count.

It was the American fleet.

"Fighters!"

Captain Yoshino was pointing at one of the carriers, a dozen aircraft circling above it like flies.

Onda had already come out of the turn and was advancing the throttles, straining the engines as he pulled back on the yoke. Their only hope was to climb back up and hide in the clouds. Slowly, agonizingly slowly, the Renzan ascended.

Yoshino: "They've seen us. They're coming up!"

Onda went on the interphone: "Otani! Turret gun! Yagi! Get on the tail gun!"

Yagi leaped out of his seat in the radio operator's compartment and disappeared through the rear door, scrambling back to the tail gunner's position. After the long hours of pent-up tension, he was hungry for action. He squeezed into the narrow space, settled into the rear-facing seat, and plugged in his helmet.

"Two fighters approaching," he said, cocking the twenty-millimeter Type 99. "Six hundred meters out." He flicked off the safety, sighting on the growing black dots.

"Don't fire. Wait until they do," said Onda. He was hoping the Americans had been confused by the sight of them appearing from seaward rather than from the land. Caution might buy them enough time to get back into the clouds.

Yagi, squinting through the thick ballistic glass: "Three hundred meters . . . Two hundred meters."

Onda turned to see an aircraft, blue with a white star, coming into view outside his starboard-side window. It was a Corsair. It was so close that he could see the American pilot staring at him.

"Onda!"

It was Yoshino. Onda turned to see his copilot staring at a second Corsair on their left. Then the two fighters were peeling away.

Yagi's voice in the earphones: "They're coming around—"

A stream of bullets shot past the cockpit, followed an instant later by the sound of Yagi returning fire from the tail gun and Otani from the turret. The Renzan lurched. Onda felt something give with the rudder. He fought to control the aircraft as the world turned white.

Keizo Kan sat frozen in his lonely seat in the radio operator's compartment, waiting for another burst of machine gun fire to rip through the plane. It didn't come. Finally he noticed the uniform white through the window over his head. They were in clouds. The Americans couldn't see them. And if the Americans couldn't see them, they might survive.

It was the second time he had lived through an enemy attack in an airplane. The experience did not get easier with repetition. His heart was beating so hard that it left him feeling ill, as if the terror had damaged the organ. He unsnapped his face mask, which had been hanging under his chin, and cast it aside as he took in deep breaths. A wave of heat swept over his body. He unzipped his flight suit and pulled it open, letting in the cold air. The helmet went next. He pulled it off and laid it in his lap, not noticing the hair from his head that came off with it.

"Tama Airfield. Tama Airfield."

The crippled Renzan had continued west through the clouds and was descending now that they were well inland, away from the American fleet patrolling the coast. Captain Onda was flying at 400 meters, hopefully low enough not to be spotted by prowling enemy aircraft. He would have preferred to fly even lower, hugging the ground, but he didn't dare—not on three engines and without a functioning rudder.

"Tama Airfield. This is Ko-G8-3. Are you there?"

Another banking turn, 30 degrees, the Renzan clumsily yawing. The terrain below was mountains scarred by clear-cutting, large swaths completely denuded of trees. Onda, Yoshino, and Kamibeppu were all scanning the sky for fighters. If there was an attack, it would come from above. PO Yagi remained at the tail gun, watching behind.

Flight engineer Otani had his eyes on the fuel gauges. The needle for the Number Two engine was reading effectively empty. Number One and Number Four engines had another twenty minutes at best.

"Tama Airfield, this is Ko-G8-3. Do you read me?"

The headphones crackled. A clipped acknowledgment. Nothing more.

"Tama Airfield, I've lost the rudder and an engine. I'm coming in."

The terrain was flattening. Onda brought the Renzan down another 100 meters, approaching the airfield from the south. Sweat glistened on his face. Yoshino beside him kept craning around in his seat, looking from the gauges to scan for threats in the sky.

There was the town of Hachioji ahead, the thread of the Tama River beyond it. Then the airfield came into view.

Onda banked right, yawing wildly, and began his final approach.

"Flaps fifteen," he said.

Yoshino confirmed: "Flaps fifteen."

"Landing gear down."

Yoshino threw the switch. A whine and chunk confirmed that the wheels had descended and locked.

"Landing gear down."

Flight engineer Otani tapped one of the gauges. Number Two engine was running on fumes now. It would die at any moment. His mind went to the 1,400 liters of fuel still in the outboard tanks, the foul fuel they didn't dare use. If they crashed, the Renzan would become a fireball. They would all burn.

They were passing over the Tama River, not much more than a stream amid a wide swatch of wetland. A freight train line, a village, a cluster of barracks.

Two kilometers out now, altitude one hundred meters. The Renzan's tail slewed to port. Onda brought it back. It was like skating on ice. He reminded himself that his eye level in the cockpit was four meters up off the ground.

"Thirty meters," said Yoshino.

Onda throttled back on the three functioning engines. Number Two engine died.

"Ten meters. We just lost Number Two."

The Renzan came down hard, its starboard wheel exploding. It bounced and came down again and veered to the left, sending men who were watching from the side of the runway scrambling for safety. Yoshino throttled down. Onda, fighting with the controls, muscled the plane back to center.

"Brakes!" said Yoshino, willing them to stop, stiff in his seat.

Onda heaved down on the pedals and brought the big plane to a halt at the north end of the runway.

The engines were silent. The hatch was open. Kan climbed down the ladder and stood on firm ground for the first time in eleven hours, the phantom roar of the engines still in their ears. He felt empty. His legs were weak. He wanted nothing more than to lie down and sleep.

Something touched the top of his head. He looked up. A drop struck his face.

It was starting to rain.

TWENTY-FIVE

"COWARD!" COLONEL SAGARA HAD ROARED INTO THE PHONE. CAPTAIN ONDA HAD BEEN ON THE other end of the line, calling from Tama Airfield to inform him of the Renzan's return.

"How dare you return! What happened to your fighting spirit? You didn't prepare yourself properly! You lost your nerve! You've dishonored yourself!"

The colonel continued ranting until he heard the sound of weeping at the other end of the line.

He fell silent, his lips quivering.

His face slowly relaxed.

"All right," he said, finally ready to listen. "Tell me what happened."

It had been Number Two gasoline in the Renzan's fuel tanks. The barrels had been labeled "No. 1 Gasoline," with an octane number of 91, but they had actually contained Number Two, octane 87. And it had come from here, Army Fuel Headquarters.

Sagara looked out at the disguised refinery complex, still untouched by American bombers, as his staff car passed through the front gate. He was in Fuchu, a half-hour drive west from his War Ministry office in central Tokyo. Tokyo Racecourse, closed since 1943, was visible to the south, its stables housing Australian prisoners of war. To the north, the sprawling cemetery where Sagara's father was buried. The sharp sulfur smell of rotten eggs filled the air.

As for the engine flameout, that had been caused by A-Go having found its way into three outboard tanks, the wretched gasoline-alcohol mix that was used only for training and had sent so many trainee pilots plummeting to their deaths. A-Go was not intended for use in combat. And it certainly was not to be used in high-altitude flight. Two members of the ground crew at Tama Airfield had already been demoted for this slipup. But the trouble had started with the mislabeled fuel—the fuel that had come from Army Fuel Headquarters. Sagara was going to have a word with a Colonel Hattori about it.

He struggled out of the back seat of his staff car and limped into the refinery's headquarters building. He was finding it difficult to walk today. The midnight return from Tama Airfield in the cramped motorcycle sidecar had somehow damaged his leg.

He passed through the entrance and made his inquiry.

He regretted his harsh words to Captain Onda. For he now realized that fate was at work. With the Renzan's return, an opportunity had presented itself, a chance to correct War Minister Anami's order to attack Tinian Island. It was Anami who had forced him to give up his vision, to stray from his destiny, his preordained path. Use the heaven-sent atomic bomb to attack a military target after the Americans had destroyed so many Japanese cities? No, he would not make that mistake again. The time had come for independent action.

A clerk appeared and led Colonel Sagara down a hall.

Luckily, the aircraft could be repaired. The wrecked engine was being replaced with a nearly new Homare 24 salvaged from a grounded Saiun reconnaissance plane. And the damage to the rudder had turned out to be only a severed cable. A bigger job, already under way, was to strip out all the guns and armor. The Renzan had to be as light as possible for its new purpose, its *intended* purpose. And that meant the man

Yagi was no longer needed. Including a navy man, not to mention a Korean, had sullied the purity of the mission and brought them bad luck.

He arrived at Colonel Hattori's office and was shown inside. The two men were of the same rank. They settled into facing chairs and the meeting took an informal tone.

"Yes, well, it's unfortunate if a labeling error occurred," said Hattori, after Sagara explained what had happened. "But you know the situation. The aviation fuel we're producing is going to frontline bases. If you received any from us, of *any* grade, I'd say that was rather generous on our part, wouldn't you?"

"It was responsible for the failure of an important mission," Sagara said, struggling to keep his temper in check. Offending Hattori would not serve his purpose.

"An important mission?" Hattori raised his eyebrows, interest piqued.

Sagara didn't respond.

Hattori's eyebrows subsided. He leaned back and crossed his arms, like closing a door. It was then that Sagara noticed the black-bordered photographs on the shelf behind him. The man had lost two sons in the war.

"Do you know what has been happening at the Imperial Palace?" he asked.

Hattori nodded. "I've heard rumors."

"What would you do if the war ended? If we allowed ourselves to surrender?"

"I would kill myself," Hattori replied without hesitation.

Sagara made up his mind. This was a man to be trusted. And his assistance was needed.

"It was a mission to attack an American base in the south," he explained. "But the target is changed now." He went on to lay out the broad strokes of the new mission.

Hattori's eyebrows rose again, this time in wonder. "Is that even possible?"

"Entirely possible. We have the weapon. And we have the plane."

"So what are you asking?"

Sagara leaned forward, his eyes bright. "I need at least sixty-five barrels of the highest-quality aviation fuel you have. Preferably refined from southern crudes. Or Omonogawa."

"Impossible! Even the Emperor couldn't get that. We don't have it. It's all gone."

Sagara let out a growling breath. "I need high-grade aviation gasoline. What can you give me?"

Hattori began shuffling through papers on his desk. He arrived at one and studied it with pursed lips. "I shouldn't be offering you this," he said, "but we have some stocks of experimental fuel, high-quality aviation gasoline refined from pine root oil. I think we could manage sixty-five barrels."

"Pine root oil!" Sagara erupted out of his seat at what felt like an affront. "I need proper aviation fuel, not some experimental tarry stuff! Put that in your trucks!"

Hattori, equally affronted, rose up to face him. "Our pine root aviation fuel isn't tarry! It's every bit as good as Number One gasoline. Even better!"

The two men settled back into their seats and scowled at each other.

"Do you have any idea," grumbled Hattori, "what that program has cost us? Our soybean oil distillates have been disappointing, I admit. But our pine root oil program *has* been successful. We've refined aviation gasoline of the highest quality from pine roots."

Sagara's scowl began to fade. "All right," he said without enthusiasm. "Tell me about it."

Hattori took a moment to master his clearly offended feelings. He grudgingly located a report and handed it to the colonel.

"These are our test results for aviation fuel refined from pine root oil using high-pressure hydrocracking." He turned to the second page and pointed to a chart. "Look at that. Octane 93. Octane 94.5. Octane 97. Extremely high grade."

Sagara was nodding. The numbers were impressive.

"The only thing I can't speak to," continued Hattori, "is long-term performance. Beyond fifty hours, I can't guarantee there won't be some residue buildup in the engines. But that shouldn't be a problem with this mission you're proposing. How long a flight, do you think?"

"Around fifteen hours," said Sagara, scrutinizing the paper.

"Then it shouldn't be a problem at all. But why don't I call in the lieutenant who did the engine testing. He can give you all the information you need."

The aviation gasoline from pine root oil was gratefully accepted. Colonel Hattori agreed to have it sent to Tama Airfield the next day. After shaking Colonel Sagara's hand and seeing him out of his office, Hattori sat back at his desk, in front of his dead sons, marveling at the audacity of the mission the War Ministry officer was proposing. Could it succeed? If so, it would be a fitting blow to the Americans. Just retribution.

He gazed at the map adorning his wall and traced the route across the Pacific Ocean to the target.

"San Francisco," he murmured.

TWENTY-SIX

KEIZO KAN STARED DOWN IN HORROR AT THE MAP THAT CAPTAIN ONDA HAD UNROLLED ON THE low table, following the lines on the onionskin overlay moving east.

"San Francisco?" His voice was strangled.

"Colonel Sagara told me to thank you," Onda quietly replied, laying his hand on Kan's shoulder. He had been subdued ever since their return. "If you hadn't brought Project Fu-Go to our attention, he never would have had the idea. The Fu-Go people had only limited information on conditions heading south. But here . . . "—he tapped the wavy lines overlaid on the map—"they knew a great deal about these Pacific Ocean air currents. They used them to send their balloon bombs to the United States, thousands of them. They assured the Colonel that they're consistent at high altitude, up around 10,000 meters. They always blow east from Japan. The speed varies, it's generally higher in winter, but the currents always move east."

They were seated in a circle on the floor in Onda's room in the barracks, Onda to Kan's right, navigator Kamibeppu to his left, co-pilot Yoshino and flight engineer Otani facing, companionably sharing a cigarette, passing it back and forth.

PO Yagi wasn't with them. He had been removed from the mission, his role eliminated along with the tail gun. He had done nothing more than nod when Captain Onda informed him, his manner restrained after the harrowing experience on the plane. He was now representing the Navy in a lowlier fashion, helping the mechanics and ground crew strip weight from the Renzan and install auxiliary fuel tanks in the bomb bay alongside the Daikon.

Yagi's absence left Kan feeling gutted. The thought of sitting in the radio operator's compartment, completely alone—how would he bear it? And with the target now to be San Francisco . . . He should never have mentioned Fu-Go. Stupid! Why had he tried to be helpful?

Otani was sucking air through his teeth, looking doubtful. "Ten thousand meters . . . We never got above eight thousand. We need better fuel."

"And we'll have it," said Onda. "The Colonel has made arrangements at Army Fuel Headquarters for proper aviation fuel this time. No more Number Two gas. This will be high octane. We should receive it today."

"No more A-Go?" said Yoshino with a chuckle, making light of the near catastrophe the volatile alcohol fuel in the outboard tanks had caused.

"No more A-Go," said Onda, smiling. "Let's leave it for the trainees."

Kamibeppu was still overwhelmed by the yawning expanse of ocean, three times farther than he had ever navigated before. "That must be at least 9,000 kilometers," he said.

"Closer to 8,500," said Onda. "Normally that would be beyond the range of even the Renzan. But by flying at high altitude, we'll be able to ride the air currents blowing up there, a river of air. So no headwind this time. We'll have a powerful tailwind. It could add an extra 200 kilometers per hour to our speed. That would make it a fifteen-hour flight, but we should be able to manage eighteen hours if we have to. It'll be risky, of course, but the only risk is the distance. The Americans won't be expecting us to fly all the way across the Pacific, and they won't be able to spot us at 10,000 meters. They won't see us until we're on our final approach."

Onda patted Kan on the knee. "That's when I'm going to need you, Sensei. You studied in America. You speak English very well, I believe."

Kan gave an involuntary start. He had slept only fitfully in the twenty-four hours since their return and was feeling light-headed and jumpy. "I can speak English," he said, "but my accent isn't good."

"Well, it will have to do," said Onda, unfolding a map of San Francisco and spreading it out over the larger chart of the ocean. It was a prewar street map, full color, showing the city in detail. "We'll drop down to 400 meters and approach from the west." He ran his finger along the map's most notable feature, an immense rectangle of green stabbing more than five kilometers inland from the coast. "Golden Gate Park," he said, reading the name. "We use this as our guide. We fly in low, following the north edge of the park, and detonate the bomb here, right at the center."

Onda was tapping the target.

"San Francisco City Hall. A large domed building, open space all around it, looks just like the Capitol Building in Washington. What could be better than that? We can't miss it. If the effect is anything like Hiroshima and Nagasaki, immediate blast damage and then the fires will destroy most of the city."

Onda turned to Kan.

"What I need from you, Sensei, is to speak English to the Americans for the final few minutes, if we're challenged. There's a good chance we'll be challenged. Say that the plane is having mechanical trouble, that we're lost, that our compass is broken—anything to keep them confused. Can you do that?"

Kan gazed down at the map. He had lived across the bay from San Francisco for three years, when he was studying at the University of California in Berkeley. He had completed his doctorate there. He had met Noriko there. He had wandered the streets of San Francisco and visited the sights there numerous times—including City Hall, where the bomb was to be detonated. He and Noriko had walked past the distinctive dome on the very evening he had so awkwardly revealed his love, the very evening they had agreed to marry.

His eyes shifted northwest to Noriko's street, hilly Buchanan Avenue where it intersected with Pine. He returned to City Hall and continued east to the distinctive triangular intersection. Yes, the Warfield theater was marked.

Where they had seen Garbo and Taylor in *Camille* . . .

The room started to swim. Kan placed his hands on the floor for support.

"Are you all right?" said Onda.

Kan squeezed his eyes shut as an image of the terrifying final moments flashed through his mind. He saw the coastline approaching over an ocean of blue, Golden Gate Bridge off to the left, the green rectangle of park down below, the network of streets. He saw himself stammering into the radio, trying to speak through his terror, his hand on the trigger, waiting for Onda's instruction. He saw Noriko's mother in her apron covered with daisies staring at the distant plane from her porch and being blinded by an intense flash of light.

He felt Kamibeppu's arm around his shoulder. He felt Onda examining his injured right hand, so much worse looking now, the skin torn by his thick glove on the plane.

"Are you all right, Sensei?"

The spell passed. Kan opened his eyes and looked around at the concerned faces.

"It's all right," he said. "I'm all right."

"Good," said Onda. "Because we're going to need you." He looked at the others, the sparkle coming back into his eyes. "If we test the engines this afternoon and everything is all right, we should be able to leave tomorrow. What do you say?"

Copilot Yoshino, navigator Kamibeppu, flight engineer Otani—they all solemnly nodded.

"All right," said Onda. "If the engines check out, tomorrow we go."

•   •   •

Kan spoke to PO Yagi after lunch, as they were making their way from the mess hall. They detoured behind the pilot training school building so they wouldn't be overheard.

"The Yankees deserve it," said Yagi, unmoved by the audacity of the new target. "They deserve a hundred attacks after what they've done to our cities. Don't you want revenge?"

"Yes, of course," said Kan, annoyance coming into his voice. "But think about it. If we succeed . . . "

He fell silent. He had bottled up his private thoughts, his dangerous thoughts, for so long that he no longer knew how to express them.

They continued on for another moment in silence. The runway came into view.

The runway. It would be Kan's last contact with the ground. He had been lucky once. That would not happen again. The Renzan would roll down the runway and lift into the air and he would never again set foot on the earth.

Yagi inclined his head toward Kan's ear and lowered his voice. "Over there," he whispered, jutting his chin toward the far side. "See the firing range? It's unguarded. And there's no fence. I checked. See those berms? Wait until it's dark, then go through there, between those berms, then turn north and go to the conduit and follow it east. There are hardly any people over there. No one will see you."

Kan gazed longingly across the runway.

"Onda can take off without you," whispered Yagi. "There's no need for you to go. Why should you go?"

The vision of escape faded as Noriko returned to Kan's mind. What would happen to her? If only he could speak to her one last time.

"Wait until dark," Yagi was saying. "Then just walk away. It'll be easy."

Kan continued to gaze at the runway.

He lowered his eyes and shook his head sadly.

"I can't."

TWENTY-SEVEN

THE FREIGHT TRAIN SLOWED TO A CRAWL AS IT APPROACHED THE TOWN OF MATSUDO, THE rail yard visible around the curve in the tracks up ahead. The bearded stranger with the bag full of watches eased himself off the roof of the boxcar where they were riding and climbed down the ladder affixed to the side. It would be dangerous, he said, to stay on the train any longer. As it neared Tokyo there would be more guards at the stations.

Noriko Kan warily followed him off the roof and onto the ladder. She had known this man for scarcely two hours, ever since he had beckoned to her to join him on the passing freight train and save herself a long walk.

"Make sure you hit the ground running," he said before letting go. He landed expertly, his legs pumping, then slowed to a walk.

The thought flashed through Noriko's mind that she should stay on the train and leave him behind. He was likely a draft dodger or a deserter, for he was a perfect specimen for military conscription, healthy and well-built and no more than thirty under the scraggly beard hiding his face. He called himself Ogawa, no doubt a false name, a traveling repairman of watches and clocks. It was a lucrative trade, he said, since new timepieces were no longer available on the market and even broken ones were worth a good deal. He had dozens of watches in his old army rucksack that he intended to barter for land in Tokyo, which was going for cheap. "You don't have any land in Tokyo for sale, do you?" he had teased, grinning at her beggarly appearance. "I'll buy it!"

The freight train continued on into Matsudo, leaving Ogawa behind. Why had the man even been riding on a freight train? If he had the wherewithal to buy land, he could afford a train ticket. This suggested that there was something criminal about him. On the other hand, he had been generous in sharing his food.

"Come on!" Ogawa called out after her. "They'll be patrolling the yards!"

Noriko looked ahead at where the tracks split into sidings and this time saw that there was indeed someone up there—a station guard or just a person walking along, she couldn't tell. If it was a guard and she was caught, she would be doubly in trouble, first for illegally riding a train, second for having no papers.

She jumped off the train, landed awkwardly on the siding, and fell. Ogawa jogged up and helped her to her feet.

"Are you all right?"

Noriko gingerly examined her scraped elbow and tested her ankle. "Yes, I think so."

They found her shoe in the undergrowth and started walking, veering away from the train tracks to follow a road heading southwest. Ueno Station was no more than twenty kilometers farther along. Noriko decided that she would walk the rest of the way, that she would take no more chances with trains, regardless of what Ogawa might do. If her strength held out, she would reach the Riken by late afternoon.

"You mentioned Hiroshima and Nagasaki," she ventured, returning to something Ogawa had said in his disjointed monologue before they jumped off the train.

"That's why I'm going to Tokyo. Like I told you. Now is the time to buy land, before it all ends."

"But . . . what happened?"

He gave her an incredulous look. "You haven't heard? Everyone's been talking about it."

Noriko shook her head.

"Well, I hope you don't have family there," Ogawa airily said. He stopped himself, turning serious. "You don't have family in Hiroshima or Nagasaki, do you?"

"No."

"Good. Because they aren't there anymore. The Americans wiped them out with only one bomb. Genji bakudan. Genso bakudan . . . "

Noriko felt a stab of recognition.

"Genshi bakudan?"

Ogawa snapped his fingers. "Genshi bakudan. That's it! So you *have* heard. One bomb to wipe out a whole city. As powerful as all the bombs in two thousand B-29s. Even the *great* Imperial Army can't stand up to that. They're finished. The bastards are done."

His sarcasm and open sedition shocked Noriko almost as much as the news that the Americans had used atomic bombs, a weapon that her husband, Keizo, had privately assured her would take many years to develop. She looked around, fearful that someone might have overheard.

"That's why I need to get to Tokyo," Ogawa continued, oblivious. "Everyone thinks it's going to be next, so now is the time to buy up property cheap. I bet I can get two thousand tsubo of land with these watches."

He gave her a sidelong look, an appraising look. "You can come with me. A little more weight and some new clothes and you'd look all right. It's been lonely for me, you know. On the road."

"Thank you for your kindness," Noriko murmured, resolved to part ways with this man. She thought for a while about how best to do it, then started putting a slight hitch in her step.

Ogawa didn't notice. They were on the other side of Matsudo now, having bypassed the rail yard, and were veering back toward the train line. The trestle bridge over the Edogawa River was visible up ahead.

Noriko affected a more pronounced limp and started groaning a little.

"What's the matter?" Ogawa asked.

"I must have twisted my ankle jumping off the train."

He took her by the arm. "Let's go on a little farther. Then we can rest."

They pressed on, Noriko working hard to maintain her limp. They crossed the bridge over the Edogawa, looking down at the sluggish water as they walked on the ties. There was a town on the other side, one of the dozens of outlying communities ringing Tokyo. They passed a weaving factory, a paper mill, a chemical plant on the right side of the tracks. All closed.

"You see?" said Ogawa, pointing ahead to another bridge over the next river. "There's the Nakagawa already."

"I'd like to rest for a moment," Noriko said.

Ogawa gripped her arm more firmly. "Let's get across first."

They crossed the steel bridge over the Nakagawa and entered the town on the other side. There were signs of bomb damage here, a factory with its smokestack knocked down and one side caved in and the blackened squares where blocks of wooden houses had stood. Then, as they crested a rise, the vista of Tokyo came into view, a seemingly endless plain of destruction disappearing in the haze far to the west.

"Aaah," said Ogawa, letting out an exclamation as he stopped to take it all in. He momentarily forgot about Noriko and let go of her arm. She thought about running but knew that would be useless. He was stronger and faster than she was.

She moved to the side of the road and sat down.

"We're almost there," said Ogawa.

"I'm sorry," said Noriko. "I need to rest."

A look of irritation clouded Ogawa's face. He started looking around. "All right. Let's go over there under those trees."

He took her by the arm and led her toward a grove that had escaped the ax and the saw, a secluded spot. Noriko was afraid now. She no longer had any doubt about his intentions.

They sat down under the branches, out of sight of the road and the scattering of houses along it. Ogawa opened his knapsack and produced two more balls of millet and rice, one for Noriko and one for himself.

"Thank you," she said.

He took out a little packet of salt and seasoned the ball in Noriko's hand.

"Thank you," she said again.

Ogawa began greedily eating. Noriko was looking around. She noted a broken tree branch a few steps away.

"Go ahead," said Ogawa, taking another bite. "Eat. It's for you."

Noriko forced herself to nibble. She was hungry, but her nerves had closed up her stomach.

Ogawa had finished now and was starting to watch her, a different kind of greed in his eyes.

His hand crept over. He started stroking Noriko's leg. She pulled back.

"So coy," he said, grinning. He moved closer and became more aggressive.

Noriko finished her meal with Ogawa tugging at her trousers. She knew what she had to do now.

"Don't tear them," she said.

"Well, then help me a little."

Mustering all her courage, she gave him a lascivious smile. "Close your eyes."

Ogawa, excited by this, eagerly closed his eyes.

"Now turn around."

Ogawa turned.

Noriko picked up a fist-sized rock she had spotted. She raised it, hesitated for only a moment, then brought it down on Ogawa's skull.

He let out an animal yelp and his whole body went stiff. He lurched up and wheeled about, his eyes wide.

"Why did you do that?"

"I'm sorry," said Noriko. She reared back again with the rock and smashed it down on Ogawa's forehead, dropping him to the ground.

She stood over him, shocked, looking down at his body. Had she killed him? It certainly looked like it, seeing blood oozing from his scalp. He didn't appear to be breathing.

She looked at the stone in her hand, a bloody scrap of Ogawa's skin and hair adhering to it.

She cast it away. Her first instinct was to run, but she didn't. She looked around, suddenly fearful that she might have been seen. No one seemed to be about. No one was watching.

Suddenly Ogawa came back to life, drawing in a long, ragged gasp.

Noriko started backing away.

Ogawa was drawing himself up onto his hands and knees now, his head hanging down.

His back arched. He vomited up his meal.

Noriko turned and ran.

She didn't go far. The thought of Ogawa coming up behind her drove her into hiding a few hundred meters farther down the tracks, peeking out from behind the crumbling remains of an abandoned house. Finally, just as she was about to give up, she saw him passing, rucksack on his back with his hoard of watches. He was walking slowly and kept raising his hand to his head. Noriko felt a flood of relief that she hadn't killed him—relief mixed with remorse, for he didn't look at all like a threat now, only a pathetic, stoop-shouldered figure stumbling along, someone who had given her food.

She waited until he was out of sight down the line before coming out from behind the wall. She followed him west for a time, keeping well back, then branched off onto a road. It wouldn't be much longer now. She could see the Arakawa drainage canal up ahead, the twin steel trestles that crossed it leading into Adachi district. The Sumida River was only a short distance beyond that. Fortunately she would cross the Sumida well to the north of the Umamichi neighborhood where they had once lived, and the Kototoi Bridge where she had spent that terrible night in the river. She did not want to see those places again.

The energy from the food Ogawa had given her was almost used up. She was desperately tired. The hum approaching in the distance therefore took some time to enter her brain. When it did, she started scanning the sky, her heartbeat increasing. It took her a moment to spot the source, three specks to the west, heading her way. They were too high to see clearly, but there was no mistaking what they were. A trio of B-29s. Her logic told her they were likely observation planes and therefore harmless. But the animal inside her, responding to the sound of the engines, made her afraid.

She could see something else now, a cloud gently descending. She didn't know at first what it was, her eyes locked on the bombers as they passed overhead and banked left over Tokyo Bay to return to the south. Then the cloud was nearing the ground and she could make out that it was a rain of paper, tens of thousands of leaflets that the bombers had dropped. Most were falling to the west to blanket the ravaged city. Some, however, were being blown closer, fluttering down to settle on the road up ahead.

She continued on to where the leaflets had fallen. People were exiting nearby houses to join passersby in chasing down the half sheets of blue paper to read the message from the sky. Noriko had seen several leaflets dropped by American bombers earlier in the summer, warning the Japanese people that their own government was leading them to destruction and promising further horrors if Japan continued to fight. She picked up one of them now, assuming it contained a similar message. One glance at the official-looking prose and she knew it was different.

"To the Japanese people," it began. "The Japanese government, acting on the wishes of the Emperor of Japan, has informed the Allied powers of the United States, Britain, the Soviet Union, and China that it wishes to end hostilities and bring the war to an end. Below is the full text of the message we received. On the other side of this paper is our reply. We urge your government to accept our terms for an honorable surrender so that you may begin the work of building a new and peace-loving Japan."

Noriko read both sides of the leaflet. The government's peace overture had specified only one condition, the preservation of the Emperor, and the Allied response did not seem to preclude this. She looked about her, astonished, as the enormity of this news soaked in. First the Americans had destroyed Hiroshima and Nagasaki with atomic bombs, demonstrating their irresistible power, and now the Japanese government was suing for peace. The realization washed over her that the war soon would be over, that there would be no Final Battle, that peace could come without the sacrifice of the One Hundred Million.

"Don't touch them! Don't touch them!"

Noriko let go of the leaflet as if it had burst into flames, instantly obeying the command even before she saw the policeman. He was advancing down the street, picking up leaflets and shoving them into a sack as civilians, wary of his uniform, melted away. She backed away, then turned and hurried off. The policeman did not try to stop her. He did not even seem concerned.

More leaflets ahead, littering the street and settled on rooftops. People were cautiously retrieving them and retreating indoors or around corners to read them. After checking that no police or soldiers were around, Noriko slipped into the narrow space between two houses where she saw that one of the blue papers had lodged.

She snatched it up, shoved it into her shirt, and continued on her way.

The area around Ueno Station was even more decayed and dismal than when Noriko had last seen it in June. The streets along which she was walking were lined with piles of rubble, mostly smashed brickwork and tiles, debris that could not be recycled or burned in fires for cooking. Drabness was everywhere, dusty grays and browns. The only dash of color came from the gardens, the squares of greens and yellows flourishing in the ash-enriched soil where wooden houses had stood. Tokyo, the greatest metropolis in Asia, was reverting to farmland.

She stole looks at people as she continued along, her arms protectively crossed. They appeared exhausted and beaten, their faces showing no sign that they had seen the leaflet. Or perhaps they had seen it but didn't believe it, passing off any talk of peace as an American trick. She thought again of Ogawa and his watches, anticipating the coming of peace while everyone else was still mentally mired in war. Maybe he was right. Maybe these dispirited, hopeless people would be willing to sell him the remains of their destroyed homes for a functioning watch.

She passed under the train tracks. On the other side was the middle school where more than a hundred people had roasted in the air raid in April. Now she was passing Komagome Park, its trees all burned on the same night, reduced to black stumps. And then she was there, at the front gate of the Riken. The iron gate itself was gone, long since melted down for bullet casings and artillery shells. A frayed and sagging length of rope now replaced it.

She stepped over the rope and entered the defunct research complex, looking furtively about, feeling like an intruder. No guard was on duty. The grounds seemed abandoned. She started for the dormitory where she and Keizo had lived following the loss of their house. Was he there now? Did they still have the room?

There was a young woman squatting outside the ramshackle building, washing clothes in a basin. Noriko knew her. Seeing this friendly presence, the first in two months, made her legs feel weak.

"Yokoyama-san?" she said, tentatively approaching.

Sumi Yokoyama, Dr. Nishina's secretary, looked up from her washing.

"Yes?"

She rose and dried off her hands, taking this gaunt, ragged woman for a stranger. Noriko found herself so overcome with emotion that she was unable to say anything more. She stood there, hugging herself, tears welling up in her eyes. It was only then that recognition burst in Sumi's face and she erupted: "Kan-san!"

Sumi Yokoyama was even kinder than Noriko remembered. She unlocked the dormitory room Keizo still occupied with their few possessions. The small urn containing their daughter Aiko's remains was still there, alone, on the shelf. Seeing it, Noriko felt her legs give out completely. She would have fallen if Sumi had not caught her. When she recovered, Sumi helped her wash herself and dress in clean clothes.

"But you don't think he's in trouble?" Noriko asked, having heard Sumi's explanation of Keizo's absence.

"Oh no," Sumi assured her. "Nothing like that. The War Ministry needed him for something, but he couldn't say what, only that he would be away for a few days. He left with a young officer, a very nice man, and we heard nothing from him until he telephoned two days ago. He asked if you had arrived. Isn't that strange, that he knew you were coming!"

"But he's all right?"

"Oh yes." Sumi Yokoyama's expression clouded for only a moment before her smile reasserted itself. "I'm sure he'll return shortly. But come, we must go and let Dr. Nishina know you're here. He's leaving for Hiroshima on Thursday. He's been asked to join the scientific team being sent down there to investigate the damage. Isn't it horrible what happened? Oh, he'll be so glad that you're here."

They headed across the Riken compound to Building 29, where Dr. Nishina both worked and lived, sleeping on a cot in his office. The outer meeting room was incredibly cluttered, books and papers piled all over and covered with dust, the blackboard on the wall a mass of smeared diagrams and calculations. It had been a long time since anything had been cleaned.

Sumi Yokoyama excitedly burst into Nishina's inner office without knocking. "Sensei!" she exclaimed. "Look who's here!"

She instantly fell silent, for Dr. Nishina was occupied on the phone. He looked up, slightly annoyed. Then he saw Noriko and gave a visible start.

The two women bowed, embarrassed, and began to back out of the room.

"Just a moment," Nishina said, speaking into the phone.

He beckoned to Noriko and held out the receiver.

"It's your husband," he said.

Noriko stood there, shocked, unable to move.

"Come," Nishina urged her. "Come and speak to your husband."

Noriko stepped forward and cautiously took the receiver.

Nishina motioned Sumi Yokoyama from the office and followed her out, closing the door.

TWENTY-EIGHT

"HELLO? IS THAT YOU?"

It was Noriko's voice on the other end of the line. A jolt of shock passed through Keizo Kan, followed by a wave of relief and emotion. He had placed the call to the Riken expecting to be disappointed again, suspecting that Colonel Sagara had been lying, that Noriko had not been released.

He mastered himself and cast a nervous look around. The clerk was the only one in the office. He was at his desk, head down, preoccupied with his work.

"Noriko?" he said, holding his damaged hand over the mouthpiece.

"Yes. I'm here." Her voice was weak. He could scarcely hear her.

"Are you all right?"

"Yes."

"Are you—are you safe?"

A pause before she replied. "Yes, I think so. Where are you?"

Kan's eyes darted to the window, scanning for trouble, then back to the clerk. The young man's head was still down.

"I can't say," he whispered.

Kan had not asked Captain Onda for permission to make the call. He was sure he would receive another refusal. He had gone to the headquarters building on his own, found a quiet office with a telephone on the wall, and told the young clerk in an imperious tone that he needed to use it. The clerk, recognizing him as the older civilian on the Renzan's no-return crew and no doubt important, ushered him to the unit and returned to his desk.

"When will you return?" Noriko asked, breaking the silence.

"I don't know." Kan's mind was racing. Everything had just changed.

"Are you all right?"

"Yes. I'm fine."

"Husband . . . I'm sorry."

"It's all right," Kan replied, beset by another wave of emotion. "Everything is all right."

Escape. That was what he needed to focus on now. If Noriko was free, Colonel Sagara could no longer use her to control him. That meant he could escape now. He could slip away from the airfield after dark, like PO Yagi suggested.

"Hello? Are you there?" Noriko asked.

"Yes, I'm here. Are you alone?"

"Yes."

"No one is listening?"

"No. They're outside." Noriko was whispering now, too.

"We have to leave," said Kan.

"Why? Is something wrong?"

"We just have to leave."

Kan racked his brain trying to think of a plan. He would meet Noriko . . . where?

"Keizo . . . "

At what time? If he escaped tonight, when would he reach Tokyo?

"Keizo," he heard her repeat. "The war is ending."

Kan's eyes went back to the window, watching for trouble. "What do you mean?"

"I have a leaflet. The government has said they're going to sur-render."

Kan stood still, confused. He was so focused on his vision of get-ting away that it was difficult to turn from it and absorb what Noriko had just said. So it was true. It was more than true. Actual steps had been taken to surrender.

"Do you have the paper?" he said, looking out the window. There was someone out there, someone coming this way.

"Yes."

"Read it to me."

Noriko began reading the leaflet: "'The Japanese government, act-ing on the wishes of the Emperor of Japan, has informed the Allied powers of the United States, Britain, the Soviet Union, and China that it wishes to end hostilities and bring the war to an end. Below is the full text of the message we received . . .'"

Kan listened with his eyes locked on the approaching figure. It was Captain Onda, heading toward the headquarters building.

Onda passed out of view, making for the main entrance.

"I have to go now," Kan whispered, interrupting Noriko before she had finished.

"Keizo—"

Kan hung up the phone.

"Thank you," he said to the clerk. He moved toward the door, ex-pecting Onda to burst in.

He reached the door and looked out. The hallway was empty. Onda must have gone to the base commander's office.

Kan stepped into the hallway and headed for the exit at the oppo-site end of the building. He was too agitated to think clearly. He started walking, not really aware of where he was going, past warehouses and the training school buildings, past the mess hall, past the barracks.

He came to the main gate, the most direct way to the road leading to Tokyo. As an escape route, this was of course out of the question. There was a guard post here, a fence extending in both directions, and houses nearby—houses occupied by people who would see him even if he got past the sentries.

He headed toward the north end of the runway, walking along the perimeter fence as if taking an afternoon stroll. The northwest corner of the airfield, beyond the scattering of buildings, was overseen by a single guard post—an unmanned guard post, Kan discovered as he drew nearer. No one was in sight. The fence was rusting to pieces.

He would leave after nightfall. With the airfield in darkness, total blackout conditions, no one would see him. Once beyond the airfield, he would make his way to the Riken and meet Noriko and together they would disappear. Where would they go? He hadn't worked that out yet. For how long? Only a short while, if the government truly was making moves to surrender. It was hard to imagine that the war could end without Japan's total destruction, but between what Colonel Sagara had said and the information on the leaflet, Kan now believed it. The war was going to end, and soon. What would he and Noriko do after that? He had no idea.

He reached the northeast corner of the airfield and continued to follow the fence down the east side. It opened onto the firing range where the Renzan had been towed to test its guns. The place appeared deserted, just as Yagi had said.

Kan looked back at the runway and the hangars and buildings beyond it. He had walked not much more than a kilometer, at a moderate pace, but it had left him breathing hard.

No one was watching. He was alone.

He entered the firing range, passing between the earthen berms rising to a height of three meters. Another berm straight ahead showed signs of recent firing, Yagi's and Otani's handiwork with the guns, but everywhere else was thickly covered with grass.

Kan continued on past it, screened now from view from the airfield. A little farther on and he came to the far side of the range—unfenced, unguarded, open scrubland beyond.

He had just escaped. He didn't need to wait until dark. He could keep walking and be halfway to Tokyo by nightfall.

He stood there, looking eastward, gazing at freedom. There was a dirt track off to the right, heading away from the airfield in the direction of the capital. No one was on it. No one was about.

Yagi's words sounded inside his head: *Onda can take off without you. Why should you go?*

He didn't move. He knew that he couldn't. If he escaped now, the mission to San Francisco would go ahead without him just the same, and if successful, it would wipe out a whole city. He would have helped to destroy a whole city, a city of people, women and children, a city transformed into a hellscape like he had seen at Hiroshima. Was his hatred of America so great that it could support such a burden?

And then there would be what would happen to Japan. The destruction of San Francisco would surely derail the move toward surrender. It would embolden the hard-liners in the Army to fight on and prompt the Americans to exact a terrible revenge. Complete annihilation would be the only possible outcome.

If he escaped now, he would be sacrificing all of Japan to save his own skin.

The work of repairing the Renzan bomber and preparing it for its new mission had continued around the clock and was now almost complete. A heap of metal, mostly armor plating, lay on the floor of the hangar, a reduction in weight of more than two tons. The replacement Homare engine was installed, mechanics making final connections. The severed rudder cable was replaced and the blown wheel repaired. The bullet holes were patched up, squares of unpainted metal on black. And the tail gunner's compartment had been stripped bare. Twenty-millimeter gun, belts of ammunition, ammo racks and gunner's seat—it had all been removed, a savings in weight equivalent to 300 liters of gas.

Kan found PO Yagi taking a cigarette break at the back of the hangar.

"Could you make the call?" Yagi asked, looking up through his smoke. He was stretched out on the floor, a piece of wood for his pillow.

Kan nodded. He motioned toward the office against the back wall. Yagi got up and followed.

"The war is ending," Kan whispered, closing the door. "The Americans are dropping leaflets on Tokyo. The government has accepted the terms of surrender."

"Leaflets," Yagi dismissively snorted. "Enemy propaganda. It's just a lie."

"No, I don't think so. It had the actual communications printed on it, the government's message to the Allies. My wife read it to me over the phone. The war is ending."

Consternation came into Yagi's face as he puffed on his cigarette. Kan could imagine what he was feeling. There was not supposed to be a future beyond the Final Battle, the titanic clash that would occur when the Americans began their invasion of Kyushu. It was Japan's inescapable fate. There was no room for hope.

"If your wife is free," said Yagi, "you can leave. You don't need to go on the mission."

Kan looked toward the closed door, the Renzan bomber outside.

"I can't."

"Let them go!" Yagi hissed. "They can kill themselves just as well without you."

"But if they're successful, if they attack San Francisco—"

"Let them! The Americans deserve it! How many of our cities have they destroyed? Fifty? Sixty?"

Kan let out a weary sigh, rubbing his forehead, which was starting to ache. He had never revealed his thoughts on the war to anyone apart from Noriko, and even that had been just a few whispers. They were dangerous thoughts, illegal thoughts, thoughts that could get him arrested and thrown into prison.

He looked at Yagi. Could he trust this man with what he was about to say?

"In my last year in America," he began, "my professor arranged for me to take the train from San Francisco to Chicago, to attend a conference at the university there. He said it would be a chance for me to see how big the United States was. I think he wanted to impress me. It was three thousand kilometers. City after city. Factory after factory. Fields of grain extending all the way to the horizon. Endless resources. And when I reached Chicago, there was still more than a thousand kilometers to go to New York—a thousand kilometers more of factories, America's industrial heartland.

"So when I heard about the attack on Pearl Harbor . . . "

Kan glanced at the closed door. He leaned closer to Yagi and lowered his voice.

"When I heard about the attack on Pearl Harbor, I knew in my heart it was a disaster. There was no way we could beat them. But we all cheered. I cheered! I convinced myself for nearly three years that we deserved an empire, that we could somehow build a new world. And look what it's got us. We're getting ground into dust. Or we give up and save the little that's left and try to start over.

"But Colonel Sagara won't allow that. Remember what he said before we took off, about how we were also fighting enemies in the highest levels of our own government who were trying to surrender? This is his plan. He wants this attack on San Francisco not just to hurt the Americans. He wants it to stop any move to surrender so that the war will continue, so that we keep fighting until all of Japan is burned up and every American he can take with him is dead, until everyone and everything has been sacrificed for his honor. And we keep going along, doing as we're told, following orders, pretending that—" Kan's voice started to break. "Pretending that losing people we love doesn't hurt us, that it serves some sort of purpose."

He looked at Yagi with tears in his eyes. "Why do we allow ourselves to be treated this way?"

Yagi gazed back, a hard look, appraising. And Kan began to think he had just made a mistake.

"So what are you proposing?" said Yagi at last. "To go along and detonate that thing over the ocean? Like you already tried to do?"

Kan didn't answer. He looked down at his hands.

"Because if that's what you're thinking," Yagi continued, "I'd say you were a fool."

Kan heard the navy man draw in a last lungful of smoke, the dry tobacco emitting a crackle. The sounds of the stub being ground into the ashtray. The squeak of the chair as he leaned back. Then the familiar sound:

"*Humph.*"

Kan looked up.

Yagi was smiling. "You know, it would make me sad to see you do that, Sensei. I don't have any friends left."

Their eyes met. And Kan knew that Yagi wouldn't betray him.

"What if there was another way?" he whispered.

Yagi's eyes narrowed. "There's often another way," he said.

Kan silently read the navy man's face for a moment. Then he took the plunge:

"I've been thinking of sabotaging the Daikon."

Yagi slowly nodded.

"If I could make some sort of timer," Kan said, caution falling away. "But a clock . . . how do I set it? I don't know when Onda will take off. I don't know when the plane will be out at sea."

He looked over at the shelves lining the wall, cluttered with gauges and small parts and miscellaneous bits of equipment.

"If there was some way to use barometric pressure," he said. He went to the shelf and began sorting through the detritus of dozens of aircraft. "The plane will be flying very high . . . "

Yagi's eyes were on the ashtray. He considered it for a moment.

"What about temperature?" he said.

TWENTY-NINE

IT WAS A BLACK-PAINTED METAL ASHTRAY WITH A DIAL THERMOMETER ATTACHED, A promotional item with the name of the instrument manufacturer printed on the dial. Judging from the chips and scratches and residue buildup, it had been in use since before the war.

The thermometer was affixed to the ashtray by a thumbscrew underneath. Yagi was able to remove it with his fingers. He cupped the thermometer in his hands, checking that his body heat was moving the needle. It did. It worked.

He nodded to Kan. Kan moved the ashtray, minus the thermometer, to the shelf, where he hoped it wouldn't be noticed, and led the way out of the office.

The hangar was almost deserted. Only two mechanics were working on the Renzan, their attention on one of the starboard engines. Then Kan saw the tank truck parked outside and off to the left, Captain Onda and others gathered around it. The promised gasoline from Army Fuel Headquarters had arrived.

They slipped into the workshop and closed the door.

The job of converting the thermometer was easily completed. Yagi, with his two good hands, did the work. First he removed the glass covering, held in place by a screw-on brass band, exposing the dial and the needle. He drilled a small hole in the dial face—at the minus-fifteen-degree-centigrade mark, they decided after a whispered discussion. The temperature inside the Renzan would certainly go well below that. He then inserted a small nail into the hole. The final step was to attach a length of wire to the nail and a second piece of wire to the pin holding the needle—carefully, so the movement of the needle would not be impeded.

The result was an open circuit that would close when the temperature fell. After the Renzan took off and began its climb, the needle of the thermometer would creep its way to the left, closing the gap between its tip and the nail. Twenty degrees, ten degrees, zero, minus five, minus ten, minus fifteen. Contact. The needle would touch the nail, completing the circuit, at an altitude of around 6,000 meters.

Kan wound the tails of wire around the thermometer, his right hand almost useless, and put it in his left pocket. He picked up the pliers with his left hand and awkwardly reached around to slip them into his right pocket. The twisting motion made him feel dizzy. He grabbed onto the desk to steady himself.

Yagi was sourly watching him the whole time. His eyes went to Kan's swollen and cracked hand, almost useless, then back to his ashen face.

"Are you sure you can do this?" he said.

Kan curtly nodded. He took a moment to prepare himself.

He went to open the door.

Yagi put his hand on the handle to stop him. He looked again into Kan's face, this time with real concern.

He motioned toward the chair where Kan had just been sitting. "Step up onto that."

Kan looked at him, puzzled.

"You have to climb into the plane," explained Yagi. "Then climb down off the catwalk to get at the wiring. Show me you can at least step up on that chair."

Kan regarded the challenge. The seat was no higher than his knees. He went to the chair and got one leg up on it, holding on to the back for support. A grunting, heaving effort, and he tried to stand up.

He couldn't. His legs were too weak.

Yagi let out an annoyed growl and held out his hand. "Give it to me."

"No," Kan began to protest. "I should be the one—"

"Shut up. Just give it to me."

Kan hesitated. He knew his strength was failing, but this latest display of weakness had shocked him. How would he even climb into the plane? Yagi was much more able to do it. But why would he jeopardize himself? The question hovered in the scientist's mind.

His shoulders sagged, relenting. He was so very weary. He handed over the thermometer and the pliers. Yagi shoved them into his pockets and turned to leave.

"Wait."

Kan took off his watch and held it out. "I asked you to look for my watch," he prompted. "I thought I left it on the plane."

Yagi nodded his understanding and took the watch. He exited the workshop into the open space of the hangar. The Renzan was parked ten paces away.

He went back to work, cleaning up the scattered pieces of metal that still lay on the floor, the armor that had been stripped from the Renzan, carrying them to the side of the hangar and piling them out of the way.

Kan held back, trying to appear nonchalant as he surveyed the scene. The Army Fuel Headquarters truck had just departed. Men were returning to work. There were seven or eight within sight of the plane: two mechanics working on the newly installed engine, putting the cowling panels back in place; a handful more occupied with other tasks; two armed soldiers standing guard at the front of the hangar, facing out.

And here was Lieutenant Kamibeppu, the navigator, walking his way.

"We have the fuel," Kamibeppu announced. "We'll soon know if the engines check out."

Kan nodded.

The bomb bay doors of the Renzan were closed. To gain access to the Daikon, which was sealed inside, Yagi would need to climb up to the flight deck, pass through the rear door of the compartment, and climb down into the bomb bay to work in the dark. There was a flashlight in the radio operator's compartment, in a cabinet beside the desk.

Kan continued to loiter, his eyes going from the plane to Yagi to the diminishing pile of metal still to be moved, Yagi's only reason for being so near the plane. The hatch on the underside of the fuselage behind the cockpit was open, the ladder in place. Could Yagi climb up it and get inside without being seen? Not with Kamibeppu standing here, watching. If the lieutenant left, however, he might have a chance, the mechanics being preoccupied and the inboard engine blocking their view.

Yagi was down to the last armload. He was taking his time now. He carried it to the side and set it on the pile. A glance back at Kan and Kamibeppu. He turned back to the pile and did a little rearranging. Then he was strolling back to the plane, looking around for any overlooked pieces. There were none. The floor was clean.

A nod of satisfaction at a job well done. Another glance at Kan. Then he was backing away.

Kan grimaced and let out a groan, holding his stomach.

"Still having trouble, eh?" said Kamibeppu, turning away from the plane.

Kan groaned again and doubled over, attracting Kamibeppu's full attention and assistance.

He straightened up, sighing with relief as if the spell was passing. "Thank you. I'm all right now," he said.

He looked over at the plane. No sign of Yagi.

Kamibeppu hadn't noticed. He remained with Kan for another few minutes, then walked away.

•   •   •

Yagi stood still in the space behind the cockpit, listening for trouble, a shout from Kamibeppu or one of the guards, the sound of boots as they ran over to order him out of the plane.

He heard nothing, only the sound of his heartbeat. He waited for it to slow. Then he took off his boots.

He passed through the door at the rear of the flight deck, moving silently in sock feet. He traversed the catwalk leading back, crossing over the Daikon down below in the dark of the bomb bay, auxiliary gasoline tanks in place on either side. A second door opening into the radio operator's compartment, light flooding down from the window in the fuselage overhead. He set his boots on the floor, found the flashlight kit in the storage cabinet, checked it. It worked. He hitched the battery unit around his waist with the attached belt and clipped the lamp to his shirt.

There were two things he needed to do. First, he had to cut the wire running from the Daikon to the guillotine switch and splice in the thermometer. Second, the guillotine switch mounted on the radio operator's desk, the bomb's trigger, had to be disconnected, reversed, and reinstalled so that it would appear closed when in fact it was open. When the setup was complete, the only thing keeping the Daikon from exploding would be the four-centimeter arc from the thermometer needle to the nail in the dial face at minus fifteen degrees.

He returned to the bomb bay and flicked on the flashlight. The auxiliary tanks, capacity 1,500 liters each, left little room to move around. He unclipped the lamp from his shirt and directed the yellow beam down the side of the space, following the course of the wire.

There. In the final meter and a half, before it entered the tail end of the weapon, a protruding flange in the airframe screened the wire from view from above. And the Daikon would hide it from below when the bomb bay doors were open. Install the thermometer here and it wouldn't be seen.

Yagi clipped the lamp back onto his shirt, stepped off the catwalk and climbed down, placing his stocking feet with care so as not to make any noise. He wedged himself into position beside the Daikon, removed the pliers from his pocket and cut the wire.

"All set?"

Yagi froze. It was Captain Onda, outside the plane.

A second voice: "It's ready." One of the mechanics.

Boots on concrete. Onda walking toward the front of the hangar. Then his voice raised to a shout: "All right, bring it over!"

The sound of a tractor starting in the distance. Getting louder, approaching. Yagi silently removed the thermometer from his pocket and began to splice it into the cut wire, lines of strain now creasing his face.

The tractor entered the hangar, the roar of its engine reverberating off the walls, then abating to idle. Yagi finished the job and climbed back up onto the catwalk. The clank of metal on metal, then a jolt that nearly threw him off his feet and the plane was moving. He recovered, slipped into the radio operator's compartment and closed the door.

The movement stopped. The Renzan had been towed only a short distance, onto the tarred gravel outside the hangar. Yagi sat at the radio operator's desk, disassembling the guillotine switch as he listened to the tractor back away, then fall silent. Then he put the switch back together. When he was finished, it looked just as it did before, seemingly in the "off" position on the right, the attached bracket locking it down as an added precaution. But with it reversed, the switch was actually in the "on" position. When the plane's electrical system was turned on, the only thing required for the Daikon to explode was for the thermometer needle to move to the left and touch the nail at minus fifteen degrees.

Would a good shake to the plane be enough to jar the needle across that small space?

Footsteps outside. The squeak of wheels. The creak of a pump. They were fueling the tanks.

They were going to test the engines.

Yagi was trapped in the plane.

He returned the flashlight to the cabinet above the desk and looked around the cramped compartment. It was just an empty box with two seats and a desk, no place to hide. He went to the rear door and peered through into the waist gunner's compartment, even more bare. A glance through the door would reveal him.

He looked down and saw his bare feet. Even more incriminating than his mere presence. He put on his boots.

He passed through the forward door and crept across the catwalk to the flight deck. The situation here was no better. The flight engineer, Otani, would be seated right there, commanding a view of the entire rear half of the space. That left only the cockpit, where Onda or copilot Yoshino soon would be seated, and the navigator's position, fully visible to everyone outside through the glass panels of the nose.

A head appeared at the hatch directly below. Yagi jerked back and closed the door and stood motionless in the dark on the catwalk. He heard someone climbing up into the plane. If they opened the door, they would see him. Moving as quietly as he could, he stepped off the catwalk and climbed down into the shadows, down until he was crouched between the starboard-side auxiliary tank and the Daikon.

It was Otani, followed by Onda, taking their seats. Yagi could hear their voices but not make out their words, procedures being called out and repeated, the clicking of switches.

A hum from inside the aircraft. The Renzan's electrical system had just been turned on. That meant the Daikon was now live, held in check only by the quivering tip of the thermometer needle. Yagi's eyes, which had been locked on the door above leading to the flight deck, dropped to the black metal of the gun barrel a handbreadth from his face.

The first engine coughed to life, then another, then all four engines together. They rose to a collective roar, steady and pure.

The testing of the engines had been ongoing for twenty minutes, Yagi crouched beside the Daikon the whole while, his mind going over various explanations for his presence if he was discovered. Nothing came to him better than the search for Keizo Kan's watch, still in his pocket.

A light came on in the bomb bay. Yagi lowered his head, expecting the door from the flight deck to open above.

The light went out. Back on again. Off.

Onda was testing the plane's electrical systems.

The bomb bay doors started to open, letting in the waning daylight and the engines' full roar. Yagi willed them to close. They didn't. Instead, the engines began to subside, the whine diminishing in pitch as the propellers slowed to a stop.

Silence. Yagi looked down through the open bomb bay doors at the gravel, expecting at any moment for someone to duck under and look up and see him hiding inside. He was completely exposed.

"The fuel is excellent!" It was Onda, calling out his side window to the mechanics.

The tread of feet above Yagi's head and forward. Onda and Otani were leaving the plane. Yagi climbed back up to the catwalk, repeatedly glancing down, expecting a head to appear at any moment.

He eased the flight deck door open a crack and listened. He heard nothing. He opened the door farther and peered through it. The flight deck was empty.

He entered and crouched down in the corner, beside the flight engineer's seat. The hatch leading out of the plane was right there, by his feet.

He waited, listening to the voices outside, Otani and Captain Yoshino, the copilot, conversing with Onda. They sounded to be in good spirits. The test of the fuel and the engines clearly had been a success. Were they looking up into the bomb bay, checking the Daikon? Yagi thought he heard Onda say at one point, "Where's Yagi-heisō?"

The murmurs subsided. Yagi heard them move to the left, then behind him, then over on the right. The crew was walking around the plane.

Onda's voice again, raised and clear: "All right, take it back into the hangar. We go in the morning! Yoshino, shut it down!"

Yagi slipped out the rear door of the flight deck and back onto the catwalk a moment before Yoshino's head popped up through the hatch. He continued on back to the radio operator's compartment and stood inside, listening at the door. He heard the bomb bay doors close, returning the bomb bay to darkness.

The tractor started up. The Renzan was towed back into the hangar. Yoshino completed the shut-down procedures and exited the plane. The voices outside diminished as people walked off.

Yagi waited. The light entering the compartment through the window above was becoming a deepening orange. He checked Kan's watch in his pocket. Six-thirty.

He left the compartment and returned to the flight deck and lowered his head through the hatch, scouting around. No one in sight but the guards at the front of the hangar, facing out.

He eased himself through the hatch and climbed down the ladder. He stepped away and gazed up at the plane, acting as if he had just come over for a look. He turned and casually began strolling away.

"Yagi-heisō!"

It was Captain Onda. He had just appeared at the entrance.

"Yagi-heisō. Where have you been?"

A dozen lies raced through Yagi's brain. He felt the weight of Kan's watch in his pocket and the story began to form on his lips. But that would mean admitting he had been in the plane.

He lowered his eyes, acting sheepish.

He inclined his head toward the workshop where he and Kan had assembled the Daikon. "I'm sorry," he said. "I fell asleep back there."

Onda continued to look at him with what seemed like suspicion.

Finally a wry smile came onto his face and he checked his watch. "Well, you'd better hurry or you'll get no dinner."

Yagi continued on to the mess hall. He found Kan waiting there, scarcely able to contain his agitation. He answered the scientist's questioning look with a nod and they proceeded inside together.

"I didn't need it," he whispered, returning Kan's watch. "But I'm not sure about Onda. Now we have to go."

THIRTY

THEY WAITED UNTIL ONE O'CLOCK IN THE MORNING, STARING UP AT THE MOSQUITO NETTING as they lay on their futons, listening as the sounds in the barracks gradually subsided. Finally silence. Hopefully, everyone was asleep.

PO Yagi got up and slipped into the hallway. Most of the doors were open to let in whatever breeze was blowing. Darkness in all the neighboring rooms. Except one.

"Onda's still up," he whispered, returning and closing the door. "We'll have to be quiet."

They moved about the room in silence, folding up their futons and stowing them against the wall, together with the equipment Kan hoped would be sent back to the Riken. He had already burned the farewell letter he had written to Noriko, along with his will. Yagi had similarly disposed of the letter to his sister. Kan had seen him crumple it up in disgust.

They went to the open window. Faint light was filtering through it, a half-moon drifting in and out behind low scudding clouds. Fortunately their room was on the ground floor. They would be able to climb out this way rather than having to traverse the hall, doors open on both sides, floorboards creaking.

Kan touched Yagi on the shoulder. "Are you sure you did it correctly?" he whispered.

Yagi gave him an angry look. He had already explained where he had spliced the thermometer into the Daikon's detonating wire and how he had reversed the switch. But Kan couldn't be reassured.

Yagi slipped out the window first, then helped Kan follow, a clumsy, awkward wriggle, too much noise. They put on their shoes and stood with their backs to the wall, screened by a line of young maples, looking around, listening. The airfield was in total darkness. The only sound was wind rustling the leaves.

The crunch of boots on gravel. Yagi's hand on Kan's chest, holding him still. They froze as a soldier walked past, a rifle slung over his shoulder—one of the guards that patrolled the airfield at night.

The guard was heading away from the runway. They waited for him to disappear around the corner, then moved off in the opposite direction, Yagi starting out low and gliding smoothly, Kan struggling to keep up at a shambling trot that soon slowed to a walk.

They continued on to the far side of the runway, skirting the south end, Yagi taking Kan by the arm to urge him along. By the time they reached the firing range and the grassy berms rising up in the dark, the scientist was gasping for breath. Yagi roughly dragged him a little farther into the range until the berms were screening them from the airfield. Finally he let Kan drop onto the grass, his chest heaving. He looked around for a moment, scanning for trouble, then sank down beside him.

Slowly, Kan's breathing recovered. He sat up. He became aware that his right hand, throbbing with pain, was wet. Yagi's rough handling had broken more skin.

"I'm sorry to be an annoyance," he whispered. "But when you spliced the thermometer into the—"

Yagi silenced him with a glancing cuff to the head.

Click.

The beam of a flashlight stabbed through the darkness.

Yagi lay down on the grass, pulling Kan with him. The light passed over them, searching the berms.

The sound of a rifle being unshouldered, a round being chambered.

Footsteps approaching.

"Is somebody there?"

It was another guard—a young one judging from the voice. Kan pressed his head into the grass, not daring to breathe.

The footsteps drew nearer. The flashlight beam danced and flitted in Kan's peripheral vision. The guard seemed to be focused on the area beyond, unaware that Kan and Yagi were now almost under his feet.

"Is somebody there? Show yourself!"

The footsteps continued on past them. Then the light was gone, the guard turning off through a gap to search the other side of the berm.

Yagi's iron grip on Kan's arm yanked him to his feet.

Air raid sirens started to wail behind them as they hurried away.

Kan thought at first that it was an alarm being raised because they had escaped. But then came the drone of engines, approaching from the south, followed by B-29s passing overhead—dozens of them, silhouettes in the clearing night sky, backed by the moon.

They continued on through the dark, Yagi leading the way. Tama Airfield was soon behind them and they were skirting the outer perimeter of the neighboring Tachikawa arsenal complex, Yagi scanning for sentries as they went. He had slowed his pace, but Kan was still gasping and struggling to keep up. It was clear that to make it to Tokyo they would need transportation.

Turning south, they came to the Chuo line and followed it east to what a weathered signboard announced was Kunitachi Station, little more than a platform set among fields. The tracks from here ran straight to Shinjuku Station, with the Riken and Noriko not many kilometers beyond that. But there were no trains. Enemy bombing had destroyed the tracks in too many places for even irregular service to be maintained.

At least the way to Tokyo was clear. Kan and Yagi continued along the tracks of the derelict line, walking under the dead electrical wiring. A settlement up ahead, a huddle of houses and abandoned factory buildings, no dogs left to bark. The breeze had died down. The only sound came from crickets and bullfrogs and the scuffing of Kan's feet. He was beginning to stumble. He wouldn't be able to continue much farther.

It was a truck that saved them. It chugged up behind them on a parallel road, headlights doused, sparks shooting from the charcoal firebox attached to the engine. Kan was unable to do anything but turn and stare. It was Yagi who scrambled across the ditch and onto the road and held up his hand to bring the vehicle to a stop. He conversed with the driver and produced a few coins from his pocket. Then he beckoned to Kan.

There was no room for them in the cab, already crowded with the driver and his family. Yagi helped Kan climb up into the back, scraping more skin off his hand. As the truck ground into gear and set off at a speed not exceeding twenty kilometers per hour, Kan lay back on a bed of cabbages and looked up at the stars showing through the scattering of clouds, overcome by a weariness that seemed to penetrate to his bones. Yagi, stretched out beside him, took advantage of the respite in tension and was soon softly snoring. As uncomfortable as the cabbages were under his back, Kan drifted off as well, a jumble of images cascading through his mind as he sank deeper. Tama Airfield. The Renzan. His neglected vegetable plot at the Riken. The Daikon. An atomic detonation consuming San Francisco.

He couldn't see Noriko's face . . .

He was jarred back to the present by the truck braking to a halt. He sat up, his heart thumping, fearing that they had come to a checkpoint, a guard post.

Yagi was already alert. He was crouched behind the cab, peering forward.

Yagi's shoulders relaxed. It was only the driver, getting down to feed more charcoal into the firebox to keep the engine going. Yagi lay back down and closed his eyes with a sigh.

Kan looked around. No more fields now. Houses on both sides, barely discernible shadows. They were getting into the city.

The driver climbed back into the cab. The truck started again.

Off to the left, to the north, the horizon glowed orange.

THIRTY-ONE

THE CALL ROUSED COLONEL SAGARA FROM A RESTLESS DOZE AT FIVE O'CLOCK IN THE MORNING. It was Captain Onda at Tama Airfield on the other end of the line.

"We've searched everywhere," Onda was saying. "As soon as it was discovered they weren't in their room. I'm afraid they've deserted."

"Fucking dogs!" Sagara shouted. "I want them arrested!"

"Yes, Colonel. The Kempeitai have already been alerted."

"I want them *shot!*"

"Yes, Colonel. But I don't think this should affect our mission. Lieutenant Otani can move back when we're on our final approach and operate the switch."

"Of course it doesn't affect the mission. You said the fuel is good, didn't you?"

"The fuel is excellent," said Onda. "And the aircraft is ready."

"All right. So the operation goes ahead as planned. Be prepared to take off!"

Sagara slammed down the receiver and threw himself back in his chair, a high-pitched whine sounding in his ears. He squeezed his eyes shut and shook his head, trying to dispel it.

The past sixteen hours had seen things take a dire turn, with the Supreme War Council meeting through the afternoon and the cabinet in the evening. The deadlock remained, but there was a palpable sense that the Badoglios, those favoring surrender, were gaining momentum. By nightfall, a premonition of defeat had begun to permeate through the War Ministry hallways, clerks scuttling down the stairs with armloads of documents to burn in the courtyard. Colonel Sagara had had several confrontations about it but was forced to give up and retreat to his office. The crumbling discipline was more than he could contain. He took a sleeping pill some time after midnight and lay down to rest.

The whining was maddening. Sagara stuck his fingers in his ears and agitated them up and down, without effect.

He hoisted himself to his feet and stumped into the hall. His clerk was not on duty. All was quiet. For a few brief hours, the Ministry of War was asleep.

He continued around the corner to look out a window of the conference room on the far side of the building, monitoring the situation in the northwest. The night sky there was glowing orange, as if the sun that was about to rise had shifted to the wrong side of the horizon. But it wasn't the sun. It was a city ablaze. The Americans had attacked Kumagaya and it was being consumed in an inferno. There were rumors that another atomic bomb had been dropped, but the colonel knew that this wasn't true. The B-29s, estimated to number around one hundred, were not Special Task Planes. They had all used V500 call signs. That meant they were from Guam.

The whine in Sagara's ears grew louder. He stuck his fingers in his ears and palpitated them, more violently this time. The ceaseless tone was maddening. He tried striking his ears with his open palms. It did no good.

A flutter in his chest, the whine rising to a scream. Then tightness gripped his heart, giving it such an agonizing squeeze that his legs turned to jelly and he fell to the floor.

He lay there in the dark, taking shallow breaths, the room roaring and spinning around him.

Slowly the pain subsided and the room settled. He became aware that his left arm was numb. And his tongue—it had turned into a lump of dead flesh in his mouth.

He gave himself another few minutes, staring up at the ceiling painted ocher by the fires devouring Kumagaya. Then, very carefully, he got to his knees.

"You don't look well, Sagara-chūsa."

It was Colonel Takeshita, entering Sagara's office at seven o'clock in the morning. Sagara was lying on his cot, a physical wreck, an intravenous needle stuck in his arm. On the inside, however, he was feeling much better. The bottle attached to the needle, now almost empty, contained an alarmingly potent dose of the "vitamin shot" that he had bullied from the medic. This, coupled with the Philopon tablets he had taken, had had a wonderfully reviving effect on his brain.

"I'm quite all right," he said, slurring his words. He swung his legs off the cot, placed his feet on the floor, took a grip on the side table, and cautiously stood up. "There. You see? Now, I hope you have good news. Because if the . . . "

He paused, choosing his words carefully to refer to the planned coup d'état.

"Because if the *action* doesn't go ahead now, then there really is no point. I think you've all waited too long already."

"It has to be today," said Takeshita, looking strained. "We've just heard that a special conference has been called at the Imperial Palace. The Supreme War Council, the full cabinet, top military leaders, and government officials—all of them together in the Emperor's presence. Prime Minister Suzuki has planned a move, I think. I fear War Minister Anami will have a difficult time holding firm."

Sagara stroked the numb side of his face. This was bad. The last time such an extraordinary meeting took place in the Emperor's presence had been on December 1, 1941, to confirm the plan to attack Pearl Harbor and declare war on the United States.

He removed the needle from his arm. He moved to his desk, holding on to a chair en route, and sat down. His left leg and left arm were working. Somewhat.

"And I'm afraid that's not all," continued Takeshita. He reached into his pocket and extracted a sealed letter. "The War Minister has rescinded his order for the attack on Tinian Island. He says it cannot proceed, that the situation is too delicate now. He told me to place this in your hands and ensure that you understand it."

Sagara took the letter and stared at it for a moment.

He opened it and took his time digesting the hastily written words. War Minister Anami was countermanding his order to attack . . . Tinian Island.

"Do you understand the War Minister's order?" asked Takeshita.

Sagara folded the letter, returned it to its envelope, and set it on the desk.

"The War Minister asked me to get your clear confirmation," pressed Takeshita. "Do you understand his order that I have just placed in your hands?"

Sagara took a deep breath, inflating his meager chest, and let it out.

"War Minister Anami has rescinded his order to attack Tinian Island," he affirmed. "The War Minister has ordered me not to proceed with the attack on Tinian Island. I understand."

Takeshita nodded with relief. "Good. Good. I'll let the General know."

Sagara rose from his desk after Takeshita left and made his way to the window. He used the cane that the medic had provided and which he at first had angrily cast away.

He froze, catching sight of himself in the mirror over the sink. His face was gaunt, his eyes sunk into their sockets. And his hair—when had it turned gray?

He continued to the window and looked out at the devastated city, aware that he was now in a similar state. He rubbed his left arm. It had minimal feeling. He wiped the spittle collecting at the side of his mouth, which he could no longer fully control. And the ringing in his ears . . . his body was falling to pieces. Why? What did it mean?

He contemplated this for a time, going over the events of the previous two weeks. There was no doubt that destiny had been guiding his actions. But what if the physical toll on his body was also part of a higher plan? What if the chains binding his flesh to his spirit had been weakened on purpose to prepare him for death?

He imagined sacrificing himself in the coup d'état that would be launched within hours. He could hunt down Prime Minister Suzuki, either at his residence or when he arrived at the Imperial Palace, and shoot him in the head. The image gave him pleasure. But it did not feel right.

And then he remembered the burning city. When the pain seized him and he collapsed two hours before, he had been watching Kumagaya aflame. He had "died" watching a burning city. His death linked to conflagration.

His eyes suddenly grew wide. He understood. He was destined to die . . .

On the plane.

He returned to his desk and called Tama Airfield. He waited as Captain Onda was summoned.

Was that all? He was meant to occupy Keizo Kan's seat, to take the place of a deserter, a traitor? Was that the culmination of his destiny, merely to operate the switch?

No, there had to be something more.

It would reveal itself.

"Onda-tai-i," he said when his aide came on the line. "Hold your departure. I've decided to accompany you."

·   ·   ·

The colonel ignored the regulation concerning the conservation of fuel and rejected the indignity of a motorcycle sidecar. He took a staff car the forty kilometers to Tama Airfield. There would be no repercussions. He would not be coming back.

The Renzan bomber was sitting in front of the hangar, a fuel cart beside it, pumping gasoline into the outboard tanks. The car pulled up beside it and the driver helped Sagara out. Captain Onda jogged over from the hangar to greet him, followed by Captain Yoshino and Lieutenants Otani and Kamibeppu. Their faces clouded as they drew near and saw the colonel's condition.

"Sagara-chūsa," Onda exclaimed.

"I'm all right," said the colonel, speaking slowly and carefully. It was not easy using his tongue.

He surveyed the Renzan parked in the morning light. The small squares of metal where the bullet holes had been repaired were now painted, restoring the bomber to perfect blackness. If the high-altitude air currents were as predicted, they would fly into night and reach the target at dawn.

The men were gathering around. Sagara turned to face them, looking from one to the next, reading their determination, their dedication, their courage. These were truly the best of Japan. He could not wish for better. The thought stirred a wave of emotion that made his eyes glisten.

He mastered it and removed the letter from his pocket, War Minister Anami's letter countermanding the order to attack Tinian Island.

"I have just received this from General Anami," he said, holding the envelope up. He cast a knowing look around at the group. The right side of his mouth rose in a ghastly lopsided leer. "We have been ordered to proceed with the attack on San Francisco."

The crew was nodding, enthusiasm rising.

Sagara tucked the letter back into his pocket. "Onda-tai-i," he said. "Are we ready to go?"

"Just another few minutes to finish the fueling," Onda replied.

"Excuse me, Sagara-chūsa," said flight engineer Otani. "But we've been hearing rumors from Tokyo." He glanced at navigator Kamibeppu. "It's had some of us concerned."

"You don't need to worry about that," Sagara said. "Everything is in hand, I can assure you. There have been plans in place for some time to deal with the Badoglio clique, and loyal forces in the Army are about to take action. By this time tomorrow, the Suzuki government will have been swept aside and General Anami will be in charge. It will be a one-two punch, our attack on the enemy on the far side of the ocean, a harder blow even than was struck at Pearl Harbor, and the establishment of a military government here at home. By this time tomorrow, Anami will be premier and Japan will be on the right path!"

The crew broke out in a cheer, slapping one another on the back.

The fuel cart was disconnected and wheeled to the opposite wing.

THIRTY-TWO

KEIZO KAN AND PETTY OFFICER YAGI LEFT THE TRUCK AT IKEBUKURO STATION, IN A MARKET on a street behind what was left of the station building. It wasn't much of a market, just a few grim vendors selling off the last of their household possessions to buy food. But it was still early, seven o'clock in the morning. Soon there would be more.

The appearance of the truck caused a flurry of excitement, people flocking around it to buy the cabbages off the back. The driver and his wife and daughter squatted on the pile, snatching money and doling out the precious cargo. Yagi had already secured six heads with the money he had in his pocket. They proceeded northeast, Kan's legs working again after the rest in the truck. There was something strange in the air, a tightness in the faces of people passing by, but it did not register in the front of his brain. He was too worried about being arrested. He shot wary glances at every soldier and policeman he saw, but they seemed oblivious to his presence. Gradually he began to relax. They continued on, past Sugamo Prison, then turned east under the elevated tracks of the Yamanote Line.

They had not gone more than a kilometer when Kan began to

stagger with fatigue. He was sweating heavily and wincing as he cradled his injured right hand, the pain now almost more than he could endure.

He stumbled. They stopped and sat down to rest, Yagi placing his bundle of cabbages between his feet. He broke off two leaves, handed one to Kan and started gnawing on the other. As he ate, Kan stared at what was left of a bank across the street, the concrete shell still standing but completely burned out. Nothing remained of the wooden structures that had existed on either side of it, just piles of charred sticks. It was the same in every direction, as if a giant had stomped Tokyo flat and set fire to the wreckage.

"Where did you get those cabbages?" A passing woman had stopped, her eyes on Yagi's bundle.

Yagi jerked his thumb up the road. "Back there. Behind Ikebukuro Station." Then, when the woman started off in a hurry: "Don't bother. They'd all be gone now."

The woman turned back, disappointed. Her eyes returned to Yagi's precious bundle.

"Would you sell me one of those?"

Yagi shrugged. "Maybe. Depends."

The spirited haggling that followed attracted others. In just a few minutes Yagi had sold all the cabbages for nearly three times what he had paid. He chuckled with satisfaction as he stowed the proceeds and resumed gnawing on a leaf. A generous handful had somehow ended up hidden under his shirt, enough to keep him and Kan going all day.

"All set?"

Yagi helped Kan to his feet and they again started off, Kan hanging on to the navy man's shoulder now for support.

He stopped.

"It's not much farther," he said. "I'll be all right from here. You don't need to come."

Yagi lowered his head and didn't reply.

"It could be dangerous," Kan pressed. "There's no need for you to involve yourself in my trouble."

Yagi looked around at the wasteland of the city. His own city, Osaka, which he had not visited in three years, would be in a similar state. He scratched his head, looking almost sheepish.

"I'll tell you what it is," he said. "Right now, I don't have anywhere else to go."

They continued east, walking in the shade under the Yamanote Line's elevated tracks, then turned south. They were close now. Kan knew this neighborhood well. He had strolled here many times while working at the Riken, taking a little exercise while he mulled over a problem. Now he was struggling just to stay on his feet.

The familiar street, heaps of rubble lining the sides, derelict streetcar tracks down the middle. The remains of the dispensary operated by the friendly old couple, now dead. The cemetery on the right, graves untended. Then a final turn and there it was: the Riken.

The sight of it gave Kan a burst of energy to walk on his own. He led the way to the entrance and looked in from behind the gatepost. No vehicles, civilian or military, were visible inside. No soldiers or police appeared to be waiting to arrest them. The place was just as he had left it, forlorn and abandoned, a lifetime ago.

"'Institute of Physical and Chemical Research,'" murmured Yagi, reading the sign affixed to the gatepost.

They passed inside and turned right to skirt around behind Building 43, gutted but still standing. Kan was not sure what he was trying to avoid, but it seemed a good idea to stay out of sight.

They passed the razed foundation of Building 49, the former home of Project Ni-Go, the neglected plot of sweet potatoes a riot of green in the ashes. He could see Building 29 now on the far side of the compound, one of the few structures that had escaped the flames in the spring. Should he head there, to Dr. Nishina's office? No, he would go to the dormitory first.

The dormitory building, like the rest of the Riken, was deserted. Kan paused at the door and looked about. Where could Noriko be?

Yagi, spotting a laundry area behind the building, skirted around back for a quick wash.

Kan headed inside. He went down the corridor, stirring motes of dust that hung in the air. The door to his room was unlocked. And inside . . .

He scanned the room. A pang hit him when his eyes touched on the urn. Aiko's remains. The space appeared tidier than he had left it. The bedding in the corner was neatly folded, pillow on top.

With rising excitement, he went to the dresser and opened the drawer where Noriko kept her few items of apparel, not much more than one change of clothing.

It was empty. Noriko had been here. She had changed into clean clothes.

He staggered from the room and down the hall to the toilet. Noriko wasn't there.

He heard voices. He hurried to the back door and threw it open. Yagi was standing there, conversing with a woman who had been washing clothes in a basin, her bare arms wet, her hair pulled back to reveal a gaunt face, which she was now hiding behind her hands as she burst into tears.

"Noriko!"

Kan stumbled down the steps and threw himself into his wife's arms and together they wept.

"You made it back," he sobbed. "You made it back. That's wonderful. I'm happy."

They clung to each other for several minutes, crying. To give them a little privacy, Yagi turned away and began noisily washing himself. When they finally let go, it was to examine each other with tender concern, stroking their faces and shoulders, touching hair, touching hands. Keizo was gutted to see Noriko so thin, just as Noriko was dismayed by his haggard appearance and the condition of his hand.

"What happened to you, husband?" she asked.

Keizo tried to smile. "I had a little accident. It's all right."

Yagi, ablutions finished, was beside them, drying himself with his shirt.

"This is Petty Officer Ryohei Yagi," said Keizo, wiping his eyes. "A friend of mine. Yagi-heisō, this is my wife, Noriko Kan."

Noriko smiled. It lifted Kan's heart even further to see it. "Yes, we just met," she said, giving Yagi a bow. "I'm very pleased to meet you."

Yagi bobbed his head as he finished toweling himself. "Likewise."

Noriko turned back to Keizo. "Shall we go to see Dr. Nishina and Miss Yokoyama? They've been so anxious about you."

They headed around to the front of the dormitory building, arm in arm, Yagi holding back as he put on his wet shirt. The drone of an airplane rose in the distance.

They froze.

An olive drab army truck was parked across the compound. A soldier was entering Building 29. He was facing away. He hadn't seen them.

They ducked back behind the dormitory, out of sight, and began to retreat.

"Stop!"

They wheeled about. A second soldier had stepped out from the front corner of the dormitory, holding a rifle. He was wearing a white armband with two characters printed on it in red: *Kem Pei*. Military Police.

"Are you Keizo Kan?" he said, slowly approaching.

Keizo, overcome with fear, didn't answer. He and Noriko clung together as they backed away.

"I said stop!"

They stopped.

The drone of the approaching aircraft grew louder.

The soldier drew nearer, aiming his rifle at their chests. "Are you Keizo Kan?"

Keizo felt his knees go weak. "I am," he stammered.

The sound of aircraft engines rose to an intense reverberation.

The kempei soldier looked up. A large bomber, painted black, was passing overhead.

He collapsed to the ground, felled by a massive blow to the head by Yagi, who had circled around the other side of the building and come up from behind.

Yagi snatched up the rifle and stood over the body, ready to use the stock as a club. But there was no need. The man was unconscious.

A glance over his shoulder. No sign of the second soldier. And the army truck was out of sight, screened by the corner of the building.

He looked at Keizo and Noriko, wide-eyed with shock.

He cast the rifle away and seized them by the arms.

They started to run.

THIRTY-THREE

THE TAKEOFF HAD BEEN FLAWLESS.

The Renzan's four Homare engines had risen to 2,500 rpms when Captain Onda advanced the throttles, a collective 8,000 horsepower, their full potential, a pure and harmonious sound filling the flight deck.

The brakes were released. The Renzan started rolling. The additional weight of fuel the aircraft was carrying had been more than offset by the removal of armor. Onda could feel the difference in the way they were gathering speed. He kept the plane on the ground until most of the runway was used up, then pulled back on the yoke and took to the air.

Altitude 100 meters. The Renzan rising.

Altitude 200 meters. Farmland disappearing.

Altitude 300 meters. They were approaching the hills.

Behind the flight deck, on the far side of the catwalk, Colonel Sagara sat alone in the radio operator's compartment, facing the guillotine switch. It had been a humiliating struggle to get into his flight suit, Onda assisting. And the manhandling that had been required to get him up into the plane had been worse. But he would need only his right hand to detonate the bomb.

He grimly regarded his left hand, the fingers curled up and useless. His body was broken. He knew it. Was this why fate had directed him onto the plane? Because operating the switch was the only thing he was still physically able to do?

The compartment tilted, the Renzan coming onto a new heading. Sagara closed his eyes and felt himself move with the plane, a part of the machine. He contemplated the gasoline flowing through the lines, feeding the engines, the aviation gas he had fortuitously acquired from Army Fuel Headquarters, refined from the roots of pine trees. How appropriate it was that they were relying on the indomitable pine, the eternal pine, for their flight. The literal essence of the earth, pine tree roots dug from the soil of the homeland, would power them across the ocean to destroy San Francisco.

The Renzan leveled out and continued its climb. The drone of the engines rose to a frequency that caused the door of the cabinet on Sagara's left to begin sympathetically buzzing. It was closed but had not been properly latched.

The noise gradually intruded into the colonel's thoughts. He opened his eyes. His gaze fell on a pair of pliers sitting on the side of the radio operator's desk before him. Fibers were clinging to its jaws. They matched the asbestos insulation on the wire leading to the guillotine switch. The scientist Kan and the navy man, the Korean, must have left the pliers sitting there after installing the switch.

"Careless," he muttered.

He snatched up the pliers with his good hand and turned to stow them in the cabinet, alongside what he glimpsed was a flashlight. He closed and latched the door to stop the buzzing.

He settled back in his seat. The cabinet was silent.

That's when it hit him.

He shouted through the interphone to the cockpit: "Onda! Did you check for sabotage?"

A crackle in Sagara's headphones. Onda's voice, confused: "Sabotage, Colonel?"

"The bomb!" Sagara roared back. "Did you check the bomb!"

The flight engineer, Lieutenant Otani, was sent back from the flight deck. Sagara had already decided that it would be pointless to try to check the bomb itself. They were not familiar with its inner workings, and in any event there was no way to get at it, given the lack of space inside the bomb bay. But there would have been no space for Keizo Kan or Petty Officer Yagi to get at it either. If they had committed an act of sabotage before deserting, the triggering wire was the more likely target. It would have been easy to access. It might have been cut.

Otani took the flashlight from the cabinet and began examining the wire. The portion from the guillotine switch down to the floor was intact.

He opened the door at the front of the compartment, letting in a flood of cold air, and stepped onto the catwalk. He directed the flashlight beam down into the darkness, tracing the wire on its snaking course. He could see no obvious sign of a break.

He climbed down off the catwalk and followed the wire.

The Renzan was over the ocean now, heading east at 6,000 meters. It had already picked up a powerful tailwind, allowing Captain Onda to level out at a lower altitude than planned and still stay on schedule, giving Otani in the frigid bomb bay time to examine the wire leading up from the bomb.

"I've found something."

Otani's voice coming through the interphone was quaking with the cold. He had connected his headset in the bomb bay, but there was no rheostat there to plug into to heat his flight suit.

"A dial of some sort," he was saying. "It's been spliced into the wire. It looks like a thermometer."

Onda's voice, anxious: "Can you remove it?"

A pause.

"It's very cold," said Otani. "Difficult using my hands."

Colonel Sagara in the radio operator's compartment was rocking back and forth with the tension. This was the moment. This was his purpose. This was why fate had led him onto the plane.

He spoke into the interphone: "Be careful. Don't touch it. Describe it to me."

A pause.

"A nail has been inserted into the dial face," replied Otani, his voice shaking. "One end of the wire has been attached to the nail, the other end to the needle." Another pause. "The needle is almost touching."

Sagara's mind was racing. An image coalesced: the wire routed through the thermometer, the gap between the needle and the nail, the needle advancing as the temperature fell. When they touched, that would complete the circuit. The atomic bomb would detonate . . . if the triggering switch was already on.

His eyes went to the guillotine switch.

He reached out to it and lifted the locking bracket.

He hesitated.

"Otani, don't let the needle touch the—"

He was engulfed by a bright light.

THIRTY-FOUR

THEY HEADED SOUTH AND EAST TOWARD ASAKUSA, INSTINCTIVELY DRAWN TOWARD THE place where their home had once stood, Keizo Kan staggering with his arm around Petty Officer Yagi. They had reached the drained pond on the edge of Ueno Park when Keizo's legs gave out completely and he sank to his knees. Yagi went off in search of water, leaving him lying on the grass, Noriko cradling his head.

"What happened to you?" she said, anguished, looking into his face. "How did you hurt your hand? Why are you sick?"

He wanted to tell her everything, the whole story, but in his exhaustion it all seemed like a jumble. "There was a bomb," he began. "A plane crashed in Yamaguchi Prefecture. An American plane. I was called to the Ministry of War." He fell silent. He did not know how to continue. He needed a few minutes to rest.

He looked up into her face. It was so thin. And the lines of stress . . . He knew she had suffered. But in her eyes, gazing down into his— behind the sadness he saw tenderness and love. It was a look he had not seen in a long time.

"I'm sorry," he whispered. "I'm sorry I wasn't a better husband to you."

"No, don't say that." Tears came into Noriko's eyes. "It was me. I couldn't—"

Her voice broke. She lowered her head until their foreheads were touching. They sat silent together as their souls reconnected.

"Do you remember when we came here with Aiko?" Keizo said after a time. "We rented a boat. There were lotus blossoms everywhere. And the elephant took your handkerchief at the zoo."

Noriko smiled at the memory. "It's all so different now," she said, looking around. There was no longer water in the pond. It had been transformed into a rice paddy. And Ueno Zoo, visible off to the left, the screen of trees scorched and leafless—it had been closed two years before, in anticipation of the air raids. All the animals had been killed.

Yagi returned with some water, which revived Keizo a little. The navy man sprawled on the grass beside him and took out his crumpled cigarette pack.

"Last one."

He cast the empty pack aside and lit the bent cigarette, drew in a lungful of smoke and gazed up at the sky. He passed it to Kan for a puff, then took another.

"Well," he sighed, "I suppose that does it for me. Hitting a kempei soldier . . . We should split up."

He watched a cloud drifting by low overhead. At least he had a little money in his pocket. If he could scrounge up more vegetables, he could do more buying and selling. And he still had his dice.

A distant flash, like lightning on the horizon, illuminated the sky in Yagi's peripheral vision.

He turned to look.

He sat up.

He rose to his feet, gazing intently toward the east.

"Look at that."

In the direction of the flash the sky was showing the subtle hues of a rainbow, reds and greens and yellows and purples. The ethereal display lingered for a moment, then faded away.

"Did you see that?" he said, turning to them.

"Was it lightning?" asked Noriko.

A smile spread across Yagi's face. He slapped his knee and let out a laugh. "It worked! Do you see that, Sensei? I *told* you I did it right!"

"What was it?" said Noriko.

Yagi was looking down at Kan. "I *told* you I did it right! Didn't I tell you? We did it!"

Kan was nodding, his eyes on the sky where the colors had been. He looked up at Yagi. "I think you're right. We did it."

Noriko was looking at them both now. "What did you do?"

"Top secret," said Yagi. "You'll have to ask your husband to tell you."

He took a final drag on the cigarette, his chin thrust triumphantly into the air, then ground the butt into the dirt.

"Well, I'd better be off."

Keizo struggled to sit up. "But where will you go?"

Yagi looked around at the desolate city—burned-out buildings, empty lots, rice growing in a manicured pond that had been an urban attraction.

The side of his mouth rose in a crooked smile. "*Humph.* I have no idea."

He adjusted his shirt, smoothed down his hair, put on his cap.

"Well, so long," he said, laying his hand on Keizo's shoulder. He gave it a final pat and was gone.

Keizo watched him head off down the street, then settled back, his head on Noriko's lap. His eyes drifted closed. His body relaxed. He allowed himself to be carried away by fatigue.

"Keizo . . . Keizo, are you all right?" Noriko's voice sounded distant, but at the same time very close.

He smiled and nodded. The pain from his injured hand was receding, along with the anxiety, along with the fear. He was with Noriko again. Nothing else mattered. They were together ·in this moment. Peace was descending upon him. The world was put right.

Was this what it felt like to be dying?

The gentle touch of Noriko's hand, stroking his forehead. A hint of breeze on his face. The earth warm under his back. Then something else, a presence that seemed to embrace them, suffusing the dark behind his eyelids with an expanding, welcoming, loving marigold glow.

He opened his eyes and looked up at his wife.

"I can feel Aiko," he whispered. "I know she's all right."

Tears of joy welled up in Noriko's eyes. Then her face crumpled in a look of anguish.

She broke down, clutching him in her arms.

"Oh, please don't leave me," she wept. "Please don't go. I couldn't bear it. I need you. Garbo loves Taylor!"

He raised his hand and brushed the tears from her cheek.

"And Taylor loves Garbo. Taylor loves Garbo so much."

EPILOGUE

A CHEER ROSE FROM THE 80,000 FANS CROWDING MEIJI JINGU STADIUM, RENAMED STATESIDE Park with the American occupation. The Japanese All-Stars had kicked off the seventh inning with a single in their game against the visiting San Francisco Seals, the score still 0–0. Would the All-Stars finally win a game for Japan against the Seals on their 1949 Japan Goodwill Tour? They were certainly putting up a better showing than the Yomiuri Giants had made in their earlier 13–4 loss to the Seals.

"Look at that," said Noriko Kan, directing Keizo's attention to the group of Americans seated a few rows farther down and over to the left. They were on their feet cheering again, dumbfounding and delighting the Japanese fans all around them. Why would Americans cheer for a Japanese team playing one of their own? But there they were, yelling and clapping along with everyone else. It made Noriko proud to see them. The things she had loved about America—it was restoring her faith.

"They live here," Keizo rationalized as they sat back down and the tumult subsided. "They're rooting for the home team."

The age gap between them appeared wider now, four years after the war. Noriko, at thirty-three, was still quite youthful and attractive in a flower print skirt and white blouse, her looks and figure almost fully restored. Keizo looked much older, in his late fifties, although he was only forty-two. He had a paunch and his hair had turned gray, and there was a slight shuffle in his step when he walked.

The boy in the row in front of them turned around to gape at Keizo's maimed hand. It was missing the index and middle fingers and looked like a claw. Keizo regarded him as the lad sucked on his candy and stared.

"You have a crab hand," the boy observed.

"My dad can snip off your nose with it," said Keizo's and Noriko's son, Koji. He was three. He turned to Keizo. "Go on, Dad. Show him."

Keizo did the trick, hiding his good hand in his claw, making the snip and a *snick* sound with his mouth and protruding his thumb.

"There," he said, displaying the nose. "Now I have it." A darting motion back at the boy's face. "And now it's back on."

Everyone seated around them started laughing, but no one louder than Ryohei Yagi. He roared out a guffaw and slapped his knee and knocked over an empty beer bottle under his feet.

They had chanced on each other a month before, as Kan was on his way from the Tokyo College of Science, where he was a professor of physics, to the new home he and Noriko had built in Asakusa. He was mounting the steps at Iidabashi Station when a familiar voice called out behind him, "Sensei! You're alive!" He had turned to see Ryohei Yagi transformed—dapper suit, snappy fedora, radiating energy and visibly prosperous.

They went to the first bar they came to and began to catch up, starting with the day after they parted, when the Emperor made his speech announcing Japan's surrender and the end of the war. Kan had been lying in a crowded hospital ward, expecting to die, when he heard it. But he hadn't died. Instead, after losing all his hair and two amputated fingers, the Americans found him. He was taken to a U.S. Army hospital and interrogated for nearly three months while he slowly recovered from what was being called radiation sickness. When he was finally released in December 1945, it was with the threat that he would be sent to prison for the rest of his life if he ever revealed the existence of the atomic bomb the Japanese had recovered from the crashed B-29. He had been required to sign a sheaf of papers pledging to keep what he knew a secret. Forever.

"Did the Americans . . . " Kan looked searchingly into Yagi's face, unable to say the rest.

"Arrest me?" said Yagi. "Oh sure, they got me. Picked me up in early October."

Kan hung his head in shame. "I'm sorry. I couldn't help it. I gave them your name."

Yagi laughed. "No need to be sorry, Sensei. I should thank you."

Kan looked at him, confused. "But didn't they lock you up?"

"Sure they did. But I didn't mind. Gave me three meals a day and a bed while they asked me their questions. I told them my memory would work better if a little payment was made. So I walked out of there with a nice wad of cash."

Kan's eyes grew wide. "You asked the Americans for money?"

"Why not? I gave them valuable information, information they wanted. Wasn't that worth something? And it set me up. Give-and-take, right?"

They stayed together drinking for two hours, Yagi shockingly forthcoming about how he made his living and asking Kan what he knew about pachinko game machines. The former navy man had used the money from the Americans as seed capital to start a thriving black-market business, forging connections with supply clerks at U.S. military bases all across the Tokyo region. Kan also gleaned that Yagi was an important figure in some sort of ethnic Korean organization. He would later learn that it was a yakuza syndicate called the Tosei-kai, the Voice of the East Gang.

When they finally parted, both fairly drunk, it was with a vow to meet again soon.

• • •

Ninth inning. The Seals were up, the score still 0–0. Yagi, throwing himself into the spirit of intercultural cheering, was roaring encouragement in English to the American coming to bat, outfielder Dick Steinhauer with eleven hits in the series. "Come on, Dik-ku Su-ta-in-hau-wa!"

Crack! A home run into the right-field bleachers. Seals win 1–0. Another loss for Japan. A murmur of disappointment rose from the stadium, but only for a moment, and certainly not from Yagi. He was smiling.

"But we lost," said young Koji, looking up at his face.

"We came for a good time," said Yagi. "And we had a good time, right? So we won!"

Hearing those words, Noriko felt the last of her reserve fall away. She decided she liked this man.

They joined the throngs making for the exits. The nearest station was sure to be crowded, so Keizo and Noriko decided to walk to Harajuku Station instead. They said their farewells to Yagi and set off, Noriko holding Koji's hand. The little boy was already a strong walker.

The tickets to the game had come from Noriko's employer, the American Forces Radio Network, where she worked as an interpreter and hosted the morning show *Let's Speak Japanese*. She had suffered no repercussions for her propaganda broadcasts during the war. Unlike her colleague Ikuko Toguri, facing a prison sentence after being famously labeled "Tokyo Rose," Noriko had given up her U.S. citizenship and therefore could not be accused of treason. It made Noriko sad to see Ikuko singled out for punishment for what all the Nisei broadcasters at NHK had done, simply because she had kept her American passport. Ikuko had never even used the name "Rose." She had always referred to herself in her broadcasts as "Annie." Noriko didn't tell anyone at American Forces Radio that if there had been an actual Tokyo Rose, it was her. Even her former NHK colleagues didn't seem to remember that she had used that name early on. And so Noriko, like Keizo, had secrets to keep.

They crossed the fetid culvert known as the Shibuya River and arrived at Harajuku Station. The wooden structure had survived the war, spared by the flames that had consumed the buildings around it and blackened the trees on the other side of the tracks. The trees were growing back now, flourishing in the ash-enriched soil. They formed a wall of green tinged with fall colors all along this section of track, where the Yamanote Line skirted Meiji Shrine and Yoyogi Park.

They bought tickets and passed through to the platform and found a place to wait against the wall, under the clock. They were soon joined by two young Americans in uniform—Marines—talking loudly about baseball. Noriko overheard them mention the name of the Seals' famous manager, Lefty O'Doul.

"Were you boys at the game?" she asked.

The Marines turned to her and brightened, surprised by her perfect English. "Yeah, we were. You too?"

Noriko began chatting with them. She had always had an easy way with strangers. And her experience working at American Forces Radio had dissolved the bitterness she had felt toward her former country and its people. The Marines were stationed at Yokosuka, she learned, and one of them knew San Francisco. It pleased Noriko to talk about her old home.

Keizo listened for a while. Then his mind drifted to the drawings in his pocket, designs for currently available pachinko machines that Yagi had given him back at the stadium. Yagi was planning to open a chain of gaming arcades that he was going to call Lucky Daikon Pachinko. "Because everything I have I owe to the Daikon," he said. But he wanted better machines, machines that would make the game more unpredictable and dynamic, like gambling. Could Kan come up with something? Kan had agreed to try.

Daikon.

Yagi's mention of their code name for the bomb had brought the riddle again to his mind. It was only after the war that Kan realized why the word had made him uneasy. It was when he was in American custody and caught sight of his interrogator's notes written in English, the word *DAIKON* spelled out in capital letters. There, between the D and the N, was the name of his daughter. Aiko. "Child of love." What did it mean, the love that was his daughter inside the hate of the bomb? It was like a paradox, a Zen koan to meditate on to achieve understanding. Was it an insight into his own real nature, into the contradictions of what it meant to be human? He pondered this for many days. Then he was released and carried on with his life.

The second Marine took out a cigarette and lit it with his fancy lighter. He tapped out another and offered it to Kan.

"Thank you," said Kan in English. It was good American tobacco, a Camel. "I will save it for later."

The train was arriving. It pulled into the station and squealed to a stop. The two Americans stepped into the current of bodies and let themselves be carried along into the car. Keizo held back for a moment, under the clock, tucking the cigarette into his pocket. He would smoke it after dinner, sitting on the back veranda overlooking his garden.

He put his arm through Noriko's and took Koji by the hand.

They followed the Americans onto the train.

SOURCES AND ACKNOWLEDGMENTS

THE IDEA FOR *DAIKON* CAME TO ME MANY YEARS AGO. I WAS READING ABOUT THE *ENOLA GAY* and the Hiroshima mission, and it struck me how uncertain the first atomic bomb was. It was experimental, not fully tested. The scientists who built it were confident it would work. It *had* to work. It was physics. But the men tasked with delivering the weapon were not nearly so sure.

Unlike the first atomic bomb tested at Alamogordo on July 16, 1945 (which was a static test of an implosion-type plutonium bomb, not the uranium-gun-type design), the Hiroshima bomb was to be dropped from a plane at a high altitude to detonate automatically above the ground. This meant that a complex detonation system involving radar units, barometric switches, batteries, wiring, connectors, and electronics had to be added to what was otherwise a simple design. And all that complexity increased the chances for failure. In practice bomb runs prior to the Hiroshima mission, there were instances where dummy bombs equipped with the same detonation system either failed to explode or exploded too early, moments after leaving the plane.

Physicist Luis Alvarez, who was sent to Tinian as part of Project

Alberta, the team that assembled the atomic bombs, would later recall witnessing one such failure: "I watched, with field glasses, the bomb being dropped from the bomb bay of a B-29 flying over the ocean, north of Tinian Island, and we were simultaneously listening to radio signals from the bomb. At a certain height above the ocean, the 'proximity fuzes' were to send out a signal, and also release some puffs of smoke. You can imagine our consternation when neither the signal was emitted nor were the puffs of smoke visible—the dummy bomb simply splashed into the ocean" (John Coster-Mullen, *Atom Bombs,* 26).

Morris Jeppson, assistant weaponeer aboard the *Enola Gay,* which dropped the Hiroshima bomb, put it this way: "There was a lot of concern at the last minute that the fuzing was not reliable" (Coster-Mullen, *Atom Bombs,* 26).

This possibility that the bomb might fail gave me the idea for a novel. It would proceed from the question: *What would have happened if the atomic bomb dropped on Hiroshima failed to explode and the Japanese recovered it?*

To imagine an outcome, I studied what was happening in Japan at the time, starting with William Craig's *The Fall of Japan,* Thomas Coffey's *Imperial Tragedy,* and Stanley Weintraub's *The Last Great Victory.* The main point of tension in those closing days of the war was between the hard-liners, particularly in the Imperial Army, who wanted to fight on, and those wanting to surrender. Some of these hard-liners knew that the war was lost but rejected the terms of unconditional surrender. They were determined to fight until the Allies relented and offered more favorable terms. Others, like Colonel Sagara in this story, believed that some sort of victory could still be achieved; that if they continued to fight they would eventually break the Americans' spirit. And if they didn't, the Japanese people would all perish with honor, fighting to the last, "until we eat stones." For the Sagaras in the Imperial Army, millions of Japanese dead was preferable to the disgrace of surrender.

I found the expression "eat stones" in Russell Brines' 1944 book

Until They Eat Stones. I have never seen it mentioned elsewhere. Brines writes: "*Ishii wo kajiru made,* say the commoners; *Ishii ni kajiritsui te made mo,* say the educated. The phrase means they will continue the war until every man—perhaps every woman and child—lies face downward on the battlefield" (9). I originally intended to call this novel *One Hundred Million Eat Stones.*

The methamphetamine drug to which Colonel Sagara is addicted became available in Japan in 1941. It was marketed under the name Philopon, a combination of the Greek words *philo* (love) and *ponos* (labor). It was widely distributed during the war to boost endurance in combat and increase home-front production, and it led to an addiction epidemic after the country surrendered. Philopon was declared illegal in 1951, but it would remain a problem for years. By 1954, there were 1.5 million addicts in Japan.

The character of Dr. Keizo Kan is loosely based on three men involved in Japan's atomic bomb program, Project Ni-Go: program head Dr. Yoshio Nishina, one of Japan's most eminent physicists at the time; Hidehiko Tamaki, leader of the theory team and the first man Nishina recruited; and Masa Takeuchi, head of the separation team, the position Kan holds in the story. Some of the sources I used for Project Ni-Go: Robert Wilcox, *Japan's Secret War*; Kim Dong-Won, *Yoshio Nishina: Father of Modern Physics in Japan*; Nuel Pharr Davis, *Lawrence and Oppenheimer* (for Kan's fictional time at UC Berkeley); Kenji Ito, "Values of 'Pure Science': Nishina Yoshio's Wartime Discourse Between Nationalism and Physics, 1940–1945," *Historical Studies in the Physical and Biological Sciences* 33, no. 1 (2002): 61–86; Tristan Grunow, "A Reexamination of the 'Shock of Hiroshima': The Japanese Bomb Projects and the Surrender Decision," *Journal of American–East Asian Relations* 12, no. 3/4 (2003): 155–89; and Keiko Nagase-Reimer, Walter Grunden, and Masakatsu Yamazaki, "Nuclear Weapons Research in Japan During the Second World War," *Historia Scientiarum* 14, no. 3 (2005): 1–38. The atomic accident in chapter 8 and Seaman Wada's and Keizo Kan's subsequent symptoms of radiation exposure were inspired by the stories of Manhattan Project scientists Harry Daghlian and Louis Slotin, who were accidentally irradiated during experiments with atomic bomb plutonium cores shortly after the war. The song Kan sings in chapter 16 is "Oka o Koete" ("Crossing the Hill") by Ichirō Fujiyama, 1931.

Investigations into the feasibility of building an atomic bomb were begun in Japan in April 1940. An atomic bomb program, under Lieutenant General Takeo Yasuda and funded by the Imperial Japanese Army, was launched in the spring of 1941. It was based at Japan's premier scientific research center, the Institute of Physical and Chemical Research in Tokyo, commonly referred to by the acronym "RIKEN," and was code-named Project Ni-Go, the Ni coming from the name of its head, Dr. Nishina. In comparison to the American program to build the bomb, the Manhattan Project, Project Ni-Go was tiny. Its staff of researchers never numbered more than twenty and its budget totaled the equivalent of half a million American dollars, less than a thousandth of what the United States spent to develop the bomb.

Because of these constraints, Project Ni-Go concentrated its efforts on only one element, uranium, and pursued only one method of enrichment, gaseous thermal diffusion. A sixteen-foot-high thermal diffusion separator was built and installed in Building 49 at the Riken, and efforts were made to enrich uranium in gaseous form. But every test was a failure. By the time Building 49 was destroyed in an air raid in April 1945, no uranium had been enriched.

Japan also had a second atomic bomb project, funded by the Imperial Japanese Navy, which had initially rejected the idea of developing such a weapon prior to 1943. It was based at Kyoto Imperial University, under Professor Bunsaku Arakatsu, and was code-named Project F-Go, the "F" standing for "fission." Arakatsu's team, like Nishina's in Tokyo, focused on the element uranium, but pursued a different enrichment method using a device called an ultra-centrifuge. A design was completed in July 1945, but the machine still hadn't been built when the war ended. The Project F-Go story, incidentally, was the inspiration for a Japanese film, *Child of the Sun* (English title, *Gift of Fire*), that aired on NHK in August 2020.

For Noriko Kan, I borrowed elements from the real-life story of Iva Ikuko Toguri, aka Tokyo Rose, as revealed in Masayo Duus's biography *Tokyo Rose, Orphan of the Pacific*, and in the declassified FBI files on Tokyo Rose. The trouble Noriko encounters at NHK is drawn from an account in these FBI files of a Filipino staffer who had dalliances with some of the female Nisei workers, which caused feelings of jealousy. For the Tokkō "Thought Police" (full name Tokubetsu Koto Keisatsu) and the Kempeitai military police: Richard H. Mitchell, *Janus-Faced Justice: Political Criminals in Imperial Japan*; and Raymond Lamont-Brown, *Kempeitai: Japan's Dreaded Military Police*.

More than any other character in *Daikon*, Petty Officer Ryohei Yagi was inspired by a real person: Japanese actor Toshiro Mifune. It is not widely known, but Mifune served for six years in the Japanese army. He was drafted in 1939 in Manchuria, where he was born and grew up, and went off for training thinking it would be great fun. It wasn't. Mifune would describe what followed as "six months of getting beaten up. It was a nightmare." He resolved to get out of the army as soon as his mandatory period of service was up. But then the Pacific War started and any chance of being discharged disappeared. Trapped in the army indefinitely, Mifune became rebellious and never rose above the rank of private first class—a Japanese version of Private Angelo Maggio in *From Here to Eternity*. At the end of the war he was doing manual labor at Kumano Airfield, a kamikaze base on Kyushu, and taking farewell photographs on the side for the young pilots before they flew off to their deaths. In later years, telling his son about his time at Kumano and the young pilots he knew there would reduce Mifune to tears.

The idea of making Yagi Korean came from my own affection for Korea, where I was born and grew up and about which I've written three books of history, starting with *The Imjin War: Japan's Sixteenth-Century Invasion of Korea and Attempt to Conquer China*. The oil tanker Yagi served on, the *Iro*, was an actual ship, the details and movements

of which are available online at http://www.combinedfleet.com/Iro_t
.htm. Background for Yagi's encounter with the bomb came from U.S.
Naval Technical Mission to Japan Report O-06, "Japanese Bomb Dis-
posal Methods," which includes a translation of a firsthand account by
Technical Lieutenant Kikuo Nishida, "Reports on the Bomb or Shell
Disposal in the Japanese Navy," October 1, 1945.

The atomic bomb plays such a central role in *Daikon* that it is almost a character unto itself. I needed to visualize it in detail, its inner
workings, to write about PO Yagi and Keizo Kan taking it apart and
putting it back together. Unfortunately, none of the books I consulted,
starting with Richard Rhodes's *The Making of the Atomic Bomb*, came
anywhere near providing the depth of detail I needed. Then I discovered John Coster-Mullen's *Atom Bombs: The Top Secret Inside Story of
Little Boy and Fat Man*. Coster-Mullen's book is not so much a narrative
history as a compendium of research on the Hiroshima and Nagasaki
bombs gleaned from declassified documents, interviews, and deductions to fill in redacted gaps. How big were the uranium rings? How
many were there? How much did they weigh? What color were they?
How were they held together? How long was the gun tube? What did
the initiators look like? It's all in Coster-Mullen's book, along with a
wealth of photos, illustrations, and plans. I could not have written *Daikon* without this invaluable source.

I was also fortunate to correspond with George "G. C." Hollowwa,
a radar weaponeer with the 509th Composite Group at Wendover,
Utah. "My specialty was weapon fuzing" was how Hollowwa described
his role to me. "I assembled approximately 10 to 15 test Little Boys and
performed the in-flight test drops. I also assembled and drop tested an
equal number of Fat Men." Hollowwa shared with me a wealth of detail about the Hiroshima bomb and B-29s, and fielded such questions
as, "Could the Hiroshima bomb have been a dud?"

There really was a Special Intelligence Unit in Tokyo that was
monitoring the B-29s on Tinian, Guam, and Okinawa as described in
Daikon—in particular the V600 "Special Task Planes," which were the

B-29s of the 509th Composite Group. The Japanese network NHK aired a documentary on this subject in 2011 entitled *Genbaku tōka ikasarenakatta gokuhi jōhō* ("The Dropping of the Atomic Bomb: Top Secret Information That Wasn't Used").

Another useful source that contributed realism to *Daikon* are the maps of Japan made by the U.S. Army in 1945–46 in the Perry-Castañeda Library Map Collection at the University of Texas (https://maps.lib.utexas.edu). I relied on these maps heavily while writing this book, particularly the "Tokyo and Environs" map series, which shows detail down to individual buildings, extending out as far as Tama Airfield.

I was fortunate to have access through my alma mater Queen's University in Kingston, Ontario, to the full run of the *Nippon Times* newspaper for the months of July and August 1945. This was a valuable source for all sorts of details, and also contributed dialogue to the story. When Kan is waiting for the train at Hiroshima station, for example, the speech broadcast over the loudspeaker is taken almost verbatim from a speech printed in the *Times*, as was the pep talk given by the commander to the kaiten trainees in chapter 11.

For the preface: "Beta Calutron Operations, June 24, 1944–May 4, 1947," John Coster-Mullen, *Atom Bombs*, 286; "Transportation of Critical Shipments," Memorandum from Major J. A. Derry to Admiral W. S. DeLany, August 17, 1945, *Atom Bombs*, 284; Doug Stanton, *In Harm's Way: The Sinking of the USS* Indianapolis *and the Extraordinary Story of Its Survivors*, 29; Lieutenant Haynes quoted in Richard A. Hulver, *A Grave Misfortune: The USS* Indianapolis *Tragedy*, 14.

For the description of Tinian and the B-29 mission in chapter 1: Harlow Russ, *Project Alberta: The Preparation of Atomic Bombs for Use in World War II* (contains detailed maps of Tinian); Paul W. Tibbets, *The Tibbets Story*; and *Enola Gay* crew member interviews in the Beser Foundation Archives.

On Japanese aircraft, in particular the Nakajima G8N Renzan: René Francillon, *Japanese Aircraft of the Pacific War*; Robert C. Mikesh,

Japanese Cockpit Interiors (contains a photo of the Nakajima G5N cockpit, a close approximation to the Renzan's). To better imagine the interior of the Renzan, which is not well known, I studied the American B-17 bomber, from which the Renzan was largely derived.

On Project Fu-Go and the Japanese discovery of high-altitude, high-speed air currents blowing across the Pacific, later known as the "jet stream": Ross Allen Coen, *Fu-Go: The Curious History of Japan's Balloon Bomb Attack on America*; Robert C. Mikesh, *Japan's World War II Balloon Bomb Attacks on North America*.

On kaiten (human torpedoes) and Hikari Special Attack Unit: Yutaka Yokota, *The Kaiten Weapon*; Michael Mair and Joy Waldron, *Kaiten: Japan's Secret Manned Suicide Submarine and the First American Ship It Sank in WWII*.

On the kamikaze experience: Yasuo Kuwahara and Gordon T. Allred, *Kamikaze: A Japanese Pilot's Own Spectacular Story of the Famous Suicide Squadrons*; Raymond Lamont-Brown, *Kamikaze: Japan's Suicide Samurai*; Ryuji Nagatsuka, *I Was a Kamikaze: The Knights of the Divine Wind* (who writes of the difficulty pilot trainees had with inferior "A-Go" fuel, which resulted in numerous deaths).

On life in wartime Japan: Thomas R. H. Havens, *Valley of Darkness: The Japanese People and World War Two*; Samuel Yamashita, ed., *Leaves from an Autumn of Emergencies: Selections from the Wartime Diaries of Ordinary Japanese*; Eugene Soviak, ed., *A Diary of Darkness: The Wartime Diary of Kiyosawa Kiyoshi*; Mary Kimoto Tomita, *Dear Miye: Letters Home from Japan, 1939–1946*; Women's Division of Soka Gakkai, *Women Against War: Personal Accounts of Forty Japanese Women*; Youth Division of Soka Gakkai, *Cries for Peace: Experiences of Japanese Victims of World War II*; Frank Gibney, ed., *Sensō: The Japanese Remember the Pacific War: Letters to the Editor of Asahi Shimbun*; the novels *Confessions of a Mask* by Yukio Mishima and *Grass for My Pillow* by Saiichi Maruya.

On the atomic bombing of Hiroshima: John Hersey, *Hiroshima*; Kenzaburo Oe, *Hiroshima Notes*; Paul Ham, *Hiroshima Nagasaki*;

Charles Pellegrino, *To Hell and Back: The Last Train from Hiroshima*; Michihiko Hachiya, *Hiroshima Diary: The Journal of a Japanese Physician, August 6–September 30, 1945*; Hiroshima Peace Culture Foundation, *Eyewitness Testimonies: Appeals from the A-Bomb Survivors*; Diana Wickes Roose, *Teach Us to Live: Stories from Hiroshima and Nagasaki*.

The appearance of pine root oil in the latter part of *Daikon* has a larger significance than might be immediately apparent. The catalyst for the Pacific War was Japan's need for oil, made pressing by the Western powers' oil embargo. The Imperial Japanese Navy temporarily neutralized American power in the Pacific with the attack on Pearl Harbor and made a thrust south, seizing the oil fields of Borneo and Sumatra to meet the nation's energy needs. But the Japanese advantage did not last. As the United States geared up for total war, the tide turned against Japan. And as the Americans inexorably advanced on the home islands, methodically destroying Japanese shipping, oil supplies were choked off and the fuel situation became dire.

Numerous sources were investigated in Japan as possible alternate fuels, the most promising among them being pine tree roots. A nationwide campaign was launched to exploit this resource with the slogan: "Two hundred pine roots will keep a plane in the air for an hour." The result was environmental devastation, the land itself suffering in the final year of the war along with the people. A staggering 14,000 squares miles of forest was cut down, much of it pine trees. Hillsides were denuded and the resinous roots dug up—a massively labor-intensive job undertaken by armies of older men, women, and children. These roots were then chopped up or sawed into pieces and boiled in stills to extract a crude oil that could be refined into gasoline. Wholesale deforestation ceased with the end of the war, but the damage continued to play out with erosion and insect infestations. It would take many years for the land to recover.

For all its shortcomings in cost and labor, aviation fuel refined from pine root oil was of high grade and its use in *Daikon* not so farfetched. See, for example, U.S. Naval Technical Mission to Japan, "Japanese Fuels and Lubricants, Article 4, Pine Root Oil Program," February 1946: "It has been definitely shown that an aviation gasoline of 91-95 octane number (with 0.15% lead) can be produced in yield of about 50% from pine root oil by means of high pressure hydrocracking." (Lieutenant S. Inaba, research period December 1944–August 1945, quoted in "Japanese Fuels and Lubricants, Article 4, Pine Root Oil Program," 105.)

Two American air attacks against Japan are described in *Daikon*: the atomic bombing of Hiroshima on August 6, 1945, and the firebombing of Tokyo on the night of March 9–10, 1945, known as the Great Tokyo Air Raid. The Hiroshima and Nagasaki atomic attacks loom so large in our memory today that they have overshadowed the Great Tokyo Air Raid, which claimed 100,000 lives in one night and left one million homeless. It was in fact the most destructive air raid in history. In comparison, the immediate death toll at Hiroshima was in the range of 70,000 and at Nagasaki approximately 40,000, rising respectively to 140,000 and 74,000 in the coming months and years as victims died from their injuries and the lingering effects of radiation exposure. (A useful source on the number of deaths caused by the bombs is Alex Wellerstein, "Counting the Dead at Hiroshima and Nagasaki," *Bulletin of the Atomic Scientists*, August 4, 2020.) Sources I used for the Great Tokyo Air Raid included Robert Guillain, *I Saw Tokyo Burning*; Edwin Hoyt, *Inferno*; and the firsthand accounts recorded in Haruko Toya Cook and Theodore F. Cook, eds., *Japan at War: An Oral History*. In this latter book I was particularly influenced by Kazuyo Funato's account of finding her mother the morning after the air raid, Kazuyo's baby brother no longer on her back. "Father said, 'What's happened to Takahisa?' My mother was silent . . . 'You made it back, you made it back. That's wonderful!' was all my father could say . . . Although Mother never expressed it in words, I think she had the most difficult time. She had let the child on her back die. We don't know if she left him somewhere, or whether he just burnt up and fell. Once people who were trying to collect records on the Great Air Raid pleaded with us to ask her, but we couldn't. She's now eighty-eight years old" (348–49). This unfortunate woman Mrs. Funato is a real-life counterpart to the fictional character of Noriko Kan, unable to speak of the death of her daughter, Aiko. Keizo Kan's words upon reuniting with Noriko in chapter 32 were inspired by what Mr. Funato said to his wife when he found her the next day.

If so much death and destruction could be caused by conventional bombing, what purpose, if any, did the atomic bombs serve? An argument in their favor is that they gave the Japanese a much-needed shock. A fanatical mindset was prevailing in Japan not unlike what would later take hold in North Korea. Japan's military leaders were determined to continue the war and were prepared to sacrifice millions of lives to do so. Massive civilian losses were acceptable to them. And the Japanese people, convinced by government propaganda that the Americans would slaughter them en masse when they invaded, were ready to comply.

The awesome power of the atomic bombs knocked Japan off this path to destruction. It pushed the Suzuki cabinet and the Supreme War Council to the point of crisis and prompted Emperor Hirohito, hitherto silent, to speak. The Emperor's unprecedented speech to the nation's assembled leaders on August 14, 1945, was the first real expression of concern for the suffering of the Japanese people, who had not entered into the Imperial Army's considerations at all. The Emperor's plea that they must "endure the unendurable" and surrender reduced everyone present to tears. It silenced the hard-liners, broke the deadlock, and ended the war.

Had the Hiroshima and Nagasaki bombs not precipitated this chain of events, the war would have ground on and the death toll would have been staggering. To begin with, the firebombing campaign against Japan that had already claimed so many lives would have continued, and with increased intensity. By way of comparison, in the month of March 1945, which included the Great Tokyo Air Raid, a total of 13,800 tons of bombs were dropped on Japan. By September 1945, with the war in Europe over and America's full military might directed against Japan, U.S. air forces were prepared to drop 115,000 tons of bombs every month.

Then there would have been the casualties in Operation Downfall, the Allied invasion of the Japanese home islands, slated to begin on Kyushu on November 1, 1945. American casualty estimates varied but easily could have topped 200,000. This in large part is why 85 percent of Americans at the time approved of the use of the atomic bombs—because they did not want any more of their men to die. On the Japanese side, the death toll would have been vastly higher. By way of comparison, 142,000 Japanese, including 42,000 civilians, were killed in the invasion of the small island of Okinawa earlier in the year. The number of dead in the invasion of Kyushu would have dwarfed this. And then there would have been the invasion of Honshu. And then there would have been the mass starvation. The Japanese people, already starving in August 1945, would have faced a full-blown famine going into the winter, with food production plummeting and the rail system for moving nutrition around largely in ruins. Even with the war ending when it did, mass deaths from starvation were only narrowly averted by occupation forces bringing in massive amounts of food aid to get the country through the first difficult months. Had the Pacific War continued into 1946, the number of Japanese killed outright or dead from starvation would have run into the millions.

This is the fearsome calculus that comes into play when the Pandora's box of war is opened. No one understood this better than Mitsuo Fuchida, the Japanese navy pilot who led the first wave of planes in the attack on Pearl Harbor. Fuchida visited Hiroshima on August 7, 1945, the day after the atomic blast, to survey the damage. "It was like an evil nightmare," he would recall to University of Maryland historian Gordon Prange two decades later. But he did not resent the Americans for it. "That was war . . . If Japan had had the atomic bomb we would have dropped it on the United States." The Mitsuo Fuchida of

1945 "would have been willing, even proud to strike such a devastating blow for his country." Fuchida saw the bomb's demonstration of power as a way to end the war with some of Japan's dignity intact, for even the most determined warrior could not stand against such a terrible weapon. He immediately telephoned the Navy Chief of Staff and said, "Japan should sue for peace at once. Please go straight to the Naval General Staff and pressure them to act!" (Prange, *God's Samurai: Lead Pilot at Pearl Harbor,* 150–53).

Could the war have been ended in August 1945 without using atomic bombs against Japanese cities? Could an attack on a purely military target, for example, or a demonstration on an uninhabited island for the Japanese to witness—both of which were suggested—have sufficiently shocked the leaders of Japan to surrender? In isolation, perhaps not. Combined with a few words of assurance, however, and the outcome might have been different. An earlier draft of the surrender terms in the Potsdam Declaration included the stipulation that Japan would be allowed to continue as a constitutional monarchy and retain its emperor. This line was removed from the final draft of the terms that were transmitted to Japan, undermining those leaders seeking to surrender and prompting the hard-liners to dig in their heels. Why was this sentence deleted? Was it simply out of concern that it would convey weakness and encourage the Japanese to hold out for concessions? Or was something deeper going on, a plan to ensure that the war would continue long enough for the atomic bombs to be used—that the bombs *had* to be used to intimidate the Soviet Union, which was poised to declare war on Japan and advance into its colonial possession Korea? As historian Tsuyoshi Hasegawa sums up, "The rejection of the Potsdam Declaration [by Japan] was required to justify the dropping of the bomb" (*Racing the Enemy: Stalin, Truman, and the Surrender of Japan,* 152).

Despite the widespread support the atomic bomb had in the United States, numerous people involved in its creation and use harbored misgivings. Albert Einstein would come to regret signing a letter to President Roosevelt in 1939 warning of the potential threat of Nazi Germany's conducting atomic bomb research and urging the U.S. government to launch its own program. He would later describe this as the "one great mistake in my life" (Ronald T. Takaki, *Hiroshima: Why America Dropped the Atomic Bomb*, 137). The day after the bomb was successfully tested on July 16, 1945, sixty-eight Manhattan Project scientists signed a petition to President Truman urging him not to use it, asserting that with Germany defeated it was no longer needed. A key sentence: "Thus a nation which sets the precedent of using these newly liberated forces of nature for purposes of destruction may have to bear the responsibility of opening the door to an era of devastation on an unimaginable scale" (letter reproduced in Kai Bird and Lawrence Lifschultz, eds, *Hiroshima's Shadow*, 553).

President Harry Truman himself was initially against using the bomb against Japanese cities. As he wrote in his private diary on July 25, 1945: "I have told the Sec. of War, Mr. [Henry] Stimson to use it so that military objectives and soldiers and sailors are the target and not women and children" ("Truman at Potsdam," *American Heritage*, June/July 1980). The Target Committee rejected this idea and came up with a list of five cities. After receiving reports of the devastation wrought at Hiroshima and Nagasaki, Truman halted delivery of further atomic bombs.

General Dwight Eisenhower, Truman's successor as president, recoiled even more strongly from the idea of using nuclear weapons. He would later recall having dinner with Secretary of War Stimson in July 1945 when a cable arrived informing Stimson that the Trinity test had been successful and the bomb was ready to use. "The cable was in code, you know the way they do it. 'The lamb is born' or some damn thing like that. So then he told me they were going to drop it on the Japanese. Well, I listened . . . But I was getting more and more depressed just thinking about it. Then he asked for my opinion, so I told him I was against it on two counts. First, the Japanese were ready to surrender and it wasn't necessary to hit them with that awful thing.

Second, I hated to see our country be the first to use such a weapon. Well . . . the old gentleman got furious. And I can see how he would. After all, it had been his responsibility to push for all the huge expenditure to develop the bomb, which of course he had a right to do, and *was* right to do. Still, it was an awful problem" ("Ike on Ike," *Newsweek*, November 11, 1963, 108).

I would like to end with a heartfelt thanks to my agent, Warren Frazier of John Hawkins & Associates, who saw promise in an earlier draft of this story and helped shape it into its present form. It was a revelation to me that an agent could devote so much time and energy to the creative side of a novel and have such a profound and positive editorial impact. I could not have completed *Daikon* without Warren's encouragement, guidance, and insightful suggestions. My special thanks also to Jofie Ferrari-Adler at Avid Reader Press for his creative input, which helped to further improve the story; to Julianna Haubner and Jessica Chin for their careful editorial work on the manuscript; and to Iori Kusano for her authenticity read that helped me correct several missteps in writing about a culture that isn't my own.

ABOUT THE AUTHOR

SAMUEL HAWLEY was born and raised in South Korea, the son of Canadian missionaries, and taught English in Korea and Japan for nearly two decades. He is the author of the nonfiction book *The Imjin War*, the most comprehensive account in English of Japan's sixteenth-century invasion of Korea and attempted conquest of China. He currently lives in Istanbul, Turkey. *Daikon* is his debut novel.